Death of an Avid Reader

Also by Frances Brody

Dying in the Wool
A Medal for Murder
Murder in the Afternoon
A Woman Unknown
Murder on a Summer's Day
A Death in the Dales

Death of an Avid Reader

A Kate Shackleton Mystery

Frances BRODY

Minotaur Books

A Thomas Dunne Book
New York

A THOMAS DUNNE BOOK FOR MINOTAUR BOOKS.
An imprint of St. Martin's Press.

DEATH OF AN AVID READER. Copyright © 2014 by Frances McNeil. All rights reserved. Printed in the United States of America. For information, address St. Martin's Press, 175 Fifth Avenue, New York, N.Y. 10010.

www.thomasdunnebooks.com
www.minotaurbooks.com

The Library of Congress has cataloged the hardcover edition as follows:

Names: Brody, Frances, author.
Title: Death of an avid reader / Frances Brody.
Description: First U.S. Edition. | New York : Minotaur Books, 2016. |
    Series: A Kate Shackleton mystery ; 6 | "A Thomas Dunne Book."
Identifiers: LCCN 2016016837 | ISBN 9781250067395 (hardcover) |
    ISBN 9781466875708 (ebook)
Subjects: LCSH: Women private investigators—England—Fiction. | Murder—
    Investigation—Fiction. | BISAC: FICTION / Mystery & Detective /
    Traditional British. | FICTION / Mystery & Detective / Women Sleuths. |
    FICTION / Mystery & Detective / Historical. | GSAFD: Mystery fiction.
Classification: LCC PR6113.C577 D43 2016 | DDC 823/.92—dc23
LC record available at https://lccn.loc.gov/2016016837

ISBN 978-1-250-06750-0 (trade paperback)

Our books may be purchased in bulk for promotional, educational, or business use. Please contact your local bookseller or the Macmillan Corporate and Premium Sales Department at 1-800-221-7945, extension 5442, or by email at MacmillanSpecialMarkets@macmillan.com.

First published in Great Britain by Piatkus, an imprint of Little, Brown Book Group, an Hachette UK company

First Minotaur Books Paperback Edition: September 2017

10 9 8 7 6 5 4 3 2 1

Dedicated to Geoffrey Forster, for many years librarian of the Leeds Library.

*'A circulating library in a town is as an evergreen
tree of diabolical knowledge'*

Richard Brinsley Sheridan

One

The newspaper item had been clipped, framed, and now held pride of place on the library's landing.

June 21, 1923, *Leeds Herald*
In a momentous discovery, the Leeds Library on Commercial Street has added the finest of jewels to its crown. Founded in 1768, this venerable institution already houses Selby's Ornithology, rare and magnificent coloured plates of birds; the works of St Thomas Aquinas; an enviable collection of Reformation and Civil War pamphlets and two hundred and one volumes of the *Encyclopédia Méthodique*. Scholars and visitors will now flock to our fair city from London, Edinburgh, from across Europe and beyond for a mere glimpse of its latest treasures.

A bequest was made to the library by a local gentleman, recently deceased and whose family remain anonymous. A tea chest of books was unpacked. Among the volumes lay the rare 1825 reprint of the first edition (1603) of *Hamlet*. The astonished and delighted librarian, Mr Samuel Lennox, reports that he has already dusted off several other much-prized volumes, including Captain William Bligh's *Narrative of the Mutiny on the Bounty* (1790), and Richard Sheridan's *A Trip to Scarborough*, both beautifully bound by Edwards of Halifax.

"We are privileged to have such a cherished and priceless collection in our midst," said Mr Lennox. "Researchers and scholars will be assured of the warmest welcome."

Dr Potter stood at the top of the library stairs. He read the article and scratched his head. 'What will Lennox do next? Send a personal invitation to every book thief in the country?'

Two

The letter came by first delivery, along with the usual bills and charitable requests. The envelope was of good quality, neatly addressed and with a London postmark. I resisted until I had eaten a slice of toast, and then slit it open with my *Present from Robin Hood's Bay* paper knife. Embossed paper bore the Coulton coat of arms.

> *22 October, 1925*
> *Cavendish Square*
> *London*
> *Dear Mrs Shackleton*
>   *On a matter of delicacy, I pray you will meet me on Tuesday next. Knowing you are a member of the Cavendish Square Ladies' Club, I suggest we meet there.*
>   *Yours sincerely*
>   *Jane Coulton*

Folded inside the note was a cheque, drawn on Coutts Bank. One hundred guineas! This must be serious.

My Aunt Berta once pointed out Lady Coulton when we

were at some long ago charity auction, an evening do at Claridge's. 'She turns heads, Kate. Study her.'

Study her I did. She was beautiful, with an air of dignity and slight reserve; tall, with a good figure, graceful neck, regular features, and something I described to myself as brilliance, crowned by abundant coppery golden hair decorated with diamond-studded combs that sparkled under the glow of the chandelier. Cousin James was there that evening. He turned unusually poetic. 'Her eyes, such a greenish-blue, as of the sea and sky on a grey day.'

It was his period for falling in love with figures from paintings. He had waxed lyrical over Elizabeth Siddal as Ophelia and so I could see why Lady Coulton enchanted him.

That must have been thirteen years ago. I was twenty-one, and nothing bad had ever happened.

Lady Coulton must be fifty years old now.

I pushed away my breakfast plate, reached for the writing case and replied to her letter, agreeing to meet on the day she suggested.

My house is of a modest size being the old coach house that once formed part of a grand estate in Headingley, North Leeds. The whole dwelling would fit easily into Lady Coulton's entrance hall, leaving a ballroom-size space for dancing.

I keep newspapers and magazines for far too long, according to my housekeeper. They are in a pile on the piano. Lifting down back copies of *The Times*, I turned the pages, looking for a mention of Lord or Lady Coulton; he speaking in the House of Lords, she at some social event. Nothing.

I would have liked one clue, however tiny.

Why is it that useless snippets of information lodge in the brain? It did not help to remember that, when in the country, Lady Coulton bred Beagles. Did she now prefer the country and her dogs, I wondered. Perhaps some squire or gamekeeper had caught her eye. I could not imagine Lady Coulton allowing herself to be blackmailed. Had the staid Lord Coulton taken up with a Gaiety girl? They had sons. Perhaps one of them had turned to gambling, or espionage for a foreign power.

When I bought the railway tickets, deciding to go to London and back in one day made me feel important, adventurous, and superbly discreet. I would lessen the chance of bumping into friends, arousing curiosity and having to come up with an explanation for my visit.

Now the day arrived. I dragged myself out of bed before daylight, recognising my plan as the worst idea since going to the fancy dress party as Vladimir Lenin, just because I had that false beard.

What if Lady Coulton's task required me to stay in London? I would need to shop for underwear, and arrange to have a trunk sent.

I dressed and stumbled downstairs. Fortunately, my trusty housekeeper, Mrs Sugden, was already up and about. An early riser, she was thoroughly dressed in her dark serge skirt, hand-knitted twinset and tightly-laced shoes, her grey hair done up in plaits.

Standing at the kitchen table, I drank tea while Mrs Sugden wrapped slices of bread and butter and a piece of a cheese and packed them with an apple in a brown paper bag.

Although her hair has turned grey and her bossy fussing would win her a gold medal, she is not yet forty.

'Ladyship or not, she has a cheek, asking you to rush off to London. If it's so important, why doesn't she come here?'

'Because she is paying, and paying well. And thank you but I don't need to take a snack. You have it. I'll eat breakfast on the train.'

'I can't imagine a breakfast on the train will be worth eating. How can it be?'

'I'll let you know.'

'I'll put this food in your satchel.'

'I was going to take my black bag.'

'It's elegant but it holds nowt. You don't have to impress them London types.' She picked up *The Strange Case of Dr Jekyll and Mr Hyde*. 'Is this little book going in?'

'Yes, just for amusement. I'm going to Cavendish Square, and it features in the story. Dr Lanyon, Dr Jekyll's former best friend lives there.'

'Then let's hope you don't bump into him.' She pulled on her coat.

'Are you going out, at this hour?'

'I'm walking up the road with you, Mrs Shackleton, to see you off safely and shut the garage door behind you.'

It was very kind of her. Such thoughtful gestures remind me that I made a fortunate choice when I engaged her all those years ago, at the end of the war.

Sookie the cat looked up from her spot on the hearth, opening a sleepy eye as we left the kitchen.

As she closed the door behind us, Mrs Sugden gave a hearty sigh. 'It's a pity I can't drive. You should have asked Mr Sykes.'

'No need. I can park by the railway station and then drive myself home.'

In early morning darkness, we walked in silence to my garage. There was a sharp chill in the air. Spectral grey mist curled through hedges, as though some celestial giant had blown ghostly smoke rings. It gave me a strange feeling to witness this gossamer vapour that in another hour would be gone. A small mound of dead leaves had gathered where the cobbles dipped. The leaves scattered when a sudden breeze whooshed them to nooks and crannies new.

My sage green autumn suit with its warmly lined three-quarter jacket has deep pockets. I touched my train ticket with gloved fingers, to make sure it was still there.

I house my car in a former stable, rented from the owners of the mansion at the top of my road. I opened the double doors and handed the keys to Mrs Sugden. The motor started without complaint. I edged forward, turning onto the narrow road.

Mrs Sugden closed the garage door. 'Have a good journey.'

'I'll try.'

'Be careful of them Londoners, Mrs Shackleton. If this business was straightforward, her ladyship wouldn't be sending two hundred and more miles for you.'

I waved goodbye, and drove away. On Woodhouse Lane, the pavements were busy with men and women walking to work. The lucky ones wore winter coats and the unlucky, or hardy, huddled in their jackets and home-knitted scarves. They wore caps, trilbies, berets or headscarves. One jaunty young woman sported a fine tam o' shanter with a big red pom-pom.

Carefully, I waited to proceed as a blinkered horse patiently drew its cart into Cardigan Road.

A tram rattled by, both decks packed, standing room only. Cyclists dodged daringly across the tracks.

It took me another fifteen minutes to reach the station. As I drew into the yard, an elderly porter came to the car.

'Luggage, madam?'

'No. I'll be returning this evening.'

He stared. 'Is that so, madam?'

This would be a tale for the supper table when he arrived home. 'You'll never guess what happened to me today. I parked a motorcar for a mad woman, off to London and back in a day.'

I slipped him a florin.

The Ladies' Waiting Room was empty. A small fire gave out very little heat. Sitting on the bench did not melt the ice in my veins. I fetched a chair and placed it almost on the hearth. I was early for the 7.50 a.m. train which would arrive at King's Cross at 11.30 a.m. Since Lady Coulton had failed to state a time, I had telegraphed the club to say that I would be arriving at noon. I settled down to read my book, and wait for the train.

Of course, I could not settle. I bought a newspaper, and went to the platform far too soon. The train was still being cleaned, but since the first class carriages were swept and dusted first, a porter opened the door and directed me to my seat.

Contrary to Mrs Sugden's dire warnings, the cooked breakfast was very good. I chose ham and eggs, which came with fresh rolls.

Through the train window, I looked out onto a landscape

of pit shafts and slag heaps. An itchy uneasiness settled like dust in every part of my being.

Mrs Sugden was right to set a big question mark above Lady Coulton's motive in sending for me. I have a well-known London counterpart, with offices in Mayfair. This lady detective prides herself on investigating society cases of infidelity, blackmail and burglary as well as smuggling, and espionage. Her ladyship could have gone to her.

Lady Coulton was taking no chances. Engaging a detective close to home might be risky. Her 'matter of delicacy' must be scandalous, deadly secret and entirely indelicate.

Three

Having taken a cab from King's Cross, I arrived at Queen Anne House, number 28 Cavendish Square, at noon. This former hotel was opened in June, 1920, as a club for women of the Voluntary Aid Detachment. I was proud to be at the opening ceremony, and visit every time I come to London.

Alfred the porter has worked here from the first. He welcomed me and we exchanged a few words.

'I have a telephone message for you, Mrs Shackleton. Your guest will be here at two o'clock and won't be lunching with us.'

'Thank you, Alfred.'

I smiled. The club has modest fare and moderate charges, for members on a limited income. I doubted that the one and threepenny lunch would suit Lady Coulton's tastes.

In the dining room, not wishing to be drawn into conversation, I sat as far from the door as possible, at a small table. There were two choices for mains and pudding. I plumped for meat and potato pie followed by jelly and custard.

By quarter to two, I seated myself in one of a pair of wing chairs, by the lounge window. I would see Lady Coulton crossing the square.

As the French clock chimed two, Jane Coulton came into view.

A few moments later, a man in a black coat and homburg hat appeared, dogging her footsteps. He kept a steady distance between them, at one moment pausing when her steps became a little slower. When she reached the club's entrance, he waited, watching her as she stepped inside. Who was he, and why had he followed her? He walked on, out of sight. Perhaps I was mistaken.

Jane Coulton swept into the room, led by Alfred. I remembered that quality of confidence and something that I was too naïve to have been able to put into words when I saw her all those years ago: sexual magnetism. Alfred, accustomed to important personages, is not unduly deferential and so it seemed to me that his awed manner towards her stemmed from something else, an acknowledgement of her beauty and elegance.

'Your guest, Mrs Shackleton,' he announced in hushed tones.

He glanced sideways at her, hovering as she slipped the mink coat from her shoulders and handed it to him. I greeted her.

Before she took a seat in the wing chair opposite mine, her eyes darted about the room, which, apart from us and the fleeing porter, was empty.

'You have come up to town today?' She spoke as if for the benefit of any person or persons hiding behind a sofa.

'Yes, by the 7.50 train.' I resumed my seat.

'The North was once so very far away.'

She did not appear greatly changed since the last time I saw her, at the charity auction. Perhaps we fix a first image so firmly in our minds that we go on seeing it the same way. If anything, she looked more striking. Her coppery golden hair, under the neat hat, was a little grey at the temples, her cheek bones more prominent. In this intimate setting, her dignity and reserve gave way to an ease of manner that comes naturally to my mother and aunt. They would have been brought up in the same circles, and came out into society a few years sooner than Lady Coulton.

She had a fragile, almost brittle quality that I had not noticed before. Her face bore traces of powder and a touch of rouge. Perfectly bowed and gently pencilled eyebrows raised a little as she appraised me. I hoped my own appraisal was not so obvious.

She thanked me for coming and enquired about what sort of lunch the club served, all the while making a shield of a shiny crocodile-skin handbag, as if it might escape from her and find its way back to the Zambezi.

'I asked to meet you here because it is close to home. I can slip out unnoticed.'

Had she been unnoticed, though? I wondered whether to tell her that I thought someone had followed her.

'My Aunt Berta probably mentioned to you that she and I lunch here occasionally.'

'She did. But she knows nothing of this meeting. Shall you be seeing her during this visit?'

'I shall see no one, except you. A taxi will take me back to King's Cross.'

It would be the four o'clock train, if she was quick about

it; or the 5.45 if she took her time. The 5.45 did have the advantage of a restaurant car.

'This is a delicate matter.'

'You are assured of my discretion.'

She placed her bag on the low table. 'It is not always easy for me to get away these days. If someone discovers that I was here, it is because I am in sympathy with the idea of a club for girls and women and may take some sort of interest, you understand?'

'I understand.' She had no interest in the VAD club but preferred not to be seen with me at the Ritz or the Savoy, where her chums would gather. I did not mention the man who may have followed her. I could be mistaken. If questioned at home, she had her story carefully worked out. But why was leaving the house so difficult?

I waited.

She glanced at her kid gloves, as if considering whether they had become part of her hands.

'Is there anything you wish to ask me before you give me your confidence?'

'Be a dear, order me a gin and tonic and something for you. I can't just plough on cold as it were.'

The club has no bar, but I knew that Alfred would be willing to oblige. Since there have been complaints about the availability of alcohol, he does not provide drinks for everyone who asks, only for those he knows will be discreet. I found him in the corridor and whispered my request, making hers a double and mine a straightforward tonic. She need not know that I intended to remain stone cold sober.

Lady Coulton drew off her gloves. 'Perhaps you know my husband is an invalid?'

13

'No. I had not heard, though I did notice that he has not lately been reported as speaking in the Lords.'

She smiled. 'Yes, he always had to make his views known, never one to snooze through the sessions.'

'How is he now?'

She made a hopeless gesture. 'Critically ill, but being nursed at home. His room is full of contraptions and frightfully efficient nurses. He is sleeping, but asks for me constantly, for no reason. Sometimes in the afternoon he has a burst of energy and imagines he could stroll across the square without becoming exhausted.'

Alfred brought our drinks on a tray. He lifted the glasses onto dainty mats, surreptitiously gazing at my guest as if memorising her beauty.

Lady Coulton took a sip. 'His illness does not stop my daughter-in-law from sizing up the house for improvements. She and my son will give up the Chelsea House. They expect me to retire to the country, when the inevitable happens.'

'And will you?'

'Certainly not.'

Not until she had taken a large snifter of gin did she begin her story, which then came out so straightforwardly that I felt sure she must have been planning to do this for months, if not years.

'I have a daughter.' She held my gaze as if daring me to judge or contradict.

You have never spoken those words before, I thought. After a long moment, she continued. 'My husband is unaware of her existence – not just he, the world is unaware. Her twenty-fourth birthday was 10th July. She was born in 1901, when my husband had been serving in South Africa for well over a year. It was quite a worry, an unlucky situation. We had been married six years. My sons were then aged five, four and three. My son Noel is an MP. My youngest, Geoffrey, farms in Rhodesia.'

'And your eldest died on the Somme. I'm sorry.'

'Thank you. He was the best, of course.' She shrugged and took another sip of gin. 'When I knew I was to bear a child, I went to Scarborough, on the pretext of taking the boys to the seaside. That is where I gave birth. The boys were too young to understand. Their nanny, who had been my nanny, took care of them during my confinement. The baby was left with my nanny's younger sister, Mrs Wells, a resident of Scarborough, the reason for my choice. Her name is on the child's birth certificate. I dared not risk a scandal, you see. My husband would have felt obliged to divorce me. It was around the time when he had succeeded to the title. I would have lost my boys, lost everything.'

'And what is it you want me to do, Lady Coulton?'

Of course I already knew, before she spoke.

'I want you to find her. Oh I can't acknowledge her, even now, but I want to know if she is well, and whether there might be something I could do for her. I never had a daughter, you see.'

This struck me as an odd thing for her to say, but of course she meant that she had no *legitimate* daughter.

I took out my notebook. 'What are the full names on the birth certificate?'

Her fingers touched her throat, as if the gesture might help her say the words. 'Parents, Jeremy and Jennifer Wells. My daughter's given name is Sophia Mary Ann.' She watched

15

me write the names and date of birth. 'I have always wondered how Sophia turned out and whether she married.'

'Do you believe she is still in Scarborough?'

'It is possible. I stopped receiving communications long ago, in 1911. They came through my nanny, you see, and she died. Well, there you are, that is my sorry tale. You are from the North. I suppose Scarborough is not too far from you.'

'Not far. About sixty miles.'

'Well?'

'Was Sophia told of her true parentage?'

'That I do not know. My name would not have been mentioned to her, but it is possible that the child sensed she was of different stock, and she may have picked up a hint. I would simply, at first, like to know where she is, whether she is well and in what circumstances.'

'I will do my very best.'

'Thank you.'

'What other details can you give me?'

She leaned forward to retrieve her handbag. She opened the bag and took out a professionally-produced postcard size photograph. 'This is Sophia.'

In the centre of the picture, leaning against a polished, wood-frame chair with tapestry upholstered seat, was a plump, well-cared for child, about three years old. She wore a white cotton or linen dress trimmed with broderie anglaise, ending just below her knees, frilled white socks and strapped black shoes. Someone had told her to point to the open picture book that lay on the chair. With her right arm, she leaned on the seat. The forefinger of her left hand pointed towards the book, but she looked into the camera. Her fair hair fell in waves almost to her shoulders. It was centre-parted and tied in bunches with two white ribbons. She had a pretty, heart-shaped face, dark eyes and snub nose, above shapely, unsmiling lips.

In the background, from left to right, was a curtain, a window seat, the bottom three small panes of a window, and a plant stand holding a fern-filled jardinière.

The reverse of the postcard gave the name of the photographic studio: Felton, Photographer, Bingley.

'Why Bingley, I wonder?'

'I don't know. Perhaps Mrs Wells visited a friend or relative there. This is the only photograph I have of the child.'

'Did Mr and Mrs Wells have other children?'

'No, they were childless and the proprietors of a fishmonger shop.'

The word 'fishmonger' brought a look of intense sadness to her face. I thought she might burst into tears, but she took another drink.

'When did you last have word about Sophia?'

'Before Nanny Tarpey died, in 1911.'

'Did you attempt to keep in touch?'

'I wrote to Mrs Wells, expressing condolences at the loss of her sister and saying that if there was anything I could do for her, she must let me know. I trusted she would understand me and that if there was something she needed for the child, she would tell me.'

'And was there anything she wanted?'

'Oddly, no. I received a rather sniffy note saying that they were all very well, thank you for asking.' She leaned back in her chair. 'It made my heart sink. She was telling me to keep my distance and not interfere with the child she now thought of as hers.'

'I suppose that would explain the silence.'

She delved in her bag for a scrap of paper. 'This is the last address I have for Mrs Wells.'

I took out my notebook and slid photograph and address in the back.

'What will you do?' she asked.

'I will go to Scarborough and call at the address. We may place an advertisement in newspapers, anyone knowing the whereabouts, that sort of thing. A hint of some advantage will bring replies, and then we will sift through them and follow up those that seem genuine. What else can you tell me about Mr and Mrs Wells?'

She looked blank, and then admitted that apart from knowing he was a fishmonger, and she was the nanny's sister, she knew very little.

'What about Sophia? Did she have any distinguishing birthmarks?'

'No. She was perfect in every way.' She took a handker-chief from her bag. As she put it to her nose, I caught a whiff of smelling salts.

After a moment, she leaned back in her chair, as though suddenly tired.

'Did you leave anything with her, some trinket or memento?'

'I couldn't, you see. She was supposed to be Mrs Wells's child. One thing did occur to me . . . '

'Yes?'

'Scarborough, the east coast, there was a bombardment in 1914. I have always worried, and sometimes dreamed that my child was killed. So much news was censored then.'

'That was reported, and there were fatalities, though

Hartlepool took the brunt. I would have remembered had a thirteen year old girl died.'

'Would you?'

'Yes. A baby was killed, in a Scarborough park.' We were silent for a moment. I could see I had not convinced her, so added, 'I think you can be almost certain that your daughter was unharmed.'

'I hope you're right.' She sighed. 'I took a risk in writing to Mrs Wells six months ago, under the pretext of asking about the upkeep of Nanny Tarpey's grave. I received no reply.'

'There could be any number of reasons for that. Sometimes letters go astray.'

'Or Mrs Wells may have thrown my letter on the fire.'

There was very little to go on, and we both knew it.

I don't know why I asked my next question. 'Did you remain in touch with Sophia's father?'

'No.'

'Did he know you were to have his child?'

'Certainly not. He . . . he was a young man, someone who came to the house in the country, to do cataloguing in the library connected with some old diaries belonging to my father-in-law. I was alone with the children, and very few staff.'

She had told me what I needed to know in order to search for her daughter. But what intrigued me was what she did not say. Who was the passionate young man who danced into her life so briefly? How must she have felt, giving birth to a child and then handing the baby to a stranger, to be brought up under another name?

I tried not to make a connection with my own experience, but it was difficult not to. My mother was born into

19

the aristocracy, married an up-and-coming police officer and was childless for longer than she liked. They adopted me from the widow of a police constable, my father, who died suddenly of a heart attack, leaving my natural mother with too many mouths to feed. But from an early age I had known that I was adopted. Did Sophia Wells know? How extraordinary it would be to live into adulthood, certain of your identity, and then to have that certainty ripped away.

My own birth mother had handed me over to her late husband's superior officer and his wife when I was just a few weeks old. My father kept her informed about me. When I eventually met this stranger, this mother, I discovered that the family had always talked about me, and followed my progress, long before I met them. My birth mother said she was glad that I had done so very well. It left me with an odd sense of obligation. I felt as though there was something I should do or say, but did not know what. 'Glad,' was the word my birth mother had used.

Lady Coulton wanted that same small gem of gladness: the knowledge that her daughter was safe and well.

Finding Sophia Wells should not be too difficult. Knowing what to say to her might be tricky. Lady Coulton seemed not to consider that, and only concentrated on the finding part. Perhaps she was right to take one matter at a time.

I privately decided to try and find Mrs Wells first, and discover what she had told Sophia.

'What were the financial arrangements?' As I heard my own question, for the first time it occurred to me that my father must have paid for me. Did he go on paying, in the form of supporting that other family, the constable's widow and her children?

Perhaps the shock of the thought showed in my face, because Lady Coulton gave me an odd look.

'I gave Mr and Mrs Wells a lump sum when they took Sophia. After that it would have been difficult. My husband and his accountant kept control of our finances. It would have been difficult for me to go on paying Mrs Wells without raising suspicions. It is different now. I have more freedom.'

'From what you say, Mrs Wells may have come to regard Sophia as her child and as the years passed, that feeling would become stronger.'

She flexed her fingers. 'Just so.'

Sophia was the daughter of a fishmonger and his wife. A gulf separated Mrs Wells and the woman who faced me, with her carefully manicured nails, delicate way of crossing her ankles, the haughtiness that she conveyed by a mere jut of her chin. I wondered in what ways Sophia may have remained her mother's daughter. What gestures she might employ, whether she had that same sideways glance that Lady Coulton gave now, when someone walked into the room and took a seat, well out of earshot.

'If I find Mrs Wells, she is almost certain to guess what is behind my search.'

'Yes, I see that. But I am sure you will think of something, a reference to her old nanny's employer, something of that sort.' Once more she delved into her handbag. 'My nanny and her sister were quite plain, to put it kindly. In the postcard, as a child, Sophia looked like me when I was that age. That is why I have had to hide the photograph for years. She has probably grown into a beauty. She must look in the glass and know that she is from a different stable to Mr and Mrs

21

Wells.' She handed me another photograph. 'Here I am, in my twenties, the age Sophia will be now. She may still look like me.'

This was also a postcard-size photograph and had been tinted. 'It's from a painting, I think?'

'Yes. The portrait was commissioned on my engagement. Coulton calls it the *Symphony in Blue*.'

She wore a long gown that revealed her shoulders. In her right hand she held a rose. Her gaze challenged the painter with grave dignity, as if she cared not a jot what he saw. She knew she was a beauty. Unconventionally, her long hair fell loose to her shoulders, more in the way an artist might pose his model than as a painter would portray a lady. The impression was of languidness and a lazy grace.

'May I keep this, for now?'

'Yes.'

'If she does resemble you, and you hope to be reunited, won't the likeness between you speak the secret you have kept all these years?'

'I will worry about that if it happens.'

'Am I to give her a hint if I find her? What do you intend?'

'I am not sure.' She sighed. 'It's too ridiculous, I know. I began to dream of Sophia when my husband first took poorly. The day after my last dream, I escaped the sick room and met your aunt for lunch at Claridge's. Berta talks about you, her niece the detective. That was when it occurred to me that it may be possible to find Sophia.'

She did not go so far as to admit that in spite of her many friends she was lonely. She did not need to.

An uneasy feeling crept over me, an excess of caution. So

many sayings tell us to let sleeping dogs lie, don't rock the boat or lift the stone.

'I will see what I can do. How shall I contact you if I have further questions, or something to report?'

After a few more words, our interview reached its conclusion. I walked with her to the door, where Alfred produced her coat.

I watched her go. She crossed the square.

There he was again, the man in black. He seemed to appear from nowhere. Keeping a short distance, he followed her, almost as if ready to pounce.

Not pausing to pick up my coat, I went after them.

Lady Coulton went in the front door of her house.

The man in black took the steps down to the servants' quarters.

Was the ailing Lord Coulton, or one of their sons, paying this man to spy on her ladyship?

Now I wished I had told her my suspicion that she was followed, but it was too late to warn her.

Four

The next morning, we were on the train to Scarborough. Jim Sykes, a former policeman, is a stickler for wanting to do things in an orderly fashion. He had a face on him.

'Spit it out. What's the matter?'

'Never mind, we've done it now.' He is good at sulking.

'Go on, say it.'

'Proper preparation prevents poor performance.'

'Yes, and . . . ?'

'I don't like this jumping straight in business. Another hour and I could have checked *Kelly's Directory of the North and East Ridings* in the Central Library.'

'We have an address for Mr and Mrs Wells: Wells's Fresh Caught Fish, Victoria Road.'

'They may have moved.'

'Then we'll be on the spot. I want to start sooner rather than later. The days turn dark so early now.' I made a conciliatory gesture. 'Here's the guide book, and you have the map.'

'Yes.'

'Well then, what more do we need?'

He sighed. 'All right. Have it your own way.'

As we reached York, he unfolded the map. 'It's no distance from the station to Victoria Road.'

'This might be the most straightforward job we have ever had.'

Beyond York, he had overcome his sulk and treated me to snippets of information from my *Black's Guide to Yorkshire*. 'Scarborough is rightly known as Queen of English Watering Places.'

'And where's the King of Watering Places?'

'It doesn't say. Bognor, probably.'

Our train chugged through the flat East Riding land-scape where fields lay fallow, their washed-out colours changing from mustard to brown to a muddy grey, so sludgy that it made the slate sky bright by comparison. My novel was Winifred Holtby's *Anderby Wold*, set in just this landscape. I imagined the fierce farmer heroine, Mary Robson, driving her cart along a winding lane, full of energy and determination about her imagined and imaginary future.

Sykes stared glumly across the barren land. 'Typical. We have a paid for trip to the seaside and it couldn't be in July, could it? No. Has to be at the dead end of the year.'

'Cheer up, Mr Sykes. The sky is trying to show a touch of blue. Look, there's a patch big enough to mend a hole in a shirt. It could be bright in Scarborough.'

'Bracing more like.'

'If we find out what we need to know quickly, I'm all for a stroll along the front and a decent lunch. I might walk up to St Mary's and pay my respects at Anne Brontë's grave.'

Sykes scowled. 'Don't include me in the pilgrimage. I've

no truck with graveyards. Let the dead in peace to get on with being dead. I'll wait till I'm carried there.'

'What would you like to see, besides the sea, time permitting?'

'I fancy a stroll up to the castle. I always try to drag the kids there but they prefer the beach and the rides.'

Arriving in a place associated with holidays and endless time for strolls and enjoyment lifted my spirits, but not for long.

As the carriage door slammed shut, I caught sight of a tall figure in black coat and black homburg. Something about the way he moved made me think that I had seen him before. Straight away, I thought of the man who had followed Lady Coulton to and from the club.

I touched Sykes's arm. 'Don't look now but I think someone is following us.'

Without needing to speak further, we made our way to the buffet bar. I found a seat in a corner. Sykes went to the counter to order.

There was no sign of the man in black, though I had felt so sure.

I explained my suspicions to Sykes, adding that even though Lady Coulton was followed, there could be no question of the person knowing what she and I had talked about in the club.

'How long have they been married?' he asked.

'Almost thirty years.'

'The husband will know she had a lover. He may know about the child, even if he says nothing.'

'I don't believe he does know.'

'In any case, it is a bit late in life for him to be spying on her.'

When we finished our tea, we took the precaution of separating, each making our way, in a roundabout fashion, to Victoria Road.

Confident that I had not been followed, as I stepped between a tramcar and a delivery van, I caught the whiff of fresh fish as a woman hurried by carrying a shopping basket.

Sykes approached from the other direction, pulling down his hat as a sharp gust of wind blew up from the North Sea. 'Who'll do the talking?'

'If it's Mr Wells, you. If it's Mrs Wells, I'll ask to speak to her privately, saying we have an acquaintance in common.'

'It could be the daughter, Sophia.'

'We'll think of something.'

Sykes could not resist his little jibe. 'If I'd been able to look at an up-to-date directory, we would have known what to expect.'

'It's more interesting this way.'

There had been a change of name. The sign above the shop read, Scarborough Fresh Fish.

To his credit, Sykes did not say I told you so.

Inside, a dapper chap with fair wavy hair and a small moustache finished serving a customer.

Sykes introduced himself. 'Am I speaking to Mr Wells?'

'Oh no, sir. Mr Wells died a long time since. My name's Richard Bryam. We took over from Mrs Wells. She kept the shop going until the lease expired in 1912 and then decided it was too much for her. Mind you, if I'd known what was coming, I would have had second thoughts. It was a devil of a job for the fishing once war was declared.'

'We're trying to trace them, for a friend of the family.' Sykes handed him our card.

Mr Bryam wiped his hands on a tea cloth and looked at the card. 'Mrs Wells and the girl stayed in Scarborough for a bit, but I heard they went away.'

'Do you know where she moved?'

'I'm sorry, I don't.' His eyes narrowed. 'Are you chasing her for money? I wouldn't help no one who was hounding a widow.'

It was my turn. 'Nor would we. Truly. This could be to her advantage. Mr Bryam, do you know what school Sophia attended?'

'You've got me there.' He went to the door between the shop and the house and opened it. There was a smell of baking buns. 'Madge! Lady here has a question.' A slender fair-haired woman appeared. 'They're asking about the Wells family and which school the lass went to.'

She wiped her hands on her apron. 'She was a pupil at Queen Margaret's, a right bonny, clever lass.'

'Where is Queen Margaret's School?' I asked.

She looked at me, judging me to be neither bonny nor clever. 'On Queen Margaret's Road. Where else would you put it?'

'Might Mrs Wells have kept in touch with any particular neighbour?' Sykes asked.

'Likely enough she did. No one had a bad word to say about her.'

We thanked them, and left the shop.

'Something tells me you won't be marching up to the castle after all, Mr Sykes.'

'And Anne Brontë will be lonely in her grave, heaving a sigh that you didn't visit.' Sykes turned up his collar.

'I'll go to the school. You make some enquiries among the neighbours. Someone must know where they went.'

'Right.'

'Let's meet in two hours at Ellingham's on St Nicholas Cliff. *Black's Guide* gives it a good recommendation.'

Sykes tilted his head and raised his eyebrows. 'So you did do some preparation, when it comes to food.'

We sheltered in the entrance to an alley while Sykes unfolded his map. 'Queen Margaret's Road . . . It's not above a mile . . . back along the way we've come, then right . . . '

'It's too cold to be guessing my way. I'll walk back to the station and take a taxi. I think Lady Coulton will run to that.'

Queen Margaret. Walking back the way I had come, I racked my brains to place her. She married a mad Henry and started the Wars of the Roses single-handed. Is that what one must do to have a school named after one?

Queen Margaret's School did appear fit for a queen. The wide entrance led to a tiled hall, its walls adorned with glass cases displaying shields and trophies, tributes to the achievements of former pupils, including Winifred Holtby, who had qualified for Oxford.

It must have cost Mr and Mrs Wells dear to send Sophia here. Even if she had won a scholarship, there would have been the price of a uniform and the cost of books, racquets and hockey sticks.

I had been adopted out of poverty into a more than comfortable station in life. Had Lord Coulton not been out of the country when his wife became pregnant, Sophia Mary

Ann would have had a title and leisure. On the other hand, she would have missed her fine education at a grammar school, and may have been packed off to Switzerland to be 'finished'.

A young teacher came hurrying down the stairs, carrying an armful of papers. 'Hello. Can I help you?'

Twenty minutes later, I sat in an airy study opposite a middle-aged woman with a serious face and benevolent, bespectacled eyes. Her desk was clear, except for a diary and a pen and ink stand. On the window sill stood a blue vase, filled with bronze chrysanthemums.

I handed her my card and explained, in part, my mission to trace Sophia Wells.

'Thirteen years ago.' Her eyes narrowed as she tried to remember the name. 'The register will jog my memory.'

From a filing cabinet, she drew out a register, and read through the names. She looked across her glasses at me. 'No Sophia Wells on the 1912 register.' She took out another register, and this time came upon the name. 'Sophia Wells. She was withdrawn from the school in 1911. Now I recall her. She did very well, high marks in all subjects. We were sad to lose her but I believe she and her mother were removing to Leeds. I remember because I started my teaching career at Thoresby High School for Girls. I mentioned that school, in case Mrs Wells was able to let her daughter continue. I felt a little sorry for Sophia.'

'Why was that?'

'She was teased sometimes, accused of smelling of fish. You know what girls can be like. I had a sharp word in assembly, not specifically about her you understand, but about accepting people for who they are and not judging because of their background.'

'I wish I had been at a school like this.'

She smiled. 'We do our best. Sophia did have one good friend, Bella Davidson. Bella taught here for three years. She is now head of English at a school in Manchester. It's an outside chance, but if you wish I will write to her and ask whether she stayed in touch with Sophia.'

'Thank you. That would be most kind.'

She glanced again at my card. 'I've never met a private detective. Perhaps you will come and talk to our sixth form sometime, and tell them about your work.'

Seated by the window in Ellingham's restaurant, Sykes and I placed our order with a waitress whose apron was so well starched it could have walked out of the building and lived a long life on its own terms.

Sykes examined his right hand. 'It's a long time since my knuckles have knocked on quite so many doors. I went the length of Victoria Road and some of the side streets.'

'Did anyone remember them?

'They remembered them all right. One old lady spoke of little Sophia rolling up her sleeves and helping in the shop. She remembered her sweeping the flags. They were a nice family, well liked. Wells was a big fellow, red-faced and jolly. He slapped a fish about as if he could bring it to life and coax the creature into swimming again. His wife was tall and thin, and when they were in the shop together it was non-stop repartee. The pair of them could have earned a good living on the stage, apparently.'

'Somebody must know where they went.'

'The old lady said they moved to Belmont Road after Mrs Wells gave up the shop. It's on the other side of the bridge. I went there but couldn't find a soul who remembered them. Happen they didn't stay long.'

Over our fish, chips, peas and bread and butter, I told him about my visit to Queen Margaret's School. At least there were two possible leads: Thoresby High School, and the old school friend, now head of English at a Manchester school, who may be in touch with me.

When we left Ellingham's, we consoled ourselves with a walk along the Foreshore, as far as the pier. We stood and looked out to sea, watching the waves roll in, listening to them crash against the sea wall.

I liked what I had heard about the little family and felt sorry that their hard-earned life had changed so abruptly. Still, it was good that Jennifer Wells had chosen to take herself and Sophia to Leeds. We would advertise in the newspapers, and hope for a good result.

We walked back to the station through the evening gloom.

Sykes armed himself with newspapers from W H Smiths. I bought Winifred Holtby's *The Crowded Street*.

We had a carriage to ourselves, so could spread out.

Sykes is one of those people who simply must read aloud any interesting titbit that catches his eye.

'Price increases. Revolution in the air again. If we'd never come off the gold standard we wouldn't have had to return to it would we?'

I cleared my throat, and read a few lines from my newly purchased novel.

'All right, so you're not interested in economics.'

'I just don't want to hear any more about the gold standard.'

He stayed silent for several miles.

'Listen to this then, "Haunted Yorkshire Mill Girl, beset by poltergeists, spends time at the British College of Psychic Science." When she is in a room, furniture shifts. Sounds like my Rosie, only with her it's deliberate. Oh, hark at this. Our mill lass doesn't even have to be in the room. Ornaments fly about. Very heavy furniture lifts of its own accord. But several weeks being studied and helped has reduced the psychic activity.' He turned the page of the newspaper. 'I'd say the mill girl came up with a good wheeze for free bed and board. I might invite a poltergeist to visit me.'

'Psychic scientists would jump at the opportunity to observe you.'

At that moment, we entered a tunnel, the train lurched and the carriage became pitch black.

Sykes flicked on his lighter and the small flame gave a strange glow to his rugged cheeks. 'The poltergeists,' he joked.

I did not answer. Somehow the change of pace and sudden darkness seemed an ill-omen. We had drawn too many blanks for comfort.

After two or three minutes, the chug of the engine returned to normal and we were once more on our way.

When we left the train at Leeds, I saw him again, the tall man in the black hat and coat. This time, he was ahead of us, disappearing along the platform.

Sykes read my thoughts. 'Worry not, Mrs Shackleton. He is a travelling salesman, with a notebook in his pocket for repeat orders.'

I was not convinced.

Five

The next day, Sykes continued work on our only other case which concerned a bank clerk suspected of devising an ingenious fiddle. The man had been seen splashing money about, and treating a lady, not his wife.

I drove the short distance to Thoresby High School for Girls, a solid, utilitarian building of smoke-darkened red brick. Early-bird girls gathered in clusters by the gate, looking so very young, clad in gabardine raincoats, school hats and stout shoes. Unless Sophia Wells had stood out in some way, perhaps, after all this time, the staff would not remember her.

Entering the main doors before being summoned by the bell gave me an odd feeling of breaking the rules. Inside, the building was not dissimilar from the school I had attended, with the broad corridor, wide staircase and that school smell of washed floors, running shoes and chalk.

A tired-looking cleaning woman, fastening the buttons of her coat, showed me to the headmistress's office. The nameplate read, Miss D. Emerson.

I knocked.

She called for me to come in.

A middle-aged woman with a pleasant pudding face and wearing sensible tweeds and brogues stood by the desk, papers in her hand. She looked at me, seeming not in the least surprised to be interrupted by a stranger.

I apologised for the intrusion, introduced myself and said that I hoped she might help me trace the mother of a former pupil.

She hesitated.

'Miss Blondell from Queen Margaret's School recommended me to come here, Miss Emerson. I know it is a long time since Sophia Wells was a pupil here, but I have been asked to trace Mrs Wells by a client and have news which would be to her and her daughter's advantage.'

I gave her my card.

In the corridor, the school bell rang.

She glanced at my card. 'Do you always turn up without writing for an appointment, Mrs Shackleton? Is that the modern way?'

Any moment now she would give me one hundred lines to write, or demand that I learn a poem from the *Treasury of Golden Verse*.

'If you'd like me to come back at a more convenient time . . .'

'No. Since you are here, see my secretary, Miss Stafford.'

She opened the door to an adjacent office. 'Miss Stafford, perhaps you can help this lady. She is a detective, trying to trace the family of one of our former pupils and assures me that it is not in connection with some felony but may be to their advantage.' The bell stopped ringing. She handed Miss Stafford my card, saying, 'Doesn't do to be late for assembly.'

With that, she left.

There is something about Peter Pan collars that makes a person look most efficient. The gaunt Miss Stafford wore one. Her office was small, not much bigger than a cupboard but a cupboard where there was clearly a place for everything and everything stacked and packed.

'What's the girl's name, and when was she here?'

'Sophia Wells. She would have come here from Scarborough in 1912. Her date of birth is 10 July, 1901.'

'Ah yes, I remember a girl coming from Scarborough. Her name wasn't Sophia. Got off to a difficult start.' She bobbed down and opened the bottom drawer of one of the filing cabinets. After peering at names on the closely packed files, she withdrew a heavy-duty board folder. She placed it on the desk, untied its faded pink tape and withdrew a register. 'Here we are.'

Opening the register, Miss Stafford glanced at the names and tapped the page with her nicotine-stained finger. 'Ah, you're right. Sophia Mary Ann Wells. She chose to be known as Mary Ann. We always ask if a girl has a middle name which she prefers. When changing schools, it sometimes helps a child to have a fresh view of herself. Next of kin, mother, Mrs Bradshaw.'

'Mrs Bradshaw?'

'They lived on Compton Road.'

Being quite good at reading upside down, I had already made a mental note of the address that Miss Stafford was now writing for me.

So Mrs Wells had remarried; an unwanted complication.

She handed me the scrap of paper. 'I do hope something beneficial comes to them as a result of your enquiries, after

Mrs Bradshaw's bad luck. Of course they may well have moved. Mary Ann will be twenty-four years old now – how time flies.'

'What bad luck did Mrs Bradshaw have?'

'It was so unfortunate. Her husband worked in tailoring, making uniforms, at Montague Burtons. He came out after his late shift one night, to make his way home. He was knocked down by the vehicle that had come to pick up the uniforms.'

'How awful.'

'Yes, twice widowed. I hope she was more fortunate the third time.'

'The third time?'

'I often saw girls with their mothers in town on a Saturday, and I saw Mary Ann and her mother on Boar Lane one day, after the war. Mary Ann was working in some office. I remember thinking what a shame she did not stay in education longer.'

'What age did she leave school?'

'Sixteen.'

'And Mrs Wells, Mrs Bradshaw, married a third time?'

'She was about to, though I know no details. She was a hard worker, and a sensible woman.'

For my own purposes, I wished that she had not remarried. Perhaps Sophia, having changed her name to Mary Ann, may have decided to take the new stepfather's name, just to baffle me.

'Might Sophia have given the school as a reference? If Mrs Bradshaw remarried, they may have left Compton Road. I am wondering whether there may be a more up-to-date address on your files.'

'I can't easily put my hands on that sort of correspondence. We have a nightmare of archives. The teachers get at them and they have no sense of leaving something as they find it.'

'Do you remember what year you saw Mrs Bradshaw and Mary Ann in town?'

'It was after the war, but not so very long after. Perhaps the spring of 1919. I know I was out to buy a hat for a wedding and had very little luck in the matter.'

'Did Sophia have any particular friends here, that you remember?'

'Now that I couldn't say. If anyone knew, it would be a teacher. But you know girls. Friendships flare up and burn out for no reason.'

'You said she got off to a difficult start here.'

'I don't know whether that is worth mentioning now, or whether it is fair to do so.'

'I am used to keeping confidences, Miss Stafford.'

'It was to do with a tortoise shell comb. One of the girls said it was hers, and that Mary Ann had taken it, accused her of stealing. Mary Ann said she found it on Woodhouse Lane and finders keepers. It was sorted out but girls took sides, as they do. After that, if anything went missing, there was this bad atmosphere and suspicion of Mary Ann.'

'Do you remember all your former pupils this well?'

'Heavens no. It was her coming from Scarborough, then the business with the comb, and other items that inexplicably disappeared, then her being top of the class and so good at netball. She blossomed, you see. I also remember her because of her mother.'

'Because of the husband's terrible accident?'

38

'Well yes, but something else. She was such a capable woman. During the war, we dug up part of Woodhouse Moor, to grow potatoes and cabbages, be self-sufficient for the war effort. Mary Ann's mother came to help. Only one other mother did so. Mrs Bradshaw was cheerful, jollied the girls along, you know. She was very good with a spade, and quite an inspiration to the girls because she worked at Barnbow, the munitions factory, and this particular morning was one of her very rare off-duty times.' She touched her cheek. 'The poor woman had that yellow tinge, a jaundiced look from working with the gunpowder.'

I thanked Miss Stafford for her time. My next call would take me even farther back into Sophia Mary Ann's life, to the photographic studio where she was captured on plate at the age of three.

Driving along Bingley High Street brought back memories of my first professional engagement. Over there was the Ramshead Arms where Sykes and I had discussed that tangled case. I spotted the familiar café with its check curtains where my erstwhile chum Tabitha had nervously smoked cigarettes while explaining that she wanted me to try to find her father, long after everyone else had failed.

Remembering that, I tried not to feel despondent about the present search. After all, I had only just begun. Having found lost sheep before, I must be able to do it again.

The photographic studio was on the same side of the High Street as the café, between a newsagents and a draper's shop. I parked outside, feeling a bit of a guy in my motoring coat, a great fleecy swaddler. There were display photographs in the window, including a bride and groom in the doorway of the old church. At least the business was still under the same management. The name *Felton Photographic Studios* was etched on the window and on the frosted glass of the door.

The clapper rang as I entered the premises.

The place was beautifully kept, with the wooden floor and surfaces well polished. An ornamental plant stood in the corner and there were two chairs for customers, one of them the same as appeared in the old photograph. Heavy drapes on the right must lead to the studio area. I was about to take a peek when a woman emerged from the rear of the premises.

'Hello. Can I help you?'

She was about sixty, gaunt with pale blue eyes, her hair done up in a bun.

'I hope so. It's a slightly unusual request.'

She glanced at me carefully and beyond, through the window to my car. 'Oh? Well we manage all sorts here. Mr Felton is out on a job but I can take your details.'

'I'm really here to try and trace someone.' I handed her my card. 'The person I am looking for is Mrs Bradshaw, formerly Mrs Wells, maiden name Tarpey. She brought her little girl here to be photographed, over twenty years ago.'

'Over twenty years ago?' She caught her lower lip between her teeth. 'Oh dear. I don't think I'll be able to help with that.'

I placed the photograph of little Sophia on the counter. The woman looked at it without saying a word, and then left the counter, went to the drapes and drew them back. 'The studio has hardly changed. So you've come to the right place. We've different backdrops. If Mr Felton was to take the picture now he'd probably set the kiddy on a little horse.'

She was right that the setting had not changed. There was the same plant stand, jardinière and perhaps the same fern. 'The little girl is Sophia Mary Ann Wells.'

The woman smiled indulgently. 'If you knew how many pictures Mr Felton takes you wouldn't ask. This would have been taken by his father and I know for sure he hasn't kept all the old records.'

'Do the names Wells or Tarpey ring any bells, Mrs . . . ?'

'Watson. And no, I don't know anyone by that name.' She picked up a pencil and wrote "Wells" on the back of my card. 'What did you say the other name was?'

'Bradshaw.'

She wrote that too. 'I can ask Mr Felton when he comes in.'

'Thank you. There will be a reward for any information leading to my finding the lady and her daughter.'

'Will there now? Well then I wish you and them luck.'

She looked past me, to the door. It opened and two women bustled in, a mother and daughter, bringing a cold draught and a buzz of excitement. It was my guess that they were here to arrange a wedding photograph.

I thanked Mrs Watson and left.

Leaving my motor parked near the studio, I walked along the High Street, trying to imagine what had brought the Wells family here all those years ago. It was too far to come simply to have a photograph taken. There must be some family connection with the area.

Crossing the Packhorse Bridge, hearing the gurgle of the water, I made my way to the ancient church, All Saints. There, I wandered through the churchyard, reading the inscriptions on the headstones. Several bore the name

41

Tarpey, the family name of Lady Coulton's nanny and her sister.

Here was the connection I had been looking for. Someone in Bingley must know the family and have information. It was time to advertise.

The office of the *Bingley Bugle* was opposite the café.

On the sloping desk, I wrote my announcement requesting information about Mrs Bradshaw, formerly Wells, maiden name Tarpey, and Sophia Mary Ann Wells.

I handed my announcement across the counter to an ancient elf-like figure with a wispy beard. He peered at my writing through thick spectacles, as if checking for a secret code or spelling mistakes. For a mad moment, I thought he would come up with some useful information about those I sought.

His voice seemed to come from a deep barrel. 'This week's edition came out this morning. It'll be next Thursday now.'

I paid him.

He wrote a receipt and the date my insertion would appear: Thursday, 5th November. Bonfire Night.

'Do you know the family?' I asked.

'I do not and I do not want to. No good will come of enquiring after Tarpeys round here.'

'Why not?'

He looked across at me, eyes twinkling, and gave a toothless grin. 'You'd have to go to the churchyard to find a Tarpey.'

Six

On Friday morning, I motored to the town centre, parked on Commercial Street, delivered announcements, and paid for insertions and box numbers in six newspapers: the *Yorkshire Evening Post*, the *Post*, *Daily News*, *Skyrack Express*, the *Herald* and the Northern edition of the *Daily Chronicle*. This felt like desperate measures but I was terribly disappointed that all the personal enquiries had so far come to nothing. Everyone reads a newspaper, even if only when it is wrapped around fish and chips or being scrunched in a ball to light a fire. Someone must know Mrs Jennifer Bradshaw and Sophia Wells.

I had parked by the Leeds Library and needed to pop in and speak to the deputy librarian, in the hope that she would relieve me of a rather odd task I had agreed to and that given my enquiries now struck me as irksome.

Dr Potter was bouncing up the stairs at the same time, carrying a hessian bag of books to be returned. He is a charming man, tall with a slight stoop, thinning hair, oodles of enthusiasm for life and a talent for waylaying people he likes to talk to. A renowned mathematician, he looks the part, thoughtful, every inch the learned man. Yet he has a theatrical quality, too. Even in winter when others are muffled, he wears an elegant white silk scarf. When he chats and smiles, he becomes so animated and expressive in speech and gesture that he has occasionally been mistaken for a Frenchman.

He tipped his black fedora. We exchanged a few words, pausing on the spacious landing at the top of the stairs.

Mid conversation, he came to an abrupt halt as something on the wall caught his eye. 'What's Lennox put up now?'

It was a newspaper article from a couple of years ago that had been cut out and framed. It boasted of the library's valuable stock. Dr Potter scratched his head. 'What will Lennox do next? Send a personal invitation to every book thief in the country?'

'He's naturally proud of the library's acquisitions.'

'So he advertises to the world. A big mistake.'

'The *Gazette* is hardly the world.'

'My dear Mrs Shackleton, there is no need for him to shout from the rooftops. Half of our shareholders are unaware of what books lurk on the shelves. That is one of the library's charms. And not every proprietor is as upright as you and I. The tales I could tell about one or two individuals would curl your hair.'

'Really?'

'Yes, but not now.' He rested his arm on the banister. 'I am recruiting supporters for a matter that will come up at a special meeting.'

'I'm unlikely to come. I'm very busy just now.'

'Oh but you must. You see, we have the opportunity to move to more suitable premises where there would be excellent security for valuable acquisitions. It is not to be missed. I shall circulate a paper.'

'You sound like a salesman, Dr Potter.'

'Oh dear, do I? Don't let my enthusiasm put you off.' He moved as if to open the door, and then delayed. 'Have you noticed something odd going on lately, little huddles and whispers?'

'I haven't been into the library for a week or so. Who was huddling and whispering, do tell.'

'Oh far be it from me to say a word about our dear president, our librarian and his deputy ... ' Dr Potter has a waspish sense of humour and I am glad he shares his little jokes with me rather than making me the butt of them; though perhaps he does that too. He lowered his voice to a whisper. 'Where is the lovely counter assistant, Miss Montague? A charming young woman, most obliging.'

'I can't remember when I last saw her.'

'Quite so. Our pre-Raphaelite beauty has disappeared. This may be a case for you, our own private detective.' He spoke light-heartedly but something in his eyes belied the tone.

'I hope not. Have you asked about her?'

'Perhaps that will come better from you. But I miss her. She was the only counter assistant who would willingly go into that dreadful basement – skip down there at a moment's notice' He twinkled, taking the merest pause for breath. 'Talking of which, a little bird tweeted a ghostly tale. I have something that may intrigue you, a personal item of historic interest.'

The trouble with Dr Potter's flow of words is that he invariably makes me feel like a music hall straight man, there

45

to give encouragement and prompt the next outpouring. He moved nearer the door. 'It's a magazine I wrote as an undergraduate, when the world was young. I only ever brought out two editions, and this copy was my last hurrah as a journalist. You'll find two articles of particular interest, or I'll eat this moth-eaten fedora.'

The door of the library opened. Chuckling, Dr Potter nodded to the man who was leaving and we both stepped inside. 'Follow me,' Dr Potter whispered.

He led the way to the shelves where pamphlets are kept in box files. Bobbing down, he withdrew a box, opened it and took out several sheets of printed papers, bound together with string. No one speaks in the library. He mouthed, 'Read this.'

I took it from him. With a gallant bow, he waved me to the counter before him.

Mr Lennox himself was there. He entered my item in the alphabetical register and in my personal ticket book.

I engaged in a little silent lip-speaking. 'Where is Mrs Carmichael?'

He nodded in the direction of the committee room.

I tapped on the door, opened it and popped my head round.

Mrs Carmichael, deputy librarian, raised her eyebrows and smiled a greeting. She is about fifty, soberly dressed, and with salt and pepper hair. She radiates efficiency and would be excellent at evacuating a building in the event of a fire. Either she was born that way, or her inner calm is hard won. She wears a wedding ring, but there has never been mention of a Mr Carmichael.

She set down her pen and pushed aside a minute book.

'Come and sit down, Mrs Shackleton. You're here about this evening.' She looked pleased, as if something important had been decided in her favour.

'Yes. I could have spoken to Mr Lennox, but he is busy on the counter.'

Now I felt guilty, because I was going to let her down, and I could not even plead a more pressing obligation. Until there was some response to my newspaper announcements, or a lucky find by Sykes in the area of Compton Road, there was nothing more I could do about tracking down Sophia and her mother. It was only that I wanted to keep my concentration on the case, and not be caught up in some matter to do with staff discontent at the library. 'The thing is, Mrs Carmichael, I was never sure from our telephone conversation quite what was expected of me this evening. As it happens I have rather a lot on just now so I am hoping that whatever it is can proceed without me.'

Even to myself, I sounded wishy-washy. To say no having once said yes is such bad form. Yet sometimes I say yes too easily.

The weight of disappointment in her face would have launched a ship from its moorings.

'Oh Mrs Shackleton, please do not retreat from this. I cannot be present myself, you see, and no one else . . . we have kept it quiet, except for a few individuals.'

'But what am I expected to do? You said on the telephone that staff are uneasy about working in the basement. You want to be able to reassure them. Mustn't their unease be to do with poor lighting, or a damp atmosphere? We have proprietors who are expert in that sort of thing.'

She clasped her hands and leaned forward, staring at the

table as if something in the grain of the wood might give her inspiration. When she looked up, her words came slowly. 'I expect you have heard stories of the haunting, that the library has its ghost?'

'It was mentioned to me once. I did not pay much attention.'

She sighed. 'Then you are going to think me a very superstitious woman.' She played with her wedding ring. 'I am not superstitious. I was brought up in a rational household. My father was a solicitor, though he died when I was very young. My mother, too, studied law and worked as a clerk until her marriage. She was active in the rational dress movement. I married a rather jolly man, fond of jokes, and in the end we did not suit each other. I am telling you this because I do not want you to laugh at what I have to say.'

'I wouldn't laugh.'

She took a deep breath, placing her palms flat on the table, as if instructing her hands not to fidget. 'The stories have always been about a former librarian haunting the place. But that is not all. There is something strange about the basement, several of us have felt it, a powerful feeling that comes over one suddenly, a cold chill, creaks and groans.'

'This is a very old building.'

She continued as if I had not spoken ' . . . a rush of cold air. I have experienced it myself. The librarian's wife, Mrs Lennox, she was a sensitive, as they call such people. Mr Lennox confided in me that she had second sight. Two years ago, she came to help unpack books. Afterwards, she was white and shaking. She would say nothing but she looked at me with such . . . I thought it was pity, at having to be here, in this place. A week later, she took to her bed and never recovered. There is something evil at work here.'

This was upsetting to hear, but it gave me a perfect excuse. 'Then what you need is a man of the cloth, the vicar from the parish church, or the minister from Mill Hill.'

'We have such a man. He will be here this evening.'

'That's all right then.'

'It is Father Bolingbroke. He is a Roman Catholic priest, versed in these matters, here on a sabbatical, studying the works of St Thomas Aquinas. Mr Lennox has prevailed upon him to bless the building.' I waited. Something told me that I was not off the hook. She leaned forward and this time clasped her hands as if in prayer. 'He needs two acolytes who know the library and who are completely trustworthy. You are one. Mr Lennox is the other.'

'Could you not take my place?'

'I am a coward. Something in me revolts against the whole idea. I feel I would be overcome. You have the courage to do it. Afterwards I will be able to tell the counter assistants that you were here. That will make a difference.'

This was very flattering, but also absurd. I did not want to ridicule her fears and while I wondered how to respond, she continued. 'It was Dr Potter who suggested you.'

'Was it indeed?' I must remember to thank him, and find some way to return the favour.

'He said that as the only lady on the committee, you are the perfect choice as far as discretion. Also, he believes that it would be difficult to enlist a staunch Protestant, or a strict non-conformist. They wouldn't do it. A Catholic would need permission from a parish priest. A fervent atheist would laugh. Say you will, Mrs Shackleton.'

'So it's because of my sex and lack of religiosity.'

'Not only that. Dr Potter thinks highly of you as a detective. He paraphrased Shakespeare. There is more on heaven and earth and in our basement than we dream of. He said that if anyone could discern the "more" that is in our basement, it would be our lady detective.'

He would have had his tongue firmly in cheek, but there was little point in saying that. Mrs Carmichael had me cornered. It was time to recognise defeat. I agreed as graciously as annoyance would allow.

'Oh good. Thank you very much.'

Leaving Mrs Carmichael to her work, I took my leave.

I treated myself to lunch at Schofields. I would have preferred this to be a celebration for finding Sophia and her mother. Instead, it was my consolation for having to wait and hope. After that, I looked about the town for an hour or so. When I emerged from Marshall & Snelgrove, I was dismayed to see fog floating through the streets and to breathe in that horrid sulphurous dampness.

Time to go home.

This would not be the best of evenings to return to the library after hours in order to help lay a ghost, or a legion of ghosts.

Having parked near the library, I hurried back in that direction. That was when Miss Merton, my neighbour, hailed me. An avid reader, maker of jams and chutneys, she is housekeeper for her brother, the professor. They live directly opposite me. She bustled towards me, being a person who walks like a crowd, dangerously swinging her string bag full of borrowed books into the thigh of a passing businessman. With her other arm she held a shopping basket.

'Mrs Shackleton, what a blessing to see you! Are you driving home?'

'Yes. Would you like a ride?'

'That is most kind.'

She is a little taller than I, sparsely built but well insulated in her dark tweed coat and broad-brimmed hat. 'It was raining when I left the house. My dratted umbrella let me down. I took it to the man in the market to fix the spoke, which you think he could have done there and then but no. "Come back tomorrow." One can get nothing done these days. And how I hate this fog! It plays havoc with my catarrh. A person like me, with narrow nostrils, has a hard time of it. You are fortunate to have broad nostrils.'

We were by a plate glass window as she said this. I glanced at myself and at her in the pane. Fog prevented a nostril comparison. She stepped out smartly, not needing to avoid a puddle because of her stout galoshes.

'I am so glad to have bumped into you for another reason than the fog and your kind offer. I was hoping to have a word.'

We had reached the car. Once we began our journey, the noise of the engine and my need to concentrate on the road as patches of fog grew dense meant that we did not have that word. We shared some desultory comments, shouted above the noise, random remarks of little consequence.

'Look! There's another one.' She was pointing at a group of children on the corner of Woodhouse Moor.

'Another what?'

'Guy Fawkes. Penny for the guy on every street corner. We're a week off the 5th of November. They do it earlier every year and all they want is to buy firecrackers.'

After we arrived back at our road, she stayed with me until I put the car in the garage.

A couple of boys were dragging a huge branch out of the wood. 'I don't hold with it, and not just because Guy Fawkes was Catholic.'

'Well there's no stopping Bonfire Night, Miss Merton, like it or not.' We walked down our street together. 'Come in and have a glass of something with me. It's such a chilly night.'

'Thank you. I don't mind if I do.'

We came through the front door. She unbuttoned her tweed coat. I took it from her and hung it on the hall stand hook. She slipped off her galoshes to reveal soft black leather shoes.

It took only moments for me to pour fortified wine with a dash of quinine and put out a few crackers and slivers of cheese. Miss Merton settled herself in the drawing room.

We sat either side of the fire.

She took a sip. 'Nothing like a medicinal wine.' In the same slightly complaining tone as she had told me about the broken umbrella, she said, 'I hope you are successful with the library ghost.'

'You know about tonight?' So much for Mrs Carmichael's assertion that the business was being kept quiet.

'Only because I reported seeing the ghost myself, last week.'

'Really?'

'I was there for a *Father Brown*. One is always secure in the hands of G K Chesterton.'

For the briefest of moments, it struck me that she did not

look at all secure. Her air of discomfort made me wonder whether she would rather talk about something else. But my curiosity was aroused.

'You really and truly believe you saw a ghost?'

'I would not swear, but it seemed so.' She adjusted her footstool. 'My brother pooh-poohs it, and of course I would not breathe a word about it in the presence of university people, not with Theodore up for the post of vice chancellor.'

'Mrs Sugden mentioned that. It's quite an honour.'

'So I keep telling him.' She leaned forward, lowering her voice. 'The vice chancellor is provided with fine accommodation. You may have seen the official residence.'

'I have indeed.'

'I hope I did not tempt fate by taking a little peep around the grounds. It has an apple orchard. To be mistress of such a house would be a full-time occupation.'

'Would you like that?'

'I have a very good apple chutney recipe, though I won't tempt fate by counting the apple trees before Theodore is appointed.' She took out a dainty hanky and blew her nose. 'But you asked me about the ghost.'

'Yes.'

'Theodore says that what I saw was a figment of my imagination. It's true that when I was a girl, often I would run down the stairs very fast. As I neared the bottom, I would see a small dark figure lurking by the newel post. It would disappear as I drew closer, but seemed real enough, just as the ghost seemed real. But I shouldn't influence you.'

'Please don't stop now. You saw a ghost.'

'Very well, if you insist. I was in the reading room, by the fire with *Pickwick Papers*. I must have dozed a little because I was conscious of reading the same paragraph twice. Something made me look up. I saw the figure, not the small figure I saw as a child but large, dark, looming. He was there, and then he melted as it were into the bookcase by the far wall. He disappeared into shelves that held the *Parliamentary Papers*.'

'And do you read some significance into that?'

'I don't know what to make of it. Until I saw him for myself, I blamed the counter assistants. You would think that intelligent young women with responsible positions would be above gossiping and chit-chatting but believe me they do more of that than any factory lass who wouldn't be able to hear above the din of machinery. "Quiet please" the sign in the reading room says. We are asked not to talk because of the disturbance to other readers. Do they observe that silence? They do not. Whenever the librarian and his deputy are elsewhere, one hears them. Chitter chatter, chitter chatter like a family of monkeys. When there are two of them you'd think it was a tribe.'

'I hadn't noticed.'

'They were particularly at it that day and that's what I blame for my apparition. They are conjuring the ghost by their interest.'

'What were they saying?'

'They were talking about sounds emanating from the basement, unexplained noises, and then the dark-haired one, she told that old story about the ghost of a librarian and said something had touched her hair, and she felt a cold breath on the back of her neck.'

The room was growing dark. Shadows lengthened on the

ceiling. I picked up the tongs and placed a few more coals on the fire. It crackled and glowed red before orange flames began to lick their way to the shiny new cobs. 'You've given me the shivers.'

'Well there you have it. I am glad that you agreed to take part in the ceremony. Theodore is surprised, although he has a great deal of time for Father Bolingbroke.'

Miss Merton is a convert to Catholicism, which I believe is genuine. Mrs Sugden claims it is entirely for the purpose of annoying Professor Merton, who strictly conforms to non-conformity.

She reached out her elegant hand and with long, thin fingers, snared a cracker and a morsel of cheddar, taking a dainty bite.

I refilled her glass. 'Until recently, I had no idea the place was haunted.'

She sipped her wine. 'That is not surprising, since you hail from Wakefield. I expect there are many old Leeds tales that have passed you by. This one dates to the last century, before the invention of electric lighting, which my brother believes counts for a great deal in the way of dispelling strange phenomena.'

The bright fire provided its own images of faces, deep caves and strange landscapes. She stared into the flames, as if her story lay somewhere between the red glow and the leaping dark orange tongue.

'It's over forty years since it was first seen, by a new young librarian, a Mr John McAllister, just twenty-four years old. It was night time and he was working late, and alone. He saw a light in one of the rooms but when he went to investigate, the room was in darkness. That's what they say.

I should hate to be alone in there at night even now that we have electricity. I shudder to think of it.'

'Just a light, he saw a light?'

'Not only that. As he was leaving, hurrying to catch the last train, he caught a glimpse of someone turning to look at him, a tall man with a shimmering face and hunched shoulders. John McAllister thought someone had broken in and he rushed to fetch a revolver and shouted, hoping a passing constable might hear. His account is written down in the library files, and locked away.'

'Perhaps someone had broken in.'

'No. The doors were all locked, yet the apparition vanished.' She paused and took another bite of cheese and biscuit. 'This is very good cheese. Is it Wensleydale?'

'Lancashire.'

'I prefer Wensleydale.'

'What happened next?'

'I've no idea. But the word is passed on through the staff. They all know about it and say nothing.'

'The story is probably embellished as time passes.'

We sat in silence for a moment. If McAllister had missed his last train, for whatever reason, he would have had much explaining to do when he got home. What had he been drinking, as he worked late and alone? Or perhaps he had not been working at all, or had not been alone. A spectral visitation would provide a most original excuse. 'Sorry I did not come home last night, dear. I was detained by a ghost.'

Miss Merton smoothed her skirt, glanced at the fire and then looked at me, perhaps sensing my disbelief. 'That is how the story is told. There was a kind of corroboration, from a most reliable quarter.'

'Oh?'

'A priest told Mr McAllister that the description of the ghostly intruder fitted the deceased librarian, Vincent Sternberg, who died in post.'

'I understand now how the staff could be unsettled, especially on these dark nights.'

'The counter assistants should not be whispering these stories. I saw the ghost. They did not. I wouldn't dream of gossiping about it.'

'Of course not.' I left a discreet pause. 'And was that the end of the matter, regarding McAllister I mean?'

'Some of the younger staff kept up the stories, held séances when the library was closed, claimed that they heard groans in the basement, a knocking sound behind a bookcase. Volumes would mysteriously leave their place and be found elsewhere. The bell that Sternberg used to summon staff was said to ring when no one touched it. Lamps would suddenly extinguish themselves when there was no draught.'

I smiled. 'Young people working in a library are no different from those working anywhere else. They must have a little amusement.'

If we had not been sitting by firelight, I may not have asked my next question.

'Miss Merton, what does your church teach about ghosts?'

'I will partake of another small glass, Mrs Shackleton, if I may.'

I obliged.

She took a sip. 'When a person dies, they are judged and go to Heaven, Hell or Purgatory. It happens in an instant. No souls hang about waiting to hear, Am I to ascend, descend or hover somewhere in-between. But it may just possibly be that in Purgatory God allows the soul to linger in those places familiar during life, perhaps to inspire prayers for the dead. If that is so, what better time than the approach to All Hallows' Eve? But of course there is another possibility. Such visions as people claim to see in churchyards and old buildings may be demons, disguised as the once living, whose purpose is to draw men and women away from faith. The library staff should be discouraged from dabbling. The way they are going, it would not surprise me in the least if some of the younger people, for a prank, tried another séance. That would be most regrettable. I would feel it necessary never to set foot in there again, G K Chesterton on the shelves or no G K Chesterton.'

A sudden loud knock on the door startled Miss Merton. 'Excuse me.'

Reluctant as I was to break off our conversation, I went to the door. Before I reached it, the urgent knocking began again.

'All right! I'm coming.'

I opened the door to a small creature with the face of a demon. He looked up at me. 'There's a racket in your garage, Mrs Shackleton.'

This was the time of year when children played tricks on their elders, most usually knocking on doors and running away, or stretching string across a gateway.

'You don't catch me that easily. It's not Mischievous Night yet.'

He took off his mask. It was Thomas Tetley, a sturdy ten-year-old who lived along the lane just below my house. The elastic of the mask had ruffled his brown hair. 'I'm not kidding. There's a funny noise an' all. Did your cat run into the garage?'

There would be a group of children hiding somewhere, waiting to see whether I would fall for their nonsense.

'Thank you for telling me. Now don't you have to go home for tea?'

Miss Merton was behind me, slipping on her coat and galoshes. 'My brother will think I lost myself in the fog on the way home. Thank you for the hospitality, Mrs Shackleton, and the conversation.'

Thomas stood back to let her pass.

I walked her to the gate. The fog had lifted a little. It occurred to me that there was something else she had wanted to say. Only rarely did she or I step into the other's house.

She paused. Glancing at the waiting Thomas Tetley, she spoke in a low voice. 'There was something I meant to tell you, warn you about. None of us is safe. Be careful, you and the child.'

Seven

Thomas scratched behind his ear. 'I'm not kidding, Mrs Shackleton, honest. Something is alive in your garage and making a right old racket.'

My young informant once more assumed his demon mask to trot up to the garage with me. We walked through swirls of fog with small gaps of clear air between, as if the god of dirty weather liked to tease. Living north of the city, the theory goes, one should avoid the worst of the fogs that descend on the town and the industrial areas in the south, east and west. But like disease and good and ill luck, fogs sometimes break boundaries and seep into new territory.

My car had been tucked away for an hour or so, since I returned home with Miss Merton.

By the garage, we stood and listened. No sound emanated from behind the wooden doors. I inserted the key in the padlock and partially opened one of the double doors. Now was not the time to worry about rats. Perhaps an army of them had moved in to occupy an old worn tyre that leaned against the back wall. I planned, when winter changed to spring, to give the tyre to the local children to attach to a branch in the wood. If there was a creature lurking, perhaps it would be more scared of us than we of it. Leaving the door ajar would give it the opportunity to run away. Edging the door open, I half expected Thomas to run off and shout the late October equivalent of 'April Fool!'

We stepped into the garage. Now was the moment for a horde of giggling children to leap from behind the car and then rush off telling tales of how they fooled the lady detective. None appeared.

'I definitely heard it.' Thomas's words through the mask sounded odd and clipped, like a puppet's voice, like Mr Punch. He produced a torch from his pocket.

The silence was absolute.

Thomas played the flashlight's beam over the car, and into each corner, sweeping light from floor to ceiling. 'It must have heard us.'

'What do you think it was?'

'I don't know. It chattered.'

'Earlier you said it could have been the cat.'

'Well it might have been. It made a scratching noise at the door.'

Bravely, Thomas bobbed down. He shone his torch under the car. 'Nothing.'

The canvas flap by the driver seat was slightly raised. I pointed. 'Here, direct the light here.'

He did so, and then shone the beam around the motor's car seats. He gave a sharp intake of breath. 'Shut the big door, Mrs Shackleton, or it will get away.'

I did as he said, creaking the door shut.

Thomas shone the light on the flagged floor, to guide me back.

I took the torch from him and directed the beam around the interior of the car. Curled in the dickey seat at the rear was a small, trembling monkey, dressed in a red, yellow and green horizontally striped knitted coat with pearl buttons. It covered its eyes and peeped through its fingers, like a child that believes it can see you and you can't see it.

I turned to Thomas. 'Is this some trick? Did one of you children run in after me and put it there?'

I could not see his face but there was hurt indignation in his voice. 'I wouldn't put a monkey in a cold car, in the dark.'

'Well where did it come from?'

The monkey removed its paws from its face but still cowered at the far side of the seat.

I handed the torch back to Thomas. 'It must have climbed in when I was in town.'

He shone the torch once more, before pointing the beam away from the creature. 'It's shivering.' In the dim light, our shadows loomed large on the far wall. The place did not seem like my garage at all but outside of time and space. 'Don't let it run away, Mrs Shackleton. It might die.'

'It will have to be returned to its owner, whoever that is.'

'Don't you even recognise it?' His voice held a note of reproach verging on disbelief.

'Should I?'

'Well yes, if you're a proper detective. It belongs to the organ grinder. He came round here ages ago but I haven't seen him since the summer holidays. My mother said he keeps to the town, where people pay him to clear off, and to the poor districts, where people pity him. He plays a little organ on a one-leg stand.'

'We'll have to do something to coax him out of that

corner. I hope he won't bite.' I reached out a hand. 'Come on, monkey.'

Thomas raised the demon mask to the top of his head. 'He might be scared of me, think I'm the devil or something.'

'Perhaps we'll have to come back with nuts, give him one, put a little trail of them, to build up his confidence.'

'He likes music. He likes what the organ grinder plays.'

'I don't have a barrel organ handy, do you?'

'No, but I know one of the songs the organ grinder plays. Our choirmaster taught us. Shall I sing it?'

'Well yes. I can't think of a better idea.'

Holding the flashlight quite still, Thomas began to sing in an exquisitely pure voice that bore no relation to the creaking music of a barrel organ. It was a song from *Rigoletto*, *La donna è mobile*.

As he sang, the monkey became alert in a very different way. It stared at Thomas as if hypnotised. After a long time, it switched its questioning gaze to me.

'Start the song again,' I whispered.

Tentatively, I held out my hand, and waited.

Slowly the monkey raised itself and swayed towards us, half walking, half crawling. It paused for several seconds and then raised a paw.

As I reached down to it, the creature leapt at me with a sudden movement, clinging to my chest and snuggling up as if it mistook me for its long-lost mother. Its tail flicked back and forth. In the light directed upwards from the torch, I saw that it was dark brown, with a ring of fluffy white hair around its head. Thomas wisely continued singing as he reached for the motoring blanket. The torch made lines of light as he moved. He set his torch on the floor and wrapped the blanket around the monkey, all the while continuing to sing.

Here was a child who would go far in life.

'Come on, monkey.' I passed the garage keys to Thomas. 'I'm going to take you home, and find your master. He should keep a closer eye on you in this foul weather.'

We left the garage. Thomas closed the door, clicked the padlock shut and turned the key. I stroked the monkey's head, reassuring it, as Thomas talked to me. 'Did you see the organ grinder in town, Mrs Shackleton?'

'No, not since the summer. Perhaps he lost his monkey in the fog. It must have climbed into my car for shelter.'

As we walked back down the road, the monkey's eyes darted from Thomas to me, but it seemed content, making no attempt to leap free and run away.

Thomas reached out a finger and held the monkey's paw. 'What if I take him home?'

'Your mother might not be happy about that.' I stopped myself from reminding him that he had wanted one of Sookie's kittens and his mother had said no. 'I'll make some enquiries. Come back tomorrow and by then perhaps I'll have found the organ grinder. Have you time to run an errand and earn tuppence before your tea?'

'Yes. I'll do it for nothing if it's for the monkey.'

'Then come inside. I'll give you a note for a gentleman in Woodhouse.'

'That man who works with you, the policeman?'

'He's not a policeman.'

'He looks like one.'

I smiled. Out of the mouths of babes. Sykes prides

himself on not looking like a policeman, but he can't help it.

Thomas followed me inside. He sat by the fire, in the chair earlier occupied by Miss Merton. I handed him the monkey to hold.

Leaving them for a moment, I went into the dining room that doubles as my office and wrote a note to Sykes, asking him to keep his ear to the ground for news of the organ grinder, and explaining that I had the monkey. It was an odd thing to have to write, but Sykes is very good at picking up titbits of information. His sources are many and his contacts legion.

I walked back into the parlour.

Mrs Sugden had heard me come in. She frequently speaks from a different, room, knowing her voice carries well. She started to talk as she walked along the hall.

'What time do you want to . . . ' The word 'eat', which would normally have followed 'What time do you want to', evaporated as she stared at Thomas and the monkey and they stared back at her. Reading her dismay, the creature hid its head under the blanket.

'What have you got there, Thomas Tetley?'

'We think it's the organ grinder's monkey.'

'Well where's the organ grinder?'

'We don't know. Mrs Shackleton is going to find out.'

I raised an eyebrow for Mrs Sugden. What else could one do?

Mrs Sugden pursed her lips. 'Is this your family whistle?' She gave a short, a long and a short whistle. Quite tuneful.

'Aye.'

'Then you've been whistled for, half a dozen times. You better get yourself and that creature off home.'

'What about the note to take to Woodhouse, Mrs Shackleton? I'll still do it.'

'It's all right. I have to go out again. I'll deliver it myself. Anyway, it's too foggy for you to be staying out much longer. You'll end up with a sore throat and lose your singing-to-monkeys voice. If your mother ticks you off, tell her about the monkey, and that you were helping me.'

The monkey did not want to be prised from Thomas, but reluctantly, eventually, it let me take its paw, and made little cries as Thomas went into the hall.

At the front door, he turned. 'You'll let me know what happens?'

'I will.'

When he had gone, Mrs Sugden said, 'Are we taking monkeys as clients now?'

'Where are those hazelnuts?' I opened the cabinet. 'Are they in here?'

'They're for Christmas. I've put 'em somewhere. Don't ask me where.'

It is very annoying to have groceries I buy and pay for hidden from view. 'Then where are the dates?'

'They're for Christmas an' all.'

'We'll get some more.' I pounced on the box of dates. 'It'll have to eat.'

'How did it find its way here?'

'It must have popped into my car when I wasn't looking. I gave Miss Merton a lift up from town and neither of us noticed it.'

'Shouldn't the thing be wearing a collar and lead?'

It was a good point. 'I suppose so. I hadn't thought of that.'

'Has it bitten you yet?'

'Not yet.'

'It will. And its fleas will eat you up, and me, and the cat.'

'I don't think fleas would survive in this weather.'

'Oh they will, under its armpits, believe you me.'

'I didn't know you were such an authority on monkeys.'

'You don't need to be an authority to recognise that a wild animal doesn't belong in a civilised home.'

I opened the box of dates. She glared. 'Don't blame me if I can't get any more and we're date-less for Christmas.'

'Do you think it will swallow the stones?'

'Your tea's ready. Happen you'd like it to have that.'

'I'll be through in a few minutes.'

The monkey eyed the dates.

'Wait on, don't be in such a rush.'

Taking stones from dates is sticky work and when an impatient monkey watches every move and makes small grabs, that does not make the task any easier. The poor thing was hungry. When the monkey had eaten all the dates, I gave it the box to play with and went to wash my hands, leaving the monkey to amuse itself. Taking apart a date box can be quite engrossing.

I went into the kitchen to eat as we had no fire lit in the dining room. Mrs Sugden took my food from the oven and put it on the table, lifting the pan lid that had covered it. 'Don't blame me if it's not piping hot.'

Sausage, mash and peas, still piping hot.

The monkey appeared in the kitchen and sat on the rag rug in front of the range. Having peeled away the fancy paper from the date box, it fiddled with the balsa wood lid, separating the edge from the top. It worked with such delicacy that it was a joy to watch it make a mess, spreading paper and wood across the floor.

Mrs Sugden folded her arms. 'Is it stopping the night?'

'I don't know where else it will go.'

'Where will it sleep?'

'We'll think of something.'

This called for a diversion. Nothing pleases Mrs Sugden more than to have a little research to carry out. While her housekeeping skills are first class, the work does not satisfy her natural curiosity and retentive mind.

'It would be a good idea if you could look up what type of monkey this is. Then we'll know its habits. If I have to advertise for its owner, I can give a proper description.'

'I should think "monkey in a poorly knitted coat" would be sufficient.'

'There are lots of kinds aren't there? It's not a chimpanzee. I'd feel very foolish to just say brown monkey with a whitish circle of hair around its head and a tail as long as itself.'

'I hate long tails. Rats have long tails. I suppose I could look in your Mees' *Children's Encyclopaedia*.'

'What a good idea.'

She was very slightly placated and slapped a cup of tea on the table while the monkey tactfully kept out of view. It even avoided tearing the bottom of the date box into tiny pieces, until she had left the room.

The monkey climbed onto a chair, staring at my cup of tea.

'Want some?'

It pursed its lips.

I poured tea into a saucer. 'Sugar? One lump or two?'

I stirred in a sugar lump.

This was the right thing to do. Monkey must have been well trained. It picked up the saucer and slurped the tea.

A few moments later, I went back into the drawing room where Mrs Sugden sat on the piano stool, an encyclopaedia open on the piano lid, under the glow of the lamp. She tapped at a picture. I stood beside her and looked at a photograph of a monkey that could have been cousin to this one.

'It's a Capuchin, said to be bright and intelligent. They like to swing through the woods and they're not too fussy whether they eat nuts, berries or insects. They come from the Amazon.'

She glanced at the monkey. It was beside me, holding the hem of my skirt, its head tilted, listening to Mrs Sugden's every word. She softened a little. 'Poor little mite. He should have been left to swing through the trees. If he swings through our trees he'll die of frostbite before you can say bananas.'

She closed the book and returned it to the shelf. 'Better shut them curtains. Don't want neighbours looking through thinking we've started a menagerie.' She paused as she closed them and glanced at the house across the way. 'You gave Miss Merton a lift up from town?'

'Yes.'

'Did she say anything?'

'I was very surprised that she accepted my invitation to step inside and take a glass of wine. She doesn't usually.'

'And what did she have to say may I ask?'

I had no hesitation about telling Mrs Sugden what Miss Merton had to say. The two are thick as thieves on all sorts of matters.

'Her brother, Theodore, is in line for the post of vice chancellor.'

'Did she tell you he has a rival?'

'No.'

'Well he has, and a very popular rival, a clever mathematician, Dr Potter.'

'Then I hope she won't raise her hopes too much.'

'What else did she say?'

'She told me a ghost story, about the spectre of a librarian who haunts the Leeds Library.'

Mrs Sugden made a clucking noise, expressing disapproval. 'That's not why she came in. I'm surprised you didn't winkle it out of her.'

'She hinted at something before she left, that she meant to warn me, that we're not safe.'

'She's worried about her brother. I think he's receiving funny letters. I was there two days ago when the postman came and she turned white when he handed her an envelope. I didn't deliberately read it, but I could see that it was addressed to the professor, the name and address written in block capitals, the kind of writing that would let a person disguise their handwriting.'

'Isn't that reading rather a lot into the delivery of a letter?'

'Well all I can say is I've never seen her so on edge. I wouldn't be at all surprised if someone is blackmailing him or threatening him in some way.'

'She mentioned nothing like that.'

'She wouldn't would she? Not unless you provided the opening. When she's summat of importance to say, she never does anything less than go all round the houses before she gets to it.'

'I'll speak to her tomorrow, if I can find a way of doing so without being intrusive. She'll be interested to know how I get on tonight at the library.'

Mrs Sugden's face expressed utter dismay. 'You're going out again in this fog?' She stared through a gap in the curtains. 'If ever there was a night for keeping out of harm's way, this is that night.'

Eight

Mrs Sugden made no further comment about my venturing out on such a night, but I could see that it was hard for her to keep quiet. She put the kitchen fireguard in place, a concession to the monkey who, after a drink of milk, had curled up on the rug next to my bemused cat, Sookie. Sookie had hissed, resenting the intrusion into her realm, but the monkey skilfully ingratiated himself. Now they both slept. Mrs Sugden, who would normally retire to her own quarters at this time, brought in her knitting, to sit by the fire and keep an eye on the little primate.

'No good will come of it,' she called into the hall as I wrapped a scarf around my nose and throat and set off to see Jim Sykes before catching the tram.

Sykes lives a short distance away. I cut through the wood and the back streets to his house. Sophia and her mother Jennifer had lived on Compton Road, with the ill-fated second husband, Mr Bradshaw. Reaching Beulah Street, I thought how wonderful it would be if Sykes opened the door and said, 'I've found them!'

It would have been wonderful, but only the opening of the door part came true.

'Come in! I was going to call round soon as we'd finished tea.'

The family was gathered at the table, each with something to say, and offering me a chair.

'I'm not staying more than a couple of minutes.'

'She's come to talk to me, not you lot.'

'Any news?' I asked.

He shook his head. 'Nothing, or I would have been round to see you like a shot. I enquired with neighbours, the post office, and all the shops. The newsagent remembers Mrs Bradshaw coming regularly for a paper, but no one knows where they went when they left the area.'

'That's a pity.'

'But it's good that she buys the local paper.'

'Yes. I paid for the insertions today. They will be in tomorrow's editions.'

Sykes put on his cheerful voice. 'With a bit of luck, mother or daughter will read the announcement on Saturday and write to us on Sunday. Who knows, perhaps by Monday there will be something to collect from the box numbers.'

'That would be excellent.' I pulled my scarf tight. 'Best be going. I'm off to catch the tram to town. I'm expected for a meeting at the library.'

Sykes's wife, Rosie, looked up from dishing out potatoes. 'Jim, won't you drive Mrs Shackleton?'

'I don't need to be driven. Safer on the tram in this weather.'

Sykes took his coat from the hook. 'Then I'll walk you to the stop.'

73

Rosie picked up a plate. 'I'll put your tea in the oven, Jim.'

I did not object to being walked to the tram. Mentioning the monkey in front of the Sykes's three children would have caused far too much interest. He listened as I gave an account of finding the creature, and asked him to keep his ear to the ground for news of the organ grinder.

'A monkey like that's a valuable commodity. I wonder what's happened to the man. I'll have a word with the local beat bobby. He might know something.'

Our conversation was cut short as the tram arrived.

I settled into my seat. Street lamps shone dimly through the gloom, blobs of dark mustard paste. Here and there I saw the dim outline of a familiar building, transformed into something strangely Gothic: the university, the chapel, and later Becketts Bank, alerting me to give a nod to the conductor who rang the bell.

Perhaps this would be a good night for a departing ghost. Fog would seep into the building, swallow up the spectre and slide away through gaps in the window frames.

I hopped off the tram and walked for a few yards, the weather turning a simple journey into an adventure. When turning the corner, I heard the muffled voice of the news-paper seller.

He stood close by the gas lamp, cap pulled down, muffler tightly wound. A short man, he wore a greatcoat that was too large. Its shoulders hung about his upper arms. The cuffs were turned up but even so reached his fingertips.

I bought the evening paper with a sixpence and told him to keep the change.

As he thanked me, the muffler slipped. His mouth hung lop-sided.

'Have you been here long?' I began, by way of starting a conversation.

In answer, he held up his right hand for inspection. I peered closely and saw that he was missing a finger and thumb.

'I been here twelve years, ever since I lost two digits and was let go from my job as a joiner. Not that I couldn't have shifted just the same, but I was slowed down, see. Nobody wants a man who's slowed down.'

'I see. Well I noticed you here earlier and . . . '

'I come here from Morley. No man wants to be seen in a reduced state in his own town. So we flitted here and the better for it.' He coughed and spat politely, keeping his phlegm well away from me. 'Late ed-i-tion. Read all abaht it.'

'Did you see the organ grinder today?'

'I heard nowt and seen less, specially since this fog come in.'

'Thank you.' It had been worth a try, but this would be no kind of day for playing tunes and gathering pennies.

It was not yet 6.30 p.m. I took a flashlight from my pocket. Not that it did a great deal of good, but I could see my own feet and a little space on either side. I walked the length of Commercial Street, glancing in doorways. On the far corner was a glowing brazier and the welcome smell of roasting chestnuts.

The chestnut seller was a small man with a big head. It was as if his body had forgotten to grow and sent all its power into his head, arms and hands the size of shovels.

I bought a bag of chestnuts. 'Have you seen the organ grinder today?'

He stamped his feet and rubbed his hands, holding them

over the coals. 'There'd be nowt doin' for him on a day like this.'

'I have something that belongs to him. Do you know where he lodges?'

'No idea, missus.'

Another customer came for chestnuts.

I turned away, warming my hands on the bag.

A narrow alley, Change Alley, runs along the back of the library and adjoining shops. I entered the alley with some trepidation, knowing it to be a haunt for ladies of the night. Fortunately, the weather kept such ladies and their gentlemen at bay and the place was deserted. I walked along the alley from the Lands Lane end, torch in one hand, chestnuts in the other. In two places, steps lead down to basement entrances. At the first spot, I flashed the torch, not sure what I was seeking. Was the organ grinder homeless, or hurt? Near the second set of steps, a back entrance to the library, I spotted something amid the debris of empty cigarette packets, the page of a newspaper, a torn brown paper bag. As I bobbed down to look, chestnuts fell to the ground. Food for rats. I half-expected an army of them to come running.

My find was a tiny scarlet fez with black tassel, just the right size for the head of a Capuchin monkey.

The rest of the alley revealed nothing of interest. I tucked the fez in my satchel, along with the flashlight, and walked round to the library's main entrance which faces south on Commercial Street.

The librarian opened the door on my first ring. He gave a quick smile of greeting: 'Nasty night.' His eyes darted beyond me, looking left and right as though expecting to see someone else. I stepped inside. In a trice he closed the door. 'Don't want to give the impression we are open for business.'

Mr Lennox is what I suppose people call a rangy kind of man, who swings his arms and takes long strides over short distances. Had there ever been a ponderous bone in his body, he must have had it surgically removed. This excess of physical movement is not matched by decisiveness. He usually waits to see which way the wind blows before making a decision.

We mounted the broad staircase. 'Father Bolingbroke will be here shortly. He has gone to the Cathedral for a supply of blessed candles and holy water.'

The fog had followed me in and crept up behind us, adding to that already sulphurous smell that had built up during the late afternoon and evening.

'Is it thick up your way?'

'It is. I came on the tram.'

'I am much obliged to you, and sorry to bring you out on such a night.'

At the top of the stairs, he pushed open the door. I stepped into the deserted main room, where the fire had been allowed to burn low. The electric lights glowed brightly, surely a disincentive to any wandering spirit.

A cheerful fire blazed in the committee room. Mr Lennox shut up a ledger that lay open on the long table. He drew a comfortable chair close to the fire for me, and sat down opposite.

My throat and nose were dry from fog. I wondered whether he would offer a drink. He did not.

'Father Bolingbroke won't be long. He will be praying for the strength to do a thorough exorcism.'

This sounded alarming.

'What are we to do?'

'We will walk the building. He will bless each room, paying particular attention to the corners, I understand. Any lingering spectre will be encouraged to continue its unearthly journey and cease to haunt the material world where once it dwelled.'

'Does he really need two attendants?'

'We are the witnesses, and will report to the committee, and reassure staff and nervous library members.'

'Do you believe the building is haunted, Mr Lennox?'

'It is not a matter of what I believe. The committee has agreed and even those not of his persuasion place great trust in Father Bolingbroke.'

'Do you?'

'Oh yes, fine chap, was an army padre. He was with the missions before the war and the stories he can tell! We're very fortunate he has come to spend time at the library during his sabbatical.'

'Why? I mean, why has he come here?'

Lennox stared at me, surprised that any living soul would question the value of a stint in this hallowed place. 'We have the complete works of St Thomas Aquinas.'

I did not know whether to be pleased or disappointed that Lennox no more believed in a ghost than I did. But I could see that the arrival of the charismatic priest would appeal to members of the committee. They were giving the clergyman access to the library's treasures. As true Yorkshiremen, they might as well avail themselves of his services while he was here, to expel the ghost, whether it existed or not.

Of course it could backfire. Lennox and I would be weak

links in the armour of righteousness. The ghost would take umbrage at our disbelief and dig itself deeper into the book-cases.

A neutral topic was in order. I remembered my conversation with Dr Potter earlier in the day, about the counter assistant he had taken a liking to.

'I haven't seen Miss Montague lately.'

He gazed at a print on the wall. 'Ah. No. You wouldn't.'

'Why?'

'She left our employment rather suddenly.'

The interruption, when the doorbell rang, brought a look of undisguised relief to Lennox's face. He bounced to his feet. 'Here comes Father Bolingbroke.'

Alone in the brightly lit room, I felt the weight of silence. It was easy to imagine that panels by the fireplace might slide open to reveal a secret passage, or that behind a bookcase a hidden room concealed ancient bones.

Footsteps broke the silence.

Father Bolingbroke strode, smiling, into the room and filled it with his presence.

'Mrs Shackleton, so good of you to come.'

A tall, broad-chested man with gentle eyes, he has a face out of a medieval painting: pale, prominent forehead, long pointed nose, sucked-in cheeks and a jutting chin. His appearance should be grotesque but is somehow attractive. Although he has taken up residence in the library only since September, he has been the victim of much hospitality, which he bears in a kindly, accepting manner. I suspect that all his life, like a popular library book, he has been in demand.

He handed his dark felt hat and threadbare coat to Mr Lennox. He took a large white hanky from the pocket of his

79

cassock and blew his nose loudly enough to alert any ghosts that they had better watch out. 'Something to cut the fog, you say, Mr Lennox?'

The priest took Mr Lennox's seat while the librarian disappeared across the corridor for glasses.

'God bless you, Mrs Shackleton for taking part in His work. That you are here will greatly reassure the ladies. May we set this spirit to rest if it is benign and if it hovers here in order to beseech prayers. If it is a demon, I will cast it out in Jesus's name.'

The librarian produced glasses and a bottle of stout. He glanced at me with a question. I nodded. Stout is not my first choice of drink but since nothing else was on offer it would have to do.

As we sipped our stout, and there was no further talk of the task in hand, the two men discussed St Thomas Aquinas. I considered mentioning the organ grinder's monkey but disliked to lower the tone. There are certain people who are always ready to regale listeners with something odd that happened to them today. Now that something odd had happened to me, I felt unable to say a word about it.

When we had finished our stout, the priest produced two candles and squashed their bottoms into the waiting brass holders. Taking a taper from the jar on the mantelpiece, he lit the candles and handed one to each of us.

He took a missal from his pocket, opened it and murmured a prayer.

Lennox and I dutifully added the amen.

'I'll start at the top,' Father Bolingbroke announced briskly, as if intending to produce a broom and give the place a good clean.

From the committee room he led the way up the staircase to the balcony, followed by Mr Lennox. I brought up the rear, hoping the ghost was not tagging along behind laughing or, worse still, ready to grab me.

In procession, we walked around the balcony as the priest murmured prayers and incantations. Lennox managed the situation better than I, quick with his amens and good at shielding his candle. Given that two out of three of us did not believe in ghosts, the procedure had a seriously unreal feeling to it. I detached my thoughts and began to glance at the titles of volumes. I did not usually come up to the balcony. It brought me up short to see the title *Dead Souls*, by Gogol. I snapped myself back to attention. If there really were a ghost and it refused to leave, then I might be to blame for not being sufficiently wholehearted.

Father Bolingbroke had certainly familiarised himself with the labyrinthine layout of the library and missed no small room, no nook or cranny. He led us at a cracking pace. Any watching spirit might feel dismay at being dubbed unclean and summarily cast out. He beseeched any lost soul not to linger in this material world, this vale of tears, clinging on in a place from whence its companions were long fled. Prayers would be said. Deliverance would be at hand.

When we had walked the entire library, Father Bolingbroke led us to the basement entrance. He opened the door.

I did not relish going down there.

Lennox's comment did not help. 'Father Bolingbroke, this is where my late wife said she felt the cold air of the afterlife. Staff call it the tenth circle, where hell freezes, reserved for souls who deface library books.'

Father Bolingbroke ignored these comments and cast a careful eye at our candles, which burned steadily. 'Is there electric light down there?'

'Yes but it is not well lit.' Lennox stepped through the door and flicked a switch. 'Wait here until I call, when I have the lights on.'

He picked up a flashlight.

In solemn silence, the priest and I waited. Through the open door to the basement, I watched as the librarian sped down the steep dimly-lit steps with the agility of a ballet dancer.

It was a good three minutes before he returned, white-faced and trembling. Never have I seen such a total transformation in a person. We both stared at him. He blocked the doorway, so we could not see beyond him.

The expression on Father Bolingbroke's face changed from serene holiness to panic. He stepped back a little, as if some evil power was at this very moment attempting to throw him off course. I half expected him to hold up a crucifix and denounce the devil and all his pomp and works.

Lennox swayed. I feared he would fall. At the same time, Father Bolingbroke and I each took an arm and led him to the nearest chair.

'There has been a most terrible . . . an accident.'

'What kind of accident?' I asked.

'A bookcase toppled. There is someone under it.'

'Stay here, dear lady.' Bolingbroke thrust his missal and candle at me. 'Are you up to showing me where, my dear Lennox?'

Lennox did not answer.

Hoisting his cassock, Bolingbroke headed for the basement door.

Mr Lennox looked deeply shocked. I had left my satchel by the counter. I fetched it and took out the flask of brandy. 'Here, take a drink. Give yourself a moment to recover and then telephone for an ambulance and the police. I will go downstairs and help Father Bolingbroke.'

Feeling a sudden horror of becoming trapped in the bowels of the building, and the lights going out, I propped open the basement door with a chair.

Nine

Hurrying down the worn stone steps, I touched the wall more for reassurance than for balance. The steps dipped in the middle from generations of use. Gripped by an irrational fear, I forced myself to continue. What if more people trod their way down these stairs than ever stepped back up? Spiritualists believe that just on the other side of some part of our everyday world is a portal into the beyond. Would this basement provide the entrance to hell?

Lennox may have panicked, and only imagined that there was a body under the books.

The atmosphere changed. Breathing in rank air, with the faint whiff of a distant sewer, I stepped across the cold flagged floor, shivers tickling the soles of my feet and shooting ice into my veins. In the stillness, I thought I heard the rush of the river under the ground. I wanted to call out to Father Bolingbroke, but felt a choking sensation in my throat. Hearing a faint noise, I moved through the narrow space between two high shelves of musty volumes. At the end of that passageway, I saw that a free-standing bookshelf had toppled. It leaned precariously against a bookshelf that was attached to the wall on the left. The sound came from there.

In the dim light, I made out the figure of Father Bolingbroke, on his knees with his back to me. He was moving books. That had been the sound I heard. A mountain of volumes lay on the floor, having fallen from the tipped shelf.

Startled by my footsteps, he turned suddenly. 'Stay back!'

There was no choice but to stay back. The space was too narrow for more than one person. As I stared, I realised that the fallen volumes took the shape of a burial mound. I saw the toe of a black shoe protruding through the books.

Surely being hit by falling books was not fatal. If the person were still alive, he needed to be able to breathe. I must be at the other end, and take the books from the man's head. What was Bolingbroke thinking of?

Hurrying, I walked behind the fallen bookcase so that I could reach the head of the person who lay wedged. He must be freed.

I knelt as close as I could and began to move books, hurling them aside. Dust and the mouldy smell of old print caught my throat. How tall you are, I thought.

And then I saw the battered black fedora. Time stopped as I picked it up by the brim and set it carefully to one side. I knew, but did not want to know. The hat was as familiar to me as the man. It belonged to Dr Potter. My job now was to be quick, be quick about it. Don't let your hands shake. Look what you are doing.

His grey hair had kept its careful parting. His head lay to one side, at an awkward angle. Blood congealed at the back of his head, where he had taken a bump, or been hit.

I stared into unseeing eyes, once grey, now shot through with blood. Dr Potter's face was red and distorted, his dark tongue protruding. The elegant white silk scarf tightly encircled his throat. In some futile hope that I was wrong and he might breathe again, I loosened it. The skin on his neck was red where the scarf had choked him. This could not be accidental. Dr Potter had been strangled. Knowing he was dead, I still felt for a pulse.

Father Bolingbroke was suddenly by my side. 'Who is it?'

There was no pulse. I could not move or speak, but knelt there, staring, willing this not to be true.

The priest helped me up. 'There's nothing more to be done for him in this life. Who is it?'

'Dr Potter.'

'Give me a moment with him.'

I stood, rooted to the spot. Gently, Bolingbroke put his hands on my shoulders and led me back to the space beyond the fallen bookshelf. 'Go back upstairs, Mrs Shackleton. I will pray for him.' He turned back.

Stumbling, I retraced my steps. Looking back, I glanced at Dr Potter's highly polished black boots, lightly coated with dust, so strange and unreal. A small volume caught my eye. It rested near his heel. I recognised it as one of the library's treasures, sometimes on display in a glass cabinet. I bent to pick it up, which seemed an absurd action but also somehow fitting.

When I reached the stairs, Lennox was calling. 'Where are you?'

There was fear in his voice.

We met halfway. There was a long, awkward moment when he froze and I could have squeezed passed him.

'There is no point in going down there, Mr Lennox.'

He let out his breath and turned.

I followed him back up.

At the top of the stairs, when he was seated once more, I broke the dreadful news. 'Dr Potter is dead.'

'Dr Potter?'

He looked so pale, so shaken. There was something odd about his response, as if he was not surprised about the death but about the identity of the deceased.

'Did you telephone the police, Mr Lennox?'

He shook his head. 'I didn't. I hoped I was mistaken.' He stared at me. 'Dr Potter. What was he doing there?'

'I don't know. Father Bolingbroke is with him, giving him a blessing.'

I was still holding *Gothic Ornament*.

He stared at it, his mouth dropping open. 'What . . . ?'

'We had better telephone.'

As we climbed the stairs to the balcony, my legs felt heavy as lead. If the ghost I did not believe in had appeared at that moment, I would have not have been surprised.

I pushed open the door marked *Private*.

Inside, I placed the valuable book on the table.

Lennox stared at it, as though it might offer an explanation. '*Gothic Ornament*. Why was *Gothic Ornament* in the basement?'

I picked up the telephone receiver and handed it to him. He shook his head and took a step back. 'You say he is dead. Could you be mistaken?'

'No.'

'Then *you* tell them.'

Within moments, I was connected to Leeds City Police.

When I reported the death of Dr Potter, under suspicious circumstances, it was as if someone else was speaking.

After I replaced the receiver, Lennox said, 'Suspicious?' He sat down in his chair. 'How could this happen?'

'Does he have a family?' I asked.

'I don't think so.'

'The police will need his address, his next of kin.'

'It's in the share register.' He stood, as if suddenly glad that he could do something. He opened a drawer of the filing cabinet. In the silence of the room, it made a grating clatter. He took out a folder and placed it on the desk.

He opened the folder and took out a list of names, neatly typed in alphabetical order.

Dr Potter had two addresses, one the Department of Mathematics at the university, and the other 'The Big Bothy', Weetwood.

Mr Lennox is a man of methodical habits. He placed a ruler under the name and address.

Once more *Gothic Ornament* caught his eye. He picked it up, walked to a cupboard, opened it and placed the book inside.

As if this action had broken a spell, he came back to the desk, picked up the telephone and dialled a number. 'The Leeds Club,' he said to me, putting his hand over the mouthpiece. After a moment he said, 'I need to speak to Mr Castle.'

'Don't say anything over the telephone, Mr Lennox. We must wait for the police.'

'He must be told. We cannot keep this from the president.'

'The police will tell him.'

Lennox cleared his throat. 'It's me, Lennox.' A pause. 'Yes, I'm still at the library, and something has occurred. I wish you would come.'

I did not want to listen any more. I went downstairs to do what one must in these situations: find the kettle.

Only when I was alone, in the tiny room not much bigger than a cubbyhole, lighting the gas ring to heat water and staring at the blue flame, did it fully hit me how appalling this was. Dr Potter is such a brilliant man, so charming, so full of life.

Just a few short hours had passed since we met on the stairs and he joked about Mr Lennox having framed that old cutting about the library's acquisitions. Had Dr Potter intended to play a practical joke by taking a valuable book into the basement and then saying, I told you to be more careful with our treasures, Mr Lennox?

Everything about our encounter took on a new significance: the recommendation that I read his undergraduate magazine articles from forty years ago, about the ghost, and about a disappearance. What was it he had said? Where is the lovely counter assistant? She was the only one who would go willingly into the dreadful basement.

I wished I had known him better. Dr Potter was a bright light in a dull world, always slightly comical in committee meetings yet with an underlying seriousness, as if about to immerse himself in the most important business of . . . what? Mathematics, I supposed. What were his personal circumstances? I had no idea. The question never arose. But he was always alone. What else might he have said to me had we spoken longer?

*

Inspector Wallis arrived, with Sergeant Ashworth and PC Hodge, the beat bobby. That was only the start of the comings and goings. They were followed by a medical man, the coroner's officer and a photographer. Finally, stretcher bearers, accompanied by Sergeant Ashworth, took away Dr Potter's body.

Father Bolingbroke had left after giving his address to PC Hodge. I could have left too but was anxious to give an account of my chat with Dr Potter earlier in the day, while it was still fresh in my mind, just in case there was some clue as to why this terrible thing had happened.

I had heard Mr Castle arrive from the Leeds Club that is in the adjacent street, a few yards away. Mr Lennox greeted him with great relief.

I was once more tucked away in the little room with the kettle but overheard Mr Castle and Mr Lennox. I caught snippets as they talked, Lennox reliving his experience.

'Dreadful ... knew straight away ... saw his pale fingers ... dead ... *Gothic Ornament* ... a mistake ... wrong ...'

Mr Castle spoke in low, measured tones of reassurance. ' ... not wrong ... poor Potter ... such a brain ... where is ...'

I heard my name, and Lennox saying he thought I had left with Father Bolingbroke.

Reluctant to be drawn into conversation, I slipped away to the ladies' room where I washed my face, looked at my blotchy skin in the mirror, and tried to keep from crying.

When I emerged, I heard footsteps, followed by the click of the door closing. I went to look out of the window into the foggy night. After a few moments, two figures came out of the doorway below, Castle and Lennox, library president and librarian. Castle is over seventy years old, but strong and upright. Watching them from above, it appeared that the older man was almost supporting Lennox who leaned towards him. When they disappeared into the gloom, the window turned grey-black and blank, as if a blind had been drawn down.

I was aware of someone nearby and turned to see PC Hodge.

He gave a small, friendly smile. Sympathetic. 'Quite a shock for you, madam. Are you all right?'

'Yes. The librarian, Mr Lennox, took it very hard. I think that helped me to steel myself.'

'That's the way sometimes, Mrs Shackleton. The sergeant has gone to the mortuary, with the deceased. I'm to take your statement, but is there anyone you would like me to telephone for you?'

'No, I'll be all right, thank you.'

'Let's find a couple of chairs, eh?'

We walked towards the committee room. 'With Mr Lennox gone, who will lock up the library?'

'The inspector has taken charge of the keys. The library won't be opening tomorrow morning. We'll take care of that, too.'

Once we sat down, the constable took out his notebook. 'I know the chap who works with you, Jim Sykes.'

Something in the constable's voice told me that he and Sykes probably did a good turn for each other now and then. 'I'll tell Mr Sykes you were here.'

Before we had time to begin, a piercing noise interrupted, the sound of a police whistle, coming from the basement.

'Sorry about this.' The constable put the notebook back in his pocket as he hurried away.

The clock on the mantelpiece ticked loudly. The fire crackled.

I should not be here. I have a case in hand. Perhaps it was to escape from the awfulness of the present, but a thought struck me. There was another way we might trace Sophia Wells and her mother. Mrs Bradshaw, having experience of work in a fishmonger's, may have returned to that work. I must remember to tell Sykes. He could make enquiries along the wet fish row in Kirkgate Market. One of the stall holders may know of the family from Scarborough.

Not much more than five minutes had passed when the constable returned, a little out of breath. 'You are a nurse, Mrs Shackleton?'

Sykes must have told him. 'Yes, I served with the Voluntary Aid Detachment during the war.'

'You better come. There's another one, in a bad way.'

Following PC Hodge, once more I took the steps to the lower floor.

I had begun to realise how large an area the basement covered, extending the width and length of the entire building, which includes adjacent shops. PC Hodge thankfully made a wide detour, avoiding the area where the bookshelves had tumbled, or been toppled, onto the unfortunate Dr Potter.

At the far side, in a corner, a few yards from the steps that must lead to the alley where I found the fez, I saw the inspector. He was standing over someone who lay very still.

I caught the smell from the poor creature before properly seeing him.

Inspector Wallis shone his torch on the man who was curled in a foetal position.

'I'd be obliged if you'd take a look at him. No broken bones that I can see but he is in a bad way.'

As I bobbed down, I realised why the inspector had not wanted to come too close to the man. I knelt beside him. His breath came in short, rasping gasps. He shivered. His forehead burned with fever. Looking into the man's mouth, I saw that his tongue was coated. There was a strong smell of diarrhoea and urine. A sudden coughing fit racked his body; congested lungs.

As the inspector said, no bones were broken.

'He has broncho-pneumonia. The sooner you get him out of here into the warmth the better.'

Burly Constable Hodge needed no other prompt from me. He took up his position, waiting a second or two for the nod from his boss, then handed me his torch and picked up the man in his arms. As he moved him, the stench became stronger. God knows how long the poor man had lain there.

'I'll follow you up,' the inspector said. 'Hodge, telephone for an ambulance.'

'Sir.'

As the constable and I moved away, the inspector shone his torch around the floor where the man had lain.

Holding the flashlight, I led us back, keeping to the wall.

At the bottom of the stairs, Hodge said, 'You better go first, madam.'

The constable made his slow way behind me towards the only warm room. Looking a little red in the face, he lay down his burden on the hearth rug. 'He's skin and bone, but heavy.'

There was a drop of stewed tea in the pot. I poured a cup, added sugar, and put it to the semi-conscious man's lips. Constable Hodge raised the man's head. Between us, we managed to help him take a few drops.

'What's your name, chum?' Hodge asked.

The man groaned and wheezed. He was beyond saying his name. Perhaps he was beyond reach of being kept in this world. His breath was laboured. He made a rattling sound as he exhaled. His chest rose and fell under the colourful waistcoat.

'I'd better phone for that ambulance.'

'The office is up the stairs, off the balcony.'

'Thanks.'

The man's hair was black and wavy and his eyebrows bushy. He sported a sorry stage-villain handlebar moustache. Under his pallor, olive skin gave him a foreign look and the suggestion of a life lived outdoors. He wore a knitted waist-coat in garish colours, green, red and yellow. I had seen those colours before, and not long ago. The garment was simply made; knit a row, purl a row. Whoever clicked nee-dles for the monkey's coat had also produced this colourful creation. It was the work of a child, an inexpert knitter, or perhaps the man himself; the organ grinder who had lost his monkey.

As he moved, the man winced. There was something heavy strapped to his middle. It was a makeshift money belt, with tapes slotted through a hessian bag. I undid it for his comfort, and then glanced in the bag: gold sovereigns, and plenty of them.

It was the action of a few seconds. I heard a sound, reached for my satchel and put the bag of sovereigns and the tapes inside. I could not have said why, except that it seemed the right thing to do. Once I had done it, I fastened the satchel, telling myself that all our efforts must be on the man himself, without the distraction of something that might suggest guilt or raise suspicion. He needed to be in hospital, not in a cold cell.

Inspector Wallis opened the door and stepped inside. 'How is he?'

'Badly. I could do with a wet towel for his forehead. There's a gentlemen's lavatory . . . '

He spoke somewhat brusquely. 'Right. I'll fetch a towel.'

Inspector Wallis and I have twice come into contact with each other and each occasion has been somewhat fraught. The first time was when my Scotland Yard friend, Marcus Charles, came north and took charge of an investigation that Inspector Wallis would have preferred to deal with himself. The other occasion was social and should not have caused rancour but I believe he had taken against my outbidding him at a charity auction for a hideous indoor plant that I imagine neither of us wanted. I would not have minded but my bid was entirely accidental. I had been adjusting my hat.

This evening would provide ammunition enough for Leeds City Police to shoot scorn at their local lady detective. What was she doing in the library at that time on a Friday night? She was shooing away ghosts and ghouls, with a papist priest and a helpless librarian.

The inspector returned with a damp towel, which he had folded. He handed it to me. I placed it on the man's brow.

We were kneeling on either side of the patient, Wallis leaning forward. I moved back slightly, so that our heads would not touch.

I watched as the inspector searched the man's pockets. Looking at the top of Wallis's head, at his blond wavy hair, I had the odd sensation of seeing a Viking searching a vanquished opponent on the battlefield. The wavy hair must have been a trial to him as a boy. When he looked up, having found a couple of tab ends, matches, and a rosary, I noticed his deep blue eyes and dark lashes that a woman might envy. He stood, went close to the fireplace and threw the tab ends and matches into the fire. 'What are his chances?'

I thought the man may hear me and so simply said, 'He needs a bed bath, a nightshirt, and a poultice to ease his chest. He will feel better for being clean.'

If he did not recover, then at least he would meet his maker in a respectable manner, having had a little comfort.

'I suppose he'll want this by him.' Wallis handed me the rosary, letting it fall into my hand.

I put it back in the man's pocket and stood.

'PC Hodge tells me you waited behind to make a statement, Mrs Shackleton.'

'Yes. I may have been one of the last people to have a conversation with Dr Potter. We spoke on the landing earlier today.'

Hodge knocked and came into the room. 'Sir, they won't take him at the Workhouse Infirmary. Full up and had one of their outbreaks. He can be accepted at the General Infirmary. I said yes. Hope that's all right, sir.'

Why was Wallis frowning? 'Inspector, that will be the best place for him. Not so far to travel and our patient will stand a better chance, particularly if they have enough staff on hand to take care of him straight away.'

'Why wouldn't they, Mrs Shackleton?'

'They'll be doing the changeover between day and night shift. Occasionally, someone is left waiting on a trolley.' I had left my scarf on the chair and now wound it loosely around the man's throat. 'When he is taken to the ambulance, we can cover his mouth with the scarf, to protect him from the cold air.'

Inspector Wallis spoke to Constable Hodge. 'After we've finished here, go up to the infirmary and keep an eye on him. I want a statement as soon as he recovers, if he recovers.' Wallis turned to me. He hesitated, as if what he was about to say came with some difficulty, and that he may be weighing a past resentment against present expediency. 'Madam, you would be doing the police force a service if you would travel with him. I want this man kept alive.'

'So do I, Inspector.'

We both knew that he might hold the key to Dr Potter's murder.

Wallis regarded me as useful, but probably a nuisance. I regarded him as a detective without experience in a murder enquiry. I hoped he would call in Scotland Yard, but something told me he would want to try and solve this case himself.

I did not trust him.

Ten

The two ambulance men wore navy uniforms and caps. One was short, the other tall. As they carried the stretcher bearing the sick organ grinder, one man raised his arms and the other bent his knees.

Constable Hodge opened the library's outer door.

In France during the war, the Ford Model T field ambulance had been the last word. Here, in peacetime, it seemed incongruous to see its solid, square outline in the quiet, foggy street. Three men came out of the nearby Mitre, and stopped for a moment to watch the stretcher being manoeuvred into the back of the ambulance.

The taller of the two ambulance men then went round to the driver's side of the vehicle and climbed in the cab. The other man stayed in the back of the ambulance for another moment or two, fastening belts to keep the stretcher in place. He then reached out to me.

'Up you come.'

He jumped out, shutting the doors behind him.

Constable Hodge opened the door a fraction, long enough to say, 'All right, Mrs Shackleton?'

'Yes thank you.'

'I'm to come along later, so I'll see you there.'

He closed the rear door as the engine cranked into life.

My semi-conscious patient wheezed. His chest rattled. I pushed at the flat pillow to try and give him more support and would have liked to raise him up but he was so exhausted that I merely rolled him onto his side and hoped that he would survive the short journey that lay ahead.

He still had my soft scarf around his throat and mouth which might give him a little protection against the icy chill. When the damp towel I had brought to soothe his brow became warm from his burning forehead, I took off a glove and lay my hand on his brow. He burned with fever, yet he shivered too. I tapped lightly on his back, hoping it might give some slight relief to the congestion in his lungs.

In the darkness of the ambulance's interior, I listened to the sounds of our journey: the rasp of the wheels as the vehicle crossed tramlines, the regular thumpety-thump on the cobblestones, and the drone of the engine. He coughed again. I held him steady when we turned a corner, stilling his arms when he began to flail and throw off his blanket.

During the first part of the journey, I had my bearings. After five minutes of attending to my patient in darkness, I could not guess our position. Finally, the ambulance came to a halt.

'Won't be long now. You are at the hospital. You'll be taken care of.'

In the cab, driver and stretcher bearer were talking quietly.

The door opened. The driver held out his hand to help me down.

As the pair lifted the stretcher, the shorter of the two spoke to the sick man. 'Did we rattle you, pal? We're tekin you in now.'

I closed the vehicle's doors.

The Infirmary building loomed darkly in the fog, huge, forbidding as the Castle of Otranto. Nothing about this day, this evening, felt real.

This building should be familiar to me since I had been shown all around it, and was last here when the plaque was unveiled, commemorating the staff who had fallen in the Great War. At the time, I had not wanted to see Gerald's name there, still hoping that my husband could be missing, and that he may return.

In the lobby, a porter came to meet us, wheeling a trolley. Expertly, the ambulance men rolled the patient from stretcher to trolley.

The driver spoke to the porter in a hushed voice. 'This lady's from the police. She's a nurse and will be in attendance. A constable will be here later.'

They took their leave.

The porter said, 'We're on the second floor, nurse.'

As we walked towards the lift, I breathed in hospital smells. Disinfectant. Anxiety. Efficiency.

He pressed for the lift and said quietly, 'Wrong un is he?'

Being 'from the police' gave me a very good reason not to reply. But being polite costs nothing and sometimes pays dividends.

'He has pneumonia.' This did not answer the porter's question, but stopped him from asking another.

In the lift there was a different smell: cabbage, boiled fish, body odour.

We rattled to the second floor.

He opened the lift doors and wheeled out the trolley, thanking me when I closed the doors behind us. Perhaps I might very soon be expelled from the scene; a hospital matron being a law unto herself. I followed the porter along a corridor at the end of which were double doors. He used the edge of the trolley as a battering ram to open the doors.

A little way into the ward, we paused by a table, lit by a dim lamp. A pen lay on a set of patient's notes beside a medication log. The chair had been pushed back.

From the nearest bed came gentle snoring. As always in such places, when patients are supposedly settled down for the night, there was one who moaned loudly. There was always one.

Each bed was separated from the other by precisely the same distance, as if measured by a ruler. I thought of the dead mathematician, Dr Potter, and what brainy measurements and calculations would remain forever undone.

The ward sister approached from the far end. The porter stepped up to her. They stood a couple of feet from the table, speaking in low tones. She glanced in my direction. This might be it: my marching orders.

She came towards me as the porter turned the trolley around and wheeled it back the way we had come.

'I'm Sister O'Malley. I'm putting your man in the room at the end.'

She was in her late twenties, pale skinned with blue-grey eyes. A few strands of wispy black hair escaped from her cap.

Without another word, she strode ahead of the porter and opened the door to a room on the right, just inside the ward's double doors.

I followed her.

The room was about twelve feet long and ten feet wide, with a high window.

While the porter wheeled the patient into the room, she said quietly, 'The porter tells me you are a nurse, and with the police.'

'Catherine Shackleton, Sister. I'm a former VAD nurse, with connections to the West Riding Constabulary and I am called to help the Leeds police from time to time.'

This was true in part, although it may have given a slightly false impression. My only connection to the West Riding Constabulary is my father who is chief superintendent in Wakefield, and I once took a lost child to Millgarth Police Station.

Among many fully trained nurses there was disdain for us Voluntary Aid Detachment types, so it was best to have this out in the open. Fortunately, Sister O'Malley showed no signs of being about to snub me.

She examined the patient without speaking. Suddenly he began to cough, to choke. She glanced quickly at me. I went round the other side of the stretcher. Between us, we lifted him and sat him up. I slapped his back, so that he might bring up the plug of phlegm that threatened to choke him. I caught it in my handkerchief.

She and the porter transferred the patient to the bed.

'Do the police want you to stay with him?' she asked. When I hesitated, she continued, 'Only I'm on my own tonight. One of my nurses is sick and the other on an emergency in the women's ward.'

I want him kept alive, the inspector had said. So did I want the organ grinder to recover, not only for his own sake but because he may be able to shed light on Dr Potter's death.

'I can stay, Sister. I could start by giving him a bed bath.'

'Thank you. That would be a great help.'

I took off my coat. 'I'm not dressed for the occasion.'

She smiled. 'You'll find everything you need, including an apron, in the room on your left, in the corridor. Very bad congestion. You'll apply poultices?'

'Of course.'

'The porter tells me there's to be a constable on duty.'

'So I understand.'

'I dislike the idea of having a policeman on my ward. It seems quite unnecessary in the circumstances. Make sure the officer stays in the corridor.' She turned to the porter. 'Wait with the patient for a moment, please.' She touched my arm ever so lightly but it was a friendly touch. 'Come on. I'll show you where to find what you need.'

I followed her through the double doors and into the corridor. She opened a door on the left. It was the nurses' room.

'Here you are. I suppose this will be quite familiar.'

The room was shelved on two sides. Below counter level were cupboards, and on the counter to the left a kettle on a gas ring. The upper shelves held sheets, towels and flannels.

By the window were three separate sinks. She pointed to them from left to right. 'That one for my tea things, middle one for patients' crocks, and the one on the right for dressing bowls. That has the hot tap with sterilised water. You'll find an apron and cap in the far cupboard.'

'Thank you, Sister, I'll manage now.'

'I'll have a chair put in the corridor for the constable.'

When she left, I hung up my coat. Donning the starched

apron and pinning the cap in place created the oddest sensation. It was as if I were leaving myself behind and becoming young again, Kate the nurse. The events of the evening had unsettled me. I washed my hands, filled a basin, picked up towels and nightshirt. These actions reminded me of my younger self, eager, energetic, speeding through the First Aid and Home Nursing examinations, being told what to do and when to do it, and never flinching.

With effort, I banished the memories and concentrated on the here and now.

Back in the room, the porter helped me take off the patient's overcoat. It was thick and too big for him but could be cleaned and would see him through a few more years, if God granted him more years. Some of his garments would be beyond saving.

'You'll need more than one basin of water for this chap, nurse.'

'I know.'

'Want me to fetch another?'

'Not yet because it would be cold by the time I'm ready, but you might fetch a laundry bag and disposal bag.'

'Consider it done.'

I set to work, unlacing the badly worn shoes. They must have been on his feet for months and were stuck to his socks. The cardboard insoles, shredded to nothing, would not have kept out the cold and damp. His socks would need to be cut off, and I dreaded to think about the state of his feet. That would be a separate job.

The porter returned with laundry and disposal bags, together with a pair of scissors. 'Reckon you'll need these. Anything else?'

'Thank you, no. You've been very helpful.'

He left. The wheels of his trolley and the opening of the doors briefly broke the silence.

He was right about the scissors.

It was not too hard to remove my patient's upper garments but the lower ones were beyond saving and had to be cut off. As best I could, I kept him covered as I worked to remove his clothing, snipping through the thick tweed trousers with difficulty.

His middle was red and inflamed from the pressure of his makeshift money belt.

His face was not too dirty, so he must have rinsed it somewhere, but there was a tidemark on his neck.

Although I worked as gently as I could to get him clean, and into a nightshirt, the process must have exhausted him still more. Briefly, he opened his eyes and seemed to look at me but without making any sign that he saw me. His eyes were bloodshot and red-rimmed.

His hair needed a wash and his feet more attention than I had given him, but the poor man must rest, and have nourishment.

I returned to the nurses' room and put on the kettle to make him Bovril, searching the cupboards for an invalid cup.

When I came back to the room, the doctor was with him. I felt pleased to have made my patient presentable.

The doctor was of the old school, self-important but thorough. He nodded curtly, and then ignored me as he placed a stethoscope on the patient's chest.

'Name?'

'We don't know his name yet, Doctor.'

He picked up the chart. 'No TPR?'

'I haven't taken his temperature and pulse yet.'

He cleared his throat. 'Soon as, then.'

He prescribed cough medicine, which we both knew would do little good, and aspirins to try and reduce the fever. At the door, he turned, giving me a curious look. 'Sister said you are former VAD Nurse Shackleton?'

'Yes.'

'Any relation to Gerald Shackleton?'

Someone must have said, 'Gerald Shackleton's widow is working for the police.'

'Gerald was my husband.' As I spoke, that old lurch to the guts upset me more than I can say. People say time heals. No it does not.

'Ah. Well . . . fine chap . . . good work.'

When he had gone, I coaxed my patient into taking a little Bovril.

Something was happening to me, and it was unwelcome. Too much of the past flooded back. All those times spent trying to do my best for patients, hoping, praying, someone would do the same for Gerald if he needed nursing and was far away. Then there would be that inevitable attachment, willing a man to live while watching him die little by little.

The inner turmoil was at odds with my measured words as I attempted to soothe and reassure. 'I'm going to make you comfortable. Can you tell me your name?'

His eyelids flickered. He slumped onto the pillows, exhausted.

In the nurses' room, I made poultices, found aspirins and replenished the Bovril cup with water.

Applying the poultices seemed cruel when he was in such a weak state, but it might relieve his breathing just a little.

He was thin; I had noticed that of course, but now I saw just how thin. His forearm was narrower than mine. Skin hung loose on his wasted calves. If he lasted the night, it would be a miracle. I would not leave him. During the war, there were times when it was not possible to sit by a dying man. One had to move on and tend to the ones who might live, who might be patched up and sent back to fight another day. As I sat by this man, whose name I had yet to learn, I remembered all the men whom I had watched die. Not another. Not this one. This one will live.

'Do you hear me?' For the umpteenth time I cooled his brow with a damp cloth. 'You are going to pull through and tell me what you were doing in that dratted basement.'

He held the clue as to who killed Dr Potter. If it was within my power, he would not keep his information for the grave.

I reached for my satchel, which I had placed under the bed, and took out the hessian bag of sovereigns, intending to count the money. There was a tap on the door. Quickly, I pushed the bag under the blanket and placed my satchel on top.

It was Constable Hodge. 'Here I am, better late than never, eh? How is he?'

'Badly.'

He stepped into the room. 'He looks grey as clay.'

'He is a very poorly man.'

'Any name yet?'

'No.'

'Looks familiar.'

I refrained from saying that Constable Hodge had probably seen the man looking a little healthier than this as he played his barrel organ about the town during the summer.

My conviction that this was the organ grinder was not simply based on the colours of his waistcoat and the monkey's jacket. Man and monkey had a certain smell in common. If I was right, someone at the station would know his name. Perhaps it would dawn on Constable Hodge. Eventually.

Why was I keeping the information to myself? I could not quite put it into words. It was something to do with not trusting the inspector. I felt sure this man had done nothing really wrong, except perhaps trespass for the sake of shelter. His crime was to be in the wrong place at the wrong time. He was too weak to have committed murder.

The constable stepped further into the room. 'That sister's fierce. Insists on me staying in the corridor.'

'Where is she now?'

'Dealing with an emergency.' He looked down at the figure on the bed. 'Mind, he's looking a bit better.'

'That's because he's clean.'

A sound in the corridor prompted the constable to retreat. 'The porter's offered me a cup of tea. Do you want one?'

'No thanks. I can brew up in the nurses' room.'

'All right for some.' He gave me a friendly smile, and was gone.

When he had closed the door, I withdrew the bag. The gold sovereigns glittered. There were too many coins to count without putting them into my satchel, which I did, in tens. Fifty gold sovereigns – a small fortune. This was an astonishing amount of money for a monkey to have collected for his master.

Stashing my satchel under the bed, I sat down in the straight-back chair.

I had not intended to doze but feeling suddenly tired I slept, in spite of the discomfort.

When I woke, I could not tell whether the fog had cleared. It was impossible to see out of the window, like looking at a solid curtain of the darkest grey.

At four o'clock, my patient opened his eyes.

'Where am I?'

'In the infirmary. You'll be cared for here.'

A look of dread came over him. His lips parted wide, his chin dipped. 'Workhouse?'

'No. The General Infirmary, Great George Street.'

'Who brought me here?'

'I did.'

He shut his eyes.

'I'm going to change the poultice on your chest and on your back. Might you be able to help me?'

His already limp body drooped and wilted. After the effort of speaking, the last scintilla of energy deserted him.

While he slept, I went back to the storage room and boiled water, poured it into a basin and added Friar's Balsam. I placed this by his bed, hoping that the pungent steam might bring some relief. Sweat poured off him, soaking the sheets.

At six o'clock, I changed his nightshirt and bedding. He groaned as I renewed the poultices.

A little before seven, I set about making tea, including a cup for Constable Hodge. As I stood in the doorway of the nurses' room while waiting for the kettle to boil, PC Hodge finally took my statement about the events last night at the library.

He closed his notebook. 'The counter assistant Dr Potter was concerned about, has she left the library?'

'Mr Lennox said she left suddenly.'

'What is she like?'

'Miss Montague is in her twenties, efficient, attractive, red-gold hair.'

'And that valuable book you found, Mr Lennox was rather concerned that it was in the basement and not on its usual shelf.'

'Yes.'

He put his notebook in his pocket. 'Well thank you, Mrs Shackleton.'

After that, it was my turn to ask a question.

'Mr Hodge, if it's not a rude question, why are you here? The inspector must know that our patient isn't going anywhere. You could come back when he recovers.'

'The minute he's fit to talk, I'm to take a statement from him. You see, the question is, what was he doing in that basement? There was only the two of them there, him and the dead man. Looks bad for him.'

'But you saw the state of him. You don't believe he could have had anything to do with Dr Potter's death, do you?'

'Could be he was putting it on a bit.'

'You can't "put on" pneumonia.'

The constable watched from the doorway as I poured tea. 'That's not for me to say. But I'm here, should he come round and turn peculiar.'

So that was why he had come into the sick room earlier.

Perhaps the inspector had said that my patient might be dangerous.

I handed the constable his teacup. 'He is a very sick man and far too weak to cause trouble.'

PC Hodge held the doors for me as I returned to the room. The organ grinder was breathing heavily.

It felt like a small triumph when I managed to help him drink, putting the spout to his lips, and watching him sip sweet tea.

Sister came in just as I finished noting his temperature, pulse and respiration on the chart.

'You can add a name, Mrs Shackleton. The constable has remembered who he is. Umberto Bruno, an organ grinder.'

In the corridor, there was a clattering of teacups on a trolley, and nurses talking. Someone dropped a bedpan.

Sister said, 'That girl is so clumsy.' She moved to go, turned at the door, and said, 'Oh, I spoke to matron. She remembers you from a stint at St Mary's during the war. She is agreeable to your returning this evening, if that is convenient to you.'

This took me by surprise, but I was not sorry. If Umberto recovered during my shift, I would be able to hear his account of why he was in the basement and whether he saw Dr Potter's assailant.

'Yes. I'll be glad to come back.'

'The shifts are seven till seven. You should go home now, and get some rest.'

When she had left the room, I picked up my satchel, heavy with coins.

Inspector Wallis and his superiors had twenty-four hours after finding the body in which to request Scotland Yard to take over the investigation. If the Yard was called in after that time, Leeds City Police would have to foot the bill, something they would be most reluctant to do.

By the time I returned this evening, I would know who was leading the investigation.

I hoped for the sake of Dr Potter and Umberto Bruno that it would not be the inexperienced Inspector Wallis.

Eleven

Walking out of the infirmary, I wanted to stretch my legs which felt as leaden as the grey sky looked. But my legs didn't want to be stretched. They claimed to be tired, and so did my feet which cried out for a tram ride. Decision: should I catch a tram and rest, or walk and have a stretch? The choice was made for me because the tram came into view as I reached the stop.

The heavy satchel dug into my shoulder. This was hardly surprising given the amount of coins it contained. Like Silas Marner, I felt the urge to re-count them. A law-abiding citizen would have handed the money to Constable Hodge. The good constable would have passed it to Sergeant Ashworth. The sergeant would, in turn, have tendered it to Inspector Wallis. There were too many opportunities for something to go wrong. I am a deeply trusting person, too trusting according to Jim Sykes, but the person I trust most is me. Umberto Bruno's sovereigns would be safe in my hands, even if they should not have been in his hands in the first place.

I climbed aboard the tram and gratefully slid into the nearest seat. The conductor took my penny.

A gentle mist covered the bleached-out grass on Wood-house Moor. Pavements shone darkly from early rain.

On an impulse I decided to get off the tram at the next stop. Only after my feet touched the ground did it occur to me that it was a little early to be calling on Sykes, but he does not lie abed even at the weekend.

As I turned onto Woodhouse Street, a lad hurtling along on a bike called to me and screeched to a halt. It was Thomas Sykes, sixteen years old, bound for his work at the joiners where he was apprenticed.

'Are your mam and dad up and about?'

'Mam's still in bed. But go on, they won't mind. Dad's been out for his paper.'

He mounted the pavement and pedalled off, a danger to pedestrians but less bumpy for the rider than the cobbles.

At their house, on Beulah Street, I tapped lightly on the window. Sykes looked up from where he sat by the fire, reading. When he saw me, he came to the door and stepped aside to let me in. 'Heyup! You're early.'

'I've been in the infirmary all night.' He looked alarmed. 'I was nursing a patient.'

'I thought your nursing days were over.'

'So did I. Look, I don't want to wake the whole house. Will you come out to the café?'

He nodded. 'Give us a minute. I'll get my boots. I'd offer to toast you a teacake but I'd end up doing it for all and sundry and we wouldn't be able to hear ourselves think.'

Moments later, as we walked in the direction of the café on Johnston Street, I gave him an account of my extraordinary Friday evening.

'Well I'll be jiggered. You went looking for a ghost and found two bodies. It could only happen to you.'

I told him about Umberto Bruno, and how I realised that he was the organ grinder.

'You did better than me. I made the supreme sacrifice of going out in the fog for a couple of pints last night. You said in your note that you were parked on Commercial Street when the monkey decided to join you.'

'Yes. I found the monkey's fez at the back of the library. I wonder whether the door was unlocked and the pair of them went in to shelter.'

'I did pick up one little bit of information. It'll interest you to know that Umberto Bruno took his barrel organ into the Mitre two days ago, for safe-keeping. The landlord has it in a cupboard. He expected Umberto to come back for it, but he never turned up.'

The Mitre is the pub closest to the library and not one I would have expected the organ grinder to frequent, but perhaps the landlord had a soft spot for him.

'Did the landlord say why Umberto took it there, or did he mention the monkey?'

'No and no. Perhaps Umberto had to change lodgings. I asked but nobody knows where he lives. My guess is that he and the monkey were living rough. Do you think someone at the library felt sorry for the old chap and let him in the back door? With the weekend coming up, he might have camped out in that basement unnoticed.'

'Well no, because the library opens on Saturday mornings, and the library staff wouldn't let an outsider in.'

'Not any of them?'

'Young Bert has a kind heart.'

'It's the sort of thing a daft lad might do.' He lit a ciga-rette. 'The shops near the library have cellars. There could be another way in.'

'A tunnel, you mean?'

'Possibly, or a connecting door.'

'But I found the monkey's fez by the rear entrance.'

'There could be different ways in and out.'

We reached the café. It is opposite the chemical works and serves strong red tea in big white mugs, always with sugar, and that everlasting milk that comes with a metal top.

I ordered sausage and fried bread.

While I waited for my breakfast, Sykes briefed me on developments in our only other current case: the sad story of the bank clerk with a gambling habit. The man had been well and truly exposed. Unwilling to face the bad publicity of a court case, the bank had dismissed him without refer-ences.

'He's lucky,' Sykes said. 'Fraud of that kind, he could have ended up inside for a very long time.'

I had put my satchel under the table. The heavy coins pressed against my toes.

Only when I had eaten my breakfast did I tell him about the idea that came to me out of the blue last night.

'Sophia's mother, Jennifer Bradshaw; it's unlikely that she may have been kept on at Barnbow Munitions factory after the war.'

'It's not information that they'd part with that easily, but I can try and check.'

'You see, I think had she gone on working there she would have stayed in the Compton Road area. It occurred to me that she may have looked for work with a fishmonger, because of knowing the trade.'

Sykes smiled. 'Great minds think alike. I was going to tell you last night, except that it's not the best news. Yesterday, I visited every wet fish shop and stall within a five mile radius. No luck, though one chap in the market knew Mr and Mrs Wells from their days in Scarborough.' He reached into the inside pocket of his coat, drew out a newspaper, and pointed. 'This is encouraging, though. Our announcement was in the *Evening Post* sooner than we hoped – last night's late edition. I'll call at the offices today and see whether anyone's been quick off the mark in replying to our box number.'

'That's a boost. I'm glad you'll be following up responses because I've agreed to go back to the infirmary tonight. I had thought if there was something I could be doing towards finding Mrs Wells and Sophia, then I should be doing it.'

'Leave it with me. If mother and daughter are in this city, I'll find them. And I don't blame you for going back to the infirmary. There's probably more satisfaction in nursing than detection, especially given how many blanks we've drawn so far.'

'Nursing doesn't rule out detection. I want to know who killed Dr Potter.'

'Are they calling in Scotland Yard?'

'I wish I knew.'

Over another mug of tea, I told him about my mistrust of Inspector Wallis, and about the organ grinder's money bag.

'How much?'

'Fifty gold sovereigns.'

He let out a low whistle. 'That's an awful lot of brass.'

'It must be his life savings.'

'You don't believe that. A man like him lives day to day, hour to hour.'

We sat in silence for a while. Sykes asked for more tea.

He took a drink. 'The sovereigns could be a payment.'

'For what?'

'For murder? Murder of a mathematician.'

'Umberto is too weak and ill, and too small. Dr Potter was a big man.'

'It's not to do with size. If he caught him in the right position, he could have whacked the back of his knees, bopped him on the head, and then finished the job. Do they know how long the body was in the basement?'

'Not yet.'

I took a drink of tea. 'I thought you'd be jumping up and down because I didn't hand over the money.'

He shrugged. 'In the unlikely event the money does lawfully belong to Umberto, and stranger things have happened, he would be hard-pressed to prove it once Leeds City Police have it in their coffers. There are always stories about someone dressed in rags, living out of bins, dying in extreme poverty and being discovered to have a hidden fortune.'

'He's too ill for me to question him about it. Of course it could be awkward if he comes to consciousness while I'm not there and asks for his sovereigns.'

'Don't rule him out as a suspect, just because he is your patient.'

'He really and truly is too weak. But I wouldn't be at all surprised to have missed something important last night.'

'Not like you.' Sykes lit a cigarette.

'It was so bizarre. First, I was busy being acolyte to the

exorcist, that took a lot of concentration. Then suddenly I was required to be a nurse again. The poor librarian, Mr Lennox, went into a terrible spin of shock. He and the priest bolted as soon as they could. My detective skills fell entirely into abeyance while I was thinking about poor Dr Potter and then caring for Umberto. That wouldn't have happened to you.'

'Why wouldn't it?'

'Because your outlook is always and forever that of a policeman, I don't suppose you'll understand how it's possible to become someone else in an instant.'

'You make me sound totally blinkered. Limited.'

'Not at all. It's very useful. If you were a stick of rock, the lettering all the way through would be "policeman". It's as simple as that.'

'Detective.'

'All right, "detective" then.'

'What would your stick of rock say?'

'Oh I don't know. Daughter, widow, nurse, detective.'

'Well then, it would be an interesting stick of rock. But don't forget I'm a husband and dad.'

'I'm not forgetting that. I'm just talking about how we look at the world.'

'Do you always turn philosophical when you haven't slept?'

'I'm not a bit tired.' A sudden great yawn contradicted me.

'Come on then. Better give me that satchel before it dislocates your shoulder.'

He walked with me to my house, wanting to meet the monkey and admire the gold sovereigns.

Before he left, I put the bag of sovereigns inside the top of the piano, and locked the lid so that no one would play it.

'Now you'll know where the money is if I succumb to pneumonia, and the organ grinder lives and I die.'

'Don't die.' Sykes replaced the vase on top of the piano, 'at least not before you sign the business over to me.'

Although I had not felt tired, the moment I put on my pyjamas and climbed into bed, I was glad to stretch out and feel the cool pillow against my cheek. In no time at all, I was fast asleep.

It was late afternoon when I woke from the strangest dream. I dreamed that I was floating about the hospital, above the wards, looking down. I saw my husband Gerald, just as he was when I visited there once. He was striding along a corridor, to a door that was signed Operating Theatre. I floated in after him. He was not there. Constable Hodge wore a cloak decorated with sovereigns. Umberto, monkey perched on his shoulder, carried a candle and made a whooshing noise. He pointed to a balcony where a ghostly figure floated by.

I woke.

Ghosts. I was letting the thought of ghosts get the better of me.

After that, I did not want to sleep again.

A bath revived me, along with a dish of Mrs Sugden's rabbit stew.

Mrs Sugden cut another slice of bread. 'It's very inconvenient, having a vegetarian in the house. How do you think that organ grinder fed the creature? Not very well if you ask me.'

'If Umberto has come round when I go back this evening, I'll ask him.'

'You're going back there?'

'Yes. There has been illness among the nurses, and they are very busy. The ward sister is glad of my being there, especially as it's the weekend. I think it will be different on Monday.'

'I should say she is glad to have you there. Are you being paid?'

'No.'

'Then you're doing some hard-up woman out of a job. Have you thought about that?'

'It's temporary.'

'That's what bosses always say.'

The monkey looked from one to the other of us, as if sharing our concern.

Mrs Sugden stood up. 'That creature understands English. Are you sure his owner isn't called Dr Dolittle?'

'Not unless Dr Dolittle goes by the alias Umberto Bruno.'

She went to the kitchen. The monkey watched her go.

It was then I remembered Umberto's knitted waistcoat. I took it from my satchel and offered it to the monkey.

He sniffed it.

'Go on, take it.'

It took the waistcoat, put it on, though it swamped him, and began chattering excitedly.

'What? What are you trying to tell me? And what will we do with you, monkey, if your master dies?'

Twelve

When I returned to the infirmary, PC Hodge was at his post, in the corridor outside the ward, exchanging words with another constable who must have been on duty during the day. Both men looked cheerful. This task, though tedious, probably came as a welcome change from pounding the beat in the drizzling cold.

Constable Hodge gave me a friendly nod as I passed through the doors and into the nurses' room where I hung up my coat and put on the apron that Mrs Sugden had obligingly washed and ironed.

Sister O'Malley appeared, carrying her teacup. We exchanged a good evening and I asked about my patient.

'Not much change. He's poorly but comfortable. He managed a mouthful of oxtail soup.' She rinsed her cup and saucer under the tap. 'Oh and unless the police want you to stay here, I should be all right for staff tomorrow. I have two nurses over their bouts of flu.'

When she had gone, I filled a dish with boiling water and added Friar's Balsam. As I picked it up, Constable Hodge put his head around the door. 'Brewing up?'

'No, not yet. And are you still expecting Mr Bruno to run off?'

He smiled. 'No such luck. My colleague was here for the daytime shift. He took a statement.'

'From whom?'

He nodded his head in the direction of the ward doors. 'Chummy in there, Umberto Bruno.'

'I don't believe that.'

'No, straight up. Our Umberto was seen following Dr Potter through the alley, into the rear of the building. When tackled about it, agreed it was so.'

'He's not up to agreeing anything.'

'Well, apparently he did.'

'And who is supposed to have seen Mr Bruno following Dr Potter?'

'That I can't say.'

'Why would Dr Potter go into the library by the alley door? He wouldn't have a key. I would never be able to go in that way.'

Constable Hodge tapped the side of his nose. 'Dr Potter wasn't like you, Mrs Shackleton. He was no ordinary library proprietor. His great-great-grandfather was one of the founders. He'll have been privy to all sorts of inside infor-mation and prerogatives.' He sniffed the Friar's Balsam and turned up his nose. 'That stuff don't half pong.'

'It's meant to.' I felt slightly sick, and not just from the smell of Friar's Balsam. Surely the man could not have given a statement, except by groaning it and allowing the daytime constable to draw his own conclusions. 'Did the person who saw Umberto say whether he had his monkey with him?'

'That I don't know.' He held the door for me as I went

123

back into the corridor. 'You see, Mrs Shackleton, you look at yon fellow and you see a patient, because of the nurse in you. I look at him and I see a bit of a pest. When he's about his business with that monkey, he accosts passers-by, no better than a beggar, and we have our own poor with their mouths to feed.' In the corridor, he opened the door to the small cell-like room where Umberto slept fitfully. 'I know what I'm talking about. I've had complaints enough.'

I did not answer. He closed the door. He and I were not as pleased with each other as we had been the night before.

I placed the basin by the bed. My patient was wheezing terribly. I checked his chart and saw that his temperature had gone down by two degrees. That was a good sign. The day staff had changed his nightshirt and sheets.

It was then I thought to do something that had not entered my head the night before. I took out my notebook and recorded everything concerning the patient's condition since finding him in the basement. I entered details from his chart, including temperature, respiration and pulse. I noted when I had applied poultices, given drinks, brought in the steaming balsam, along with comments on his physical state and the way he had drifted in and out of consciousness. His only speech had been to ask where he was, and to wonder whether he was still alive; hardly compatible with giving a statement to the police.

Slowly, the evening ticked by. When Umberto showed signs of distress, I tapped his chest and back in an attempt to ease the congestion. At nine o'clock, he managed to take a few spoonfuls of broth. His weak gaze met mine, and he nodded appreciation. Perhaps he had nodded to the daytime police-man's questions, and that had been construed as assent to being seen following Dr Potter into the building. After taking the broth, he lay back on the pillow, exhausted, eyes closed.

I noted this, wishing I knew what he was supposed to have said in his 'statement'.

My world had shrunk to this small room, dimly lit by a night lamp. At about ten o'clock, I looked out of the window. The night was clearer than Friday, and I could see the shape of the Town Hall. These were rooms where my husband Gerald would have worked. Perhaps he looked out of this very window. As I thought of him, I remembered the roll of honour commemorating the infirmary's war dead and bearing his name. Yesterday morning and this evening, I had passed it without a second glance, and a lack of feeling that surprised me.

I was no longer in love with a memory. The harsh thought came to me that if we who are still here are to be of use in this world, we must break faith with the dead, and make the choice to be in the land of the living, leaving the shades behind. Gerald was never coming back. My life could go on for another fifty or sixty years, and so must I.

In the early hours of Sunday morning, I made tea for my patient, myself and for Constable Hodge.

When Umberto opened his eyes, there was a spark of brightness there.

After he took a drink of the hot sweet liquid, he murmured, 'I never been so comfortable.'

And then he closed his eyes. Part of me wished, for his sake, he might never open them again.

But he did.

'Mr Bruno, what is your monkey's name?'

His voice came out hoarse. 'Percy. He fill my purse, or try to.'

After that, he dozed and when he came to again, he asked, 'Where is he?'

'Percy? He's safe. He's well. And so are your sovereigns. I have them at my house for you.'

He frowned, as though my words made no sense.

Now that he was capable of a little speech, I would have liked him to say more, but he dozed again.

At six o'clock, I took the teacups back into the nurses' room and washed them, leaving everything tidy, ready for the day shift.

When I went back into the corridor, PC Hodge was not at his post. He must have been taking a short break himself. Or perhaps the inspector had realised the nonsense of guarding a very sick man and had put his constable back on the beat.

I opened the sick room door and saw Constable Hodge holding Umberto's arm, shaking him.

'What are you doing?'

'Waking him.'

'Why?'

'Because he needs to hear what I have to say. You might be better to wait outside.'

'I'm going nowhere. I'm nursing this man. You should leave.'

Constable Hodge cleared his throat. 'I've had my orders.'

Umberto looked up at him, confused, fearful.

'Right, so you're awake and we have a witness that you are awake.' The constable straightened his shoulders. 'Umberto Bruno, you are charged with the murder of Horatio Erasmus Potter. You do not have to say anything but anything you do say may be taken down in evidence and used against you. Do you understand?'

He brought out a pair of handcuffs.

I snatched them from him. 'Are you mad? The man is very poorly. Are you trying to kill him?'

'Madam, you are impeding a police officer in the course of his duty.'

'Then charge me.'

'I am instructed to secure the prisoner.' He softened his tone, trying to sound reasonable. 'He won't be removed yet, Mrs Shackleton. Not until the order comes through.'

Reluctantly, I returned the handcuffs. But if the constabulary thought they would pin Dr Potter's death on a sickly organ grinder, they could think again.

Having retrieved the handcuffs, the constable could not quite decide what to do. He tried handcuffing Umberto to the bed post, but it was such a stretch on the man's arm that he gave up, and instead handcuffed his wrists together.

'How can he be cared for like that? What happens when his nightshirt must be changed?'

'I will remove the handcuffs.' He sighed. 'I'm sorry, Mrs Shackleton, but you see, he was in the basement, and so was Dr Potter, and there was no one else.'

'And you think that rather than be evicted from his warm and cosy spot on a freezing flagged floor, this man would first stun Dr Potter and then, taking no chances, strangle him with his own silk scarf. You saw how sick he was. You carried him. How can you think such a thing?'

He hesitated.

'Constable, you see the state of him. Does he look like a man capable of leaping from the bed and making his escape? Take off the handcuffs.'

'It isn't up to me, madam. Orders come through the

sergeant from the inspector. If I don't follow them, my head will be on the block.'

'Then I'll speak to the inspector.'

'I know just what he'll say.'

'And what's that?'

'That you can't take chances in a case like this.'

'Where will I find him?'

'Sergeant Ashworth?'

'Inspector Wallis.'

'In his office, in the Town Hall, but . . . '

'But what?'

Whatever the constable had intended to say he thought better of it. He left, closing the door gently behind him.

What logic! The prisoner was in the basement, and so was the corpse. Ipso facto, Umberto must be the murderer.

Perhaps I had done no service by seeing Umberto through two long nights. To slip away in the throes of pneumonia would be preferable to swinging on the end of a rope.

In the corridor, a trolley announced the arrival of the early morning tea, and of the dayshift.

Bringing the chair close to the side of the bed, I sat down and took Umberto's hands in mine. 'What happened in the library basement?'

'He took my monkey.'

'Who did?'

Umberto closed his eyes.

One question had been answered: Leeds City Police had not seen fit to call in Scotland Yard. It would now be up to me to find Dr Potter's killer.

Thirteen

A light drizzle fell steadily as I walked the short distance to the Town Hall. The sound of church bells broke the early morning stillness as the Catholic Cathedral pealed out a summons to its parishioners.

Leeds CID, in the person of Inspector Wallis, had taken the most direct route to "solving" the crime of murder: find a possible witness, Umberto Bruno, and pin the crime on him.

How should I approach the inspector this time, and attempt to make him treat Umberto Bruno with some semblance of humanity?

There are several reliable ways of dealing with a man who is not a relative and not a lover. Some women play the dragon queen, so imperious as to make a man quake. The femme fatale will, at least temporarily, take a man's breath away. An old nursing friend successfully played nanny, chidingly putting officers on their best behaviour as if they were in a nursery rather than on a ward. My preferred way is to be the chum, encouraging, playing up and playing the game. That seems usually the best choice, but not easy with a man as taciturn as Wallis.

I reached the side door of the Town Hall, which is the only way in on a Sunday.

Dragon Queen-like, I announced to the commissionaire my name and business and claimed to have an appointment with the inspector. When the commissionaire did not see me on his list, I told him that was because the appointment was arranged by telephone ten minutes ago.

Without waiting for further comment, I climbed the wide staircase that led to CID headquarters.

In spite of the past four years spent investigating, I had never met any of the senior officers of the Leeds City Police in a professional capacity. It would have been so much better if my father had been superintendent here in Leeds, rather than in Wakefield. The two forces kept their distance from each other and my father rarely visited Leeds. The rivalry was unacknowledged, but real.

No one came between me and the inspector's door. By clever deduction I knew it was his room. The nameplate etched on the glass read: Inspector G T Wallis.

I tapped.

A voice called, 'Come in.'

I pushed open the door to a square office with a high window. The room smelled of ash and stale tobacco. Behind a heavy old oak desk sat Mr Wallis in his crumpled worsted suit, white shirt and navy blue tie. He stood, pushing back his chair.

I crossed the worn rug. 'Excuse my coming unannounced, Inspector.' I hoped I had struck a note between confident and friendly but suddenly felt I had struck no note at all, feeling a mess, rumpled, bleary-eyed, glad of the hat hiding my hair and wishing I had washed my face.

By now I was close enough to see his blue eyes. It is surprising how many people have odd eyes; not odd in colour but in shape. The right eye was bright, penetrating and round; the left eye, a little smaller, less intense and tending towards oval. I found this oddly disconcerting, and for a moment we simply looked at each other, as if for the first time. His fair hair shone from the application of pomade. He was more clean-shaven than yesterday. An amused half-smile curled his full lips.

'Please take a seat.'

I sat down; so did he.

'What can I do for you, Mrs Shackleton?'

'It's about Mr Bruno, Umberto Bruno.'

'Thank you for going with him to the Infirmary.'

'I was glad to help.'

'Yes, I suppose you were. Though it must have been a bit of a shock for you to first find the body of one of your fellow readers, and then some smelly fellow curled in a ball, especially when you were expecting to see something more insubstantial. A ghost, I understand?'

I let the jibe pass.

He took a sheet of paper from his desk drawer. 'You must be reimbursed for your time and trouble. If you complete this form . . .'

I took the form. 'Thank you, but that is not why I am here. I have just come from the infirmary, where I spent the last two nights watching over Umberto Bruno.'

'It was an imposition and the force is grateful to you.'

'Mr Bruno has pneumonia. It was touch and go whether he would live. It still is.'

'Oh, I think he will live. His sort do you know, surprising as it may seem.'

'I am not sure what you mean.'

He smiled. 'You served as a nurse in the VAD?'

'Yes.'

'Then you may know that many nurses have a reputation for being soft on malingerers, being easily taken in by a man capable of putting it on.'

'You speak from experience of VAD nurses?'

There was an ever so slight change of manner, annoyance at being challenged and perhaps a discomfort that told me he had not fought in the war. Well, there was nothing surprising in that. He would have been exempt from military service.

'I know enough of the gentle sex to understand that judgement may be clouded when a lady takes to nursing.'

I could have put him right, giving a host of examples of hard choices made under the most distressing conditions, but that would not have taken me an inch nearer changing his mind about Umberto Bruno. My hopes of playing the chum faded fast. 'The man is critically ill and incapable of committing the crime he is accused of.'

I expected him to correct me. Umberto was arrested on suspicion. He had not yet been charged. Wallis did not trouble himself to set me right. 'Bruno thought he had found a place to shelter, and to hide. He was wrong. Luck was on our side when he was unable to leave the scene of the crime.'

'Handcuffs are unnecessary and will make it impossible for him to be nursed satisfactorily.'

'The man is a vagrant, an intruder, with enough circumstantial evidence for him to be charged with murder. I recommend that you reserve your compassion for a more worthy recipient.'

'He is not well enough to have given a statement. The man is hard-pressed to utter half a dozen words.'

'Sometimes half a dozen words are enough.' He pushed back his chair. 'Your comments are noted. Now if you'll excuse me, I have much to attend to.'

It would have been a waste of my breath to argue. I stood. So did he.

'One point, Mrs Shackleton, that you may be able to clarify.'

'Yes?'

'The valuable library item you picked up after you uncovered the unfortunate Dr Potter.' He looked down at his notes. '*Gothic Ornament*. Where precisely was it, if you can recall?'

'Not far from Dr Potter's feet.'

'And it was you who telephoned for the police?'

'Yes.'

'And to the Leeds Club, for Mr Castle?'

'No. That was Mr Lennox. He rightly thought that as library president, Mr Castle should be informed. Also, Mr Castle gave Mr Lennox some support. You see, Mr Lennox's wife died a year ago and he is still easily upset.'

'So I understand.' He nodded briefly. 'Thank you for coming, and if you'll fill in the form . . .'

Did he think that Umberto had attempted to steal the book, and Dr Potter had intervened?

'May I ask a question, Inspector?'

'Of course.'

'I believe Dr Potter was hit before he was strangled. Was the only wound to his head, or was there some other blow?'

133

'That is not something that needs to be known. Not yet, anyway.'

'You see, Dr Potter was tall as a top shelf. Mr Bruno would struggle to reach a taper on a mantelpiece, and is as weak as a fallen sparrow.'

'It is not height that matters, Mrs Shackleton, but posture – the position of those concerned.' Inspector Wallis stroked his chin. 'You said in your statement that when you and Dr Potter spoke, he seemed to believe something may have gone missing. What did he say, precisely?'

'It was less in his words than his attitude. He was put out by the article about the library's valuable stock being on display. He was enthusiastic about the possibility of the library removing to new premises where the stock may be more secure.'

'Anything else?'

'Nothing that I didn't tell Constable Hodge. Dr Potter wanted me to read an article in a magazine he had written as an undergraduate, because it concerned the ghost, and a different disappearance.'

'Different to . . . ?'

'He thought a library assistant had disappeared. But I don't believe there is a mystery. I'm sure Mr Lennox can explain her departure.'

'And did you read the magazine?'

'No. I took it home and there has not been time since.'

'I'd like to see it, please.'

Our talk was at an end. I had given him a better account of what happened in the library than anyone else, of that I felt sure. Why did he not budge?

'What about Umberto Bruno?'

'Nothing changes. He is our main suspect.'

He walked me to the door.

Outside in the corridor, I leaned against the wall, attempting to regain my composure. I felt like smashing the glass in his office door.

As I stood there, thinking what to do next, I heard him speak into the telephone. 'Have Umberto Bruno brought in and put in a cell.' There was a pause. The person at the other end must have had the temerity to question the order. In an impatient voice, Wallis said, 'I am aware of that. Have our own doctor examine him.'

Oh no you don't. I would not let him do it, but how was I to stop him? Who could I turn to? I hurried down the broad stairway. My father is a superintendent of the West Riding force, he would be able to talk to his Leeds counterpart. In theory, that is. In practice he would not do it. He would say that it was not his concern, it would be undue interference, and the man on the spot must make the decisions.

Then it struck me. Having given houseroom to the man's monkey, why not do the same for his master? I could smuggle Umberto from the infirmary, abduct him and take him home; but how, without being seen?

Slowly I retraced my footsteps down the Town Hall stairs and out into the dismal street.

Why did this matter so much to me?

Because I felt pity for the man. Because I believed him to be innocent. Because during my wartime nursing there were so many men for whom I could do nothing. Because I felt devastated by the death of Dr Potter. I was unable to save them. I would save Umberto Bruno.

I had left my car at the entrance to the infirmary. I hurried back there now. Instead of making things better for my patient, I had made his situation worse. If the poor man was taken to the cells, he would die. Of course he would die. Case closed. There would be no need for the police to look for anyone else, and it would save the expense of a trial.

Perhaps it would be kinder to let him die. That might be preferable to wrongful imprisonment, a perverted trial and the rope.

Once back in the infirmary, I sought out matron, Millicent Formby. We knew each other from when she was a ward sister at St Mary's during the war. At that time, I thought of her as an odd old stick, though she was then not many years older than I am now. In the end, when a couple of nurses wilted under the strain and I did not, we rubbed along very well and came to understand each other.

I had to wait about twenty minutes, until she had finished ward rounds.

Finally, I found her, pen in hand, at her desk.

'Matron?'

'Kate! I heard you were here.'

'Hello, Millicent. I didn't know you were so close by. I live just up the road.'

'I know.'

'You never got in touch.'

She shrugged and smiled. I understood what she meant. We had not been great chums, though what had seemed a huge difference between us then had diminished with time.

'Millicent, you will know that Umberto Bruno has been charged with murder, and handcuffed.'

'I saw on my ward rounds just now. I've contacted the hospital chairman to protest. I have asked that the order be countermanded and the handcuffs removed.'

'Thank you. That's a relief.'

'Let's wait and see. The police may put up a good argument for keeping them.'

'I don't believe he did it.'

'Of course you don't. You always saw the best in people.'

'That was then. I've changed. But I'll swear that this man was too ill to do what he is accused of.'

'I don't know whether the man is guilty or not, but I won't have a patient handcuffed on my wards. We're not the Workhouse Infirmary where some beds are not much more than a holding cell.'

'There's something else. Inspector Wallis has ordered him to be taken to the cells.'

'That's madness.'

'It's vindictiveness because I tried to interfere. Can you stop it?'

'I can try. They won't be able to move him if the doctor and I say no. We would have to be over-ruled by the board and they won't manage to meet before tomorrow afternoon, possibly tomorrow evening.'

'That's no time at all.'

'If you think the man is innocent, try and persuade someone to believe you, and soon. Do you know a good solicitor?'

Fourteen

Did I know a good solicitor, Millicent, the matron, had asked. Yes I did: Mr Castle, library president. If anyone could persuade Inspector Wallis to show commonsense and compassion, it would be Edwin Castle, Esquire, one of the most influential men in the city. I knew where I would find him on this Sunday morning: the mayors' nest.

Mill Hill Chapel in City Square is an attractive place of worship, with a long dissenting tradition, the spot where men of importance, including mayors past and present, worship and hobnob, so earning the chapel its nickname. Built in the perpendicular style, it possesses some fine stained-glass windows. On this particular Sunday morning, a row of expensive motor cars stood parked outside. I left my car on the other side of City Square and crossed back to the pleasant courtyard, its trees now almost bare of leaves.

The service was already underway, and with a packed congregation. I slipped in at the back. A well-dressed man in a good coat and kid gloves slid along the pew to make room for me.

I looked round for Mr and Mrs Castle. He has a healthy head of white hair and wears gold-rimmed spectacles. She has a taste for extravagant hats in plum or navy. Mr Castle and Dr Potter held each other in high regard. Mr Castle told me so once, at a library Christmas sherry do, when he was marvelling at Potter's mathematical genius. At the same do, Dr Potter told me that Mr Castle was a very clever man, the glue of the library and one of those men whose presence on a committee ensured that it ran smoothly.

I could not see the Castles, but that was probably because they were near the front of the chapel. Now that I was here, the misgivings set in. Mr Castle may not yet know that Umberto Bruno had been charged with murder. The service ended as I was trying to decide how best to break the news, and ask for his intervention.

I stood to allow the people in my pew to leave, all the while keeping a watch for the Castles. Filing out was a slow business because many stopped to shake hands or exchange a word with the minister. Eventually, Mr and Mrs Castle appeared. She is in her late sixties, a little younger than he. Both are well preserved. He wore a good alpaca overcoat. Stately Mrs Castle linked his arm, her lambswool brushing his alpaca. She sported a maroon hat with high crown, broad brim and veil, the kind of hat you would hate to sit behind in a theatre. Both have a healthy look that comes from a lifetime of good food, leisure, and holidays in Switzerland.

I smiled, as if it was my habit to accost people as they left chapel.

'Mr Castle, Mrs Castle, good morning.'

She glared at me suspiciously, giving a royal nod.

He was charming, as always. 'Mrs Shackleton. You have decided to join our congregation?'

'Not exactly. I came hoping to have a word with you.'

Mrs Castle, not a person likely to win an award for subtlety, scowled.

'Of course.' He ignored the squeeze his wife put on his arm. 'My sympathy over the terrible shock you had on Friday evening.'

'Dearest, the children are coming, and the grandchildren.' She looked at me. 'And the great-grandchildren,' she added with a note of triumph befitting the fertile matriarch.

'Then I wouldn't dream of detaining you. But Mr Castle, I am wondering whether . . . ' We were by the door, and there were still people passing. I adopted a conspiratorial tone to encourage him to step aside with me, which he did, releasing his wife's steely grip. 'Have you heard that the man found in the library on Friday evening, Umberto Bruno, has been charged with murder?'

'How do you know this?'

It suddenly occurred to me that none of them knew I had been at the man's bedside. 'I was at the infirmary this morning.'

'You were at the infirmary?'

'I went with him in the ambulance on Friday evening. You know I was a wartime nurse?'

'Yes.'

'He is dangerously ill, but handcuffed. I don't believe for a moment that he killed Dr Potter, and the handcuffs are inhumane. People listen to you, Mr Castle. I wonder if you might intervene.' There was a subtle change in his posture and that glance some people give when one makes an appeal, a mixture of reluctance and vanity.

'Perhaps he is handcuffed to prevent escape, or self-harm.'

'He can barely move without help, and there is a policeman on the door of the ward.'

'Leave it with me.'

Mrs Castle was suddenly beside us and must have been listening. 'My husband has his professional reputation to consider, as well as his duties as library president. A solicitor cannot act in a way that would be contrary to a police investigation, especially when Mr Castle saw the vagrant follow Dr Potter into the alley.'

I stared at Mr Castle. 'You did? It was you who saw him?'

'I thought nothing of it at the time. Dr Potter was such an eccentric. There was no accounting for his whims, and the vagrant was some distance behind him.'

'When? What time?'

Mrs Castle stepped between us. 'Mrs Shackleton, we all know about your hobby, but please to practise it elsewhere.'

Castle said, 'It's all right, dear. Mrs Shackleton has had a shock. We all have.'

Mrs Castle was not easily put off. 'We have prayed for the repose of poor Dr Potter's soul.' There was a challenge in her voice. She suspected I had not prayed for anyone's repose. 'Come, Edwin!'

'I'll be with you in a moment, dear.'

She drew back her shoulders and threw out her chest. 'On this date in 1768, the library opened its doors for the first time. It is disgusting to commemorate that date with talk of murder.'

She strode out of the chapel.

Slowly, Mr Castle and I followed her. 'If you can spare just another moment, Mr Castle . . . '

'What is it?' he asked. 'It would be wrong of me to talk about a police investigation when I may be called as a witness.'

Mrs Castle was at the gate, turning, marching towards the row of cars.

Mr Castle exchanged greetings with several important looking men as we moved away towards the farthest tree. A sharp wind brought down a leaf that landed on his hat.

'I'm most grateful for everything you did on Friday, Mrs Shackleton. Lennox was very sorry afterwards that he lost his nerve a little, and of course Father Bolingbroke apparently had another engagement, visiting the sick I believe. I thought you had left, or I would have made sure you reached home safely.'

'Thank you, there was no need.'

'As a matter of fact I did know about Bruno. Inspector Wallis telephoned to me. It has not been made public yet.'

'I believe the police are wrong.'

'Why so?'

'There are too many unanswered questions, Mr Castle. What motive could Bruno have had for such a deed?'

'That is for the police to find out.'

'Bruno did not do it. He needs legal representation.'

'My practice does not handle criminal matters.'

'But you could look into it. Someone else must have been there. Do you know of any enemies that Dr Potter may have had, or of any possible connection between his death and thefts from the library?'

'Thefts?'

'Dr Potter suspected books had been stolen.' I was exaggerating a little, but something in Castle's manner told me I had touched a nerve. 'I can't imagine the organ grinder would have been a book thief. There must be something the police are missing.'

Mr Castle's face was a picture of surprise. 'It never occurred to me that the police could have made a mistake. It seems such an open and shut case, but if you believe there is cause for concern . . . '

'I do. Apart from lack of motive, Dr Potter was well-built and fit. Umberto Bruno is skin and bone, and besides, I have this feeling . . . '

'Ah, a woman's intuition.'

'If you want to call it that, but really to do with physical disparity between the men. I should like to take another look around the basement.'

'The police are not allowing us down there just yet. If it will set your mind at rest, I will ask them when we are allowed access.'

We walked out of the grounds together. Most of the cars had gone. Castle stood and stared. 'Oh dear. My wife misunderstood me, I think.'

There was only my car left, on the other side of City Square. Mrs Castle had deserted her husband.

'Let me offer you a lift. Mine's that blue Jowett over there.'

It would give me an opportunity to ask him a few questions on the journey.

I began with the most innocuous. 'Have you historic connections with the library?'

'Oh no, not like Potter. I purchased a share in the library as a young man, when I qualified as a solicitor. A professional man has a duty to become part of the life of the city.'

Mr Castle made no attempt to staunch my queries but in his calm lawyer's manner carefully deflected every question. He was cautious, unwilling to commit himself, and reluctant to believe that Inspector Wallis could be mistaken. 'We must remember, Mrs Shackleton, that this is a police matter.'

Of course he was right. This was not my case. But I had one more idea. The person who may know whether Dr Potter's suspicion about thefts was correct was the librarian, Mr Lennox.

There is no great distance between Meanwood and Chapeltown. Mr Lennox lived at Grange Villas, Chapeltown. I knew this because he and his late wife once held a sherry party for committee members.

It was possible that Lennox would visit his wife's grave in the afternoon and that if I called now, I may find him at home.

Within a quarter hour of dropping off Mr Castle, I drew up outside Grange Villas, a fine stone-built mansion that sometime in the previous century had been turned into flats. I do not always look through windows before ringing a doorbell but on this particular day I did, and a good thing too.

There, seated at the breakfast table, was Mr Lennox, in his dressing gown, Sunday papers on the table. Opposite him was Mrs Carmichael, deputy librarian, also in her dressing gown.

They had not seen me as they were gazing at each other.

Time for me to give up and go home.

As I drove, I considered asking Sykes to come with me to the library and bring his skeleton keys so that we could gain entry, but I could hear his arguments. The front is too exposed and with iron gates. Change Alley attracts vagrants, prostitutes and the attention of the beat bobby. Sykes would question my judgement, remind me that I have not slept, tell me that although it is Sunday, people will be out walking to and from church, and window shopping. He would tell me that police are keeping an eye on the place.

Besides, I had already interfered with the Mr Castle's Sunday mornings. Sykes must be allowed his day off.

Feeling in low spirits and the tiredness of a sleepless night beginning to creep up, I set off for home.

As I drove, words popped into my head. *The Big Bothy, Weetwood*: Dr Potter's address.

As if it had developed a mind of its own, my motor sped on, beyond Headingley, in the direction of Weetwood.

Fifteen

Big Bothy, Dr Potter's dwelling, was in one of those out of the way nooks. If I had not happened upon a couple of girls exercising their ponies, I might be looking still.

Leaving the car in a narrow lane, I walked along a track. On the curve of a bend, I saw the dwelling, a single storey, octagonal house with two chimneys, a roughcast finish and latticed windows. It stood in a meadow that in spring and summer must be glorious but now looked a sorry sight. Close by were two outhouses, presumably one of them housing the earth closet and the other a shed. A little way beyond was a paddock and stable.

Close up, I saw that the roughcast finish on the walls of the house had been decorated with tiny pebbles and fragments of coloured glass, giving the building an idiosyncratic appearance.

When no one answered my knock on the firmly shut oak front door, I peered through the nearest of the latticed windows into a library. Under the window, a sturdy desk held an oil lamp and cut glass pen and ink stand. The surface was strewn with notebooks and sheets of foolscap paper. An exceedingly large tabby cat leapt onto the desk and stared at me.

Through the next window I looked into a kitchen-cum-dining room. The window after that revealed a bedroom, furnished with a walnut bedroom suite. Beside that was a parlour or sitting room where a low fire burned. This room was comfortably furnished with large Persian rug, and well-worn chintz-covered chairs and sofa. Alcoves on either side of the fireplace housed bookshelves. In front of one set of bookshelves to the right of the fireplace, an ornate cage on a stand held a handsome parrot. Through the last window, I saw a small bedroom with cast-iron single bed, chest of drawers with jug and bowl, shaving kit, hair brush and clothes brush. On a wicker chair, lay an open book.

Every room had at least one oil lamp. Neither gas nor electricity had been brought to this spot.

I waited a few more moments, looking about to see whether anyone would return. No one did.

Following a well-trodden path to a gate in the fence, I crossed the paddock, towards the stable.

Through the half-open stable door, I heard a sound and peered inside, ready to introduce myself.

A man of heavy build and medium height had his back to me. He was hatless and wore a dark coat that was a little on the small size, pulled tightly across his shoulders. A pony stood beside him, flicking its tail. In front of them was a free-standing blackboard, the kind normally seen in a schoolroom. It was covered in large, boldly-written numbers, some of them simple, the kind children might learn in their first year at school, and others more complicated, including equations that meant nothing to me.

The man whispered into the pony's ear.

He waited.

I watched.

He whispered again, and waited.

I waited.

Nothing happened.

After a moment I backed away from the stable door, returned, and made a show of knocking on the door and pushing it open.

I cleared my throat and made myself known, apologising for interrupting him.

Man and pony turned their heads.

'Hello, sir.'

'Hello.' The man gave a deep sigh. 'Be with you in a moment, madam.' He spoke in a soft Welsh lilt to the pony as he led it back to the stall and gave it a pat.

The pony nudged his pocket.

'Right you are, Archie, though you don't deserve it, mind.' He produced an apple and held it towards the creature who took it from his hand.

As the man walked towards me, I saw that he was smartly dressed, his coat well-brushed, brown boots polished to a high sheen, his trousers a little too short. Ample grey wavy hair, centre parted, and one of those melancholy drooping moustaches gave him the appearance of an inventor of improbable machinery. He could have been any age between thirty-five and fifty.

'I'm Mrs Shackleton from the library. We were all shocked and sorry about Dr Potter's death.'

'That is kind. Thank you. I wondered if someone would come.'

'And you are?'

'I beg your pardon. I forget my manners. I am Richard

Morgan, Dr Potter's manservant, man and boy, my service interrupted only by the business that interrupted us all.'

He closed the stable door and we fell into step together on the path that led towards the house.

'Is there anyone else here with you? I'm sorry that I don't know Dr Potter's circumstances. We were acquainted through the library but I realise now how little I know about him.'

'Just the two of us here it was and powerful well we were suited.'

'It's very peaceful here.'

'Out of the way some would say, but there is a bicycle in the outhouse, see you, which takes me where I need to go. And sometimes Dr Potter pedalled his way to the university or walked to the road as far as the tram stop. That is what he did on Friday. I told the police when they came to break the terrible news and ask their questions.'

'You must have worried when he had not come home.'

'Well I did not worry, Friday night being so heavy with the fog. I was not surprised when the doctor did not return for supper. I thought the fog had pressed him into stopping at his gentlemen's club and that I would see him on Saturday. No cab driver would have inclined himself to drive up here on such a night.'

'He sometimes came home by cab?'

'Heavens no, not as a rule, but on Friday morning he let it drop that he would be coming in style, see you, and he seemed very pleased about something.'

'He must have relied on you a great deal.'

'I like to think so.'

Ingratiating oneself into a person's confidence is a despicable habit but on occasions useful. I shamelessly invented a courtesy aunt who had relied for forty years on a companion who would then have been left bereft without some assistance as to how she might find her way from her lonely situation.

He invited me indoors.

We entered a spic and span hallway with polished floor, threadbare carpet and a vase of evergreens on the table.

'Please step into the parlour. I am just about to make tea.'

I sat down on one of the chintz-covered chairs that I had seen through the window. As I did so, the giant cat stalked into the room and leapt on my knee, its weight cracking my thighbones. I stroked its head. As if in protest, the parrot by the bookcase began to squawk. The cat purred.

The parrot's squawk turned into a low chant. 'Ones two is two, two twos four, three twos six, how's your father?'

The cat's purr mounted to a deafening crescendo.

'Two and six,' the parrot squawked, 'stupid bird, stupid bird, three and four.' It then lapsed into silence, broken only by the rattle of the cage as it pecked seed.

The volume of the cat's purring increased so much that I found it disconcerting. I stopped stroking its head. It butted my hand and continued its high volume signals of content-ment. Never in my life have I heard even a baritone reach such a pitch. It was the kind of unearthly sound that might make one believe in reincarnation, the reincarnation, in a single creature, of a Welsh male voice choir.

'Eleven twelve,' the parrot said, just as Mr Morgan arrived with the tea tray. He set it down, picked up a damask cover from the back of a chair and placed it over the cage.

He then turned to the cat. 'Down, Dunce!'

Dunce ignored him.

I lifted the cat gently to the floor. It weighed as much as a trunk packed for a month's voyage. 'Why do you call him Dunce?'

'His name is Toby. We call him Dunce because he pays no heed. He doesn't try. Oh, he sits on the desk as though pretending great interest but there's nothing behind it.'

'I see.'

I did not see. Not one little bit did I see.

Mr Morgan drew up a low table, set it with a china cup and a plate of homemade biscuits. 'How do you like your tea, Mrs Shackleton?'

'As it comes, Mr Morgan.'

'One lump or two?'

'None, thank you.' Having become used to going without sugar when it was in such short supply, I had lost the taste for it.

He poured the milk, and tea of a goodly colour, and hot. 'Thank you.' I took a biscuit. 'You have a cook?'

'Oh no, madam. It is all my own work. Wouldn't do to have women about the place, begging your pardon. Not with the professor concentrating so hard on his subject.'

'What was his subject, precisely?'

'Well mathematics, of course.'

'A difficult subject.'

'Indeed, it is a subject chill and severe, with the beauty and truth of an ancient carving. But my master turned mathematics into poetry and his interests spread much wider and warmer.'

'In what way?'

'We did not say much about it, not yet. It is a great pity that so much of his work is left undone.'

151

'Did the police ask you about his work, the work that was left undone?'

'No, madam. They wanted to know about his acquaintances, what took him to the library that day, why he may have been in the basement. I am afraid I was not much help.'

'I should think you were in a state of shock.'

'Indeed I was, and most upset by their insinuations.'

'What did they insinuate?'

'One can never be sure with insinuations as they are exactly that and lacking in precision as you might say. It would shame me to repeat what I think they were implying.'

'Tut-tut. How awful for you.'

'As if he would, as if Dr Potter would take as much as a match that did not belong to him. Every book here is owned by Dr Potter or legitimately borrowed and none overdue.'

'They thought he may have books that did not belong to him?'

'My poor master, struck down at the height of his explorations and they asking me what books he has and where. Would you credit that?'

'I would not.'

'I will see that the good doctor's wishes are carried out, that his books are donated to the university, and the borrowed ones returned. Perhaps you will be so kind as to take his Leeds Library books with you.'

'He took some back only on Friday.'

'He has a special dispensation for wholesale book borrowing. There are more.'

'Yes, if you wish, but do not rush yourself. I can come back another day.'

'I will not have aspersions cast on his good name. He never returned books anything but early in all his life.'

'Your loyalty does you credit.'

'He deserves no less. He was good to me, took me into his confidence occasionally. He usually passed on his clothing to me. We are much of a size except that he was taller. But I am a dab hand at shortening trousers.'

I tried not to glance at Mr Morgan's trousers that ended somewhere above the tops of his grey socks. I looked around the room. 'And the property?'

'Rented, furnished, and paid up until the end of April.'

'And then? Do you have family?'

He shook his head. 'I have not had much time to think about my future. But I will not work for another gentleman because there would be none so interesting and important as Dr Potter.'

'What will you do?'

'It is too soon to say.'

'Of course.'

'But two possibilities present themselves. I have learned something of mathematics, have taught myself Latin and German. A man could not live with a genius and fail to catch a glimpse of life's mysteries. Some families who may not be able to afford a full-time tutor may engage a person on an hourly rate to help their children learn.'

'That sounds a good idea.'

'Education is the foundation on which we will build a new and better world.'

'And the other possibility?'

'I am not sure how I could do it. And if I could, I am not sure how I could turn it into a living.'

153

'Try it out on me.'

The cat stalked the room, stopping only to sniff Mr Morgan's shoes. The silent parrot sent waves of dark reproach from under its tent.

I took a wild guess. 'Does this other possibility have anything to do with teaching animals to count?'

His tea went down the wrong way. He tapped his chest, stood up, wiped his watering eyes and left the room, motioning me to excuse him. For an uncomfortable length of time, he coughed and choked in the hall.

A few moments later he returned.

'How did you know, about the animals?'

'The parrot has an inkling of its times tables, the blackboard in the stable is covered with sums and you were encouraging the pony to respond I believe.'

'No one told you then?'

'Oh no. Well, not unless you count the parrot who seems to know more questions than answers.'

'Polynesia is a terrible show-off. She learns by rote, that is the top and bottom of her ability, with not a jot of understanding.' He refilled our teacups. 'I hope you will keep this to yourself, Mrs Shackleton. Dr Potter was not yet ready to reveal his findings. It would have been his life's work, had the Lord spared him. He believed that animals are clever, quick-witted, and some of them more intelligent than many humans.'

'He was teaching animals his subject?'

'He began his classes a year ago, with cat, parrot and horse. He chose cat because of its loquaciousness, loud purr and sociability. But when it came to lessons, Dunce showed no interest whatsoever.'

On hearing his name, Dunce appeared from behind the

sofa as if by magic. Leaping onto the chair arm, it dug its claws in my forearm and began to paddle its paws.

'And the pony?'

'Now there's a different matter. I watched Dr Potter at work. The results would astound. When he asked Archie three plus three, Archie stamped his hoof six times. I saw it with my own eyes and have been trying to see whether I can persuade him to repeat the exercise for me.'

'I see. And this would be your other choice of earning a living?'

'I know. It sounds like a fairground trick but if you heard Dr Potter on the subject, you would understand. He knew so thoroughly what he was about, had designed a scheme of work for Archie that would have taken him through algebra. A German mathematician tried a similar experiment, and there was some testing of his theories that found him wanting. But my master, he knew how to eliminate all possibility of . . . suggestion I think it was.' He sighed. 'If only I had paid more attention to his methods.'

'Mr Morgan, to look at this from a practical point of view, and tell me if I must mind my own business, Dr Potter treated animal learning as his hobby, while drawing a salary from the university. Your situation is different.'

'This is not just about my future way of earning a living, see you. I feel a loyalty to his ambition.'

'It does you credit.'

The cat tired of distressing my sleeve and squared up to make a jump at the low tea table. 'Dunce!' Morgan shouted. It glared at him, stood down, and skulked away.

'Mr Morgan, do you know if the professor intended to add more pupils to his animal classroom?'

'Odd that you should say that. Having given up on Polynesia and Dunce, he did begin to consider that he had made unfortunate choices. Earlier this week, he wrote himself a new timetable for working with Archie and was studying it on Wednesday evening. I thought it was to make an adjustment, but when I dusted, I came across something that surprised me. It was a separate piece of paper, the start of a new timetable and work schedule. The heading said, Counting by digits, one to twenty. Well a pony has no digits.'

'Do you know what kind of animal he thought may show promise, or have special abilities?'

'He was a keen reader of theories of evolution. The great apes interested him. A book he read most avidly only last week was *The Expression of the Emotions in Man and Animals* by Mr Charles Darwin.'

'I see. And you mentioned that you thought he would be coming home in style on Friday.'

Morgan stared at his shoes. The teacup shook a little in his hand. He placed it down carefully and for a long moment held his silence. Perhaps I had said too much. I waited.

'I do not want this known by that inspector. He will misconstrue or ask me questions I cannot answer.'

'You can rely upon my discretion.'

'Dr Potter asked me to dust down the camp bed, giving me the impression that we were to have a guest.' His voice suddenly came close to breaking. 'The only guest was death himself.'

'I am so very sorry for your loss. If it is any consolation, Dr Potter was in the highest of spirits when I saw him on Friday morning.'

Morgan gave a sad smile that broke my heart. 'I don't suppose he said what made him so glad that day?'

'No, but I do have an inkling. If it is confirmed, I will come and tell you, just between the two of us, though it won't be today.'

'I am much obliged.'

The only way to confirm my surmise would be to speak to Umberto Bruno, but it seemed a good guess that Dr Potter had seen Percy the Capuchin monkey at work and been impressed by its abilities. I wondered whether Dr Potter had intended to bring both Umberto and Percy to the house. If so, the monkey had narrowly missed an opportunity to become a mathematical genius. At this very moment, it was probably following Mrs Sugden around the house, or shredding back copies of *The Times*.

Mr Morgan rose to his feet. 'I will fetch the books for you.' He sighed. 'He will never now finish *The Thought and Speech of Animals*. Borrowing from the Leeds Library prevented his university colleagues latching onto his true interests, which he knew some would roundly mock.'

A few moments later, he returned carrying two enormous bags of books. 'There are too many for you to carry, Mrs Shackleton.'

'It's all right. You might walk me to my car.'

'Yes indeed. It is most kind of you to do this.'

I rose to go. 'One more question, if I may, Mr Morgan.'

'I am at your service.'

'Dr Potter mentioned a plan for the library to move premises. Unfortunately I missed the committee meeting where that was discussed.'

'Oh that, the Stayers or Removers Jolly Sub-Subterranean-

Sub Committee. That was his nickname for the matter. It had yet to be thrashed out. He and Professor Merton were particularly looking deeply into the question, but my master was very much in favour.' There was an ever so slight narrowing of the eyes, indicating distrust perhaps. 'I should hate to speak out of turn.'

'Whatever you say will stay within these walls.'

'It was the university vice chancellorship, see you, that was the bugbear between Dr Potter and Professor Merton. It became difficult for them to discuss anything in a civil manner, not that I breathed a word of this to the police because I do not believe a man of learning like Professor Merton . . . ' He rested the bags of books on the chair seat.

'They were rivals for the post I understand.'

'Indeed they were. Not that I am a betting man you understand, but they were joint favourites.'

In spite of her cage cover, Polynesia, the learn-by-rote parrot, began to squawk.

We left the house, escorted by Dunce the cat, and walked back along the lane towards my car. I opened the car door. 'Was there much rancour between Dr Potter and Professor Merton about the post of vice chancellor?'

Morgan placed the bags of books carefully in the car. 'Oh indeed there was. It kept Dr Potter awake at night worrying about it.'

Suddenly, here was a motive. I wondered whether my neighbour, Professor Merton, had an alibi for the time of Dr Potter's death.

Sixteen

As I drove back along Weetwood Lane, the mental picture fixed itself firmly in my mind: Dr Potter and Umberto Bruno in the basement, Percy watching as money changed hands, gold sovereigns counted into a hessian bag. Umberto had found time to strap the moneybag to his belly.

How had the creature escaped from the basement when his new owner and his previous owner had become entombed there? It was Mrs Sugden who had pointed out that the monkey had no harness, collar or lead.

I tried to imagine what was going on in the men's thoughts, and to picture the scene. After two failures in his attempt to teach arithmetic to animals, Dr Potter believed himself to be on the road to success with Clever Archie. He wanted to discover whether his methods worked across different species. When parting with so much money, he would need to be sure that Percy would prove a good subject. He may well have asked Umberto to remove the collar and lead, to make sure the monkey understood commands and was not simply responding to a tug in this or that direction. That would explain why the monkey was not tethered.

Mr Bruno, feeling ill and in need of funds, would of course oblige.

If Dr Potter had intended to go home by taxi, had he arranged for a car or a cab to collect him and the monkey, and perhaps Umberto? Potter had Saturday and Sunday to see the monkey settled in. He may have planned for Umberto to come too, for a night, or the weekend, to reassure the creature.

Inspector Wallis and PC Hodge thought it possible that Umberto had killed Dr Potter. Suppose that could be so? Umberto may have wanted money and monkey. While Dr Potter bent his lofty frame to speak to Percy, Umberto had walloped him on the head and then strangled him. But if he had the strength for that, he would have had the strength to leave.

Someone else was there, but who and why?

Umberto held the answer to that question. If only he would rally, he may be able to help. There was something niggling at the back of my mind. I must be patient, and wait for a half-formed thought to turn into a definite idea.

I parked my car by the side of the infirmary.

Porters are sticklers about not allowing visitors except on the appointed day, and certainly never allowing visitors without passes. Now that I no longer had a legitimate reason for coming to the ward, and had no nurse's uniform that would allow me to pass unchallenged, I had to consider how best to find my way inside.

Bluff. Or, come into the building by a back door. I decided on the latter, and was prepared to engage in the former.

I had worn my motoring coat and hat to drive to Dr Potter's house. But I have a cape in my car. I tucked my

160

motoring coat by the dickey seat, covering the bags of books, and put on the cape. It might pass as a nurse's uniform.

I walked to the rear of the building where the bins are kept and where staff padlock bicycles. The door was open.

I took the back stairs, counting the floors until I reached the second.

Of course this brought me to the wrong end of the ward, where I would have to pass the men's beds, the nursing desk and Sister's office.

Press on. I could only be evicted.

Adopting a cheerful busy-nurse manner, I strode purposefully into the ward. Only one nurse was in evidence. I recognised her from the change of shifts. Giving her a big smile, I walked on.

Not knowing how long I might have with Umberto before the on-duty policeman intervened, I tapped lightly on his door and went inside.

He was propped up on several pillows, no doubt to help his breathing which was laboured, but he looked a little brighter in himself.

What a relief to see that the handcuffs were gone. I wondered whether Mr Castle was responsible for their removal, and hoped so. That would be one in the eye for Inspector Wallis.

'Umberto?'

He opened his eyes.

Wishing I had brought him something, fruit or flowers, I smiled. 'You look a little better today, without the bracelets.'

He glanced at his wrists and managed something like a crooked smile, murmuring a few words in Italian.

161

Whoever was taking care of him had excellent nursing skills, but poultices and balsam had not alleviated the wheeze and rattle in his chest. To fire questions at him seemed mean.

'Do you remember last Friday, when you were in the basement of the library, with Percy, and Dr Potter?'

He frowned.

'The man with the scarf.'

'He was doctor?'

'A doctor of mathematics.'

'Ahh, *si*. He want Percy. Since summer he want Percy. I say no.'

'Why did you change your mind?'

'He promise. No experiment on Percy, kindness, teaching numbers. And money, gold.' His breath whistled as he spoke.

'Your money is safe. Do you remember that I brought you here?'

'Someone I remember. You?'

'Yes. My name is Kate. Umberto, what happened in the basement?'

He glanced at his wrists, as if the handcuffs might reappear. 'When other man come, I hide.'

'What other man?'

He shook his head. 'Don't know. Angry. Angry words. And me so tired, so tired. That is why I part with Percy. I think, no more summers for me. Dr Potter, he promise to take good care of Percy. Give me money, to go home to Napoli.'

'Did you see anything at all, or hear what the men said?'

He shook his head. 'Nothing. Only I call for Percy. He

162

does not come. I think they must be gone, all gone. I'm jiggered. Want a kip.'

I smiled that he suddenly sounded like a Leeds man.

'Yes, you were exhausted.'

He began to cough.

I gave him a sip of water.

'Percy is very well. I'm taking care of him, and your money is safe. Think about Napoli. You'll be there soon. When you come out of hospital, I'll arrange your passage. I've never been to Naples. Perhaps I'll come with you.'

He laughed and it changed his face, brightened his eyes, but it made him cough too, a terrible fit of coughing that racked his body and brought tears.

I waited till the coughing had subsided.

His breath came in short, panting gasps. 'I want priest.'

'I'll see to it.'

He was shaking his head, holding up his hand. 'Good priest, Father Daley, St Patrick's.'

'Then you shall have him. I'll see to it now.' I gave him my hand and he held it in his, reluctant to let go.

'Goodbye for now. I'll see you soon.'

At least I had not said, 'Everything is going to be all right.' Usually, the words pop out when everything is far from all right.

Leaving the infirmary building was easy. No one challenged me, including the policeman who sat in the chair by the ward entrance, and the porter who did not look up from his newspaper.

Back in the car, I tore a page from my notebook and wrote, 'Mr Umberto Bruno, gravely ill patient at the General Infirmary, requests a visit from Father Daley.' I folded my card inside, and set off for St Patrick's on York Road.

I brushed away the thought that Umberto would never come to trial. Inspector Wallis's mistake would go unchallenged.

Not if I could help it.

Seventeen

Having put in two night shifts at the infirmary and had very little sleep on the third night, I still expected to wake at the usual time on Monday, but slept late and stared bleary-eyed at the clock. I slid from the bed and pulled on my dressing gown.

Gingerly, I made my way downstairs. This was Mrs Sugden's day for removing all the stair rods and setting them on the kitchen table. The smell of Brasso filled the air.

She was annoyingly cheerful. 'I've lit a fire in the dining room. I expect Mr Sykes will be coming round with replies to your advertisements.' She put a teapot on the table, between stair rods.

I poured. 'I hope he won't come before I have a cup of tea.'

'You needed your beauty sleep.' She produced a letter. 'This came by first post.'

I carried my tea and the letter into the dining room. The envelope was written in a neat hand and postmarked Manchester. The inside address was Wythenshawe, causing me a shiver of anticipation as I realised that it was from Sophia's old school friend, the English teacher.

Dear Mrs Shackleton
Regarding your enquiry about my school friend Sophia Wells, I
have not heard from her in a long time. My letter to her at
the Compton Road address came back, returned to sender. I am
disappointed that she has not let me have a new address and
so cannot help you. I only know she found work in a library.
That was the last I heard.
*   If you see her, please ask her to write and say I am still at*
my teaching post and still taking care of my sick mother.
*   Yours truly,*
*   Bella Davidson*

I put the letter on the dining room table, to show to Sykes as Mrs Sugden brought me a steaming dish of porridge. The Goldilocks complaint: my porridge was too hot.

I took out the file, containing the photograph of Sophia, aged three, and Lady Coulton in her twenties.

Turning over Miss Davidson's letter, I picked up a pencil and jotted down what I had learned. Children almost always grew taller than their parents. Sophia would be above average height, with auburn hair, if she took after her mother. She had been suspected of stealing at school, and reacted furiously, so good at sticking up for herself. If she had continued as neighbours remembered her as a child, she was ready to roll up her sleeves and get stuck in. Now I knew that she most probably worked in a library. Wouldn't it be wonderful if she had mentioned the name of the library to Bella Davidson?

I took a telegram form from the filing cabinet and copied down Miss Davidson's name and address, adding this message:

THANKS FOR LETTER STOP *AT WHICH LIBRARY IS*
SOPHIA EMPLOYED?
Shackleton

Mrs Sugden appeared, followed by the monkey.

'You haven't eaten your porridge.'

'I'm letting it cool.' I pushed the picture of Lady Coulton towards her. 'Take a look at this photograph.'

She polished her spectacles on her apron. 'She's well-to-do.'

'Don't pay attention to her dress or hairstyle. Look at her face and the way she stands, the wave in her hair. Does she remind you of anyone?'

'Is her hair the colour of this tint?'

'Yes, reddish gold.'

'Well there's one person she puts me in mind of.'

'Who?'

'The young woman who works at the library. I've returned your books to her.'

'Which one?' I tried to suppress my excitement. It seemed too much to hope that the very person I was searching for had been employed at my own library until recently and would easily be found.

'Which book?'

'No! Which assistant?'

'Well there's only one that looks like this. I don't know her name.'

'Miss Montague.'

'If you say so, you know them best.'

'If you can bear to tear yourself away from polishing stair rods, I'd like you to take a telegram to the post office please, and pay for a reply.'

'I'll do it right away. Is there owt else, because if not I'll run a few errands while I'm out.'

'No, that will do. Thank you.'

'Get that porridge down you. You look terrible. State you're in, you'd blow away in a strong wind.'

'Mrs Sugden, you are not required to be my mother's eyes, ears and deputy.'

'Well she asks me, when she telephones and you're not here. Am I supposed to lie?'

'Stretch the truth. I am very well, thank you.'

'And don't forget the stair rods are out. Your mother will blame me if you take a tumble and break your neck.'

Dutifully, I ate my porridge, went upstairs to wash and dress, and only just in time.

Sykes gave his familiar rap on the door.

I went down and let him in. He took several envelopes from his pocket and followed me into the dining room. 'Responses to our newspaper announcements.'

'Anything definite?' I knew by his face there was nothing definite, no reply from Mrs Bradshaw or Miss Wells saying, Here I am!

'Early days, so I'm not downhearted, but take a look. We have one helpful reply, a try-on from a con artist, and a nasty note from a poison pen merchant.'

The first letter had the address 27 Britannia Place, New Wortley. It read,

Dear Sir,

For information concerning whom you seek, send an unmarked
ten shilling postal order to the above address by return post.
You will not be disappointed.

   J Willoughby.

'It might be genuine.'

Sykes snorted. 'J Willoughby is getting his bid in early, while thinking of a good story that will extract a few quid from a muggins.'

The second letter was written on ruled paper, in a round, careful hand.

29 Valley Street
Leeds
Dear Sir
In answer to your advertisement in the paper, I know of a woman
who came from Scarborough to Leeds before the war. Her husband
worked in the tailoring trade, Ernest Bradshaw. I worked alongside
him at Sumries Tailoring. He referred to his wife most fondly.
She was a widow and had a daughter. He went to work at Burton's
which was closer to his home but sadly met with a bad accident.

   Yours faithfully,
   Arnold Hepplewhite

This was encouraging. 'Mr Hepplewhite is genuine. What he says about Mr Bradshaw's accident is true.'

Sykes nodded. 'He sounds a straight kind of chap, willing to do a good turn for his old workmate's family. I'll see if he can come up with anything else, as long as I can convince him I'm not a debt collector.'

'You could be mistaken for a bailiff.'

'Thank you. That makes a change from my looking like a policeman. I'll pay him a visit. He may have heard gossip through the trade, what happened to his workmate's widow, but given that I've already drawn blanks around the previous address in Compton Road, it's not highly promising.'

He was right about the third note being a poison pen letter. It read simply, *I knew Sophia Mary Ann Wells at school. She was a thief and a liar. She fooled some people but not me.*

I tried to sound hopeful. 'We only placed the announcements on Friday. People will go on reading the papers for weeks.'

'Maybe you're right. We could have a lot of folk chasing a reward by the time next week's out.' He set the poisonous letter aside and put the others in his inside pocket. 'Oh and I went to Barnbow this morning, to see whether I could glean any information about Jennifer Bradshaw. No luck, I'm afraid. They act as though there's a still a war on and treated me like an enemy agent asking for military secrets.'

I handed him the letter from Bella Davidson. 'This came from the schoolfriend. She says Sophia took a job in a library. Mrs Sugden is sending a telegram to ask if Bella knows which library, because I have a theory.'

'Oh?'

'I know it sounds far-fetched and too much of a coincidence, but I have begun to think she worked in the Leeds Library until very recently. She's the same age, carries herself well, and has a look of Lady Coulton.'

'That sounds too good to be true. But why only "think", surely you can be definite about something like that.'

'The library assistant's name is Marian Montague.'

'Well then how can it be her?'

170

'Sophia called herself Mary Ann, that's almost Marian. Some girls like to play about with different names. Perhaps her mother married a man called Montague and she took the name.'

'I'll go the register office and see if I can find out whether Jennifer Bradshaw did remarry, and if so what her name is now.' He took out his notebook. 'When did Marian Montague leave the library, and why?'

'She left not long since, but I don't know why. I'll enquire today.'

Sykes looked at the poisonous note accusing Sophia of theft. 'I wonder if there's any truth in this?'

'She was accused of stealing a comb at school. I don't believe we should take that seriously.'

'If I were deciding to follow a life of crime, I'd apply for work in a bank, not a library.'

'There have been rumours about books going missing from the library. Some of them are valuable.'

Our conversation was cut short by the ringing of the telephone.

I went to answer. 'Kate Shackleton speaking.'

'Mrs Shackleton, this is Jane Coulton.'

'Lady Coulton.' I had a sudden feeling of guilt, as though I had not been trying hard enough.

'Any developments?'

'Not yet, but we have excellent leads.'

'Good.' There was a long pause. 'I know it is less than a week since we spoke.' It would be a week tomorrow. I waited. Perhaps she had some other idea that might speed up our search. 'When we met, I told you that a certain person was very ill.'

'Yes.' She had said Lord Coulton was seriously ill. Had he died?

'That was not entirely true. That person is in reasonable health. The one who is ill is his wife.'

'Oh. I'm sorry.'

'Yes.' Her voice was rueful, slightly good-humoured. 'So am I of course. And what I did not want to say, but must, is that the doctors hold out no hope.'

She waited, but I could not think what to say, except, 'Oh . . . '

'So you see, there is some urgency. I asked if they thought it would be a year, or a few months. It may be months, but it is more likely to be weeks. It is only fair that I should tell you. I could not bring myself to do so when we met.'

'Thank you for telling me. We will redouble our efforts.'

'Please do. Goodbye, Mrs Shackleton.'

'Goodbye.'

I felt as if the floor might give way beneath me. She thought I did not care, that I was not doing everything to find her daughter, and it was true. I had spent the weekend at the bedside of an organ grinder.

What if it had been my birth mother, wanting to see me for the first and last time before she died?

I dragged myself back into the dining room, feeling that I was the one who had been given a death sentence.

Sykes looked up. 'What on earth's the matter?'

'That was Lady Coulton. What a bombshell she has dropped. She has only weeks to live.'

Sykes looked, waiting for me to say more. When I did not, he said, 'What's the matter, and when did she find out?'

'I don't know, but she knew when we met that she was ill,

and concealed it.' I dropped into the chair. 'We need to find her daughter.'

'Why didn't she tell you when you met?'

'Perhaps confiding about Sophia took all her energy and determination. I feel dreadful, and stupid for not realising she was ill.'

'Poor woman.'

'I mentioned someone followed her to and from the club.'

'Yes.'

'I thought it must be one of the staff, spying for her husband. Now I suspect the man was looking out for her, probably fearing she may collapse on the short walk.'

'Then she's brave.'

'What a performance. It must have been a terrible strain to hide her condition. I can't bear the thought that we may fail her.'

Eighteen

The hessian bags filled with Dr Potter's library books hung heavily on my arms as I climbed the library stairs. I hoped Mrs Carmichael would be at the counter because I did not want to upset one of the younger members of staff.

Of course who was at the counter but Miss Sturgeon, a slightly nervous, old-fashioned young woman who has worked here for a couple of months. She wore a grey skirt and black cardigan, with her usual spotless and crisply ironed high-necked white blouse, an antique gold locket at her throat. She recently bobbed her almost-black hair, perhaps in an attempt to look modern. Miss Sturgeon is one of the assistants accused by Miss Merton of revelling in stories about the ghost.

Fortunately, someone came in behind me so I simply put the bags of books behind the counter and said, 'I'll speak to Mrs Carmichael about these.'

'All right, Mrs Shackleton. I'll tell her.'

I walked through to the adjoining room

More seats than usual were occupied. News of Friday night's events had spread. Readers remained quiet yet watchful, alert to the slightest sound: a clearing of the throat, the rustle of a newspaper. Usually people in this room are lost in words. Now they were lost for words, waiting for an explanation of the untimely death of one of their number.

I glanced at a newspaper, and then became aware of Miss Sturgeon, hovering nearby. She whispered, 'You were here on Friday, Mrs Shackleton?'

I nodded and led us into the corridor.

She gulped. 'Mr Lennox won't say much. I feel so nervous when I'm here alone on these dark days. Poor Dr Potter. To think, I was up here on Friday, and he down there in the basement . . . What happened?'

If Mr Lennox had thought it wise to be sparse with information, I had better not say too much.

'It will all come out in time. So you saw Dr Potter on Friday?'

'Yes, when you and he came in at the same time, just before ten. No one saw him after that. I was on the counter all day. We had hardly any readers in the afternoon because of the bad weather.' She closed her eyes and lowered her head. 'It's so horrible. First we are haunted by the ghost, and then a death.'

'Miss Sturgeon, we are not haunted. This is an old building. Sometimes there are unexplained noises.'

'There is a ghost. I think that's why Miss Montague left.'

So Miss Montague had gone without fanfare or the opportunity for our stalwart Miss Heaton to take a collection for a leaving present.

'You need no longer worry about the ghost. Father Bolingbroke saw to that.'

175

'I suppose we should all be reassured, even though ...'

'Even though what?'

Her whisper became a mere movement of the lips. 'He is a Roman Catholic.'

'Catholics are very good at that kind of thing. They have had a lot of practice.'

Her look told me that she was not reassured.

I wondered what had brought about this resurgence of interest in the ghost. After all, it was over forty years since his first appearance. But if youthful imagination was to conjure him again, this season of restless souls and spectral fogs would prove the best and worst of times for a haunting.

'When did Miss Montague leave?'

'About three weeks ago.'

Although our brief conversation was muted, a stooped, elderly gentleman passing through the corridor glared at us, clearing his throat to indicate ostentatious disapproval.

'Where is Mr Lennox?' I mouthed.

'In the committee room.'

On my way, I saw Father Bolingbroke, in the new room, poring over Thomas Aquinas. I tried not to make a sound, but perhaps he is sensitive to another's presence. He turned and gave me a look of great concern before glancing about, to ensure we were alone, and no one would shush him. 'Mrs Shackleton, tell me, have you recovered from your ordeal?'

'Fully, thank you.'

'Thank the Lord.'

I could not resist, because to tell the truth I was a little annoyed by the way he rushed off with no thought for Lennox, or for me. 'Do you think we accomplished our task of sending the ghost on his travels, Father Bolingbroke, in spite of our dreadful discovery?'

'We must trust in God. I did everything I could. May God forgive the poor sinner who murdered a blameless man.'

'Umberto Bruno is innocent until proven guilty.'

'I believe he has confessed the crime, which is to the good of his soul.'

I don't quite know what expression I plastered on my face, but I took my leave and walked to the committee room where I tapped on the door.

After a moment, Mr Lennox opened the door.

He and Mrs Carmichael were seated at the long oak table. It was piled with damaged books. After glancing at them, noticing the age and the covers, I realised that here were the volumes that had fallen and covered Dr Potter's body.

In the centre of the table was Pugin's *Gothic Ornament*.

'Good morning.' My manner was a little breezy because I wanted to be sure that no look of mine betrayed that I had seen them together, in their dressing gowns, over the Sunday morning breakfast table at Mr Lennox's flat. 'Sorry to interrupt.'

Mrs Carmichael gave a small smile. 'Some tasks warrant the occasional interruption.'

'That's quite all right.' Mr Lennox pulled out a chair for me. 'I am glad you are here. I worried about you over the weekend. I felt I let you down on Friday.'

His manner was, as usual, warm and friendly. She was calm and confident as ever, if a little detached. Given that she had insisted I take part in Friday evening's venture, I was surprised that she seemed more concerned about the books

177

than anything else. She pointed out one that was very badly damaged.

He straightened a small pile of books. 'These are the volumes that took the brunt when the bookcase toppled. We are examining them to see which we will be able to repair ourselves and which must go to the bookbinder.'

'Dr Potter would have hated costing the library money.' Mrs Carmichael stretched a loving hand towards *Gothic Ornament*. 'Fortunately Pugin was not in the least damaged.'

One of Mrs Carmichael's special interests is the library's collection of Civil War pamphlets. I learned this when I had the misfortune to be co-opted onto the storage sub-committee. Mrs Carmichael put up a powerful argument against her precious pamphlets remaining in the basement after the war ended. No doubt she now felt fully vindicated.

Mr Lennox said, 'I expect you have heard that the police have charged a man with the murder of Dr Potter.'

It gave me a small shock to realise that he did not know I had gone to the infirmary with Umberto Bruno and sat by his bed for two nights. Naturally he was ignorant of the fact that I was giving board and lodging to Umberto's monkey, and taking care of his gold sovereigns.

'Yes, I did hear.'

Mr Lennox raised his eyebrows and sighed. 'Bad business. I can't decide how I feel about it all. It's such a mess. In a way, it could be a relief that some vagrant found his way in and was disturbed by Dr Potter, that it was an outsider.'

'Why do you believe that is what happened?'

'What else could it be? The police have charged the organ grinder fellow.' He blinked. 'Do you have another explanation?'

'Not yet. Mr Lennox, is there anyone else who could have been in the basement on Friday?'

'I was here from half eight till noon, when I went to a meeting at the Central Library; we like to ensure we are not duplicating acquisitions. I saw Dr Potter briefly when he came in with you, and that was all.'

Mrs Carmichael made a neat pile of books with damaged bindings. 'I was here all day, but only on the counter when Miss Sturgeon went for her midday break. Professor Merton was here in the late morning. He and Dr Potter sometimes walk back to the university together.'

Mr Lennox said, 'The police inspector tried out a ridiculous theory – that Dr Potter was stealing books, or that he caught the organ grinder stealing books.'

'What makes him arrive at such a conclusion?' I asked.

Lennox sighed. 'Because you found Pugin's *Gothic Ornament* near the body, the police seem to think that Dr Potter may have been our thief but that is not so.'

Mrs Carmichael said. 'It's such a puzzle. Dr Potter had every right to be in the basement. We cannot say that this or that area is out of bounds to a proprietor, especially one as esteemed as Dr Potter.'

Lennox nodded agreement. 'He was a man beyond reproach, entirely unworldly and interested only in his subject, a most selfless and impartial individual.'

'Mr Lennox, you just said that the police "seemed to think that Dr Potter may have been our thief". What do you mean by that?'

My question upset both Mr Lennox and Mrs Carmichael. They exchanged a look.

Mrs Carmichael said, 'Shouldn't we tell Mrs Shackleton?'

Mr Lennox made chewing motions, as if tackling a tough cut of mutton. 'We kept it quiet.' He swallowed the mutton. 'Well, not to put too fine a point on it, valuable books have been stolen.'

So that was what Dr Potter had meant when he asked me about stolen books in the same breath as he mentioned the lovely and obliging counter assistant. 'You have your own suspect, I believe.'

Mrs Carmichael's nostrils quivered with distaste. 'We certainly do. Will you tell Mrs Shackleton, or shall I?'

'We can no longer be sure,' Lennox said. 'Don't you see that?'

'I am sure.' Mrs Carmichael picked up a damaged book and moved it across the table. 'The thief was a member of staff. That is how we know it was not Dr Potter, and certainly not the organ grinder, who would not have known which books are valuable.'

Lennox barely moved his lips. 'Perhaps we were wrong.'

'We were not wrong. She hid books somewhere, intending to take them later when the coast was clear. Don't you see, that is why she had no objection to working in the basement.'

'Let us say no more.'

For a moment, neither spoke. 'Mr Lennox, Mrs Carmichael, you can't leave it like that.'

Mrs Carmichael lowered her eyes, and left the talking to Mr Lennox.

'She is no longer here. We dismissed her.'

'Who was it?'

'One of the counter assistants.'

'What did she steal?'

'William Bligh's *Narrative of the Mutiny on the Bounty*. Mrs Carmichael suspected her when the cleaner found the index card in her waste bin and asked was this card meant to be thrown away.'

'She stole more than one book?'

Mrs Carmichael sighed but took her cue. 'She denied it, of course. She went almost hysterical with rage. I thought she was going to strike me. Mr Lennox had to restrain her.'

Mr Lennox nodded grimly. He lowered his eyes, as if the memory pained him.

Mrs Carmichael continued. 'She thought that by disposing of the index cards, anyone searching through the drawer for titles would not know the books were meant to be in stock, or would assume they had been withdrawn or disposed of.'

How stupid of her not to take the cards home, I thought.

Now Mrs Carmichael warmed to her tale. 'She did not take into account that I have a shelf list and checked most carefully, cross-referencing with loans.'

The episode still rankled and it incensed her to speak of it. She made the slightest gesture towards Lennox, as if to comfort him, but made no contact. 'The person in question said I could search her locker and her bag if I did not believe her. She had never stolen anything in her life and anyone who said different was a blatant liar. That was her bluff. But I did search her bag and found Joseph Priestley's *History and Present State of Electricity*. We know she took other books, including the Bligh, but unfortunately did not have the proof.'

Why were they being so exasperating? I wanted them to speak her name. 'Who was it?'

'She has gone.' Mr Lennox looked distinctly uncomfortable, almost as if he had been the thief's accomplice. 'Mrs Carmichael pointed out that she would have had to remove the library's nameplate, a task of some skill. No doubt that is why she volunteered for the bookbinding course. Naturally Mr Castle has been informed.'

'I don't know why you are being so protective of her if you are sure of your facts. It is clearly Miss Montague. I saw her name in the minutes as having taken part in a bookbinding course, and she left three weeks ago.'

'Yes,' Lennox said. 'You would have learned of her departure at the next committee meeting, under staff matters.'

'What else went missing?' I did not yet want them to know that my interest was in the person, rather than the books.

'Walker's *Costumes of Yorkshire* and Dugdale's *Monasticon*.'

'Were charges laid against Miss Montague?'

'No.'

'Did you tell the police?'

'No. We discussed the matter with Mr Castle and decided to keep it quiet, for the sake of the library's reputation. We dismissed her without a reference. It could have been a most unwelcome scandal.'

Just like the bank clerk Sykes had been investigating. An organisation must hold onto its reputation. Take the blow and say nothing.

'I wish I had known. My assistant, Mr Sykes, is very good at instituting security into establishments.'

Mrs Carmichael glanced at a book for damage and deftly set it aside. 'Indeed. One does not expect to have to make random searches of staff leaving a library, as if they were factory workers who might wrap a length of cloth around themselves and cover it with a bulky coat.'

'I am sure we could come up with some discreet measures to minimise the risk of theft. Let us talk about it when things are a little more settled.'

How should I approach finding out more? By pretending to know less than I did.

'Remind me, what was Miss Montague's Christian name?'

Mr Lennox answered straight away, and softly, as though her name waited to fall from his tongue. 'Marian.'

'Mary Ann?'

'No, Marian.'

'Ah, I thought you said Mary Ann.'

'She may well have been a Mary Ann,' Mrs Carmichael said. 'Perhaps she lied about her name as about everything else. A pity you weren't on the appointments committee when she came, Mrs Shackleton. I expect you must be adept at spotting individuals with criminal tendencies.'

'I'm afraid not. In my experience, appearances can deceive.' Keep her on the subject, I told myself. 'I'm trying to remember Miss Montague. Didn't she have auburn hair?'

Mrs Carmichael said, 'Yes, she wore her hair long, not very well done up in a chignon, with fancy combs.'

'She was quite striking.'

Hastily, Mr Lennox stood and clumsily pushed back his chair. 'If you'll excuse me, I'll telephone to the bookbinder from my office.' Looking most uncomfortable and without another glance at either of us, he left the room.

Mrs Carmichael waited until he had closed the door. 'Oh yes, Miss Montague was striking. She turned heads.' It gave me a shiver to hear Mrs Carmichael use the same words about the library assistant as my Aunt Berta had used to describe Lady Coulton all those years ago. She turned heads.

Mrs Carmichael continued. 'At first I thought her a decent person but she had a coarse habit of rolling up her sleeves to just above the elbow, as if about to sink her arms into a tub of washing.'

Just as young Sophia Wells had rolled up her sleeves and swept the pavement outside the wet fish shop in Scarborough.

Mrs Carmichael wrinkled her nose. 'Her demeanour gave a bad impression to gentlemen proprietors. It would not have surprised me in the least if she had come to work wearing earrings.'

A dozen thoughts dizzied my brain. Mrs Carmichael's sleeves ended just above her scrawny wrists. Her hands were veined and spotted. It would not suit her to have a young, attractive woman drawing the eye of her lover. It must have been convenient for Mrs Carmichael to have Marian Montague caught stealing.

'Did she live with her family?'

'No, and there's another thing that is not to her credit. She was in lodgings, up Bayswater Road way. Said that her mother had remarried and she did not get on with her stepfather.'

'Did she take the stepfather's name?'

'Who knows? One would not know what to believe about a girl like that.' Mrs Carmichael looked at her watch. 'Oh dear, look at the time. I take an early break and must be back for my hour on the counter.'

I weighed my choices. Stay here and grill the reluctant Lennox, or see what information I could garner from Mrs

Carmichael, who was revealing an unexpected streak of malicious jealousy.

'Do you mind if I join you, Mrs Carmichael? I'm feeling a little peckish myself.'

She hesitated. 'I take a turn about town, and then eat a sandwich at my desk.'

'Then please break your habit. Let me treat you to a bite at the Corn Exchange.'

She blushed, whether from embarrassment or pleasure I did not know, but agreed.

We left the building, walked along Commercial Street and took a right turn onto Briggate.

'Tell me,' she was making an effort not to sound ghoulish, 'did Dr Potter look like himself when you found him?'

I gave her a sanitised version, which lasted as far as the café where we were shown to a table near the centre of the room.

The menu was chalked on a board.

'What are you having, Mrs Shackleton?'

'Sardines on toast, but choose whatever you want.'

When the waitress came, she hesitated and then said, 'Welsh rarebit.'

When we were alone again, Mrs Carmichael said, 'You don't fool me, Mrs Shackleton.'

'Oh?'

'You cannot help being a private investigator can you? I expect you want to know who else was at the library on Friday morning after you left.'

'Yes, I suppose I do.'

'You know how poor the weather was? Some of our Friday regulars stayed away. Miss Merton changed her

185

library book. Miss Heaton placed a collecting tin on the counter for the widow of the retired commissionaire who needs medicines. Father Bolingbroke read Thomas Aquinas. Mr Castle looked at the cartoons in *Punch*. He never borrows books, you know, not in all his years as a proprietor. A gentleman from the university spent an hour poring over the *London Gazette*. Mr Lennox and Mr Castle discussed library business with Professor Merton.'

So Professor Merton, Dr Potter's rival had been at the library. Much as I would have liked to pursue an enquiry as to who did kill Dr Potter, my first obligation was to find Lady Coulton's daughter.

'I am afraid this dreadful business has me flummoxed, Mrs Carmichael.' Slowly, I returned to the subject of Marian Montague. 'A person who does intrigue me is the dismissed library assistant.'

'Intrigue you? She is a brazen hussy and a thief.'

'Just the kind of person who is interesting to a detective. I should like to visit her, if you have no objection.'

'Why would you want to do that?'

'Are there still books missing?'

'Yes.'

'Then the least I can do is to try and retrieve them. It is my area of expertise.'

'She will have sold them by now.'

'Perhaps, perhaps not. You say she lives in the Bayswater Road area?'

'Yes, number nine, Back Enfield Street. But I don't believe you'll find her there.'

'Why is that?'

She hesitated. 'In confidence?'

'Of course.'

'I saw her, shortly after she left. I believe she is now living in the kind of slum where she belongs. A den of thieves, probably. I have not told Mr Lennox. He had a soft spot for her, many gentlemen did, and she took full advantage.'

'Dr Potter liked her.'

Mrs Carmichael pulled a face, which was meant to express contempt but merely made her look unpleasant. 'She fooled everyone.'

'Where did you see her?'

'In one of the courtyards, not far from here. I was in the market to buy an apple and came out onto Back New York Street, to walk along and eat it where no one would see me. It's so unladylike to eat an apple in the street. I saw her coming out of an alley. Well, isn't that just the kind of place one would expect to see her? She saw me and we ignored each other. I almost choked on my apple, seeing the thief at liberty, giving me a bold stare.' She looked at the clock. 'Goodness! Is that the time. I must rush.'

I left with her and said, 'Which was the courtyard where you saw Miss Montague?'

She smiled. 'I am glad I am not a detective. I expect you like to know things about the criminal classes and where they meet each other, their dens of iniquity. It's just round the corner.'

We left the Corn Exchange and walked a few yards. 'That's the place. I don't know what it's called. I hope you won't go in there.'

If entering this dismal alley might lead me to Sophia Wells, a troop of dragoons would not stop me.

Nineteen

One might pass the entrance to Danby Court on the way to or from the market without noticing it, except for the stench from the middens. Twelve paces through a narrow passageway of red brick took me across uneven cobblestones. My feet alternately squelched and crunched over cinders, spread by some enterprising soul across filthy puddles. The overwhelming feeling was of gloom. Outside, the day was grey and in here several shades darker. Ahead, and on either side, loomed tall brick houses. Outside landings hinted at a multitude of occupants.

Aware of being stared at from every side, I trod lightly, taking in everything while appearing to look at nothing and no one.

A toddle of barefoot tots played listlessly at the bottom of broken concrete steps that led to upper rooms. One of the bairns hemmed in a spider that moved this way and that, trying to reach impossible sanctuary. Two men lounged by a wall, smoking. Three women formed a huddle, chatting to each other. One was immensely stout, one thin as a length of string and the other not taller than a child and with legs so bowed they made a perfect 'O'.

'Excuse me.'

The length of string turned to me. Her eyes were hollow, her cheekbones prominent.

I remembered something a ward sister had said about a patient who died after an operation, too weak to pull through: 'Women feed their children and starve themselves.'

This was a dwelling place not for the poor who lived from week to week but for those who scraped by on pennies, day to day, hour to hour.

Counter assistants earned no fortune. Miss Montague should have afforded better than this, but perhaps not, if she had been sacked without a reference.

The three women now all looked at me, as did the children. The tormentor of the spider forgot his work. Perhaps the spider scuttled free. One of the lounging men cleared his throat and spat loudly on the ground.

'Hello. I'm looking for a Miss Marian Montague. I believe she lives or visits here?' Even as I spoke, it sounded absurd.

The thin woman shook her head. She looked at the other two and said something. They also looked blank. In unison, all three stared at me, and then looked away, as if that might make me vanish.

A prompt might help. 'She is tall and has reddish hair. She dresses well, keeps herself neat.'

Finally, the short woman with the 'O' legs answered for them all. 'You've come to't wrong place. There's no one by that name and no one fits that description.'

'Thank you.'

I hesitated, wondering whether to leave my card, and then fished one from my satchel and handed it to 'O' legs.

She looked at it upside down before passing it to the thin woman who took it carefully between finger and thumb, but said nothing.

I waited for a moment, but they had decided on silence as the group response. 'Well thank you.' I felt awkward, stupid and out of place as I walked away.

Fortunately the roads were not too busy. I drove along Briggate to North Street passing the Dispensary that is shaped like a battleship. This was where the poor took themselves with their broken limbs and damaged eyes. I passed the park they called the Jews' park, and the tailoring shops, butchers, greengrocers, pawnbrokers and engineering works. It was my guess that if you worked on North Street, it must feel like the centre of the universe.

The blundering tram made its straight way before curving onto Roundhay Road. I followed it. There is something both reassuring and stifling about tram routes and timetables. They will take you only in the allowed directions; no going off the rails.

What I found dispiriting about whole swathes of Leeds was the sameness of the brick-built back-to-back houses, the cobbled streets and the dismal greyness that hung over lives. There was a feeling that this was it. Once locked in the greyness, there would be no escape to a greener place, to a broader life, to possibilities.

Perhaps Marian Montague had wanted more. Had she really stolen valuable books? 'No one ever looks at them,' she had told herself. 'I'm clever. I can earn a little money.'

Lady Coulton's daughter might well have an inborn sense of entitlement, and the acquisitiveness of the English aristocracy coursing through her veins.

Someone who had aspired to be a counter assistant in a library must have a rich inner life, an imagination, a thread of consciousness that took her out of time and space, to wilder or more romantic places.

It was hard to make up my mind who or what I was searching for: the truth about a murder; a missing daughter; a thief; a wronged young woman.

The stench of Sheepscar Dye Works almost choked me. Now I must make a right turn, onto Holroyd Street.

Once upon a time, I hardly knew how to find my way around Headingley. Now I knew the streets of Leeds so well that I could run a taxicab service if required.

Back Enfield Street was far more salubrious than Danby Court. The end house, Marian's address, was the most impressive in the street. It was surrounded by a two-foot-high brick wall, topped by a foot-high fence. To the left of the gate was a dilapidated stable, converted into a garage; some sign of prosperity here. To the right of a green-painted door were two large sash windows, ground floor and first floor. Above them was a narrower attic window.

I knocked on the door.

After a moment, it was opened by a broad-cheeked pleasant-looking woman in a flowered pinafore.

I apologised for disturbing her and told her my name.

'Have you come about the room?'

'No.'

'Only I thought you might have seen the card in the window.'

'I'm here because this is the address I have for Miss Marian Montague.'

'You a friend of hers?'

'I'm from the library where she worked.'

'You best come in.'

I edged into the heavily furnished room, past a table and chairs, a sewing machine, dresser, and a rocker and bed-chair on either side of the fireplace.

She indicated the rocker for me, and perched on the bed-chair.

'Marian came because she saw my card in the window. Eighteen months she were here and then this.' She stood up and took a sixmo sheet of paper from behind the clock on the mantelpiece.

I took the note from her. It read:

Dear Mrs Claughton, Sorry to leave without notice. Thank you for all you have done. Marian Montague

'When did she leave?'

'Early one morning, a couple of weeks ago. A Saturday. Had her supper as usual the night before. I didn't hear a sound. She must have crept out like a cat burglar.'

'Did she take her things?'

'Yes. Not that she had much, her clothes and such, a nice brush and comb set, some photographs, and books. She didn't take all her books.'

'Do you still have her books?' I felt a shiver of apprehension. Was I about to find a stash of stolen goods?

'Well yes, I kept them because I didn't like to throw them out. Might you be in touch with her?'

'I would like to be, that is why I came.'

'Come up then. I'll show you the room. Perhaps you'll know some decent person who's looking for board and lodging. Not that it'll be available long.'

I followed her up two flights of stairs to the attic. It was furnished with a single cast-iron bedstead with brass knobs on each corner. The bed was neatly made, covered with a cream candlewick counterpane decorated with roses. On the chest of drawers stood a cheval mirror, a basin and jug and a brass candlestick. Above it were two shelves. In place of a wardrobe, someone had ingeniously fixed a rail diagonally across the corner of the room.

'My husband put up them bookshelves especially for her.' A note of hurt entered her voice. 'I wouldn't have guessed she would just go off like that.'

'Did she give any hint, any sign of something wrong?'

Being sacked from her job would be enough, I should think, but since Mrs Claughton did not know about this I was not about to tell her.

'She was sometimes a bit nervy. Once I heard her crying. Over some lad I guessed but as far I know she wasn't walking out with anyone.'

'What about family?'

'She had a stepfather. Her mother died years ago. The lass was treading her own path through the world as best she could, and making a good fist of it I thought. My children left long ago. I was fond of Marian. I'd like to know she's all right.'

'You didn't think to make any enquiries?'

'It's not up to me. She left the note and she was off.'

I looked at three books on her shelf, and opened each one,

hoping some note or photograph might fall out, but nothing did.

'I've bottomed the room. Another person might have squeezed two paying lodgers in here but that's not my way. If there's anyone else at your library looking for a place, tell them this is a clean house.'

'I will.'

'You have me worried over her now. I hope it's not some man taken advantage of her.'

'Why do you say that?'

'Well it usually is, isn't it? Though I wouldn't have thought it. Marian is a respectable girl. She didn't have much money, which of us does? But she kept herself clean and tidy, kept regular hours, was happy with her job, always had her nose in a book, spent far too much on candles, ate like a bird, but was fond of custard, never had visitors or gentlemen callers, except . . .'

'What?'

'Now that I think of it, just before she left, there was this feller. He was hovering about, out there, by the wall. I didn't like the look of him. And I never would have connected him to Marian. He looked like he was up to no good. The kind you'd imagine might be spying out a house with an open window. Not that folk round here have much to steal. Me and mine, we're probably the best off around here but that's not saying a lot.'

'Can you describe this man?'

She let out a puffing sound and pulled a face. 'He were a biggish lout, dark hair a mess, cuffs short on his long arms. Bow legs.'

'How biggish?'

'Five foot nine mebbe, same as my lad, bit of an apish look. Swaggered off when he saw me looking. Could be summat or nowt but I hadn't seen him round this end before.' She handed me Marian's books. 'Keep them for her. I hope you find her.'

'Thank you.'

There were two novels, a childhood copy of *The Secret Garden* and Compton Mackenzie's *Carnival*, along with a French improver. So she had abandoned French.

Her job, her lodgings, her French; what else had she given up? And who was the loutish youth up to no good? I felt a sudden sense of dread.

Whether or not Marian proved to be Lady Coulton's daughter, it seemed that life may have dealt her a cruel blow.

Twenty

There were too many maybes and possibilities. Longing for something I could be certain of, I began the drive home.

What I wanted was for Sykes to appear, brandishing a copy of a marriage certificate. Mrs Jennifer Bradshaw married Mr Somebody or Other Montague.

What I wanted was a telegram from Sophia's old school friend: Sophia Wells took up a post in the Leeds Library, or the Harrogate Library, or Lands End, or John o' Groats. Anywhere, as long as it was definite.

An eerie sound greeted me as I opened the front door, odd discordant strains from the piano.

I opened the drawing room door. There sat the monkey, Percy, on the piano stool, striking keys with one paw. With the other paw, he turned the page of the sheet music, and inclined his head towards me, as if waiting for praise.

'Clever Percy.'

Mrs Sugden had heard the front door. She came into the hall. 'What a racket it's making. I hid the key to the piano, but it found it. Twice. Thinks it's a game.'

'It doesn't help that I put something inside the piano that

belongs to the monkey's master. That's why it sounds so awful, and it can't be doing the piano any good.'

I lifted the top and took out the sovereigns. Immediately, the monkey became interested and began to sniff the bag.

Mrs Sugden handed me an envelope. 'This came, an answer to your telegram.'

'That was quick. I thought Miss Davidson would be teaching and not see it till she got home.' I ripped open the envelope, hardly daring to hope for some proper information at last.

The message read:

```
DO NOT KNOW WHAT LIBRARY EMPLOYS SOPHIA
STOP TELEGRAMS FRIGHTEN MOTHER STOP
SEND NO MORE
BELLA DAVIDSON
```

With a deep sigh, I handed the telegram to Mrs Sugden. 'Put that in the Coulton file folder please.'

Mrs Sugden glanced at it. 'Oh dear, you know what's happened don't you? Bella was busy at her teaching. The old mother hurried all the way to the school carrying your telegram.'

'Yes, and she's sickly. I've probably finished her off.' I flopped down in the chair. 'I am completely at a loss. I don't know what to do.'

'If you're stopping in here, I'll fetch a shovelful of the kitchen fire through.'

'No. I'll keep my coat on while I think.'

'I'll put the kettle on.'

The monkey had lost interest in the bag of coins and was

rifling through papers on top of the piano. He brought me Dr Potter's student magazine.

'Thank you, Percy.'

He nodded acknowledgement.

The magazine contained a couple of poems by other students, an account of a rag day and charity collection. There was a plea for contributions on topical interest, short fiction and poetry. I could see why Editor Potter made this appeal. Almost all the articles were by Horatio Erasmus Potter himself.

His account of the library ghost bore a close resemblance to Miss Merton's version, though with a little more detail. In the year 1884 on a dark night, gas lights having been extinguished, Mr McAllister, the librarian, was alone. He saw ghostly lights in the topography room. He caught sight of a pale face and a tall dark figure. Thinking this an intruder, he fetched a revolver and made a challenge, but the ghost vanished. In one crucial aspect young Potter's account differed from Miss Merton's. Before the librarian saw the ghostly lights and the spirit, he had heard a noise that disturbed him, a sound emanating from the bowels of the building. There was a hint that the ghostly intrusion was a student prank. The article ended with the words, 'Play up and own up! Who perpetrated this jolly jape on a serious and conscientious librarian? Read the next issue.'

But, according to Dr Potter, there had not been another issue, and he should know.

Perhaps Dr Potter's livelihood had been more secure as a mathematician, but he would have made a good writer. I flicked through his pieces. Then, as later, he had a tendency towards the scurrilous. There was an article about an

198

absconding solicitor, Mr Nelson of Nelson, Castle and Nelson. An executor in several wills, Nelson had disappeared with clients' funds. A young secretary had mysteriously gone absent at the same time. 'Had they run off together,' Potter asked in his article, 'to live a life of luxury on stolen money?'

The comment about the secretary must have been what Dr Potter was referring to when he said there was a disappearance. Perhaps he thought that Marian Montague had also eloped, carrying valuable books with her.

I wondered whether the Mr Castle in the law firm was a relation of our Mr Castle, library president.

The pages included a round-up of local news: the arrival of the fairground at Holbeck, the success of local brewers and a bicycle club outing.

I took the magazine into the dining room and placed it in my filing cabinet, out of the way of Percy.

It was no use. I had to do something more about finding Marian Montague, if only to eliminate her from enquiries, as the police would say.

Picking up the telephone, I braced myself to speak to Mrs Carmichael. It would appal her to know that I had gone in search of Marian, but that could not be helped.

She answered on the third ring.

'Hello, I'm sorry to interrupt your afternoon. After we spoke at lunch, I became concerned about Marian Montague. I wanted to see her for myself, but she seems to have vanished. She is not at her lodgings. No one in the yard you pointed out knew anything about her.'

'I don't understand. Why are you concerned?'

'It's not something I can explain, especially over the

telephone, but believe me, I have my reasons. I wonder if you might check her records and see whether there is a home address for the stepfather, or a referee who might know her whereabouts?'

She gave a great sigh, letting me know what a waste of time this was. 'I'll look, if that's what you want, but I shall have to ask Mr Lennox if I am allowed to divulge the information. Are you at home?'

'Yes.'

'I will telephone back to you.'

I could not settle to anything else but picked up a pencil and waited by the telephone. It was just possible that Mrs Carmichael would shortly tell me that the school certificate presented by Miss Montague was in a different name: Wells.

It was a good ten minutes before the telephone rang.

'Mrs Shackleton speaking.'

'Hello, it's me. A most extraordinary thing . . . her records have gone. I have the most particular filing system and there is nowhere else they could be. It would not surprise me if she found her way in here and destroyed them, so as not to be traced and charged with theft.'

'I see, well thank you for looking.'

The apprehension I had felt for Marian earlier turned to a kind of fear. I was suddenly chilly, my hands like ice.

As I disconnected the call, Mr Sykes arrived. I saw straight away that he must have had about the same amount of luck as I. None.

I picked up my mittens. 'Let's go outside and take a turn around the wood, Mr Sykes.'

We went out of the back door and through the garden onto our well-trodden path through Batswing Wood. The air was fresh and clear, the sky surprisingly blue and hosting busy white clouds.

Sykes thrust his hands deep into his pockets. 'There are no records of Mrs Bradshaw having remarried, not in Leeds anyway. As to answers to advertisements, I picked up two more and followed through but without success.'

I told him about the telegram from Sophia's friend.

He sighed. 'I've kept on trying regarding libraries. I visited Central Library and some local branches. No one has heard of her. It's as if she and her mother have vanished into thin air.'

Someone had spread crumbs on the grass for the birds. A couple of magpies pecked greedily.

'Mr Sykes, I told you about my hunch, my theory, that Sophia Mary Ann Wells and Marian Montague are one and the same person.'

'Yes. It's the kind of theory to come up with when you meet a dead end.'

'Marian was dismissed from the Leeds Library. Being a private library it is not linked in with the municipal libraries, except on a friendly basis between librarians. Anyhow, her staff records have disappeared. Am I making too wild an assumption in presuming Marian to be Sophia Wells?'

'Anything is possible. Even if you are wrong, it's worrying if a lone young woman has disappeared, thief or no thief.'

'Dr Potter was concerned about her. I see that now.'

'Our only hope is for better answers to our newspaper advertisement.'

'I can't bear to just do nothing.'

'Mrs Shackleton, tomorrow it will be a week since you saw Lady Coulton. No one could have done more than we have. It's a matter of time.' We slowed our steps as a robin perched, cocking its head to one side as if posing for a photograph. 'What else can we do but wait?' Sykes asked. 'I would suggest having a printer run off some letters that we could send to every library in the county, but we have only the friend's word that Sophia works in a library.'

'I'm going to the police, about Sophia, and Marian.'

'They'll love you, with a murder investigation going on.'

'What murder investigation? Inspector Wallis has found a convenient culprit.'

'It's too soon to feel defeated. We're not beat yet. This isn't like you.'

I stepped into a crunchy pile of leaves that had been protected against the rain.

'I can't bear to do nothing. What if while we wait and wait, Lady Coulton dies?'

Twenty-One

The corridors of police headquarters ran wick with men stomping about in an important fashion, carrying pieces of paper. I could hear the tap tap of typewriter keys and the sound of raised voices. Don't hesitate, I told myself. Act as if you belong here and know exactly where you are going.

The inspector was not in his office.

For a moment or two, I lingered in the corridor, wondering what to do.

It surprised me that I recognised his footsteps on the stairs. He has a steady, unhurried tread and shoes that made a clickety-click from the metal segs on his heels.

I stood by his door, acting sentry.

'Hello, Mrs Shackleton.' He showed no surprise.

'Hello. I've brought you Dr Potter's student magazine.'

'Ah yes, thank you. You could have left it downstairs.'

Determined not to appear the complete supplicant, I handed him the magazine. 'There's something else, something I meant to tell you, and I have a request, too.'

'Will it take long?'

'No.'

'Come in.'

This time he did not sit behind his desk but brought a chair from by the wall and placed it near the one at the front of his desk.

'What's the request?'

'One of the counter assistants from the library, Marian Montague, aged twenty-four, was dismissed on suspicion of stealing.'

'Go on.'

'She protested her innocence.'

'Of course.'

'And now she has gone missing from her lodgings. I think Dr Potter was worried about her. He mentioned a previous disappearance, which is in his article. A solicitor embezzled his clients' money and made off with a secretary. I don't see the connection but it made me wonder.'

'What is your own interest in Marian Montague?'

Was I that transparent? 'I am searching for a missing person, Sophia Mary Ann Wells. For all sorts of reasons, I believe that she may have been using the name Marian Montague.'

He raised an eyebrow. I hoped he would not ask me what reasons, but he did. 'What makes you think she is the same person?'

'Her age, appearance, that Marian could easily be preferred to Mary Ann, which was the name she used at school. Mrs Bradshaw, the mother, was about to remarry and that could explain a new surname. I have information that Sophia took a job in a library.'

'I saw your announcement in the papers on Saturday.'

'So far all our enquiries have come to nothing.'

'Surely it is early to be giving up?'

'There is some urgency to the search.'

'What have your enquiries uncovered?'

'Sophia's mother, Mrs Jennifer Bradshaw, worked on munitions at Barnbow. That was one wall we hit because they would not give out information, not to me. They would to you.'

He reached to the desk for a notepad and wrote down the names. 'I'll have an enquiry made at Barnbow. If there is a connection with the library, it could have some significance. Let my sergeant know what else you have found. And you say there was something you meant to tell me?'

'I know why Dr Potter and Umberto Bruno were in the library basement. Dr Potter bought Umberto's monkey for fifty sovereigns. He had an interest in trying to teach animals their numbers. He thought Percy, the monkey, he's a Capuchin, would make a good subject.'

The inspector leaned back, pulled in his chin and stared at me, as if I were mad. 'What? How do you know this?'

'I called at Big Bothy, Dr Potter's house, to extend condolences on behalf of the library. No one else had, you see.'

'When was this?'

'Yesterday, after I came here.'

'And after you prevailed upon Mr Castle to ... bring pressure on me to take off the handcuffs.'

'Yes.'

'You've been very busy, but how do you know Dr Potter intended to buy the animal? What evidence do you have?'

'Umberto had a heavy money bag tied to his waist, a bag of coins. I thought it must be coppers and that I would look after it for him. A sick room is no place for a dirty bag of old coins. When I saw it was sovereigns, I thought it must be his life savings and I had better take care of them.'

'You did not think to hand the money over to the police?'

'I knew he was innocent. You had not charged him. I thought you were protecting him, as a witness.'

'I had better have the bag of money. I'll send someone for it later.'

'I'll tell my housekeeper.'

'And the monkey?'

'He's at my house.'

Inspector Wallis leaned forward and put his head in his hands.

'I didn't take him, Inspector. He found his way into my car on Friday afternoon.'

'Are your sure he cadged a ride? You didn't abduct him?'

'My car was parked outside the library. I gave Miss Merton a lift and neither of us saw or heard the creature. Later a neighbour's child came to tell me that he heard sounds in my garage.'

'I won't take the monkey into custody just yet.' The inspector gave himself a little shake, and sat up straight again. 'Is there anything else you have found out?'

'Nothing important.'

'Tell me.'

'Dr Potter was all in favour of the library moving to new premises. He would have persuaded people to agree with him. He was that kind of man.'

'And the relevance of that is?'

'I don't know. Probably not relevant.'

He ran a hand over his hair, as if trying to smooth out the wave. I noticed that on his left hand he wore a signet ring, with his initials. 'There's some connection, or you would not have mentioned it.'

'Perhaps, but I can't think what. I suppose it surprises me that Dr Potter was in favour of change, given his long family connection with the library. It's a separate matter, but when I read Dr Potter's student account of a ghost, there was something odd.'

'Can you say what?'

'Not precisely. You will see he mentions that the librarian claimed to have heard a sound from the basement prior to the ghost's appearance, and it now makes me wonder.'

'What?'

He smiled, and so did I. We were both looking at insignificant details when what was at stake was so enormous. His slow and pernickety questioning, suggesting that he wanted to find the truth, sat uneasily alongside the way he had so quickly jumped to the conclusion that Umberto Bruno was guilty. It made no sense.

'Go on,' he prompted. 'What makes you wonder?'

'The sound and the way he described the apparition makes me think that it was not a ghost.'

He chuckled, crinkling the laughter lines around his eyes. 'So, unsurprisingly, the logical mathematician did not believe in ghosts. What was his explanation?'

'That it was a student prank. I think someone with a key had let himself in the back door of the library to give the librarian a scare, perhaps even young Potter himself. There was not a great age difference. McAllister was twenty-four years old.'

'Dr Potter had keys I believe, passed to him through the family.'

207

'Yes.'

'That would solve the mystery of the ghost. I hope I may be able to find the missing counter assistant for you, and for myself.'

'Thank you.' I felt glad that, needing his help, I had given him something to think about. 'You are wrong about Umberto Bruno, Inspector.'

'You have another suspect in mind?'

I hesitated. He must know that my neighbour, Professor Merton, and Dr Potter were rivals for the post of university vice chancellor, and that the professor was also in the library on Friday. Pointing fingers was not my way of going about things.

'I only know that it was not Umberto. I called to see him after I had worked out that he was in the basement to sell his monkey. He confirmed it, saying Dr Potter had wanted to buy Percy since the summer and he had only given in now because of being unwell, and I suppose penniless, though he did not say that.'

'I am glad that you agree Umberto Bruno is capable of giving a statement.'

'He didn't . . . '

'Mrs Shackleton, I will do what I can to find the missing counter assistant, for my reasons as much as yours. But you must do something for me.'

I waited.

'Keep out of this murder enquiry. Do me the courtesy of believing that I know what I am doing, and very soon I shall be putting Umberto Bruno in the dock.'

Twenty-Two

Waiting on events is the most enervating non-activity in the world. I confess to being not very good at it. It especially did not help that Percy was once more pounding the piano. I was glad of the diversion when Mrs Sugden, twitching the drawing room curtains, said, 'There he is again.'

'Who?'

'There's someone lurking about. I don't like the look of him.'

'What kind of someone?'

'A biggish chap, long arms.'

I went to the window. 'Where?'

'Disappeared again.'

'What was he doing?'

'Trying to be inconspicuous but looking about him, as if he didn't know which house to burgle. It's these dark nights when you have to watch out. Let them know your house is occupied. That's why I left a light on in here, with the upshot that our Percy found the piano key again. Music mad he is.'

I thought about poor Dr Potter and his plans to teach animals mathematics. He was right to choose Percy. If any

209

animal showed an instinct for numbers, it would be this little Capuchin, with his sharp intellect. Unfortunately, his love of music and his ability to be tuneful were seriously at odds. To save a headache coming on, I gave him the sovereigns to play with. 'See if you can count them, Percy.'

He began to sort the coins into piles.

I went upstairs to change. Percy monkey followed. He hid behind the wicker chair, peeping.

I covered my eyes. 'Go on. Hide properly. I'll count to ten.'

At this rate I would be as mad as poor Dr Potter. Quick glimpse of me aged fifty-five, dyed hair, colourful frock, touring with a fairground. Kate and Percy, the amazing double act.

'Ten! Coming, ready or not.' The clever little creature had vanished. I looked under the bed and behind the curtains. 'Where are you?'

The slightest of sounds came from the wardrobe. I opened the door. There he was, tucked behind the clothes, grasping a handful of silk, my Delphos robe. 'Found you! Come out, come out, and let go of that very carefully.' He made no move until I held out my hand.

Oh dear. I could see my business draining away. Kate can't investigate today. She has to play hide and seek with a monkey.

Mrs Sugden called suddenly from downstairs. 'Go to the front window. He's coming back!'

I was in my back bedroom that looks onto the wood. Hurrying across the landing, I went into the front bedroom and peered through the window.

The man was about five feet nine inches tall, with bow

legs and long arms. He walked with a swagger. Where had I seen him before?

He gave a quick glance about, thought himself unseen, opened the Mertons' gate, went into their garden, and peered through the front window. What a sneak; a man after my own heart.

From her vantage point at the front window, Mrs Sugden called, 'He's walking round the back.'

'Are they at home? I'll telephone.'

'He'll be through that there door and murdering them in their beds before you do that.'

'Don't be so melodramatic. They're not going to be in their beds at this time of the evening.'

'Murder at tea time, that's what it'll be. She has a strand of pearls that belonged to her great-aunt Harriet. I'm going over there.'

'Are you mad?'

'She's my friend. I'll swear that sneaky blighter has a weapon.'

Before I could stop her, the valiant Mrs Sugden left the drawing room, hurried into the hall, and opened the front door. Percy showed no sign of following but bounded towards the drawing room window to watch, no doubt having had enough of the open air and damp dark nights.

'That's it. You stay here, Percy. Practise your scales and count your money.'

I slipped on my shoes and picked up a coat from the hall stand.

By the time I went through the front door, Mrs Sugden, moving like a greyhound out of a trap, was across the street. As I reached the gate, she was disappearing round the back

of the Mertons' house. I hurried after her, across the cobbles, through the creaking front gate and up the path.

A loud bang cut the air. It was unmistakeably a gunshot.
A strangled cry followed.

'Mrs Sugden!' I practically tripped over my own feet in
the rush to reach her.

She was standing by the Mertons' back door, holding a
pistol.

Swaying as he moved, a figure disappeared into the bushes
that separated this garden from the one next door.

Mrs Sugden burst into life, hurrying to the hedge. 'Stop!'

I grabbed her arm. 'What are you trying to do, kill the
man?'

'I got the blighter in the leg. He had a rifle.'

'Stop waving that gun about.'

'I'm not waving it. I know how to use a pistol.'

'Put it away for God's sake. Now stay here!'

I followed the direction the man had taken. The thing he
had dropped was not a rifle but a big stick. I waved it at Mrs
Sugden. 'This it, then? This his deadly weapon?'

'He was up to no good.'

'Go home.'

Miss Merton opened the kitchen door.

Mrs Sugden hovered.

Miss Merton looked about. 'Is it someone letting off
bangers?'

'Yes, but they've gone now.'

Miss Merton stepped into the yard. 'It beats me why they
can't wait till Bonfire Night to let off their firecrackers.'

'He was in the garden. You go back in, Miss Merton.
You'll catch cold. I'll see if I can spot him.'

Before she had time to protest that there was no need to chase someone who had let off a banger, I pushed my way through the hedge. Twigs scratched my face. A bramble caught my sleeve. Mrs Sugden tagged along behind, the smoking gun out of sight now.

'Go home. I'll deal with this.'

She ignored my order.

'I'm not leaving you.'

There was a gap in the hedge in the next garden. Unhindered, we walked through three more back gardens almost as far as Headingley Lane, emerging through a front gate only when we reached a dense, impassable hedge.

There was no sign of the man, not on our street or on the main thoroughfare.

Slowly, we made our way back up the street. 'You go home. I'll talk to Miss Merton. And if there are still bullets in that pistol, get rid of them.'

I have never been in the Mertons' kitchen before. Everything appeared entirely up-to-date, including the shiny gas stove. Someone had been ironing. Two piles of neatly folded hand-kerchiefs stood on the corner of the dresser.

'The coast is clear, Miss Merton. Whoever it was has gone. We should all keep our doors locked on these dark nights.'

'Well thank you for being so vigilant. I'll be glad when Bonfire Night is over and done.'

'Are you alone?'

'Yes, but don't worry about me. I am quite capable of hit-ting an intruder over the head with a frying pan.'

'Where is your brother?'

213

'Working late, some tutorial with his prize student, there aren't many students he regards highly but this one brought him a particularly fine fossil, so he tells me. Have a seat. I was hoping to talk to you.'

I sat down at the kitchen table.

'Will you have a cup of tea, or something stronger?'

'No, thank you. What was it you wanted to talk to me about?'

'You first, Mrs Shackleton. Why do you want to see Theodore?'

'He and Dr Potter had a lot to do with each other, didn't they? I wanted to say how sorry I am about the death.'

'Oh, I see. I thought you were going to ask me had Theodore received death threats.'

'Has he?'

'Wait here.'

Moments later she returned with two envelopes. Holding them carefully, using only finger and thumb, she took from each envelope an octavo-size sheet of paper and placed them side by side on the kitchen table.

The first one included a neatly sketched dagger that dripped red-ink blood. Block capitals read, 'STAY PUT.'

The second featured a pistol and was equally simply worded: 'DON'T DO IT.'

'Has he shown these to anyone?'

'No, and if he knew I had seen them or was showing them to you, he would be furious.'

'What do you make of them, and what do you think he makes of them?'

'I wish I knew. He is not popular, like Dr Potter. Perhaps he took it to mean that he should stay in his present situation

214

and not let himself be considered for the post of vice chancellor.'

'These notes are so amateurish, like a student prank.'

'I am glad to hear you say that. I would hate to think someone intended to kill him. Do you think Dr Potter received similar threats?'

'I don't know.'

'Of course, Theodore pretends he does not want the vice chancellorship. He was most annoyed when I talked about the possibility of moving, and what a difference it would make, how we would need to entertain and so on. He quite blew up on me.'

'What did he say?'

She threw out her chest and pulled back her shoulders, pursing her mouth to ape pomposity. 'This is what he said. "I am a geographer. My study is the Earth's crust and the glory of the crust distilled. Such an appointment would interfere with scholarship." Or words to that effect.'

'Then why did he not withdraw from consideration?'

'Because he would love to be vice chancellor. He would kill for the opportunity.' Her hand flew to her mouth. 'I didn't mean that of course. He and Dr Potter never saw eye to eye on any matter, except evolution and even then they took different views, though don't ask me to explain beyond saying that Theodore allowed for God. Underneath it all, I believe they held each other in high regard. It made Theodore despair. He knew that Dr Potter would win any argument, not on logic or reason but because he was witty and charming.'

'There can't be any connection between these threatening messages and Dr Potter's death, not if the two of them were on different sides on just about every question. Why would someone want to kill both of them?'

'I don't know, unless it is someone who dislikes university men.' Once Miss Merton begins, she keeps up the momentum. 'My brother is a dear man, but difficult. He thinks too much. It is like living in the midst of an electrical storm – unless an electrical storm is what we mere mortals call a storm. Is it? I don't know, but I should imagine the prickly tension, the oppressive sense of thunder about to clap, the expectancy of lightning, is much the same as living with a man who permanently thinks on a high plane. He loses things and accuses me of moving them – papers, lumps of metal, measuring devices, lengths of wire, never fossils, of course, which he keeps under lock and key, as if they were diamonds.'

'He brings his work home?'

'And carries it back. Back and forth, hither and thither, sometimes trotting across to the university in the middle of the night. And as if geography wasn't enough now it is wireless sets. He is very interested in the latest developments in broadcasting, but he hates it as well. It will deteriorate into endless chatter, he says. No one will be able to think for the noise and the self-congratulation of nonentities who will creep into our living rooms across the wires. I ignore him most of the time. I have my kitchen, my favourite chair, my G K Chesterton.'

There is no point in trying to hurry Miss Merton. After a deviation in which she related the plot of a story she had just read, in which a Catholic priest turned out to be a fraud, Miss Merton finally said, 'I can see you wonder what I am building up to.'

'It crossed my mind that you may have something to tell me.'

'You are correct.'

'About your brother?'

'Not exactly, or at least not only about him. About the discussions between him and Dr Potter about possible changes at the library, a removal to new premises. They were at loggerheads over whether the library should stay in its present premises or remove.'

'Yes I did hear something about that. I thought they were of one mind.'

'So they were, in the beginning. They were trusted to recommend a reasonable course of action, which would be to do nothing. Theodore was all for staying. At least he was consistent. Dr Potter changed his mind and became an enthusiastic remover. I am afraid people may draw the wrong conclusions and believe that their rivalry and disagreements may have led to violence. They were at daggers drawn over the matter.'

She had given me something to think about. In real life, no one would kill to have their way about a library staying where it is, or removing. Academics and people who work in libraries have a different set of priorities. I tried to allay her fears, even while my own increased.

'Surely they were friendly rivals. Academic men are like that are they not?'

'Good heavens no. Believe me, Mrs Shackleton they are not. It became very bitter, the question of staying in the present library building or removing. Dr Potter tried to persuade Theodore. He came and ate with us one evening, mutton pie. They started arguing before I brought in the jam roly poly and of course being so caught up in their own ideas, they forgot my presence. And then they went into the study, to talk, and raised their voices too.'

'When did Dr Potter change his mind?'

'I don't know. But this is written by Dr Potter. It was screwed in a ball. Theodore had thrown it in the coal scuttle.'

She placed a sheet of paper between us on the kitchen table. It was written in a crabbed hand.

Reasons for removal
Premises outlived usefulness 50 years ago.
Commercial Street now Leeds equivalent of Piccadilly, no longer suitable for professional purposes
Offer of moving expenses by prospective purchaser
Albion Place site perfect
Present building will never provide sufficient shelf space; lady proprietors must have novels. What abt yr own sister and G K Chesterton?

A look of deep sadness came into Miss Merton's eyes. 'I never knew I told Dr Potter about my love for G K Chesterton.'

'Oh I'm sure you did.' I had no other basis for this statement, except knowing that she told everyone a great deal about a whole manner of subjects.

She folded the paper and put it in her pocket. 'Theodore was surprised that Dr Potter changed his mind so thoroughly.'

'Why were they chosen, your brother and Dr Potter? I know they are clever and well thought of, but so are many of the proprietors. Some have far more leisure for committees.'

She shrugged. 'Well, you know, my brother is a geographer so can be expected to be aware of shapes and how many shelves fit in a room, though in truth he is better about land, sea and rocks, and how many strata it takes to create a coal field. Dr Potter was a mathematician. It is surprising how many people think that subject qualifies a man for making pronouncements in relation to finances.'

'Yes, I suppose so.'

'What are you thinking, Mrs Shackleton?'

'It may be nothing, but the real reason Mrs Sugden and I came over was because we saw someone look through your front window and come into your back garden. He ran away when we came.'

She laughed. 'Is that all? Some naughty children have been helping themselves to our logs. Theodore has locked the logs in the shed so we should be all right now.'

'This was a man, a young man I think.'

'You don't surprise me. They never grow up, not when it comes to making a bonfire. There's a lot of competition as to who will have the best fire.' She was trying to make light of the intruder, but I could see that she was upset.

If she wanted to make light of it, so would I. 'You're probably right. We're all a little on edge after what has happened.'

I crossed back to my own house wondering about her brother, the professor. Was he a potential victim, or a killer?

I must have raised my voice much higher than I imagined because the monkey, entertaining itself by sliding down the banister, Umberto's waistcoat under its abdomen, pricked up its ears and looked at me with saucer eyes.

Mrs Sugden called from the kitchen. 'I'm in here.' She was standing at the table, slicing a very big potato. 'Thought I'd do egg and chips.'

'I don't want egg and chips.'

'You have to eat.' She continued slicing.

'Get rid of that gun. I want it out of the house.'

'Wasn't in the house. Was in my quarters.'

'Your quarters? This is my house. I will not have the place used as an arsenal.'

'I saw him off didn't I? Saved us all from being slaughtered in us beds.' She let out a cry of alarm.

She had sliced into her finger. Blood spurted across the chipped potatoes. I turned on the tap and manoeuvred her to the sink. 'Stick it under there.'

Blood and water swirled into the basin. 'The man was unarmed.'

'He had a big stick. It looked like a rifle.'

'If your eyesight is so bad that you can mistake a stick for a rifle you need a white stick yourself.'

'It was dark.'

'All the more reason to be cautious. You could have killed him.'

'I shot his leg. If I'd wanted to kill him, I'd have aimed at his head.'

'For all I know you did, and missed.'

'I did not. I know how to shoot.'

'Oh do you?'

'Yes I do.'

'Where did you learn?'

'I'm not telling.'

'Secret is it? Something you did in the war. Go on, tell me you're of Russian ancestry and you enlisted with Maria Bochkareva's Women's Battalion of Death.'

'I don't know what you're on about.'

'What then? No wonder you never talk about your past.' I produced a hanky and handed it to her. 'Wrap that round.'

She made a poor fist of folding the hanky.

'Give it to me.' I refolded the hanky. 'I took you on trust and now you pull out a gun.'

'You took me because I was the first one through the door and you were that busy listening for the telephone, waiting for a footstep on the path, you didn't pay attention to no one. You only set me on because your mother wanted to scoop you up and take you to Wakefield. This place was a pigsty.'

'You're avoiding the question.'

'What question?'

'Where did you get the gun and where did you learn to shoot?'

'My husband Ronnie brought it back from the war.'

'Lots of people brought guns back. They don't all carry bullets in their apron pocket and take pot shots.'

'It wasn't a pot shot. Ronnie taught me, when we lived beyond Ripon.'

'Why?'

'Why do you think? We were planning to rob a bank if you must know.'

'I can believe that, after tonight.' I pulled out a chair. 'Sit down for heaven's sake.'

'Anyone else would give me smelling salts.'

'Anyone else would throw you out without notice. You probably did rob banks.'

'Oh aye. That's why I'm still here. I'm waiting for people to calm down over the gold bullion I took from the Bank of England. Once they stop looking, I'll be off.' She stared at her finger. 'If I was a destitute organ grinder, you'd apply lint and a bandage.'

'And if your victim bleeds to death, the hangman will apply a rope to your neck.'

'I know what I'm doing with a gun. Ronnie taught me to shoot rabbits.'

'You don't shoot rabbits with a pistol.'

'Never said you did. The pistol were an additional skill, to come in handy if we were waylaid by outlaws.'

'In the North Riding?'

'We had it in mind to emigrate, and to have some land of our own. I was saving for our passage. That's why I went to work in munitions.'

'I didn't know you worked in munitions.'

'I was at Barnbow, number two filling station.'

'That was where Mrs Bradshaw worked, Sophia's mother.'

'Well before you ask, I didn't know her. That place was bigger than a small town.'

'Is that where you got your supply of bullets?'

'No. Ronnie and his pal Fred brought them back.'

She looked so pale that I went into the dining room and brought a bottle of brandy from the cabinet. I poured her a glass. 'When did Ronnie die?'

'Two weeks before I came to see you about this job. Influenza.'

'I had no idea it was so recent.'

'I thought it best not to say, to give the impression it was in the past.'

That explained why for that first year I sometimes thought I had employed a silent ghost.

Taking a taper from the mantelpiece, she held it to the flame of the fire, crossed the kitchen and lit the gas ring. It popped into blue life. She put the chip pan on the ring.

I went across and switched off the gas. 'Sit down. Tell me how you found your way to somewhere beyond Ripon after you'd worked at Barnbow.'

She wound the white hanky tighter round her finger. It was turning red with blood. 'By the time Ronnie was demobbed, I'd been given notice at Barnbow. Neither of us could find work. His pal said why not do some potato picking for this farmer he knew, and that there was a caravan he had use of, a battered old thing on the edge of a field. It let in the rain. But we enjoyed it, being out in the open, picking spuds.'

'It's a big jump from picking potatoes to robbing a bank.' I went to the sink, turned on the tap. 'Give your finger another rinse.'

She let the water run over her finger, leaving swirls of red in the sink. 'They lost money on a horse. We were on our uppers. Again. After a fine week or so, it did nowt but rain, chucking it down day after day. Fields turned to mud. Summat in Ronnie snapped, as if it'd been waiting to snap, and then it did. I think it was Fred, to jolly him along, said what about robbing a bank. One of them things a person might say.'

The water was running clear. I turned off the tap, and took the iodine from the cupboard.

As I dabbed the iodine on her cut, she winced. 'Fred had

meant it half in jest, about the bank, but Ronnie took it to heart. So Fred started to plan. Picked his bank, this bank in Ripon. He picked his day, the morning after market day. He and Ronnie would be there when the manager opened the door. They'd pull on balaclavas and be right behind him, gun in his back, not to hurt him, but to make him open the safe. I told them it was stupid, but they wouldn't stop talking about it, drawing diagrams. It was all that kept Ronnie going. He said my part was to be nearby with a shopping basket and take the money. No one would suspect a woman with a shopping basket.

'At first I wasn't sorry when he took poorly, thinking it would shut him up, thinking at least he won't end up in prison. The farmer sent for a doctor to come to the caravan, but it was no use.' She lifted a hand to her hair. 'It turned me grey. I was pure dark brown before that. Afterwards, a week after he was buried, I came back to Leeds, spruced myself up and went to see about a job.'

'I had no idea.'

'Well, none of us does know another's story, not really. You told me nowt. I worked it out.'

'What happened to Ronnie's friend, Fred?'

'Stayed on as a farm labourer, patched up the caravan. He kept the rifle and give me the pistol, said it might come in handy. It was my memento of Ronnie, and his big plans.'

There was a loud knock at the front door. It was a policeman's knock, forceful enough to put the panel through.

Mrs Sugden stood up, almost knocking over her chair. 'Oh my God, they've found him. He's bled to death in someone's back garden.'

'You stay here.' I walked along the hall. The knock had

startled Percy. He hid behind the hall stand. I held out a hand. 'Come on.' He let me push him into the safety of the drawing room.

I opened the door. It was PC Hodge, the beat bobby who had come to the infirmary to stand guard over the hapless organ grinder.

'Mrs Shackleton, if I might have a word.'

The night was too dark and cold to speak on the doorstep. 'Of course, Constable. Come in.'

He stepped across the threshold. In the hall, he took off his helmet, clutching it to his chest, looking a little sheepish. 'I've something to collect I believe.'

For a moment I could not think what he meant, and then I remembered. Inspector Wallis had asked for Umberto's sovereigns.

'I'll get the bag.'

'Right you are.' He waited in the hall for the moment it took me to fetch the hessian bag.

I handed it to him.

'Thank you. There's something else, Mrs Shackleton. Can we sit down a minute?'

'Yes. Come through.'

I led him into the kitchen. Mrs Sugden might as well hear if an injured man had blamed some crazy woman for shooting him in the leg. She was standing by the gas stove, having relit the jet.

The constable nodded to her.

We sat down.

He placed his helmet on the kitchen table. 'It's about Umberto Bruno. He's took a turn for the worse. He's not long for this world.'

'Poor man. I'm sorry to hear that.'

'The thing is, I thought you'd want to know. I'm right sorry, Mrs Shackleton. You did your best for him.'

'It was too late. Something should have been done for him much sooner.'

'That's true of a lot of people. It's a sad fact of life, of the world as it is.' He stared at his helmet, waiting for me to stand, to thank him, to let him go.

'Is anyone sitting with him?'

'No. I've been stood down. I'm off duty but said I'd call for this bag.'

I glanced at Mrs Sugden. 'Oh dear, poor fellow.' Showing the makings of a good character actress, she hid her relief that the constable was not here to arrest her for unlawful shooting.

'Stay and have a cup of tea, Mr Hodge. Mrs Sugden was just making one.'

'The kettle's on.' Mrs Sugden rewound the handkerchief around her bloody finger.

'I'm going to the infirmary to see Mr Bruno.'

The constable nodded. 'I told the sister you might come. The priest has been.'

'Mrs Sugden, I won't eat, but you should. Perhaps the constable would like egg and chips.'

'Oh I couldn't,' he said, but his eyes lit up.

'I'm sure Mrs Sugden will rinse her blood off the potato.'

'Well as it happens, mi stomach thinks mi throat's cut.'

Mrs Sugden and I exchanged a look. If the constable was here in the kitchen, he would not be bumping into a man with a bullet in his leg.

As I stood in the hall, putting on my coat, Constable Hodge was saying, 'That finger needs a bandage.'

'They're in yon cupboard. Can you reach one?'

'Aye.'

As I left the house, a sense of failure flooded over me, such as I rarely feel. What a great nurse, refusing to face up to the inevitable. What a great detective, to know nothing about her own housekeeper.

Umberto had been given a dose of morphine. His breathing was laboured and loud, but I knew that he would by now be feeling no pain. There would be no last words, but perhaps he could hear me.

I took his hand in mine, and placed my other hand on his brow. 'Rest. Don't fret about anything. It's all taken care of, and Percy too.'

There was the slightest pressure on my hand. I liked to think he knew I was there.

His rosary was on the bedside cabinet. When I put it in his palm, his fingers curled around it.

He would want to die in his own language. If words were forming somewhere in his brain, they would be in another tongue, a different voice, from faraway and long ago, so I spoke very little, just his name, a few words. But we held hands for hours, until all light fled. Finally, his grip loosened. Still, I held his hand until, when the sky was streaked with dawn, he died. I opened the window for his soul to fly away.

For a long while, I sat by his bed. The accusation of murder still hung over him, and would until Dr Potter's killer was found. During the night, time seemed both endless and still. I wondered about who might have murdered

Dr Potter, and left Umberto helpless in a corner. Professor Merton seemed unlikely. It is hard to imagine one's neighbour as a killer. But there was something strange going on, and it would be good to find out who was the intruder into the Mertons' garden.

I left the room before Umberto's body was taken away.

It surprised me to see Sykes, waiting downstairs. We looked at each other and I suppose he did not have to ask about Umberto.

'Mrs Sugden came to tell me. The desk porter let me sit in his room. I thought I'd drive you home. Saw your car outside.'

We walked to the door. Although the sun had risen so promisingly, it was now hidden. We climbed into the car. For no particular reason, I remembered when Sykes first came to work with me. He was mortified that he had never driven. Now he did so at every opportunity, occasionally far too fast.

I swear he sometimes divines what I am thinking.

He speeded up in the direction of Headingley. 'Go on, say it.'

'Say what?'

'Home James, and don't spare the horses.'

'Slow down! We're not in a race.'

'You can't get the help these days. I drive too fast, Mrs Sugden pulls a gun.'

'She told you?'

'She did. I could hardly credit it.'

'I'd like to know who her victim was, and what he was up to. I wonder whether he went somewhere to have his wound dressed.'

'Don't know about that. He'd be asked awkward questions if he went to the dispensary.'

'But it's possible.'

'Worth a try I suppose. One of the dispensary orderlies owes me a bit of a favour.'

'Then call in the favour.'

'I'll try.'

We drew close to the end of my street. 'Keep going, Mr Sykes.'

'Where to?'

'I want to see Dr Potter's manservant again.'

'Why's that?'

'They were close. Given that Dr Potter mentioned Marian Montague to me, I wonder if he said anything about her to Morgan, that's the manservant.'

'It's too early to see anyone yet. Normal people are sleeping.'

'I suppose you're right. Come round for me in a couple of hours and we'll go together.'

Twenty-Three

We drove north from Headingley, along a back lane deserted by all but a milk cart. I gave Sykes impressively good directions to Big Bothy. He parked in the lane, where I had stopped on my previous visit. We walked the path to the strange octagonal house that Dr Potter had called home. Perhaps it was because of knowing its occupant's fate, but it looked strangely forlorn. A bicycle rested by the wall next to the door. Morgan had mentioned that he used it for shopping and that occasionally Dr Potter cycled to work.

Mr Morgan must have seen us walking along the path because he was waiting in the doorway. The poor man looked so lonely, framed in a halo of isolation.

'Good morning, Mr Morgan. Excuse the disturbance.'

'It is no disturbance, Mrs Shackleton.'

'This is Mr Sykes who works with me. I wondered whether we might come in and have a word.'

'Of course.' The men shook hands. 'Come you through.'

It seemed heartless to come questioning him. Not only did I want to know about Marian Montague, whom I desperately hoped was Sophia Wells. If I were to clear

Umberto's name, I needed to find out what enemies Dr Potter may have made.

Morgan led us into the parlour. I sat down on one of the chintz chairs. Sykes made as if to sit in the opposite chair, but stopped mid-air.

Morgan produced a newspaper. 'Excuse the cat hairs. Dunce will sleep there and there's nothing to be done about it.' He placed the paper on the chair seat.

'Where is Dunce now?' I asked.

'Out for a stroll.'

Polynesia parrot tilted her head to one side and began to recite her two times table. The cage door stood open. She flew out and onto Morgan's shoulder. Sykes stared. I have never before seen him mesmerised.

'And what can I do for you?' Morgan asked.

'When we spoke last, you said you thought that Dr Potter had a surprise in store last Friday.' He looked at me with interest but did not muster a reply. 'I want to tell you what was in Dr Potter's mind. He intended to bring home a clever monkey for enrolment in his arithmetic class.'

Morgan's troubled face lit with sudden understanding. 'Ah so that was it. I should have guessed he was planning something along those lines. What kind of monkey?'

'A Capuchin.'

'I see. I knew he was excited about something. That explains the scheme of work for counting by digits. Where is the creature?'

'I am taking care of him.'

'Thank you for telling me. I always would have wondered.' He sighed. 'Did the purchase of the monkey in any way, shape or form have a connection with my master's death think you?'

'I do not think so, except that both men were in the wrong place at the wrong time. I am trying to form a clear picture of what may have happened. Would you mind if I ask you one or two questions?'

'Fire away.'

The parrot pecked at Morgan's ear and then began to count.

Morgan said, 'That is enough of your showing off, Polynesia. Thank you and goodnight.' He turned his shoulder to the cage. She hopped inside and he closed the door. 'Now what was that you were saying, Mrs Shackleton?'

'Did Dr Potter ever mention a helpful young library assistant, Miss Montague?'

'I can't say that he spoke much of his colleagues except that rascally Professor Merton.'

'Why is he a rascal?'

'He caused my master no end of grief. If the two of them had agreed to the removal of the library to new premises, they would have swung all the proprietors behind them. But the professor dug in his heels and was all for staying.'

'I saw some of Dr Potter's arguments for removal. They seemed to me sound.'

'What arguments?'

'Oh, Commercial Street being no longer a suitable location, now more appropriate for business and shopping. He mentioned the lack of space in the building and the prospective purchaser being prepared to pay removal costs.'

Morgan gave a small chuckle that changed his whole appearance. For a brief time, something shone in him, a glimmer of admiration for his master. 'I knew he would come up with something sound.'

232

'You mean that was not the real reason?'

'Heavens, no. None of that mattered to him.'

'Then what did?'

'He was all for staying until he knew thc full details of the scheme. The building was to be turned into a department store, see you, a grand emporium. In the basement there would be a menagerie, with every kind of exotic creature that graces the face of the earth. There would be an aquarium, a miniature jungle, a tropical world with its own boiler.'

'Yes, now I do see. I suppose he did not want to tell the professor the real reason.'

'Certainly not, because that may have given an inkling of the nature of our secret work, teaching the animals. Besides, he and Professor Merton were at each other's throats over the vice chancellorship.'

'They were rivals, I believe.'

'That is one way of putting it.'

'Was there much rancour between Dr Potter and Professor Merton about the post of vice chancellor?'

'Oh indeed there was. Dr Potter needed all his wits about him to ensure that Professor Merton would not wriggle out of the contest and leave Dr Potter to sup the poison chalice of success and swallow the degradation of drumming up funds for university expansion.'

'Neither of them wanted the job?'

'Bless us and save us, no they did not.'

'But I thought, from what Miss Merton said . . . '

He chuckled again. 'My master knew how to play a cunning game. He specially went to eat mutton pie with the Mertons and cleverly drew the sociable sister on his side.'

A cob of coal crackled and split, creating an orange and

blue flame. My barely hatched theory that taciturn Professor Merton had murdered his rival for the post of university vice chancellor curled up the chimney with the rising smoke.

I glanced at Sykes, to see whether he had any questions. He stared blithely at the gigantic cat as it strolled into the room.

Morgan rose. 'I am being a poor host. Will you take coffee? We have a bottle of Camp.'

He spoke with such pride that it would have been difficult to refuse. I agreed to coffee, and so did Sykes.

'I will ask the Reverend Jones whether he will also take refreshment. He has come from the university, the chaplain you know, here about the memorial service, and the books.' He left the room.

Sykes, fascinated by the talking parrot, crossed over to the cage. 'Hello, Polly.'

'Hello, hello,' said the parrot. 'Two twos.'

'Four,' Sykes said.

I followed Mr Morgan into the hall, intending to ask whether he needed help. It could be that some coffee other than Camp was hidden in a cupboard and I may be able to suggest a change.

The sound of voices from the study brought me to a full stop.

The man speaking to Morgan sounded strangely familiar. I drew closer to the study door.

The voice belonged to Father Bolingbroke. 'Oh yes, I will take these with me now, the Bible and this commentary.'

'That Bible, it is the one book my master said should come to me.'

'Then so it will, but I believe it will give me inspiration

for the memorial service. I know that if I read from this I will experience a powerful connection to Dr Potter, being that he held this same good book in such reverence.'

Without waiting to hear Mr Morgan's reply, I hurried back into the parlour.

The parrot said, 'What's your name, your name.'

'Jim Sykes, Jim, Jim, Jim.'

I shut the door behind me. 'Mr Sykes, the reverend in the study is a fraud. He is not university chaplain Jones, he is Father Bolingbroke, the one I told you about.'

'The exorcist?'

'The same. He is trying to steal a bible. It must be valuable. It's him. He's the book thief. Now I know why *Gothic Ornament* was in the basement. I'd lay a pound to a penny it fell from his cassock pocket. That must be why he stayed in the basement so long.'

'Three twos, two sixes . . . '

'Oh shut up,' Sykes said to Polynesia. 'Let a man think.'

'If he sees me, he'll know he's rumbled.'

The parrot tried to regain Sykes's attention. 'One and one makes two, two and two.'

Sykes scratched his head. 'Leave it to me. He has to go out of the house with a book, or he hasn't stolen anything.'

'I'll stay here. If he sees me, he'll backtrack.'

Sykes left the room. In the hall, he called to Mr Morgan.

As he did, it struck me that the bike we had seen outside may not belong to Dr Potter and Mr Morgan but could have been used by Father Bolingbroke, alias Reverend Jones. He had chosen a Welsh name to ingratiate himself with Morgan.

Knowing I should stay put, on an impulse, I left the house, seized the bike and wheeled it out of sight.

Sykes must have drawn Morgan from the study because a moment after I moved the bicycle, Father Bolingbroke came out of the front door, carrying two books.

He spotted me as I spotted him. I should not have peered round the side of the wall.

'Mrs Shackleton!'

'Father Bolingbroke, or should I say Reverend Jones?'

He laughed. 'Poor man, one has to be kind to the Welsh. I thought it would give him comfort if I used my mother's maiden name. Now, my bicycle . . . '

There was only one way to keep him from having the bicycle and that was to leap on and cycle away, which I did, but awkwardly because it was a big boneshaker. Dunce chose that moment to saunter out onto the path, refusing to give way. I swerved. The bike wobbled.

Bolingbroke came after me. 'What do you think you're playing at?'

'Stay where you are!' Sykes called.

'That is my Bible, hear you!'

I feared that Bolingbroke would outstrip the pair of them and so rode the bicycle in a clockwise circle, heading straight for him. He dodged. This allowed Sykes to seize him from behind and as he did so Morgan rescued the precious volumes. I came to an awkward stop, steadying the handlebars, leaning sideways to reach the ground. By the time I dismounted, Bolingbroke was in handcuffs.

I knew this was what Sykes had always longed to do: put the cuffs on someone. Finally, he had his wish.

'Consider yourself under citizen's arrest, sir, for the crime of theft. It will be best if you come quietly.'

Surveying our transport, I wondered how to manage the

situation, with one car and a bicycle or two between us. Then I came up with the answer.

'Mr Morgan, if you will harness the pony and trap, you and Mr Sykes could escort Father Bolingbroke to his home, where I suspect there may be a cache of stolen books. I will drive back to town and alert the librarian and the police that we have apprehended a felon.'

'Yes,' Sykes said. 'It would be an uncomfortable squeeze for four of us in the car, and undignified for a man of the cloth.'

'Not the police.' Bolingbroke stared at his handcuffs and looked at each of us in turn, as if trying to bore a hole into our souls. 'This is not a criminal matter. I am trying to do my best for the library.'

Morgan nursed the precious books in his hands. 'I will find some suitable wrapping and then see to the pony and trap. Archie will be glad of an outing.'

Bolingbroke stared in disbelief at his wrists. 'Let us go to the police station, see what they say about the illegal use of handcuffs.'

Sykes smiled. I could hear what he would say if the question of handcuffs arose. 'Handcuffs? What handcuffs? The man came voluntarily, as he should when caught red-handed by three upright subjects of His Majesty.'

'You don't know where I live,' Bolingbroke spluttered. 'And don't think I'll tell you.'

Fortunately, thanks to Miss Merton, I did know where Bolingbroke lived: on Street Lane where he paid little or nothing for bed and board with a kindly proprietress of the library. I gave Sykes the address, and then set off for the library.

Twenty-Four

'Come in!'

Mr Lennox, poring over a ledger, pencil in hand, looked up. 'Mrs Shackleton.'

'Mr Lennox.' I stepped inside and closed the door. 'I need you to come with me to Father Bolingbroke's lodgings. There has been an unusual development.'

'Oh dear, is he ill?'

'No. I can explain as we go, but it would be helpful if you bring a note of the books that have gone missing.'

Mrs Carmichael came in, carrying a file. 'Mrs Shackleton, I saw you come in. Is there anything I can do? Mr Lennox has an appointment with the auditors shortly.'

A sharp frostiness in her manner made me realise that she thought I had designs on her lover.

'It's Mr Lennox I need to speak to, but you may as well hear what I have to say. I believe we will find that your book thief is Father Bolingbroke. I and my assistant, along with Dr Potter's manservant, apprehended him at Dr Potter's house. He was helping himself to a valuable Bible and commentary.'

Lennox's eyes widened. 'Potter's *Geneva Bible?* You mean to say he just kept it on the shelf?'

'Come and see for yourself. You are the expert.'

Mrs Carmichael smiled with evident relief. 'Heavens no, you are much mistaken. Father Bolingbroke is a true scholar. The thief was . . . well, she was dismissed, as we told you.'

'And no books have gone missing since? And it was a pure fluke that *Gothic Ornament* was found where Bolingbroke had knelt to attend to Dr Potter? And you imagine that your sacked library assistant was fully aware of the value of the volumes that were taken?'

Her mouth opened every so slightly and a flicker of doubt came into her pale blue eyes. 'Everyone knows which books are valuable.'

'What did any of us know about Father Bolingbroke before he came here? You were deceived. We all allowed ourselves to be deceived by him.'

Mrs Carmichael's hand went to her lips. 'It can't be true.'

'Bolingbroke was caught red-handed this morning, impersonating a university chaplain and calling himself the Reverend Jones.'

Lennox stared at Mrs Carmichael. 'You were so sure.'

'Yes, very sure. The book was in Marian Montague's bag, the index cards in her waste bin. We both saw them.'

Lennox's voice dropped to a whisper. 'She swore she was honest. I wanted to believe her, but you convinced me.'

'You are too gullible.' Mrs Carmichael thumped her fist on the desk, which must have hurt.

His mouth tightened. 'And you are too quick to rush to judgement.'

'You wanted rid of her. Don't deny it. She had become a nuisance.'

He took a step towards her. 'No, you wanted rid of her, out of jealousy.'

I have never been sure of why anyone would want to pour oil on waters, troubled or untroubled, but I attempted to do so. 'This is no time for recriminations.' I stepped between them. 'Come with me, Mr Lennox, to Roundhay. Let us see what treasures Father Bolingbroke has in his room.'

A sudden misgiving crawled up my spine. What if Bolingbroke had already despatched the stolen books to whoever would buy them from him?

Without another glance at Mrs Carmichael, Lennox reached for his coat.

'Mrs Carmichael.' I spoke as kindly as I could in spite of her barely concealed hostility towards me for having brought such news. 'Would you be so kind as to telephone the police and ask them to come to Father Bolingbroke's lodgings as soon as possible?'

She nodded, gave a long anguished look at Lennox, and then picked up the telephone receiver. I felt a sudden pity for her.

'I'm sure you did what you thought best at the time.'

She did not look at me. 'I shall ensure the police are aware of the urgency. You see, people don't always take the theft of books seriously. I do.'

Lennox took a sheet of paper from the top drawer of his desk.

Mrs Carmichael spoke into the telephone mouthpiece. 'Police please.'

Without a backward look, Mr Lennox went out, buttoning his overcoat. I followed.

By the time the police arrived at Bolingbroke's large upstairs front room, Lennox had placed neat ticks alongside nine of the books on his list of twelve.

In spite of its ample size, the room was crowded. Mr Morgan sat on a dressing table stool; Sykes stood by the window.

Bolingbroke was seated at what would not for much longer be his desk. 'This is all an unfortunate mistake. I borrowed the books. Not being a library member, I had to do so unofficially.'

Inspector Wallis spoke softly. 'You can explain all that at the station, sir, when we take your statement.'

Sergeant Ashworth took charge of the books. 'I'll give you a receipt for these, Mr Lennox. We'll take good care of them.'

Morgan hugged the good book to his heart. 'I cannot be parted from this Bible. It is part of my master's effects, see you. His last will and testament will proclaim it mine.'

Wallis considered. 'Mr Morgan, come to the station with Mr Sykes. You can make your statements, as the arresting citizens. I will release your property to you.'

The lady of the house was not at home but Inspector Wallis took the liberty of making use of the kitchen and dining room, so that the constable and sergeant could do what was necessary by way of taking preliminary accounts of the day's events.

Bolingbroke was whisked away to the bridewell in the company of Sergeant Ashworth.

There was a moment when Wallis and I met on the landing, and I managed a brief word.

'Inspector, that copy of *Gothic Ornament* found near Dr Potter's body, do you think there might be just a possibility that Dr Potter suspected Father Bolingbroke?'

Wallis said, 'What makes you think Bolingbroke is a "Father" of any kind? I have had my eye on him. Prison pallor is a very particular shade. His real name is Aiden Parrott. He spent three years in a seminary before the war, training for the priesthood, until some altarpieces caught his fancy. The inmates at Armley Gaol preferred him to the real thing. That's probably where he stole the cassock.'

'So that was why he was in such a hurry to be away on Friday. He thought that one of you may recognise him.'

'It was enough for me to know where he was, for now.' Wallis surprised me by answering what was really in my thoughts. 'If I had not arrested the organ grinder, and with reason, we would have released him onto the street, to die a little sooner and in less comfort. You would not have liked that either, I suppose.'

This is how we all departed the Roundhay lodgings of Father Bolingbroke. Inspector Wallis, now in charge of Bolingbroke's house key, left a constable on duty outside, to await the owner's return.

Sykes, Morgan and I hovered at one side of the front porch. The constable and Lennox, who had engaged him in conversation, were at the other.

'To think I gave that rogue free run of my master's study. It is beside myself with annoyance I am.'

'Mr Morgan, he deceived everyone.'

Sykes said, 'Put it down to your good nature that you

were taken in. The man is a confidence trickster, but you had the wit to catch him out.'

'That bicycle he rode, was that stolen too?'

The constable took a sudden interest, being one of those people who can listen to two conversations at once. 'What bicycle is that, sir?'

'A boneshaker, painted green it was.'

This cheered the constable no end. 'If you will all stay here while I make an enquiry of the neighbours, I may find out about the bicycle.'

It was only then that I realised Mr Lennox and Mr Morgan had not been introduced, and so I undertook the formalities. The two men fell into conversation about Dr Potter.

Sykes and I drew apart and discussed what to do next.

Sykes glanced at Morgan. 'I must stay with him until we have given our statements. The poor chap looks desolate.'

'How will you get home?'

'I'll ride back to Weetwood with Morgan in the pony and trap. If that bicycle Bolingbroke rode turns out to belong here, I'll bring it back, and then catch the tram.'

'I'll take Mr Lennox to the library.'

The constable returned, well pleased with himself. 'The green bicycle belongs to the son of the householder.'

And so it was decided. Sykes and Morgan walked to where patient, clever Archie stood harnessed in his trap.

Lennox and I returned to the car.

He looked at his watch. 'The auditor will be at the library by now.'

'Let Mrs Carmichael deal with him. I am sure she is capable.'

'Oh, she is capable.'

'We won't go straight back, Mr Lennox. The Lake Café is in need of business in this poor weather.'

Ten minutes later, we were seated at a table decked with a blue and white check cloth next to a window, with a view over Waterloo Lake. On a fine Saturday, the place would be packed to bursting. Now, in spite of the clear pale blue sky, there were just two other customers, elderly women sitting close to the fire.

The walls were decorated with good amateur watercolours of the boating lake, the folly castle and the rose garden.

Mr Lennox ordered a tongue sandwich, and cheddar cheese on toast, with a dash of Worcester sauce, for me.

I poured tea.

He grasped his cup with both hands, like some workman outdoors in the cold struggling to keep warm. 'Why didn't I believe Miss Montague? How could I have been so stupid? And what an idiot not to see through Bolingbroke.'

'Well he's caught now. Let the police deal with him.'

'If Mrs Carmichael had not searched Marian's locker, Marian herself might have said, "What's this doing here? Who has put a book in my bag?" Why her, why pick her as his victim?'

'He is a clever crook. He knew someone would be ready to think ill of her.'

'Mrs Carmichael.'

'Mr Lennox, I know how things stand between you and Mrs Carmichael.'

He looked up. 'Do you? Has it been that obvious?'

'Not to others.'

'She stood by me, you see, all the time my wife was ill. No one knows the draining exhaustion of watching a dear one grow weaker and more helpless day by day. Pamela Carmichael was my sanity. I don't know what I would have done without her, and then, when Marian came . . .'

'Marian Montague.'

He nodded. 'Even her name is lovely.'

'Yes.'

Lennox remembered his manners, took his cup by the handle and drank.

The waitress brought our food.

Something held me back from prompting him to say more. Perhaps it was a sudden reluctance to know, to be expected to be sympathetic to the man who had betrayed both wife and mistress.

When we had finished eating, Lennox took out cigarettes, and straight away put them back. 'I can't breathe in here. And I can't go back to the library. Not just yet.'

'Let's take a turn round the park.'

He paid the bill.

Outside, the air was bracing, but with a penetrating chill.

We took the path around the lake, side by side but not looking at each other as we avoided muddy puddles.

He began to speak. 'The first time I saw Marian, it was as if something long dead came alive inside me. I thought . . . I imagined one so young and vibrant would not look at me, but she did.'

'There is quite a gap in your ages.'

'She is twenty-four. I am forty-nine, but it did not matter, not to her.'

His words came out in bursts, followed by silences in

which I listened to the wind in the trees and the call of birds.

'I am not saying I didn't love my wife, but our life was quiet and companionable. Before Marian, I have only ever once in my life felt such overpowering attraction for another human being, as if our souls called out to each other. Oh I know that sounds too Emily Brontë for the world, too romantic for someone as middle-aged and jaded as I, but it is true.'

'Were you and Marian . . . I mean . . .'

'I loved her you see. I could have sworn she felt the same. When I found out she was the thief . . .'

'You did not believe her denials?'

'At first, yes, but to have a book in her bag, for the index cards to have been torn and left in her waste bin, and her confusion. Pamela, Mrs Carmichael, was so very sure. I thought that Marian had been using me, making a fool of me'

A blackbird perched on a branch. I hoped it would sing.

Speaking almost to himself, Lennox said, 'She was so like my first true love, the woman who sent me spinning, years and years ago. That lady gave me my marching orders. I thought Marian would do the same.'

Something clicked in my head, a most unwelcome click. Marching orders meant that the "other woman" had not been his wife. I remembered the words of Lady Coulton. Someone had come to the house when Lord Coulton was away in the South African wars. A young man had arrived to do an inventory in the library.

On the lake, two swans glided by, turning their long necks, each looking at the other.

'When was it, how long ago, this great love?'

'I had just come down from Christchurch. Not being of independent means I followed a suggestion from my tutor and accepted work cataloguing in a library. I won't say where, but it was for a titled family. The lady, and she was a lady, she was married. Mrs Shackleton, that woman was the love of my life. I will never forget her until the day I die. Yet when Marian came into the library, I looked at her and for a moment thought she had returned to me.'

So I was not the only person who had noticed the resemblance between Lady Coulton and Marian. Now I wanted him to stop. But it was too late. I willed him to stop, but he did not.

'I expected Marian to rebuff me, because of my age. But she was so charming, approachable, and she had a way of letting me know that she liked me. Why did she choose me and then let me go?'

He was confusing the two loves of his life. I reminded him. 'You let Marian go.'

'Yes I did, fool that I am.'

I was not here to listen to the details of Lennox's passion for his own daughter. I needed to find her. 'Where has she gone?'

'I thought it best not to see her again, at least not yet. This changes everything. She is not a thief.'

'Do you know where she is?'

'I have an idea. I can find out.'

'Good.'

We came to a large puddle. I stepped one way round it, he the other. 'Why do you want to know?'

'Mr Lennox, she was a young female employee of the

247

library, without a family to fall back on. We have a respon-
sibility for her welfare. Will you tell me as soon as you have
her address?'

'I hadn't thought of it like that.'

'No, I don't suppose you had.'

'I should be the one to find her, and beg her forgiveness.'
He was slightly abashed, and so he should be. 'I need to make
application to a friend who made an arrangement for her. I
will let you know.'

'What kind of arrangement?'

'For her to stay somewhere, in the country.'

The clock on the boathouse told me it was time to leave.
We walked back to the park gates.

It took us a few moments to settle into our seats. I handed
him a pair of motoring gauntlets. 'This separation between
you and Marian, it may be for the best.'

'What do you mean?'

'Oh just a feeling.' I started the motor.

Providence had intervened. Bolingbroke and Mrs
Carmichael had done a great service to Marian and Lennox.
If it had not been for the false accusation of theft, Lennox
may have married his own daughter.

We did not speak again until we reached Commercial
Street. He thanked me for the lift.

It was a loose end, something I could not make sense of.
'Mr Lennox, I know this may seem an odd time to ask, but
where do you stand on the question of whether the library
should stay on Commercial Street or remove to new premises?'

'I was neutral about the business. But now I'm all for
removing.'

'Why?'

'Dr Potter put a very powerful case. He is the last man in the world to speak up for change. If Potter saw advantages in the idea of removing, believe me the whole committee would be carried along by him. Besides, after everything that has happened, rumours about the ghost, Potter's death, the horrible experience Marian has gone through, I say let us have a fresh start.'

'Yes I can see you would feel that way.'

'We have the meeting scheduled for tomorrow, where the matter was to be publicly aired.'

'I had forgotten about that.'

'It was too late to cancel. People will now come to hear about Dr Potter.'

'And will you speak about the question of removal?'

'I don't know what will be said. Officially, I am still neutral.'

He climbed out of the car and stood by the running board. 'I am going to find Marian. If she will have me, I'll marry her.'

My stomach did a somersault. Not if I find her first.

It was exactly a week since I had seen Lady Coulton. Surely something must break soon. This was it. Lennox would lead me to her. I caught his sleeve to delay him. 'How soon might you be in touch with her?'

'I hope very soon.'

'Let me know the instant you have her address. It was very wrong of you to take up with a young counter assistant, and then to cast her out.'

I sounded like one of the characters from a Sunday school prize novel, but he must be stopped from seeing her.

249

Lennox's face was full of remorse. 'Do you think I don't know that?'

'I must speak to her first.'

'To put her off me?'

'I have another reason for wanting to find her, something that is extremely urgent.'

He nodded, though whether he had taken in my words I could not be sure.

Twenty-Five

I arrived for the meeting at ten to three. Rows of chairs had been set out and already nearly all seats were taken. At the top end of the room stood a long table, set with a water jug and four glasses. About halfway down the room, I spotted an aisle seat to my right. People on the row behind me chatted in low, confidential tones, waiting to hear what would be said about the events of last Friday.

A couple of minutes before three o'clock, Mr Castle strode in, followed by Professor Merton, Mr Lennox and Mrs Carmichael.

They took their seats, not looking at us, or at each other.

Mrs Carmichael placed a notebook and pencil on the table.

Mr Castle, who is a stickler for punctuality, took out his fob watch and held it in his right hand for what seemed a long time. He then placed it on the table.

Mrs Carmichael picked up her pencil, ready to make notes.

Mr Castle looked up, his eyes searching the room as if taking a mental register of attendance. He cleared his throat before speaking. 'Good afternoon, ladies and gentlemen. Thank you for coming. This meeting was scheduled some time ago for a particular purpose. Sadly, we have been overtaken by sudden and tragic events. You have all heard by now of the distressing death of our highly esteemed friend and library proprietor, Dr Potter. It grieves me greatly that this loss occurred here in the library, the worst event of our long history. There will be services of remembrance in churches and chapels across the city this coming Sunday. This is neither the time nor place to say more. In due course, announcements will be made. Inspector Wallis and Sergeant Ashworth are here. If you wish to speak to them, or to me, please do so after the meeting.' He paused. Heads turned, including mine. Inspector Wallis was standing at the back of the room, Sergeant Ashworth beside him. Castle continued. 'I now ask you to stand and observe a minute's silence, to pay our respects to Dr Potter.'

We all stood.

During the sixty seconds of silence, my mind raced around Dr Potter, charming and witty, until Friday still brimming with the enthusiasm and impish humour of his undergraduate magazine days. He had recommended his article about the ghost, being tickled about my participation in the 'exorcism'. 'A jolly good jape,' he had written. Having suggested to the inspector that the young Potter may have been the ghost, I pictured him in my mind, using the keys that had belonged to his grandfather to let himself in the basement door, knowing the eager young librarian was working late, creating deliberate sounds, taking fright only when McAllister brandished a revolver. He then hurried down the stairs and let himself out of the front door, chuckling all the way.

But why the other article, about the solicitor from the firm Nelson, Castle and Nelson?

When the minute's silence had ticked to its conclusion, Mr Castle took a sip of water. 'Thank you, ladies and gentlemen. You may be seated.'

Chairs scraped, feet shuffled.

As he sat down, Mr Castle took a deep breath and let it out in a sigh. 'I have a motion on the table from Miss Heaton. She suggests that we arrange for this building to be blessed by clergymen of three denominations.' He paused. 'May I have a show of hands in favour?'

Out of regard for Miss Heaton, and seeing nothing but good in a blessing, I raised my hand. Mrs Carmichael stood and counted one side of the room. Mr Castle counted the other side. He jotted down the number. 'Against?'

A couple of courageous rebels, or awkward curmudgeons, raised their hands.

'Abstentions?' Mr Castle asked. There were none that I could see. 'The motion is carried. Miss Heaton, I leave you to make the arrangements.' He put his fob watch back in his waistcoat pocket. 'The matter for which today's meeting was originally arranged now pales into insignificance. Some of you may have heard of the proposal put to the committee by a group of businessmen, interested in purchasing these premises for a different use, which would entail the removal of the library. I call on Professor Merton to speak to this question.'

Craggy Professor Merton rose to his very full height, took a deep breath, sniffed, and pushed his spectacles further up his nose. 'Before I do so, I must say a few words about my colleague and close associate, our much lamented fellow proprietor, Dr Potter. He was a man of learning, an honourable man. He would have made a most excellent university vice chancellor. The world is poorer without him.'

This was the longest speech I had ever heard from my neighbour. He drew murmurs of agreement, and then continued. 'Regarding the question of whether the library should stay in these premises, or remove, Dr Potter and I looked at this matter most carefully. There was a certain attraction for Dr Potter in the idea of the removal to premises not yet built, representing a leap into the unknown. After much consideration, it is the considered judgement that we should drop this question altogether and move forward.'

Mr Castle glanced at his notes. 'Thank you, Professor Merton.' He paused. 'This venerable library must not be treated as a sinking ship. She is afloat. She has proprietors, a captain and crew who are devoted to her. She will sail on through this century and into the next without altering course or seeking harbours new.'

Murmurs greeted his words, mostly of approval, but with a single 'Shame!' and a 'Too bad'.

Mr Castle looked at Mr Lennox and Mrs Carmichael. 'Mr Lennox, would you inform the meeting of the staff view on this matter? They are of the same mind, I believe.'

Lennox remained seated. Even from where I sat, I saw his Adam's apple leap as he gulped. 'They are indeed of the same mind, satisfied with our present situation.' He paused, and reflected. Speaking once more, with all the emphasis he could muster, he concluded, 'We see no advantage in removing to new premises.'

He had changed his tune since yesterday.

Mrs Carmichael nodded, her mouth a grim line.

'Are there any questions?' Mr Castle asked.

There were two questions. A gentleman I did not know asked about some kind of permanent memorial to Dr Potter.

Miss Heaton asked whether proprietors would be kind enough to contribute to the collection for Dr Potter's nearest and dearest. The tin was on the counter.

I wondered if she knew that his nearest and dearest were a Welsh manservant, and a pony called Archie.

Mr Castle picked up his pen in a drawing the matter to a close gesture.

I stood and raised my hand. 'Mr Chairman.'

'You have a comment, Mrs Shackleton?'

'Dr Potter was highly enthusiastic about moving to new premises. It is too soon to dismiss the possibility. In honour of his memory, we should have a discussion in committee, and a vote, just as we have voted on a blessing for the building. I suggest we postpone the question.'

I sat down to a couple of murmurs of agreement.

Mr Castle frowned. Professor Merton glared at me. The two men put their heads together and exchanged a few quiet words.

Finally, Mr Castle said, 'Very well, Mrs Shackleton, we will take the matter to the committee.'

'Thank you.'

Having spoken on a sudden impulse, I could not precisely say why I had intervened, especially since Dr Potter's enthusiasm was entirely to do with the possibility of a menagerie in the basement. It just seemed to me that a lid was being put on the business far too quickly, and I wanted to know why.

Mr Castle thanked people for their attendance and closed the meeting. Library proprietors began to file out the way we had come. Mr Castle and Professor Merton had their heads together. Mrs Carmichael joined with two lady proprietors in earnest conversation.

Mr Lennox slipped away, into the passage. Without appearing to hurry, I moved after him. I caught up with him at the foot of the staircase.

'Mr Lennox.'

He turned. He was pale, and looked ill.

'You changed your mind about the removal.'

'We all thought it for the best.'

'But you were so enthusiastic.'

'An answer is demanded by the business group concerned. We were in a corner.' Something about the way he phrased his answer, made it seem personal, as though he were the one in a corner.

'Do you have Miss Montague's address for me?'

Without replying, he hurried up the stairs, entered his room and closed the door firmly.

I joined the short queue at the counter, to register attendance, and took money from my satchel to contribute towards Miss Heaton's collection.

An elderly couple had buttonholed Inspector Wallis and Sergeant Ashworth. I watched Inspector Wallis carefully extricate himself, leaving Sergeant Ashworth to deal with queries or offers of information.

The inspector came to speak to me. 'I don't believe I congratulated you on delivering the book thief, Mrs Shackleton.'

Sometimes modesty is the best policy.

'It was pure fluke. I called to see whether I could do anything to help Dr Potter's manservant. Fortunately my assistant Mr Sykes was with me, and Mr Morgan caught Father Bolingbroke red-handed.'

'Excuse me, Inspector.'

Wallis turned to see who had spoken, and was immediately engaged in conversation.

As I signed the register of attendance, I fastened my coat and adjusted my satchel. Then I noticed that the basement door was open just a fraction. Marian was the one who did not mind working in the basement. I remembered noticing a desk there, just by the small pulley lift used for transporting books between ground floor and basement.

People were gathered in twos and threes, and small groups. Looking at this bookshelf and that, I edged closer to the basement entrance. Once at the door, it was a matter of a second to slip through, and to flick the electric switch. The shiver I felt as I went down the stairs was not simply due to the change in temperature.

As I had remembered, the desk was to my right, its surface clear. I opened the drawers one by one. There were two on either side and one in the centre. In the centre drawer was a neatly written list, headed 'things to do'. A quick glance told me that there was nothing personal on the list; it was to do with cataloguing, rearranging files, searching for a title. The side drawers contained pencils, pen and ink, typed sheets whose text had been struck through, indicating the paper should be reused on the blank side.

In the last drawer was a five-tooth silver hair comb, embossed with fruit and flowers. I ran my fingers across the decoration. That was hers, I felt sure. Miss Montague always had some pretty comb in her hair.

Surely there would be nothing to find, after the police search, but all the same, I would take a look. Otherwise I would regret the missed opportunity. I walked past the coal hole. The grate above, through which coal was delivered from the street, let in a grey light. Next to that was a half window and beyond, a cupboard of a room. There was a shovel, a pick, and a broom. I realised that I still had Marian Montague's silver comb clutched in my hand so hard that it hurt.

The lighting was poor. I took a torch from my satchel and played the light back and forth. The bookshelves that had toppled were once again upright, but their stock had not been returned. It gave me goose pimples to pass so close to the place where Dr Potter had lain. I pressed on, towards the spot where Umberto had curled himself in a ball and would have died had we not found him. The floor was flagged with paving stones, and there were the marks of a broom, where it had been swept.

I had not heard footsteps, but suddenly knew someone was behind me. Startled, I turned to see Mr Castle. 'What are you doing down here, Mrs Shackleton? You could have been locked in.'

He was standing far too close. I moved aside. 'Oh I don't think so. Someone would have noticed the lights.'

'What are you looking for?'

'I'll know what I'm looking for when I see it. Isn't that the charm of our library? We come across the unexpected.' I was determined not to let him intimidate me; reminding him that though he was library president, he held only one share, as I did.

'You are being rather enigmatic.'

'All right, perhaps you can help. Where has Marian Montague gone? You, Mr Lennox and Mrs Carmichael are the only ones who know she was wrongfully dismissed.'

He is not a man to show his reactions, but I would have sworn that in the dim light, his jaw dropped. 'Why do you want to know about her?'

'She was sacked without a character and has left her lodgings. It won't do.'

Suddenly, he was blocking my way, standing close, looming over me. When I stepped aside, so did he. 'Wrongfully, why do you say that? It is a mistake to think there can be only one thief in the world.'

'There was only one thief in the library, and it was not her. Anyway, thief or not, I want to find her.'

'It must be very hard being a detective, Mrs Shackleton, imagining all sorts of terrible things. Do you think I smuggled the girl home and am keeping her in a cupboard?' He gave a mirthless laugh.

I dodged aside and began walking back towards the stairs. 'I shouldn't think Mrs Castle would want her in the house.'

He was beside me again, and the corridor of books was too narrow. 'I won't have my dear wife's name mentioned in the same breath as that woman of Babylon, excuse my language.' I glanced up at him but in the dim light could not read the expression on his face. 'She was no good. I do not expect a lady to understand my meaning. We are fortunate that she went quietly.'

I was cold, but suddenly turned colder. 'What do you mean, she went quietly?'

'You must know she tried to latch her hooks into Mr

Lennox. She would not be the first.' He put his hand on my arm. 'You are going in the wrong direction.'

'What?'

He gripped my arm. 'It's a labyrinth down here. This way for the stairs.'

'You know your way around the labyrinth then?'

His grip on my arm tightened. 'What do you mean by that?'

'Nothing. Just that I have seen enough.'

A sense of unease flooded through me, but I struggled to behave normally as we walked side by side.

When he spoke again, it was as if he had forgotten Marian Montague, or wanted to change the subject. 'You were talking to Dr Potter on the day he died.'

'Yes.'

'What did he say?'

'The usual pleasantries.'

'Scurrilous remarks more likely.' Castle uttered a small dismissive sound. 'He handed you something, a student magazine I think. Have you read it?' He tried to sound nonchalant, but there was something like dismay in his voice, or fear.

I thought about mentioning Dr Potter's written account of the ghost, but it suddenly struck me that the more relevant article may have been the one concerning Nelson, Castle and Nelson, solicitors. 'There was an item about embezzlement and a Mr Nelson and his secretary going missing.' Someone going missing, like Marian Montague. I kept my voice light, as if we were walking along the street, chatting, and not blundering about between high bookcases and turning corners. 'Were you in the same practice, Mr Castle?'

'I was. It was most unfortunate. Nelson almost ruined us. He helped himself from the estates of several clients, and then made off with a secretary. I had to rebuild the practice from scratch. I would hate people to begin talking about it again.'

'What about the other Nelson? There were two.'

'Old Mr Nelson had died. It would never have happened on his watch. His son was a disgrace to the profession.'

I had kept him talking, and given the information he wanted. While we walked, I thought we were leaving the basement, moving towards the stairs, but we had come full circle. We were back by the corner where Umberto had lain. Castle did not seem to notice. 'Where is that scurrilous magazine of Potter's? I did not know there was one still in existence, until I saw it on the list of borrowed items today.'

'I returned it.'

'No, you did not return it.' In the dim light, his eyes had an intense, almost desperate gleam.

On the stone floor, the pool of light from my torch created a world of shadows all around. We were once more near the spot where Umberto had almost died. By torchlight, the broom marks created an abstract pattern of swirls. 'Then the magazine is still in my satchel. I'll look when we're back upstairs.' I tried to sidestep.

He was in my way and jostled me. The torch fell from my hand and clattered on the floor.

He stuck out his foot and shoved me, making a sudden grab for my satchel. I fell sideways onto the hard floor, the whole of my left side hitting the ground so hard I cried out. A firecracker went off in my head, blazing through temple, cheekbone, eye socket. I felt as if my eye might pop out. As I lay there, a searing pain shot up my arm. When I tried to move, my hip and leg refused.

He was picking up the torch.

It was him, I thought. He killed Potter. He left Umberto to die. He would kill me too. With a great effort, I used my right hand, to push myself onto my knees.

Ignoring me, his attention centred on the spilled contents of my satchel. He shone the light. 'Where is it? Where is it?'

He thrust his face into mine, grabbing my shoulder, pushing me backwards. I raised my right hand and brought the teeth of the ornamental comb down his cheek. He let out a cry and staggered back, holding his face. I pushed myself to my feet, my left leg feeling useless. Grabbing at my wrist that was now throbbing with pain he shoved me against the wall. The back of my head bashed against the brick, but having the wall at my back gave me support so that I brought up my right knee and slammed it in his groin. He relaxed his grip. I pulled free and turned to run, trying to scream for help but no sound would come. My left leg felt as if it belonged to someone else.

Suddenly, Inspector Wallis stood in my way.

He leaned towards me, all concern. 'What happened, Mrs Shackleton?'

'Castle attacked me.'

'Attacked you?' Now *he* was blocking my way.

'Let me out of here.'

Castle was suddenly beside us, full of solicitude, carrying my satchel, not speaking to me but to the inspector. 'She tripped over the uneven flags and dropped her bag.' His

262

voice was calm as he turned to me. 'The contents spilled, Mrs Shackleton. One or two more bits back there. I'll get them for you.'

Wallis said, 'Good thing you came down here, Mr Castle. You could have been locked in, Mrs Shackleton.'

'That's just what I said.' Castle oozed charm to the extent that I almost disbelieved my own experience.

For a horrible moment, sandwiched between the two men, the thought came that I would never escape.

Then suddenly, the inspector was guiding me back to the stairs. 'You're safe. Trust me. He won't harm you.'

Did he believe me, or was he protecting Castle?

I ran my tongue around my teeth, feeling sure one had come loose. My cheek burned. It must be bruised. I touched my finger to the sore place and felt blood.

When we were at the top of the stairs, the inspector whispered, 'I heard Mr Castle say, "Where is it?" What did he want?'

'Dr Potter's magazine.'

'Give it to him.'

'You have it.'

'I'll put it on the counter.'

'Didn't you hear me? He attacked me.'

'I heard you. It would be your word against his.'

Back in the main room, the inspector spoke to his sergeant, who went to the counter.

Mrs Carmichael stared at me with a look of horror. 'What happened?'

Now was not the time to say, and she not the person to tell. I simply shook my head, not ready to tell the truth and cause consternation.

I picked up the magazine that the sergeant had placed on the counter. 'I'm returning this. I believe Mr Castle wants it.'

At that moment, he emerged from the basement door, carrying my satchel, moving towards me like someone on roller skates gliding at speed, someone for whom the earth's atmosphere would part as he approached.

Mrs Carmichael looked at me, about to say something else, and then thought better of it.

Castle handed me my satchel.

I raised the magazine in the air. 'It's here. I told you I'd returned it.'

He smiled, as though nothing untoward had happened. 'Thank you. I'll borrow this please, Mrs Carmichael.'

She looked surprised. 'That's unlike you, Mr Castle. You never take anything out.'

At that moment, I liked her.

Castle scowled, 'Nonsense.'

'Ah there you're wrong,' Mrs Carmichael said. 'I know I should have other diversions but it amuses me to check on borrowings. Dr Potter was the most avid reader, and you are far too busy with your legal tomes ever to make use of your personal ticket book.'

Leaving Mrs Carmichael and Mr Castle at the counter, I went to the ladies' room where I splashed my face and then ran cold water over my painful wrist.

When the door opened, I gave a start, but it was only Mrs Carmichael. I saw her in the mirror.

'Here.' She took the top from a bottle of aspirins and tipped three into my hand, filled a mug with water and gave it to me.

I took the aspirins.

She put a slip of paper in my pocket, saying, 'Read this later. Not now.'

I took it out and read it.

18 Dorset Avenue, Harehills — front downstairs room — visit me this evening

She turned to leave.

I stopped her. 'Wait! Walk back with me, to the door.'

She nodded. 'What will you do?'

'Go home.'

How did I know if I could trust her, or anyone? She may be in Castle's pocket and have slipped me knock-out pills.

We left the ladies' room. I waited. She went ahead, through the reading room and towards the counter. I walked to the exit door.

Inspector Wallis was waiting at the top of the stairs. 'My driver is at the entrance. He will take you to the dispensary. You need treatment.'

I opened my mouth to explain that I just wanted to go home. In a quiet voice, he said, 'You'll be safe in a public place.'

We walked down the stairs. I felt like an old woman, taking one careful step at a time. 'He attacked me and you are protecting him.'

'As I said, it would be your word against his.'

'Why would I lie?'

'Why would he?'

'He is important. Next you'll tell me that he plays golf with the chief constable.'

'As it happens, I believe he does.'

He walked me to the door and opened it for me. 'I don't suppose there is any point in asking you to leave this investigation to me?'

I ignored him.

Approaching the doors of the dispensary, I glanced up. A pair of carved stone cherubs gazed down, one tearful and anxious, the other smiling, presumably after the careful attention of dispensary staff.

Benches were set against the wall and across the centre of the waiting room, row upon row of people, waiting to see a doctor. Just my luck that I would be here for the rest of the day. I gave my name and details at the reception desk. 'It's only a sprained wrist.' Now I wished I had gone home and asked Mrs Sugden to bandage it for me.

The receptionist glared at me over her horn-rimmed spectacles. 'The doctor will decide what is the matter, and what is to be done. And you have a bruise on your face. The cause?'

'I tripped.'

She gave me a look that told me she had heard that tale before. 'Take a seat. You will be called.'

There was a little shuffling up to make room for me. I cursed my bad luck and settled in to wait. It was now eight days since I had seen Lady Coulton. I was so near to finding her daughter, yet so far. As I looked at the number of people ahead of me in the queue, I calculated that I would be here for at least another three or four hours. The thought of Castle kept me sitting still, budging along every ten or fifteen minutes as some of those before me were seen.

I knew where Castle lived. He knew where I lived. What was he afraid of? That Dr Potter had told me something, divulged a piece of dangerous information, but what?

A solicitor missing from Castle's legal firm, forty-odd years ago; a ghost appearing about the same time. If my head did not throb so much, I would be able to think more clearly.

I had reached the far end of the third bench when a rheumy-eyed porter with a red nose glanced about and then spoke to me out of the corner of his mouth.

'Are you the Mrs Shackleton that works with Jim Sykes?'

'Yes.'

He took the torn top of a cigarette packet from his pocket and handed it to me.

I waited a moment, until he had sidled away and then read what he had written.

Peter Donohue, 9 Danby Court, wound to his leg

This must be my day for having addresses thrust at me.

There were still two and three-quarter benches of people waiting to be seen. I hesitated only for a moment, and then left.

The porter caught up with me in the vestibule. 'Aren't you going to see the doctor?'

'No.'

'Wait on.'

A moment later, he returned and handed me bandages and pushed them into my coat pocket.

'Thanks.'

'You should have your wrist and that bruise seen to.'

'I will. It's all right, I'm a nurse.'

'Aye, they're the worst.'

'Tell me about Mr Donohue. What was the treatment?'

'He was patched up. Said he'd caught his leg on a nail, nasty wound to his calf. His mam dragged him in, fearful it would turn septic.'

So he had removed the bullet himself and kept quiet about being shot. What did Peter Donohue have to hide?

Twenty-Six

The porter had called me a taxi. It was raining when I arrived at Danby Court. The heavy overnight downpour had flooded the drains and a sickening, sour stench filled the air. I stepped carefully through the flooded courtyard but it was impossible to keep my feet dry.

I was conscious of being watched. My outfit marked me out as not belonging in this place where the inhabitants had little enough to shield them from the elements and the vagaries of ill-fortune. Short of tearing my garments to shreds, there was little I could do but press on, and find number nine.

It was at the far end of the courtyard, on the ground floor. Pity the people who lived in the cellar. Rain and filthy water teemed down the steps. Rain had also seeped under the ill-fitting ground floor door. I knocked.

The door was opened by a gaunt, skull-faced man with prominent cheekbones and ears that gave his old face a pixie quality. He stood a few feet from the door, on a pallet that, for now at least, protected his feet against the inch-deep ingress of water.

'I'm looking for Peter Donohue.'

'Oh aye, and who are you when you're at home?'

'I'm a nurse. I have fresh bandages for his leg.' I tapped my satchel, indicating that there was more in there than he could dream of.

'You best go up then.' He nodded at a staircase.

Glancing behind him, I noticed how crowded this room was, including an old and a younger woman, another man and several children. Perhaps people had come up here from the flooded cellar.

I thanked him, and climbed the stairs.

Unfortunately, the woman who answered my knock was one of the people who had been in the courtyard when I was enquiring after Marian Montague, the thin woman who had taken my card from her companion. Thanks to my occasional visits to Scotland, I do a passable Edinburgh accent, though it is a touch on the posh side for a Leeds courtyard. Keeping my head down, as though my face was still lashed with rain, I watched raindrops from the brim of my hat fall onto the toes of my galoshes. 'Is Mr Peter Donohue at home?'

'He is not. Who wants to know?'

'I'm a nurse. I've brought him dressings, for his leg.' I took the blue wrapped packet from my pocket. 'When will he be home? I'd like to take a look at his wound, see that it has not turned bad.'

'He's on the mend.'

'All the same . . . '

Someone was staring at me from the corner of the room. I risked a glance. She was lying on a narrow bed covered by an army blanket.

At first we did not recognise each other in these strange surroundings and me with my faux Edinburgh accent.

The person who was quickest on the uptake was the woman who faced me, Peter Donohue's mother I guessed.

'It's you. You was here a few days ago, asking after . . .' She stopped and tried to place herself between me and Marian Montague, for now I saw it was she, propped up on a tick pillow, the blanket up to her chin. She looked pale. Her beautiful long hair had been roughly shorn, giving her the look of an urchin. Were things so bad for her that she had sold her hair? Or perhaps this place ran wick with lice.

'Miss Montague?' I let my accent drop.

'Mrs Shackleton.'

Since the start of her employment, apart from a long chat at the Christmas social, our encounters had largely consisted of exchanging books across the counter. How had she come to this place after her respectable lodgings? The bump under the blanket gave the answer. She was pregnant.

'You're not a nurse at all, are you?' the woman said.

'Oh yes. I'm a nurse all right. I served throughout the war in the Voluntary Aid Detachment.'

'Didn't anybody tell you the war is over? First you're here asking one lot of questions, then another.'

It was her turn to fire the questions. How did I know where to find Peter? Since when had the dispensary cared enough about its patients to send out emissaries with bandages? Who had sent me and why?

She would have slammed the door in my face, except that I could see she feared I would come back with the police. Perhaps she knew that her son had been shot in the leg and perhaps she did not. But she would know him well enough to realise he had been up to no good.

In the end, after neither of us would answer the other's

questions, and when Marian continued to stare at me, Mrs Donohue made to shut the door.

I had no intention of turning tail. Before she had time to shoot a bolt or turn a key, I pushed my way in, rudely stepping across the threshold. A shooting pain ran from my wrist to my shoulder. Perhaps it was a fracture and not a sprain.

'Miss Montague, you left the library so suddenly. I was worried about you.'

'There's no need.'

'There was a terrible misunderstanding. I want to try and put it right.'

'Do they know where I am?'

'No.'

'And I don't want them to, do you understand?'

The woman intervened. 'The lass doesn't need you. I'm taking care of her now.' She turned to Marian. 'Don't worry, love. No one's going to harm you.'

What did she mean? I looked from the younger to the older woman. 'What is going on?'

'I could ask you the same thing,' Mrs Donohue said sullenly.

'All right. To stop us going round in circles, I'll tell you why I am here. The first time it was because someone saw Miss Montague coming from this courtyard. I was curious.'

'And how is it you were snooping about for my son, pretending you want to change his bandage?'

'I'll gladly change his bandage. If his leg has turned septic he risks losing it. I would like to know what he was doing in the place where the bullet was fired.'

'Bullet? He cut his leg on a nail.' She turned to Marian

Montague. 'Is she all there? This woman who doesn't know whether she's Sassenach or Scot?'

Marian did not answer. She bit her lip. Her eyes locked on mine, with a silent plea to say nothing.

Mrs Donohue once more filled the silence. 'The lass is doing well enough. I'm seeing to her, and she's not paying the kind of rent demanded from her at her last place. She's not been well, and unless you can do summat practical for her, I'll ask you to leave now and stop disparaging my lad who is out earning a respectable living this very minute, but he'll be back and he won't be pleased to hear someone accusing him of being shot.'

There was nothing more to be said for the moment. Mrs Donohue had flung open the door and stood with one hand on the knob and the other on her hip, her head tilted back, mouth grim, inviting me to leave.

With some difficulty, using only my good hand, I took a bandage from my pocket.

'Keep it.' I crossed to the bed, handing it to Marian. 'Here's my card, too, so you know where I am, should you need me, or need help.'

Marian said, 'I am quite all right, thank you.' In a softer voice, she whispered, 'I know where you are. Peter came to the wrong house.'

So the poor man had not intended to murder Professor Merton but to visit me. Of course, it was a simple mistake. We were on opposite sides of the same street and he had been confused. Since Mrs Sugden was so handy with a pistol, I guessed he would not try again in a hurry. But why had he come, and why did Marian seem so fearful of telling a straightforward story in front of her fierce protectress?

'How far gone are you?'

'Five months. I'm all right, but I slept badly, and my legs ache, that's why I'm resting.'

Mrs Donohue crossed the room. She stood, arms folded, uncertain whether to join in the conversation or order me out.

'I'm glad Marian has you to take care of her, Mrs Donohue. I'm sorry for my deception but I was concerned.'

'Well you might be,' Mrs Donohue snapped, though slightly placated. 'It's not the best start for a young couple, but they've made their bed and they'll lie in it.'

Marian bit her lip.

So Mrs Donohue thought that Peter was the father. Perhaps he was. But the quick warning look from Marian told another story. Small wonder Marian was reluctant to speak.

I noticed a shopping basket on the table and a coat over a chair. 'You were going shopping, I think. Let me keep Marian company while you are gone. And please, let me contribute to the groceries.' I took out my purse. 'I'm sure Marian would like something nourishing.'

'A sliver of liver,' Marian said. 'I have a fancy for liver and onions.'

I handed over a sovereign, half expecting her to object. She did not.

'What's up with your arm?'

'Just a sprained wrist.'

'Better use that bandage on yourself.'

'I'll do it,' Marian said. 'You go to the butcher, Mrs Donohue. We'll be all right.'

'Well then, if you're sure?'

'I'm sure.' Marian swung her legs from the bed and picked up the bandage.

When Mrs Donohue had gone, I sat on the end of Marian's bed. 'What's going on, Marian?'

'I could ask you the same. Why did someone shoot Peter when he came to bring you my message?'

'He went by mistake to Professor Merton's house, and something had been happening that made us all fearful. I'm very sorry that your friend was shot.'

She opened the bandage. 'So was he. He can't get over it. He could have been maimed for life, all so that he could ask you to meet me. I wanted you to know that I am innocent. Being sacked without a character is serious for someone who has to earn her living.'

'It will be cleared up, and I will give you a reference if you need me to.'

She sighed. 'I did a first aid course at school. Funny how things come in handy.' She put her pillow under my arm and began to bandage my wrist. 'I was worried when you found out I was here. Thought you might tell someone at the library.'

'Mr Lennox?'

'Yes. You know about us, about me and Sam?'

'Only since yesterday. He told me how much he came to care for you. He knows now that you did not steal books.'

'Of course I didn't steal books. Much he thought of me to believe that old crow Carmichael. She sacked me without a reference and he let her. Men can be so stupid. But that wasn't all.'

'Why? What happened?'

'You must swear not to say where I am. Once the baby's born, I'm going to Australia with Peter.'

'Have you married Peter Donohue?'

'No, not yet! You don't know anything, do you?'

'Obviously not.'

'I waited for Sam, Mr Lennox, on the day they sacked me. I hadn't told him until then that I was pregnant. I threatened to tell everyone, make a fuss, show him up for what he was. He called me a liar. Said I was stringing him along for what I could get. As if I would have picked a pernickety librarian if I was trying to do well in the world. But that was the least of it.'

'What do you mean?'

'I wasn't going to give up on him. Every night I went to the library. He's always the last to leave. Nothing I said seemed to touch him. She had convinced him that I was a conniving thief and a scheming tart. He shook me off, every time, and then . . . '

'Then what?'

'You won't believe me.'

'Tell me.'

'He tried to have me killed, to shut me up.'

'Never!'

'I said you wouldn't believe me. Well it's true. Ask Peter when he comes. That's why you mustn't tell anyone where I am.'

'But that's preposterous.'

'He doesn't want a scandal. Half the women in the library are in love with him. The men think he's a great chap. Who would believe me? Mrs Carmichael took one look at me and guessed my condition. Said there were places for girls like me, places where I'd never see the light of day.'

'Marian, your landlady told me that your mother died?'

'Yes.'

'I'm sorry. When?'

'When I was twelve years old. I was left with my step-father and I can't go back there. It's out of the question.'

Now my theories began to crumble. 'Tell me, were you ever known by another name, Sophia?'

'No.'

'Wells?'

'No, why should I be? I showed my references and school certificate at the library. My name is there, plain for all to see.'

'Of course.'

'Who has been saying different?'

'No one. Forget it. My mistake.' I began to feel faint. My head throbbed.

The door opened. A tall dark-haired young fellow in a shabby jacket and baggy trousers with long arms and bow legs stepped into the room.

Marian said, 'Peter, this is Mrs Shackleton, the person you were going to take my message to.'

He took off his cap. 'Oh.'

'I was telling her what happened but she won't believe me. Who would?'

'Aye,' he said.

'You tell her.'

'Me?'

'Go on.'

'Marian wanted me to tell you she int a thief.' He twisted his cap, wringing raindrops from it.

There must be more to be said, but an awkward silence hung over the three of us.

Out of desperation, I had convinced myself Marian and Sophia were the same person. Having discovered my mistake, I should go now, go home and lick my wounds.

But I could not. The injustice could not be allowed to stand. Besides, my now archenemy, Castle, had reacted so strangely at the mention of her name.

One sure way to encourage lovers to speak is to say, 'How did you two meet?'

They both smiled. Good start.

'I drew Marian's likeness.'

He went to the mantelpiece above the empty fire grate, took down a piece of cardboard and handed it to me. It was a meticulously drawn portrait, so lifelike and carefully tinted that it could have been a photograph.

'That's very good. You are an artist.'

'He is,' Marian said. 'I knew that soon as I saw his work. I used to like drawing myself so I know how good he is. His work should be hanging in a gallery, not chalked on the ground to be washed away by the rain.'

'I wouldn't take her sixpence, so she give me a box of chalks.'

'That's how we got to know each other. One day we went to the museum together in my dinner hour, to sketch the animals.'

'Some right funny looks we got there.' Peter returned the drawing to the shelf.

'Is that how you earn your living, as an artist?'

'I do what I can. Odd jobs in market. I was skinning skate yesterday. I shift bags of spuds, help some older ones set out stalls. There's nowt doing in the drawing line when the weather's bad. No-one stops to have their portrait done.'

Marian rose from the bed and went to a small brown suitcase in the corner of the room, opened it and took out a square silk scarf. 'You could do with a sling for that arm.' She tied the scarf into a sling and helped me put it on. 'What happened to you anyway?'

I realised I had been holding my arm. The bruise on my cheek was probably turning a fine shade. I did not want to talk about my misadventure in the library, but their eyes were on me with that now it's your turn to talk look.

'I was in the basement of the library looking for something that might bring me to you, Marian, since you'd left your lodgings. I tripped.' I could have told her the truth, but I did not want to go into long explanations. I was here to find out information, not to give it.

'You've come here from the library?' Marian asked.

'Yes.'

She looked suddenly worried.

Peter gulped. 'Might someone have followed you?'

'No. I'm sure not. I was sitting in the dispensary for long enough before I came here.'

'You should leave. Don't tell anyone where we are.'

'I won't. Promise. And if you want to go to Australia, well I have brothers there. I have two families, you see, and my natural family, one of the brothers went to work on a sheep farm. But I expect you'll want to be in a city, to be an artist, Peter.'

Marian shivered. She drew the blanket around her shoulders. 'Why would you help us?'

'You were unfairly treated. I can't bear that.'

I almost had their confidence, and then the door opened.

Mrs Donohue appeared, very pleased with herself, basket on her arm. 'I'll have to fry this liver on Mrs Wrigg's fire.' She put down the basket and picked up a black frying pan.

Peter said, 'She'll want a slice then.'

'I fetched her a duck egg, and one for you an' all, for your tea. Bring some fire kindling home.'

'Aye.' Peter picked up his cap. He looked at Marian. 'You all right if I go?'

'Yes.'

Mrs Donohue said, 'You'll earn no brass hanging round here.'

She dropped liver into the frying pan, with a knob of dripping, and went out, followed by Peter.

'Marian, how did you find yourself here?'

'Peter brought me. And neither of us feels safe.'

'Whatever happened, I know Mr Lennox is full of regrets.'

'I don't care what he is full of.'

'Tell me, what happened between you?'

She patted her belly. 'Doesn't take a genius.'

'When did it start? You began work at the library a little over a year ago.'

'Yes, and I saw straight away that he liked me, and I liked him, even though he was so much older. When his wife died before Christmas time, everyone was so sad for him. There was talk about not having a Christmas do, but he said we should have the usual fuddle at Powolny's, even though he was in mourning. He said life must go on. He sat beside me, and paid a lot of attention, but I never set my cap at him. If anyone says I did . . . '

'No one has said that.'

'She'll say it. Mrs Carmichael. Whenever there was something to be done after work, he would ask me, and I know that upset her. Nothing happened between us, but if our hands touched, he would blush, and so would I. For St

Valentine's day I sent him a card at work, and he knew it was from me. I meant it as a joke.' She pulled a face. 'I should have known better, should have thought about Bathsheba Everdene and Farmer Boldwood.'

'Don't make me laugh, Marian. It hurts my ribs.'

'Anyway, he had sent me a card, at my lodgings. Mrs Claughton teased me about it over breakfast, saying I had a secret admirer.

'I was in work that morning, a Saturday, and had cause to go in the basement for something. When I got there, Mr Lennox was already there and asked me what I had to do and said he would see to it. But I just stood there, not knowing whether to pass a remark about the Valentine cards.

'That was how it began between us, on St Valentine's Day in the basement of the library. Nothing much happened, but then it was out in the open between us. When we finished work, I shared my sandwich with him and we went to see a picture at the Coliseum, and we held hands.

'It was very hard to be at work after that, knowing we loved each other but could do nothing about it. At Easter he bought me chocolates. He said he could not ask me to marry him, it being so soon after his wife's death.

'In May, he asked me would I go with him to Whitby and I did. He bought me a locket and a ring which I wore in the hotel, and then afterwards on my locket chain.

'By then, Mrs Carmichael knew something was going on and was very jealous. She started to pick on me, and to say things about me, such as I was seen talking to a sailor, and then another time that I had picked up a man in the City Varieties bar, and it wasn't true. When she said she had seen me talking and laughing with a pavement artist, I said yes and what was so wrong with that. That was when he first lost trust in me, thinking I was anxious to find a proper sweetheart that I could walk out with in a regular way. I told him that wasn't true, but the damage was done and things were not the same. He believed her about the sailor, and some man in the Varieties. My condition was practically showing. She must have guessed, but he had not, and I had not told him. I was waiting for the right moment when he would stop believing Mrs Carmichael's stupid lies about me and see what she was up to.

'It was out of the blue when she accused me of stealing and produced a book that I was supposed to have put in my bag. That was 9 October, a Friday. He took Mrs Carmichael's part against me, saying why else would I have a book in my bag. Why else would the index cards be in the bin where I had been working? I went a bit mad because it was so wrong.

'All that weekend, I stayed in my room and cried and cried. Then I thought, why should he treat me this way? I must tell him that I am carrying his baby and then he will see sense. I waited for him after work, every night, telling him, but losing my temper and he said I was acting the mad woman, the complete mad woman, and I said that was better than being half mad, like him. I watched for him, Monday, Tuesday and Wednesday. He had to lock up, you see, so he could not avoid me. Each time he either tried to draw me away, where no one would see us, or he simply marched off.

'On Thursday, he wasn't there. I thought he must have gone away, that I had scared him away. And I was so tired because I pretended to come out to work each day, and I did not know how long my money would last and walked about the town and went to the museum, and tried to find some other job, any job.

'When I got back to my rooms, there was such a kind letter from him, saying he would make it up to me, and to come to the back of the library at six o'clock on Saturday morning, which was 17 October, that he had some time off and we would go away together for the weekend. He believed me. We would plan what to do, but I must tell no one, it would be our secret, and I must bring this letter, and pack a case, and leave a note for my landlady to say that I was leaving.'

The smell of liver drifted into the room. We would not have much longer before Mrs Donohue's return. 'What happened next, did he meet you?'

'I can't say, because it's not just my story from there. It is Peter's too. He won't want me to say. I just know he won't.'

'When does he finish work? I'll ask him myself.'

There were footsteps on the landing.

'If he earns a few coppers, we go to the Old Royal Oak. There's a good fire there so we make a drink last. Go there about seven o'clock. I'll tell him you're coming and I'll stay here, then his mam will stay with me.'

'Thanks for seeing to my arm.'

She smiled. 'Never mind that, just don't lose my scarf.'

Then it dawned on me. I could not walk into a strange pub on my own. She must know that. It was a ploy to be rid of me, or was it?

'Marian, have you ever walked into a pub on your own?'

'No.'

'And neither have I, and I can't can I?'

'I suppose not.'

'I'll be at the entrance to the alley at seven. Don't let him keep me waiting.'

When Mrs Donohue came in, bringing a pan of steaming liver, I began to feel weak from hunger. It was time for me to go. I would leave my car where it was, by the library, and catch the tram. This was not simply because I could not drive with one hand, but I felt anxious about going back there in case Mr Castle lay in wait.

Mrs Donohue put money on the table. 'Here's your change from the liver.'

'Keep it, please, for some coal.'

'Oh no,' Mrs Donohue said. 'We don't want charity.'

'You could give it back when your ship comes in, but I think Marian is owed it.'

Rain came down in sheets as I left Danby Court. It was difficult to know what was worse: the story Marian had told, or finding out that I was entirely wrong and that there was no connection between her and Sophia Wells. I had wanted to believe they were one and the same person, convinced myself of that, made the 'facts' fit. Now I was back at the beginning.

It was only five o'clock, but already dark. I glanced about, in the hope that Peter Donohue would suddenly appear and that I would not have to kick my heels between now and seven o'clock. There were people about, that was good. Yet I felt ill at ease. What if Castle, or Lennox, lurked somewhere watching me, suspecting that I knew too much, though precisely what I knew was not entirely clear to me.

Soaked, head spinning, hand swollen, arm throbbing, a satchel that could be snatched from me in an instant, it was madness to walk about like this. Even if I found some reasonable eating place, I would draw funny looks; something the cat left on the doorstep. I was shivering with cold. My feet were blocks of ice, my fingers icicles. Arrows of bitter wind pierced my lids and turned my mind numb. Nothing seemed real.

Go home, Kate, I told myself. Come back later. Avoid the library. If a monkey could hide unseen in the back of the vehicle, so might something, or someone, else, and driving with one arm in a sling was not a trick I felt like trying just now. I walked to the Corn Exchange, unsure which would be the best tram stop.

There was a long queue.

When someone touched my shoulder, I almost jumped out of my skin.

'You've been in the wars.' It was Sykes.

'Don't creep up on me like that!'

'I was watching to see whether anyone followed you. Your car or mine?'

'Don't ask hard questions.'

'Yours then. Don't want it left outside that library all night. Someone might get the wrong idea.'

'How did you know where to find me?'

'Chummy at the dispensary said you were there, and that he'd given you the Danby Court address. I thought about coming in, but you would have given me a rollicking.'

'It was delicate. I need to be back at Danby Court by seven o'clock, to meet Peter Donohue.'

'The wounded intruder?'

'He was looking for me and couldn't find the right house in the dark. The man is a talented artist, down on his luck. His portrait of Marian Montague is superb.'

'Go on, tell me. You're going to buy him a sketch pad, a set of crayons, perhaps some oil paints and canvases.'

'They want to go to Australia.'

'Well then, we can pay the fare to Australia. Our wonderful detective agency will go bankrupt and I'll be the one emigrating.'

We crossed the road. As we walked back towards the library, I gave him a potted version of the events of this afternoon.

'What did Inspector Wallis do when Castle attacked you?'

'He said it would be my word against his.'

'That doesn't answer my question. What did Wallis do?'

'He helped me upstairs, made me think . . . '

'What?'

'That he knew something. The police driver took me to the dispensary. Wallis said I should leave the investigation to him.'

'According to him, he already solved the crime, by charging Umberto Bruno, so he's talking about the assault on you. He must be.'

'I don't know what goes on in that man's head.'

'You could have gone to your own doctor with a sprained wrist. He packed you off in a police vehicle to the dispensary, a public place where you would be safe – for several hours, if you hadn't scarpered.'

We had reached my car. My head ached. Nothing made sense. Sykes had to help me into the car. As we set off, I thought I glimpsed the shadow of a figure behind the library gates.

Twenty-Seven

At the kitchen table, Mrs Sugden uncorked the iodine and dabbed my cheek. It stung.

Sykes soaked a bandage in cold water. 'So Marian Montague is not Sophia Wells and never has been.'

'Not even for a second.'

I was more than bitterly disappointed. I felt stupid at having convinced myself that they were one and the same person, yet also relieved that Lennox had not seduced his own daughter.

What would the odds have been against my finding Sophia Wells's father? Yet I had found him. No name, nothing to go on, and I stumbled on Lady Coulton's long-lost librarian lover, but not her daughter. That was a little bit of information I would keep to myself, not even Sykes needed to know.

Sykes put the bandage on the table for Mrs Sugden. 'You'll make a better fist of this.'

'That should see you right.' Mrs Sugden put the cork back in the iodine bottle. 'You'll find Sophia. You always find them. It's only a week yesterday since you took the train to London.'

I placed my arm on the table, for Mrs Sugden to begin her re-bandaging. 'By the time I find her daughter, it may be too late for Lady Coulton.'

Sykes gave a little sway, the prelude to one of his bad jokes, probably along the lines that at least I had been given a good retainer.

I glared at him. 'See if you can find me a sling in the first aid box. I'll wear my cape to cover it.'

Mrs Sugden paused in her bandaging. 'You're not going out again? If that lass in Danby Court isn't the one you're looking for, what else do you need to know?'

'I'm interested to find out why Marian has gone into hiding, in fear for her life. Oh and by the way, the chap you shot the other evening, he was her fiancé.'

'You want me to give you my notice over that pistol don't you?'

'After today, I have half a mind to borrow it.'

'You don't know how to use a gun.'

'It can't be that hard. Point it and pull the trigger. If you can shoot a chap in the leg, I'm sure I can.'

'But would you want to?' Sykes handed Mrs Sugden a safety pin for the bandage.

'If that pistol had been in my pocket this afternoon, Mr Castle would have been the one in need of bandaging.'

Sykes fished a large square of linen from the first aid box. 'How's this for a sling?'

There was a loud knock on the front door.

Mrs Sugden observed her handiwork, and was satisfied. 'Are we expecting anyone?'

'No.'

She marched to the door.

The voice was familiar. It was Inspector Wallis. 'Is Mrs Shackleton at home?'

'I'll just see.'

She came back into the kitchen. 'Are you at home to a plainclothes man who's carrying an ugly plant?'

'Show him into the drawing room.'

'Right you are.'

Sykes knotted the sling and helped me lift my arm into it. 'Will that do?'

'Yes. Thank you.'

He nodded in the direction of the drawing room. 'I'm not here?'

'You're not here.'

He straightened his tie. 'Should I be here?'

'Yes. You can give me a lift to town to meet Peter Donohue.'

I walked down the hall and into the drawing room.

The inspector was standing a little to one side of the fireplace. On the linoleum to the edge of the rug sat a brass plant pot containing a wilting evergreen.

He smiled. 'Excuse my dropping in, but I wanted to make sure you were all right.'

I returned his smile and gave a slight lift of my arm in the sling. It hurt. 'Do sit down.' I sat in the wing chair.

He took the seat opposite mine. 'You left the dispensary without being attended to. I sent the driver back for you.'

So he had been keeping track of me. 'It was such a long wait. I knew what to do myself, being a nurse.'

I glanced at the potted plant. We both did, for rather longer than strictly necessary. 'I hope you like it. It is a thank you for your help.'

'That was very thoughtful of you.' A smile hid my dismay, but I fear he heard it in my voice.

'I had it at home, and I know that you like rubber plants because you bid for one at that charity auction.'

'We both did, so you must like it yourself and I would hate to part you from it.'

'They collect dust. I only bid because I felt obliged to fork out for something. Oh, sorry, now I've put my foot in it. But you do like them?'

Either the man had no social skills whatsoever or he was being extremely rude. I gave him the benefit of the doubt. 'They are popular plants.'

He looked relieved, but uncertain.

'May I offer you something?'

'No, thank you. I won't stay more than a minute. I wanted to see how you are, and also to tell you that I looked into the people you thought to be missing, the library assistant Miss Montague, Miss Sophia Wells and her mother Mrs Bradshaw.'

I was suddenly aware of holding my breath. Had he succeeded where I failed?

'Regarding Marian Montague, Mr Lennox did offer to help her, but she refused. She is of age, and she vacated her lodgings of her own accord, leaving a note for the landlady.' His eyes searched my face, wondering whether I would admit to having visited the landlady myself. I did not, but waited. 'We will keep her name on record because it is possible that our so-called Father Bolingbroke had an accomplice in the library.' He fished in his pocket. 'As to the other persons, all I have is a former address on Compton Road for Mrs Bradshaw. I managed to squeeze it out of staff records at Barnbow.'

'Thank you.' He had learned less than I, or at least was deliberately giving that impression.

When he made a slight movement to go, I stood. 'Inspector, what did you mean earlier when you said I should leave the investigation to you? Is the murder investigation still open?'

'I assume you were in the basement because you thought there may be some other clue.'

'I was looking for any trace of Marian Montague. I found her comb, that's all.'

'Where?'

'In the desk drawer.'

'She did work down there.'

He had not answered my first question. I doubted he would answer another, but asked anyway. 'Why was Mr Castle so concerned about finding me in the basement, and about his magazine?'

'His story is that he felt bad about your having gone through such an ordeal on Friday, and that he came to look for you.'

'You don't believe that, do you?'

'If you want to press charges for assault, I will take the matter to my superiors, but I would have to take Mr Castle's version also. I don't know why he was so sensitive about the magazine.'

'So that's it?'

'Look, Mrs Shackleton, I admired you when we first met during that tragic Hotel Metropole business, when I stood aside for Scotland Yard, but to be honest I did not like you. I was mistaken. Now I like you. You were very plucky. I admire the way you stood up for the late Mr Bruno. I would hate to see you pursue an unpleasant court case. You must decide.' He smiled thinly. 'I have to go. Sorry.'

I walked him to the hall.

He played with the brim of his hat. 'Let me know if there's anything I can do for you in the future.'

'I will.'

When hell froze over.

He glanced at my arm, and opened the door. 'I see that you have your car back from outside the library.'

'Yes, a neighbour kindly came with me and we brought it back.'

'Good. I would hate to think of you driving with your arm in a sling.'

When he had gone, I went back into the drawing and looked through the window as his driver pulled away.

Something tugged at my skirt.

It was Percy. The monkey had been hiding behind the piano. He looked up, and with a forlorn gaze shook his head.

'So you don't trust him, Percy. You are probably right.'

We were sitting in a corner of the snug at the Palace. Peter Donohue held tight to a pint of bitter. 'I picked this pub cos I'm not a reg'lar. If we keep us heads down, no one'll bother us.'

I sipped at a brandy to thaw my blood. Sykes would be nearby, in the tap room or the lounge bar, keeping his eye on the door of the snug. The snug was soporifically warm from a blazing fire. In the corner to our left, three old women in turbans leaned forward in the comfortably upholstered seats and chatted companionably, laughing every few minutes. Opposite them, a couple of old men played dominoes at a table, contemplating the game with the seriousness of generals forming a battle plan. I understood now why people left their cold, damp rooms for a spot like this.

I had slipped Peter five bob to pay for drinks and cigarettes. The Donohues and Marian would probably talk about me. Thinks she can buy us, Mrs Moneybags.

He seemed reluctant to talk, glancing about, nervously failing to light his cigarette and then trying again.

I told him tales of the Australian outback, mainly drawn from my reading of magazine articles. Although it was true that I had a brother in Australia, we had never met. He was already there when my birth sister sought me out to help in an investigation. But I had helped, and she would tell him to do the same for me, of that I felt sure.

He blew a smoke ring. 'You think emigrating to Australia is a good plan then?'

'I do. That or Canada, which isn't so far away. My twin brothers from my adoptive family are in Canada, Eric and Dennis. I know they'd help you to a good start if I gave you a letter for them.' I thought it best not to mention that Eric works with the Canadian mounted police.

'I've a bit of brass tucked away. Things have never been as right in some ways, but it could all go wrong.'

'I understand how you and Marian became friends, but what I don't grasp is why she is so anxious, and in hiding.' Her tale of Lennox wanting here dead seemed preposterous.

'Something bad happened.'

'Peter, you have to tell me everything. If you don't, what happened to Marian could happen to someone else.'

'I could get done for what I didn't do. Who would believe me?'

'I believe you. That's enough for now.'

'You could tell just one other person and that'd be that.'

'Trust me. I know it's connected with a letter sent to her by Sam Lennox, the librarian.'

'I know nothing about him. He's just a miserable streak of whitewash who took advantage of Marian. It's his black shadow that scares me.'

Something in his words made me think back to the evening we found Dr Potter's body. Lennox's first thought was that he must contact Mr Castle. The image came back to me of the two of them. I had watched through the window as they left the library together on Friday night, leaning towards each other, disappearing into the fog.

I touched my sling, and my iodine-daubed cheek which had come out in a bruise. 'Shall I tell you who did this?'

'Somebody knocked you about?'

'Not in a way I could prove. He said it was an accident, that I tripped in the library, in the basement.'

His face, which until then had been mobile and expressive, turned to stone. He nodded slowly. 'I know who it was.'

'Peter, talk to me.'

'I'll get us another drink.'

'All right.'

I was reluctant to let him go, in case he disappeared, but he gave a nod to the waiter who had brought drinks to the domino players. The waiter came over and took the order.

Still he did not speak. Taking a single cigarette from a packet, he put it behind his ear and then slit the packet open and began to draw with a stubby pencil. The lines came swiftly, the shape of the face, the dark hair, the moustache.

It was Edwin Castle to the life, but with an evil cast that must have been in his face all along. I had never observed it until now.

He pushed the picture towards me. 'Is that him?'

'That's him, but how do you come to know him?'

He put the picture back in his pocket, as if it might prove dangerous. 'He was a school visitor when I was in infants' class at ragged school, and all the way through to top form. Every now and then he come in to tell us how we could do well in life. In the yard at playtime, he'd throw spice up in air for us to catch, toffees, pear drops, liquorice. Other times he chucked money. One day I caught two halfpennies at once. He ruffled my hair. "When you grow up, you can be my rent collector." That's what he said.'

Peter moved his fingers nervously on the table top before taking another drink. 'I'd see him about the town. He'd give me summat for running an errand to the cigar shop on Boar Lane. When I started boxing, he come to see me fight. When I did big bouts he bet on me and give me a share of winnings.'

Until he paused, I kept my eyes on Peter, and then glanced beyond him in the direction of the old women in the corner, in case my gaze made him uncomfortable.

'There was nowt doing, no jobs, so I nearly signed on for army. Castle said, "Don't do that, you won't like it." He sent me to see a man in Thrift warehouse who give me a job. One day he called in to see how I was doing, asked did I want to earn a bit extra cash. Well who would say no to that?'

'What did he want you to do?'

'Someone owed him money. I had to scare that person, make an example.'

The waiter brought our drinks. Peter paid him, and must have given a bit extra because he received a hearty, 'Thanks, pal.'

'And did you,' I asked. 'Did you scare someone for him?'

'I wished I hadn't. I didn't like doing it but he made me know that I could wave goodbye to my job at Thrift if I didn't do it. Counting all together I did that kind of job for him a few times, five I think. Next time he asked me to do summat, I refused.' He stared into the beer, picked up the glass and took a drink, leaving a froth of foam on his top lip. He wiped his lips with the back of his hand. 'I was laid off early this year. Mr Castle said there would be summat for me and when he saw me allus give me a few bob, sometimes ten bob, for doing nowt. Funny thing is, I think he forgot about me unless he saw me. So I'd want to be in his way, so he'd give me a few bob, but I wouldn't want to be in his way because . . . Well, you see why.'

'Yes.'

'One day when he saw me, things was right bad. We owed rent, couldn't get owt on tick. We'd have to flit but where to, how? Mam had slipped and hurt her ankle. It swelled and she was slow and let go from her cleaning job, told to come back when she was better. When she went back, job was filled. Mr Castle spotted me picking tab ends from gutter. Funny thing is that time, I think he'd come looking for me. He said come and see him and told me where to meet him, in back alley behind Mitre that night.'

He was taking a long time to reach the point of his story. The Mitre was the closest pub to the library. The alley must be Change Alley.

'I met him. He told me he had one last job for me and

then would fix up for me and Mam to go to London where he knew someone would provide live-in accommodation and work. I felt right glad, asked what was the to do.'

Peter's leg was moving now, up and down quickly, as though he had no control over it.

'He said there was a bad lot, a whore, trying to destroy a good man. All I had to do was put an end to trouble she caused. I knew what he wanted but played daft, saying how was I to do that. He said, put an end to her. I knew I wouldn't do it. Whore or not, I wasn't gonna do nothing to a woman, never mind murder. But we needed money, so I egged him on, said I would. I asked for summat now, to be going on with, meaning to get clear. He give fifty quid. I knew then that I'd have to go careful, because he might have someone onto me if I let him down. He reckoned no one would miss her, no one would know, that I'd see her in that back alley on Saturday morning at six o'clock. The door below the steps would be unlocked. He took me down there, showed me where I was to bury the body and where the pick and shovel was. Promised another fifty quid when job was done.'

I had meant to stay quiet but I couldn't help the words of shock. Now I understood why Marian was so scared, and Peter too.

'He told me to cut off her hair, as proof that I'd done her in, and to take the locket and ring from her throat. When I'd given him her lovely hair, the locket and the ring and the letter she would have "about her person" then he would pay me. I asked how would I know who she was? He said how many whores did I think would be in the alley on Saturday morning and she would be there and that would be the one. But once I duffed up the wrong man for him so I insisted I wanted to know, kidding on that I was right serious about it. I told him, I said, there's whores in every alley. Who's to say there won't be one at each end?

'He said, "She looks respectable, and pretty but don't let that fool you. She has reddish hair and is on the tall side. If you walk along Commercial Street tonight at six o'clock, you will likely see her standing in the library doorway, making a nuisance of herself, wearing a bottle-green coat."'

I stared at him. 'Marian? He wanted you to kill Marian?'

He nodded. 'I knew then that he was talking about Marian. He didn't know that her and me was kind of friends on account of the drawing. That I liked her, that she'd been decent to me. At just before six, I walked along that street. I saw her in library doorway. When I got to top of street, I turned round and watched her walk across to shops and look up. I suppose she saw there was no lights on, and then she went home, walked back to her digs. I followed her. I telled her.'

'She must have been horrified.'

'Not at first. She didn't believe me at first, said it was impossible. "Look at this then." I showed her the money, and I described him. She still didn't believe me, and went inside and slammed door. I hung about on her street. She came out a bit later, with a letter in her hand, saying, "Sam Lennox has asked me to meet him in the alley at six o'clock on Saturday morning," and she was crying. I said I would come for her at four o'clock that morning and I did and took her to be with my mam where she would be safe. And it was my mam who helped cut her hair, and cried as she did it, because her hair was beautiful. We told Mam that somebody would pay for it, and I would deliver. That's all Mam knows, and now you know the truth.'

His story seemed impossible to believe. All the more reason it would not have been invented.

'How did you know Castle wouldn't be watching you?'

'Are you kidding? He keeps his distance. But I took summat to bury, just in case.'

'What?'

'A Guy Fawkes in a sack. I was right worried that some copper would see me carrying a sack through town. But I know the coppers' beat times, and so did he. That cellar door back of library was unlocked, just like he told me.'

'He lives in Meanwood, that's miles away.'

'He sometimes stays in that club on the street behind.'

'The Leeds Club, on Albion Place?'

'That's it.' He lit another cigarette. 'Next time I seen the evil one, I give him Marian's hair, that he'd wanted as proof I'd done the dirty deed, and her locket, and her ring, and the letter that she had in her pocket. He asked about her suitcase. I told him that I put bricks in it and slung it in river. And he said, "Good man," and give me fifty quid.'

'We should go to the police.'

'No! That hundred quid'll take us far from here. I wanted to go straight away but Marian was sick and me Mam wasn't well.'

'You haven't done anything wrong. I think we might get a fair hearing from the police.'

'They wouldn't collar him, it'd be me. I told you cos Marian trusts you.'

'How can we stop Castle, if you won't speak out?'

'Let someone else speak out. I told you cos you said you'd help us.'

'If I type up what you've told me, will you sign it?'

'No.'

'Are you safe where you are?'

'Oh I'm safe. Nobody comes in Danby Court that doesn't belong there.'

'I did.'

'And everyone knew it.'

'The money Castle gave you, was it in coins or notes?'

'Some of each.'

'Were they new notes?'

'Some.'

'They could be traced.'

'Don't get me in bother. Don't do nowt till we've left country.'

'If I could get us into the library, would you show me exactly where you buried the Guy Fawkes?'

'I'm not off in there again.' He took the cigarette packet from his pocket and began to sketch. 'There's alley door. Them's steps. At bottom of steps, three paces along, a big bookshelf, behind that flagstones, in shadow. The evil one put a cross on the flag with chalk, so I'd know.'

How close had I been to that flagstone today, I wondered. There were brush marks, where someone had swept; perhaps to erase the tell-tale chalk mark.

We said nothing else. He downed his pint. I finished my brandy.

When we left the pub, fog had begun to roll in from south of the river.

'I'll walk you up home, Mrs Shackleton. I know where it is now.'

'No. Just see me onto the tram.'

'You sure?'

'Yes, and thank you. You were brave to tell me. I won't let you down.'

As we waited in the cold for the tram to rumble into view, a Jowett pulled in across the road. Good old Sykes. He would follow the tram.

I rode for just one stop, and then rose from my seat.

The conductor rang the bell. 'You been in the wars, love.'

'Just a skirmish.' Gingerly, holding onto the rail like an old lady, I stepped carefully from the tram.

Sykes was waiting. He climbed out of the car to help me and my sling into the passenger seat.

'Home to rest your arm?'

'Not yet. There's someone I want to see first.'

Twenty-Eight

Sykes stopped the motor in Sheepscar and listened as I gave Peter's account of being paid to murder Marian.

'It beggars belief.'

'I know.'

'For what possible reason? It's out of all proportion. Men have dropped young women in trouble since time immemorial, but murder?'

'I don't understand it either.'

'Will you go to Inspector Wallis?'

'Absolutely not. Peter and Marian trust me. There must be another way.'

'I can't think what.'

'Lennox is the weak link.'

'The librarian?'

'Yes. He can't have known what Castle planned. But if Castle told him yesterday, and now Lennox is implicated, that would explain his total change of manner between our talk in the park and yesterday at the meeting, when he was so subdued.'

'Subdued? The man should be flattened.'

'If he knows what Castle planned, and what he thinks he has done, let Lennox be the one to go to the police.'

'What do you intend to do?'

'Confront him.'

'Then I'm coming with you. You're assuming he was not in on the planned murder, but you don't know that.'

'By the lake, when we talked about Marian, and he realised she was no thief, he wallowed in self-pity about his "mistake". He wanted to make amends. I would have sworn he meant it. At the library meeting, he had completely changed, almost a different person, a man in a daze. I don't believe he knew that Marian was supposedly dead and buried, not until Castle told him, just before that meeting.'

'Surely Lennox must have known. Why would Castle have taken it upon himself to have Marian murdered?'

'He called her the whore of Babylon. The man has a warped mind.'

'Even if you are right, and Lennox didn't know until yesterday, or today, do you really think he will tell all, just because we turn up on his doorstep unexpectedly?'

For a moment, neither of us spoke.

'Sleep on it, Mrs Shackleton. This isn't the right thing to do.'

'Mr Sykes, it is the only thing to do. Lennox is not going to murder me, is he?'

'Am I expected to answer that?'

'Let's go. It's late. I don't want to drag him from his bed.'

Sykes started the engine. 'This is a bad idea.'

'Grange Villas, up Chapeltown Road, and I must go in on my own, and take him by surprise.'

'I should think you will, arriving at this time of night.'

303

'It's not nine o'clock yet.'

'Oh well, that's all right then.'

It did not take long to reach our destination.

Sykes said, 'What if your nemesis, Castle, is with him, or the inspector?'

'We would see the car.'

'And someone will see ours. I'll find a quiet spot to park.'

He turned right and right again, into a street with few houses and high walls.

'Come on then, wounded soldier, I'll walk you round.'

'No need.'

'I hate to tell you this, but under that cape, your arm in a sling looks exactly like an arm in a sling.' He took my other arm. 'I'll walk you to the gate.'

'All right, but then make yourself scarce.'

'Which is his flat, in case I need to come to the rescue?'

'It's the ground floor, but don't barge in. I'll be all right.'

The broad gate stood open. I had a feeling that Sykes would not stray far.

I walked to the main door. Surprised to find it slightly ajar, I stepped inside.

The shared entry was well kept, with a gleaming black and white tiled floor. The balustrade and banisters shone and a scent of lavender polish permeated the dark hall. An occasional table held a plant. I could just make out the shape of a telephone on the wall.

Mr Lennox's door stood open.

I stepped into the room, where only a low fire in the grate gave off a glimmer of light. 'Mr Lennox!'

There was no answer. I felt for the electric switch by the door.

At first I could not find it, but tried again, slowly sliding my hand from the door jamb until I felt the ribbed brass protrusion, and flicked the switch.

The sight made me gasp. I must have seen him straight away but my eyes refused to acknowledge the body. Instead, I stared around the room, my back to the wall, fearing someone might jump out on me.

Drawers had been pulled out, cupboards thrown open, papers and books were strewn about the floor. Finally, I allowed my eyes to rest on the figure sprawled face down on the hearth rug, one leg at a peculiar angle, as if about to mount a bicycle. Lennox's arms were raised, as though in an instinctive reaction to break a fall. The back of his head was smashed. Blood seeped onto the collar of his dressing gown. Something pink lay on the hearth rug. Bloody brains. Near him was a heavy brass poker. As if to add to the horror of the sight, a coal split and gave off a sudden blaze. Already, a faintly unpleasant smell filled the room.

How long I would have remained, staring, I do not know. Rooted to the spot, I looked all around the room. Was that a movement behind the curtain? I stared at the piano. Was someone crouched there?

A sound snapped me into life: the front door closed.

A voice said, 'Mr Lennox! You'll let all heat out of the place.'

My reaction was instant. I crossed the room, hurrying into the kitchen. There, I leaned against the wall and held my breath.

The voice came closer. 'Were you born in a field to leave the door . . . Oh, my God!'

There was a long silence, and then the heavy breathing of

panic. Footsteps retreated into the hall. I heard the telephone receiver being lifted.

In the gloom, I could make out the back door. Blindly I walked towards it, praying no fiend lurked in the shadows, and that the back door would be open. It was locked. I felt for the knob, and the key. Turning the key, I let myself out.

There was nothing I could do here, except tell the same story as the neighbour, and in doing so complicate the police investigation and delay my own.

Seeing no way out from the back of the house, save a high wall that I was not tempted to climb, I hurried round to the front, hoping the neighbour would be too concerned about being put through to the police and would not see me. He had closed the outer door.

There was no sign of Sykes.

I walked back the way we had come, trying to keep a measured stride, fighting the urge to run, run far away from the horror.

As I turned the corner, I heard footsteps behind me; recognisable footsteps. When Sykes makes haste, he does so by taking long strides so that he appears to be in no hurry at all.

'You came out of there like a bat out of hell.'

'Let's just go.'

Without another word we strode to the car, Sykes gripping my good arm through the cape. I tried not to shake, but it is not something easily brought under control.

Not until we were in the car and had driven about a mile did Sykes pull in by the side of the road.

'What's wrong?'

'He's dead.' I described the scene. 'A neighbour saw him moments after I did. He was calling the police.'

'Why did you leave?'

'It did not need two people to report the death. We have work to do, Mr Sykes.'

'Could it be a burglary gone wrong?'

'No. A burglar would look in the places people hide money, jars, vases. The vase on top of the piano was untouched, and so were the jars on the mantelpiece.'

'Perhaps he was disturbed.'

'Then he would have run away, as I did, not smashed in Lennox's head with a poker.' Sykes let out a loud breath. 'And don't say I should tell Inspector Wallis. I have no great faith in Wallis's crime solving abilities.'

'Leeds Police will call in Scotland Yard on this one.'

'Not if it's up to Wallis. He has a high opinion of himself. Either that or . . . '

'What?'

' . . . he is prepared to cover up for people in high places. This is all connected, and no one wants to see the connections.'

'We don't know that. Just because he has not confided in you, doesn't mean he isn't doing his job. A police inspector won't share information with a private detective.'

'I don't trust him. Go see my father. Tell him what happened to Dr Potter, and about Marian disappearing. I can't give Peter Donohue away, but Marian might be brave enough to say her life was threatened.'

'Your father won't intervene. There's no love lost between Leeds City Police and the West Riding Constabulary.'

'He'll think of something. The two chief constables met

at a garden party. Their wives are friends with my mother. There'll be ways and means.'

'Then you go. He's your dad.'

'Go to see them, looking like this?'

'I don't know what to say.'

Sykes drove us back in silence.

He opened the gate for me.

I stepped inside. '*Will* you go to Wakefield? Talk it over with my dad.'

'All right. If that's what you want.'

'I can't think of a better idea.'

He walked me up the path to the door. Percy was watching from behind the curtain. I put my hand in my pocket for the door key, and there was the address that Mrs Carmichael had given me. *18 Dorset Avenue, downstairs front room.*

I turned the key in the lock and went inside. From the window, I watched Sykes go. Mrs Sugden had not heard me come in, so my only explanation was to Percy.

'I'm going out again, Percy. Amuse yourself on the banister, or go back to sleep.'

The monkey, most disconcertingly, gave me a look teeming with reproach.

Doing a little manoeuvre with my left arm, I realised that I should easily be able to hold the steering wheel steady with that hand, and steer the car with the other.

I had been to Mrs Carmichael's house once before, in the spring when she was ill and Miss Heaton had taken a collection for flowers. We had driven over to deliver them. Now I realised that Mrs Carmichael's illness must have

308

coincided with the trip that Sam Lennox and Marian Montague took to Whitby.

Dorset Avenue is a hill, and the house was about halfway up. The high privet hedge was neatly trimmed, as I remembered.

Driving had not been too difficult, but climbing from the car I made an awkward movement and sent shooting pains up my arm.

I clicked open the cast iron gate and climbed the steep steps to the front door.

Not wanting to disturb the whole house, I tapped on the bay window, where a light glowed. The curtain moved. Mrs Carmichael's face appeared. She stared at me, taking a while to puzzle out who had called. I had a sudden image of her thrusting her address into the pocket of every person she met. The curtain fell. A moment later, the key turned and the door opened.

'Mrs Shackleton, do come in.'

'I'm sorry to call so late.'

She opened the door wider. I stepped inside and waited until she had locked it behind me. At the far end of the hall there was a sound. Mrs Carmichael called, 'It's all right. It's for me.'

A brief smile lit her sad face. I guessed she did not receive many callers and this would intrigue her landlady.

She had covered her work clothes with a cotton robe. 'Come through. This is my room, and I'm a bit all over the place.' She picked up a newspaper from the chair and tossed it onto the table under the window.

There was a bed by the wall opposite the window. At its foot was a single wardrobe that looked as if the door would not have enough space to open fully. A rocking chair stood by the fireplace where a fire burned, comprising a coal brick and three cobs. On the chair lay knitting needles and a partially done cable stitch cardigan.

'Sit down.' She moved her knitting to the table, beside a half-finished jigsaw puzzle and a book.

'Can I get you a drink?'

'I wouldn't mind an aspirin and a glass of water, please.'

'Of course.'

She disappeared from the room.

I stared into the fire. The image of Lennox came back to me, his head so close to the fender, the smell, and the mess in the room. Now here I was with a woman who had loved him, still did for all I knew, and I could not tell her what had happened.

Lennox's death was the kind of deed Peter might be blamed for. Castle was behind it, I felt sure, but that would not be up to me. None of this should concern me. But it did. Dr Potter, Umberto Bruno, and now Lennox. Who would be next?

Mrs Carmichael returned with a bottle of aspirin and a glass of water. It was a pretty glass, delicately engraved with flowers and leaves; a best glass.

I took a couple of aspirin. 'Thank you.'

'It's no trouble. My landlady is very obliging. We keep up the pretence that I am a cousin on her mother's side. This is a very respectable area. She does not want to be regarded by her neighbours as a person who takes in a lodger.' She picked up the poker. My hand shook. Hell hath no fury like a woman scorned. I watched her as she split the coal brick down the centre. 'That's better, bit more warmth.'

'Yes.' I now felt hot and loosened my cape with my good hand. 'Have you been out this evening?'

'No, just doing my knitting and pottering about. Let me help you.' She took the cape and hung it on a hook at the back of the door. 'It's nice to have someone else sit in this room for once.'

She seemed so different here, in this small space, with her knitting, her reading and her jigsaw puzzle. I waited for her to speak.

She took the glass from me. 'What happened in the basement today? You looked terrible when you came back upstairs with the inspector and Mr Castle behind you.'

'The story is that I tripped. I will stick to that for now.'

'Castle.'

'Has he ever done anything like this to you?'

'Not to me, no.'

'To others?'

She looked at me steadily before replying. 'I believe he has, though I would not be able to prove it. I shouldn't have asked you to come here. You don't look well, but I had a feeling that you wanted to know something, and I wondered whether I might help.'

'I am not having much luck, to be frank.'

'I am guessing you were looking for some trace of Marian Montague.'

'I was but I am not now. I mistakenly thought she was the person I have advertised for, Miss Sophia Mary Ann Wells. I know the name is different but I had reasons for assuming the two might be one and the same. Miss Wells also works in a library, though I do not know which.'

'Where did you look for Miss Wells?'

'My assistant has checked the central library and they have no knowledge of her there, or at any of the branches. Her mother worked at Barnbow but has moved from her previous address. There is a register of city authority employees that Mr Sykes managed to see, but she was not on it.'

'Does she have a library qualification?'

'I don't know. She has a school leaving certificate.'

'Come into the library in the morning. I'll make some telephone calls. One becomes acquainted with a world of people over thirty years, and there is a certain fellow feeling. Library staff may be unwilling to give information to an outsider, but I am well known, and well thought of.' She spoke rather defensively.

'I am sure you are. I did not know it was so long.'

'I was twenty when I started at the library, long before Mr Lennox came.'

As she spoke his name, once more that dreadful image of Lennox played itself before my eyes. But her words gave me an opening. 'Something puzzled me today, at the meeting. Mr Lennox had previously been so enthusiastic for the library to move premises, and also – I'm sorry to say this if it pains you – hoping to make up to Marian Montague for dismissing her unfairly. Yet today, he seemed like a beaten man. What changed?'

She leaned forward a little and folded her arms across her chest. 'I and the staff never had a fixed view about the library's future. We left that to Mr Lennox, as librarian. I don't know why or how he changed, only that he and Mr Castle had been ensconced in the office before the meeting.'

So I was right. Castle had told Lennox about the body in

the basement, but why? If it were for the purpose of changing Lennox's mind about removing from the premises, it had worked. New owners would have made alterations for the menagerie in the basement. The body would be found. I could think of only one reason why Castle had ordered Marian's death, and it was not to protect Lennox from the clutches of a whore. He was covering some crime of his own.

Mrs Carmichael waited for me to speak. She hugged her legs and rocked a little back and forth.

I did not know what to say. Was it my imagination, or had she spoken Castle's name with loathing?

Suddenly she sat up straight, as if she had made up her mind about something. 'Mrs Shackleton, why did you tell Mr Castle about that old magazine? He did not know it was in the library.'

'He asked me what Dr Potter said to me on the day he died, and what he gave me. Once he knew, he seemed anxious to have the magazine.'

'And did Dr Potter say anything of importance to you?'

'No. I wish he had. It was only about articles he had written, concerning the haunting, and a story of embezzlement.'

There was a tap on the door.

Mrs Carmichael opened it and took a cup from her landlady. 'Do you think we might run to a second cup, Mrs Harrison? My friend from the library has called to bring me a particular book.'

I exchanged how do you dos with the landlady who agreed on a second cup of cocoa, but regretted that there was only one biscuit.

Mrs Carmichael gave me her cup. 'I think this is the kind

of cocoa prisoners drink. Perhaps Father Bolingbroke is enjoying his at this very moment.'

'I'm sure it will be lights out in the prison by now.'

She watched me take a sip of cocoa. 'You found out who was stealing books. Who do you think killed Dr Potter? The library is beginning to feel rather dangerous.'

So that was why she had asked me here.

'I don't know.'

'But you have a suspicion?'

'Yes.'

'Will you say?'

'I'm sorry. It would be wrong to voice a suspicion.'

'I also have a suspicion.'

'Can you tell me?'

She shook her head. 'You won't, and so I won't. I only wish I could feel confident about Inspector Wallis.'

That made two of us.

I drank my cocoa, feeling we had disappointed each other. She wanted information I could not give. In turn, she was withholding something, but what?

When she walked with me to the front door, she seemed a little agitated. 'Be very careful, Mrs Shackleton.' She spoke as if genuinely concerned for my safety.

To make light of how I felt, I tapped my satchel and made a joke. 'Don't worry about me. I am carrying a pistol.'

She did not smile. 'Then you should have it in your pocket.'

I was not carrying a pistol, but suddenly that seemed a very good idea.

Twenty-Nine

I had slept badly, dreaming a grinning Lennox into ghastly life. With that terrible dream logic, I knew that his eyes held the image of his murderer. He was edging towards me, willing me to look into his eyes. His lips moved but I could not make out words. He was asking questions, and then telling me something. I woke feeling a cold terror and hearing a voice say, Men can breathe, eyes can see, life to thee.

It left me cold and too scared to close my eyes again. I swung out of bed.

Drawing back the curtains revealed the most glorious dawn, orange and blue and gold. The trees in Batswing Wood were not yet bare. Among the gold, yellow and brown, a few green leaves refused to die. It takes such a long time for the leaves to turn, and to fall. If I do not look every day, it can happen suddenly, and catch me out. Occasionally, there will be a fierce wind in the night and in the morning all is changed.

As soon as I had washed and dressed, not an easy business with a sprained wrist, I went into the dining room as quietly as possible, so as not to wake the monkey.

While pretending to find each animal a terrible nuisance and the pair of them a double nuisance, Mrs Sugden has given each of them a bed. The cat has a pair of old curtains in a corner by the kitchen dresser. The dining room, which doubles as my study, is now the monkey's quarters. My typewriter sits on the sideboard. In its place on top of the filing cabinet is a plywood orange box, acquired from the greengrocer. This holds a feather pillow as mattress and a blanket artistically knitted with a diamond design from scraps of brown and green wool.

Percy opened an eye, looked at me, and went back to sleep.

I reached for a pad of paper and pencil and began to jot down what Marian and Peter had each told me the evening before.

After about half an hour, Mrs Sugden appeared, still in her dressing gown. 'What are you doing up this early?'

'Just in time, Mrs Sugden. I'd like you to type something.'

She stood up straight, pulling her shoulders back, trying not to smile. 'I'll have to put kettle on first.' Mrs Sugden loves to type, having mastered the qwerty keyboard at night school. 'And I'll boil you an egg.'

'I'm not hungry.'

'Aye well you didn't eat last night and you'll likely end up chasing shadows through a long day so I'll do an egg.'

This was her olive branch regarding the gun. Normally she would have presented me with a bowl of lumpy porridge.

Percy followed her. When Mrs Sugden first accidentally let him into the back garden, with Sookie, I thought we would not see him again. But he explored a little, wearing his woolly of course, came back and pushed his way in.

Whenever he comes back, Mrs Sugden says, 'Couldn't

you have lost yerself in't jungle? Do you have to come plagu-
ing me?' Or she will open the door and shout, 'Percy! Have
yer swung yer way back to Mexico?' which is her way of
calling him in.

After I had eaten the compulsory egg, Mrs Sugden set up
the typewriter, double checking that she had the carbon
paper the correct way round.

'Fire away. I'm ready.'

Looking at my notes, trying as far as possible to use
Marian's way of speaking, I dictated her statement. Mrs
Sugden typed carefully, occasionally cursing a typing error
and insisting on erasing and back-spacing to retype. She
made no comments until both statements were finished.

'These two could write a book.'

'She could, and he could illustrate, being an artist. Do you
know, I might mention that to them as a way of earning a
living.'

'There are worse ways,' she said pointedly. 'Were you
serious about wanting my pistol?'

I thought for a moment; Dr Potter strangled; Lennox battered to death; Marian in fear for her life; my close encounter
with Castle in the basement.

'I'll take the gun, just in case.'

What puzzled me was that I had not yet heard from my
father. It worried me to think what I might have set in train
by asking Sykes to tell him about the events of the last few
days.

I was putting on my coat when Sykes came to the door.
'Before you ask, I didn't go to Wakefield. I set off to tell your
father, as you'd said, but I thought better of it before I'd gone
a mile and a half.'

'Well I'm relieved. It wasn't one of my better ideas.'

'So what now?'

'You could give me a lift into town. Mrs Carmichael, the deputy librarian, has offered to help us find Sophia Wells. She'll use her contacts in other libraries, make some enquiries.'

Sykes looked at his watch. 'Library won't be open yet.'

'I know. That's not my first port of call.'

Peter Donohue, carrying a small parcel, crossed the road from the market as Sykes parked the car. I followed him into the courtyard.

'Peter!'

He turned and waited until I caught up with him. 'What are you doing here? You'll be moving in next.'

'I've brought notes from my own bank, to exchange for the ones Castle gave you. I hope they'll be traceable to his bank. And I have a suggestion, an idea.'

We walked up the stone steps. 'Mam's out. She's filling in for a cleaner who's badly.' At the door, he called, 'It's me!'

'Hang on a minute.' The bolt shot back.

'Morning, Marian.' I stepped inside. There was a book about Australia open on the table.

Peter said, 'I brought you some tripe, Marian. I'm off back over to market shortly, bit of unloading.' There was just one chair and a stool. Peter perched on the corner of the table. 'Mrs Shackleton wants me to swap that money Castle give me, but my fingerprints will be on it.'

'Do the police have your fingerprints?' I asked.

'No.'

'Then don't worry.'

We exchanged bank notes. I put his in an envelope.

Marian watched, saying nothing as I tucked the envelope in the side compartment of my satchel. 'There's something else.'

'I thought there might be,' Marian said.

'I typed up what you told me.' I took the statements from my bag and put them on the table.

Peter rolled a cigarette, looking down at the typed pages. 'You said in confidence.'

Marian drew a sheet towards her. 'You did that, with one hand?'

'I was up early.' I waited until she had finished reading. 'It's the gist of what you told me. I'm hoping you'll agree to sign, so that we can have Castle put where he belongs.'

She ran her fingers through her shorn hair. 'His word against ours?'

'Somewhere, he has your hair, your locket, your ring. There's a Guy Fawkes buried in the basement. This won't be his only crime. Other things will come to light.'

Peter shook his head. 'Oh no. You don't catch me out like that. I'm not putting my name to owt. You said you'd keep me out of it. I don't trust coppers.'

Marian backed him up. 'Why should Peter put himself in harm's way? Lennox and Castle have the world behind them. We have no one but you, and you promised.'

'The police won't be interested in misdemeanours from the past, Peter. If you read it, you'll see I've chosen words carefully, knowing what to leave out, but including how Castle homed in on you from childhood.'

'He did. I never thought of it like that. He picked me out for his own purpose.'

'I can arrange for you both to stay somewhere out of harm's way, until the baby is born. My sister would take you in, or I have the use of a house in Robin Hood's Bay.'

Peter shook his head. 'Nothing doing.'

'What about you, Marian?'

'Yes I will, but that's different. You're asking Peter to take a big risk.'

I handed Marian a pen. She hesitated. 'And if they want me to go in and verify what I have said, someone will follow me back here and arrest Peter.'

'I will give it to the police only if I'm sure you'll both be safe.'

Marian's hand hovered above the page.

Peter said, 'Oh just do it.'

We watched her sign. 'I'd like to see their faces when Castle and Lennox find out I'm alive.'

Peter reached for his own statement and glanced at it. 'Marian's signed and so will I. I'll take my chance. You and Mam will be safe, Marian. That's what matters.'

'Thank you.' I spoke quietly, hiding my sudden misgivings. 'I'll stand by you. You can rely on that.'

'Where are you going now?' Marian asked.

'The library. I'm hoping to have some help tracing the person I'm really looking for.'

'Is she coming into money?'

'Possibly.'

'Then I wish it were me.'

Mrs Carmichael sat in Mr Lennox's chair. 'It's unusual for him to be late, but I've taken advantage and made some telephone calls for you. I've already tried Leeds and you were right. No Miss Wells in any of the Leeds libraries, and not in York or Wakefield either.'

It felt strange, sitting opposite her, knowing that none of us would ever see Lennox again.

She consulted her address book and then looked up. 'You must have awful aches and pains after yesterday. You look a bit peaky.'

'I'll survive, didn't sleep very well, that's all.'

She gave the operator the number of Harrogate Library. After a moment, she put on her telephone voice. 'Hello. Mrs Carmichael here of the Leeds Library. I wonder if you might help me.' After a moment she continued, 'We have a post available for a counter assistant and there was a young woman on our shortlist from a while ago whom I should like to contact but someone said she has found a post, perhaps in one of the Harrogate libraries. If so, I could cross her off our list. I wonder whether you might confirm that? Her name is Miss Sophia Mary Ann Wells.' Another pause. 'Thank you.' She put her hand over the mouthpiece. 'If she's in Yorkshire, I'll find her for you.' She spoke again into the telephone. 'Then I wait to hear. Goodbye.'

'They'll telephone back to you?'

'Yes.'

I waited and listened while she made calls to Bradford and Keighley, sounding cheerful and efficient. It would not be long before she heard the terrible news about Lennox.

She closed her address book. 'That is four I am waiting to hear from. I won't telephone to more until they give word.' There was a tap on the door. 'Enter!' She smiled at me. 'I could become used to this seat.'

Inspector Wallis stepped into the room, looking from Mrs Carmichael to me.

She put the address book in the drawer. 'I'm sorry. Mr Lennox is not here yet. It's unlike him to be late.'

'May I sit down?'

'Yes, of course, Inspector.'

'I have some bad news I'm afraid. Mrs Shackleton may as well stay to hear it.' He paused. 'I'm sorry to tell you that Mr Lennox was found dead at his flat last night.'

Mrs Carmichael stared at the inspector. 'How? I mean, what happened?'

'The death is being treated as suspicious.'

'You don't mean he . . . '

'He did not take his own life.'

Mrs Carmichael fumbled up her sleeve for a handkerchief. 'I don't understand. How is it suspicious if . . . Oh, oh.'

'I have a sergeant and a constable downstairs interviewing staff and readers. We have not yet told them why, but I am asking people to account for their movements between six o'clock and nine o'clock yesterday evening.'

She blinked, and blinked again, as if expecting tears that did not come. 'I was at home all evening. I caught the tram as usual, just after six. Had my tea, prepared by my landlady, and then stayed in my room.'

'Your landlady would confirm that?'

'Yes, and Mrs Shackleton came to see me at about half past eight?'

She looked at me.

'That's right. I was also at home at about six, and then met someone and went to the Palace public house between

322

seven and eight, and then home for my car and across to see Mrs Carmichael.'

'What was the purpose of your visit to Mrs Carmichael?'

'Mrs Carmichael is helping me trace Sophia Mary Ann Wells who I believe works in a library.'

He looked at her.

She nodded. 'I have been making telephone calls for Mrs Shackleton.'

'I see.' The inspector looked from her to me. He seemed to be considering whether to ask me to leave. He did not.

'Mrs Carmichael, yesterday at your meeting, I noticed that Mr Lennox's demeanour was much changed. Can you explain why that was?'

'He was fond of Dr Potter. It knocked the stuffing out of him that Dr Potter died.' She twisted her handkerchief. 'There was another reason. He developed an attachment to one of our assistants, Miss Montague. I regret to say that we wrongly dismissed her, suspecting her of theft. I dare say it was my fault for not believing her denials.'

Wallis said, 'We have not managed to interview the young lady.'

I could keep quiet no longer. 'I have.'

Inspector Wallis fought to keep control. 'Mrs Shackleton, this is not a game. What do you have to tell me?'

They both looked at me.

'She is in hiding.' Somewhat awkwardly, due to my painful wrist, I reached for my satchel. 'There's a drawing I would like you to see.'

'Let me help.' Mrs Carmichael took my satchel, extracted Peter's drawing, and stared. 'It's Mr Castle to the life.'

She handed it to Wallis.

He looked at it, and at me.

'Castle paid to have Marian Montague murdered and buried in the basement.'

'That is a very serious allegation, Mrs Shackleton.'

'Yes, and before you think it, I am not being vindictive because he attacked me.' I spoke quickly, before the inspector had time to interrupt. 'It is my belief that Mr Lennox knew nothing about Marian's supposed death until yesterday, just before the meeting. That is why he was so distraught, and why he changed his mind about removing from these premises.'

All colour had drained from Mrs Carmichael's face. Her breath came in short bursts. For a moment, I thought she would have a heart attack. I went to calm her, encouraging her to slow her breathing. When she recovered a little, she was about to say something, but Wallis spoke first.

'There is a sketch next to the portrait.'

'Yes. X marks the spot where her body was to be buried. Mr Castle chalked the paving stone with a cross. I noticed yesterday that it had been swept, probably to remove the chalk.'

Wallis looked as though he might explode. 'How long have you known this?'

Now was not the time to be precise. I hedged. 'This morning, I took signed statements from Miss Montague and the young man paid one hundred pounds to do the deed. Some of the notes he was given in payment are in an envelope in my satchel. I thought it best to have them in case they were drawn on Mr Castle's bank.'

I looked at Mrs Carmichael. She obligingly took the envelope from my satchel and handed it to the inspector.

'And you've been sitting on this information while calmly contacting branch libraries about whether they employ Sophia Wells?'

When he put it like that, my approach did seem somewhat skewed, yet it would be impolitic to say that I did not trust him.

Mrs Carmichael probably thought she was being helpful. 'I telephoned only library headquarters and main libraries.'

'Where is Miss Montague?'

The door was suddenly flung open. Marian entered, hatless, her coat open displaying her interesting condition. 'Here I am.'

Mrs Carmichael stared. The inspector and I had to turn in our seats. He stood up immediately.

Marian struck a pose like an avenging angel. 'Why should I hide? I'm safest in full view.' She strode into the room, running her hands through her cropped hair. 'Where is he? Where is Sam Lennox? Where is his friend the murderer? I demand the return of my hair. It should fetch a bob or two and I need the money.'

I stood. 'Marian, this is Inspector Wallis. He has brought us some bad news about Sam Lennox.'

She did not resist when the inspector guided her to his chair.

It was Mrs Carmichael who said in a flat voice, 'Sam is dead. Murdered.'

Marian closed her eyes. She put her hands on her belly as if to cover the baby's ears.

I went to her side. 'If it's any consolation, I'm sure Sam Lennox had nothing to do with Castle's plan.'

'Of course not,' Mrs Carmichael snapped. 'He wouldn't have had the guts.'

Inspector Wallis walked to the door. 'I'll speak to my constable. I have asked Mr Castle to join us. You ladies won't want to see him.'

Marian let out a harsh laugh. 'That is where you are wrong, Inspector. I want to thank him. He has helped me shape my future, and my fiancé's. We're to be married next week.'

My bruised cheek suddenly throbbed. My leg went into cramp. It was as if my body parts were reminding me why I wanted to see Castle charged with assault as well as murder. 'I'll stay.'

Mrs Carmichael did not budge. 'I will stay, Inspector, if it's all the same to you. I may be able to contribute some rather particular knowledge.'

There was a tap on the door. A constable put his head round. 'Mr Castle is here, sir.'

Wallis looked around the room. He went to the window and moved the curtain. 'Behind there, Miss Montague, can you manage to stay silent?'

'Probably not.'

'Try!' Inspector Wallis turned to the constable. 'Show him up.'

Castle must already have been on his way up. It was less than a minute before the constable showed him in. 'Hello,' he said cheerfully. 'More investigations?'

The inspector had remained standing. 'Yes. Please take a seat, Mr Castle.'

Castle sat in the chair opposite Mrs Carmichael. 'Where's Mr Lennox? Are you keeping his chair warm?'

Mrs Carmichael did not answer. She was breathing rather

noisily. I feared she may begin to panic. It took a lot of effort for me to stay calm myself when, nice as pie, Castle said, 'How are we today, Mrs Shackleton?'

The truthful answer would have been that I was in the mood to pick up my chair and bring it down on his head. 'I am on the mend.'

The inspector cleared his throat, as if warning us to say nothing. 'Can you account for your movements yesterday evening between six o'clock and nine, sir?'

'I was at home with my wife.'

'And she will confirm that, will she?'

'Yes, of course. What's going on?'

'Mr Lennox is dead, sir. I am investigating his murder.'

'Good God!' Castle's shocked expression could not be faulted. It gave way to outrage. 'You can't believe I had anything to do with it?'

'May I ask what you and Mr Lennox talked about before yesterday's meeting?'

Castle took a moment to answer, as if recalling something so mundane presented great difficulty after such a shock. 'Library business, nothing in particular, apart from the announcement that was to be made. We agreed it was time for some stability.' He glared at me. 'Now, of course, the business about new premises will drag on.'

'Perhaps you told him that there was a body in the basement and that if it were found, he would be blamed, because it was the body of a young woman who worked in the library and who became close to Mr Lennox.'

'That's preposterous.' In his best patrician manner, he looked from me to Mrs Carmichael. 'Ladies, you may go. You must not let this scurrilous nonsense sully your ears.'

'The ladies may stay, Mr Castle. I believe they have some-thing pertinent to say.'

'What are you driving at, man? I won't stand for this.' But stand he did, to his full height, in his long black coat, and he glided towards the door. A connection that had been just on the edge of my thoughts suddenly struck me. I felt my fists clench at the horror, at the simplicity.

'Come and sit down, sir,' the inspector said. 'I'm sure it won't take long to clear this up.'

Castle returned to his chair.

Their next exchanges were lost on me as images floated into my mind. I was in the dark library, forty-odd years ago. Mr McAllister, the young librarian, worked late, and alone. He heard sounds as he was packing up to go, but thought nothing of it. Then he saw a light.

Edwin Castle had thought the library would be deserted. He had been at work in the basement, having let himself in the back door.

My thoughts were suddenly interrupted.

No one told Miss Montague to sweep aside the curtain and stand over Mr Castle, but she did.

'Where is my hair, my locket, that stupid cheap ring?'

Mr Castle rose from his chair. He looked about the room, as if he had forgotten the location of the door. He rocked on his heels. His mouth opened and closed. 'What ... what's going on?' For the first time his mask fell. He stared at Marian Montague, and then at me, with pure hatred. 'Get these witches out of here.' He swayed and may have fallen back-wards, but suddenly, Mrs Carmichael was behind him. She held the pistol, taken from my satchel, jamming it in the back of his neck with such force that his head jerked forward.

'You won't remember me, Mr Castle.'

'Has everyone gone mad? Inspector . . . '

Until then, the inspector had been sitting in a relaxed fashion, feeling quite in charge. He stood, very slowly. Standing still as a statue he said softly, 'Steady on, Mrs Carmichael. Put down the gun.'

She ignored him. 'You know me only as Mrs Carmichael. You won't remember the nine-year-old girl, Pamela Nelson, whose father had the misfortune to be a partner in your estimable legal firm.' No one moved. 'I was afraid I would forget Dad, forget what he looked like, and so morning, noon and night, I closed my eyes to see him, and I see him still, when I close my eyes. But I'm not closing them now, because I am looking at your neck and imagining a noose around it.'

Castle gulped. He put his fingers to his collar.

The inspector's voice became almost a whisper. 'Mrs Carmichael, if Edwin Castle is guilty, he will face the full weight of the law.'

'He won't though, will he, because my father's body was never found.'

Castle choked out the words, 'I want a solicitor.'

'My father was a solicitor. You remember him, your part-ner? He was an honest solicitor. You are a crook.'

Wallis spoke as though no one in the room had a gun, and no one was being threatened, and at any moment we might all go out and choose a library book. 'Mrs Carmichael, when I came to Leeds City Police, I looked into your father's case. It intrigued me . . . '

'Intrigued? It destroyed us, the shame, the disgrace, the injustice.'

'Wrong word. Sorry. I suspected there had been a poor investigation. I will tell you, but you must give me the gun. I don't want to take you into custody. You have waited too long for justice.'

She hesitated, keeping the gun firmly jammed in Castle's neck, yet she looked at each of us in turn.

When our eyes met, I forced her to hold my gaze. 'He won't wriggle out of it, Mrs Carmichael. He made a chalk mark on the spot where Marian was to be buried. Because under another slab is your father's body. A bullet is too good for him. Let him face the full force of the law, for all his crimes.' She did not put down the gun. I kept on talking, this time to him. 'The discovery of Mr Nelson's body would have ruined you. You were the embezzler, and you killed Mr Nelson when he found out. You took no chances about excavations down there. You killed Dr Potter because he suspected something. He had remembered that Mr Nelson disappeared around the same time as a 'ghost' came into the library one night, probably to wash its hands and brush its hair after the dastardly work of burying a body. Dr Potter would have persuaded the committee to sell these premises, and the digging would begin.

'You tried to blackmail Mr Lennox, telling him Marian was buried there, and that you had her hair, her locket, and the letter that he wrote to her.'

There was a tap on the door. Moving cautiously, not taking his eyes off Castle and Mrs Carmichael, Wallis opened the door a fraction.

'Sir, we have taken statements from the staff.'

'Good.' Wallis handed him the piece of paper on which Peter had drawn Castle's likeness, and the burial spot in the basement. 'I want the flags removed in this part of the basement, and some careful digging. Send word, and then come back here.' He closed the door. 'Mrs Carmichael, the gun, if you please.'

Marian said, 'You'll find a Guy Fawkes that Peter buried instead of me.'

Wallis took a step towards Castle. 'That won't be all we find, will it, Mr Castle? It would suit you if Mrs Carmichael shot you now, wouldn't it?'

'No!'

Castle closed his eyes. His head came forward in something like a nod of defeat.

Mrs Carmichael clicked the revolver.

Castle said, 'Nelson found out about me. I had no choice but to deal with him.'

Mrs Carmichael hissed in his ear. 'My father, Sam Lennox, Dr Potter, the library's most avid reader. You killed them all. Shooting is too good for you.'

Her hand fell to her side. I took the gun. 'It's all right now. You can close your eyes and see him. Your dad will know you kept faith.'

She stared at Castle. 'I knew there was a reason you haunted the library, and that it was nothing to do with a love of books.'

We stood clear, letting the inspector do his job.

'Edwin Castle, I am arresting you on suspicion of the murders of Mungo Charles Nelson, Horatio Erasmus Potter and Samuel Lennox. You do not have to say anything but anything you do say will be taken down in evidence and may be used against you. Do you understand?'

Castle might have been a toad, croaking. 'Yes.'

The inspector stepped aside, nodding to the two constables who had appeared. One of them, holding handcuffs, glanced at the inspector, with the unspoken question, Do we use them?

The inspector nodded. 'Take him to the bridewell.'

When they had gone, the inspector led Mrs Carmichael back to Lennox's chair.

The telephone began to ring.

Mrs Carmichael neither saw nor heard.

Marian stepped in and picked up the receiver. 'The Leeds Library, Miss Montague speaking.' She listened. 'Mrs Carmichael is away from her desk. May I take a message?' She picked up a pencil and began to write. 'Thank you. I will pass that on.' She hung up the telephone, and wrote another couple of words before handing the paper to me. 'For you, Mrs Shackleton.'

The message read,

From Librarian, Keighley, Miss Sophia Wells works as a counter assistant at Bingley Library.

Thirty

She was not difficult to spot, being the only member of staff on duty at Bingley Library. A little above average height, and slender, she had a widow's peak, light brown hair, the same shade as Sam Lennox's, and uneven features. She looked more like Lennox than her mother. Slightly gangly, she was not unattractive but by no means beautiful. She had a high forehead and long straight nose. Nothing pale and interesting about her, her cheeks had a good colour. Yet she had her mother's stillness, and way of carrying herself erect. She was dressed in grey.

I glanced along a shelf of history books, and then left the library. Sykes was waiting outside.

'Don't keep me in suspense.'

'It's her. I'm sure of it.'

'So what now?'

'I wish I knew whether Sophia has been told about the adoption. If not, it would be kinder to let Mrs Bradshaw break the news.'

Sykes brandished the *Bingley Bugle* under my nose. 'The paper came out today. They may already have seen our announcement.'

As we stood discussing what to do, Sophia came out of the library wearing a black coat, a red scarf, mittens and matching woolly hat. We were to the right of the door. She turned left, and did not see us.

'Follow her, Mr Sykes. We can't afford to lose her now. Come back and find me in the café.'

Sykes is good at tailing people. He pulled down his hat.

I pretended to look in a shop window, and then another, keeping an eye on him to see which way he went. Something in the window caught my eye, a pair of earrings. When I looked again, there was no sign of Sykes.

The café had a menu in the window. I stood reading it. By the time I reached the last item, stewed plums and custard, Sykes was beside me again.

'You were right first time. She went into the photographic studio, through the shop and into the back.'

'Then that was probably Mrs Bradshaw I spoke to last week. How annoying! She could have saved us so much time. I've half a mind to go straight to Sophia.'

'It may not have been,' Sykes said. 'But it probably was. There's a youngish chap in there, the photographer I expect.'

As we went into the café, I felt a surge of relief. From our seat by the window, we would see Sophia when she returned to the library after lunch. 'We've finally pinned her down. If Sophia and Mrs Bradshaw want nothing to do with us, I can at least report to Lady Coulton that I have found Sophia, and that she is well.'

Sykes picked up the menu. 'Her ladyship wants more than that. She wants to see her daughter before she dies.'

'I expect she does. I wonder how I will manage it.'

The waitress came. We ordered soup and cheese sand-wiches.

'Will we go to the photographic studio mob-handed?' Sykes asked.

'Why not? You may have more luck with Mrs Bradshaw than I did.'

'I was thinking of the photographer. If he's still there, I could keep him talking, have my photo taken while you break the news to Mrs B., that there is no hiding place from Kate Shackleton.'

I smiled. 'You want your picture. You'll have it enlarged, framed, and hung above the stairs at home, the *paterfamilias*.'

'You read my mind.'

It was another half hour before Sophia passed the window on her way back to the library.

Sykes asked for the bill.

Slowly, we made our way to the photographic studio.

'Nice place,' Sykes said, surveying the window display. 'And is that her, the woman you spoke to last week?'

'Yes.'

'She's the right age.'

The clapper rang as we stepped inside. The woman and the young man looked up. Straight away, I saw that she recognised me, but he was the one who spoke.

'Hello.'

'Nice place,' Sykes said, turning to me. 'You were right. '

The man beamed. 'What can I do for you?'

'Mr Felton?' Sykes asked.

'Yes, that's me.'

'And Mrs . . . ?' Sykes looked at the woman, whose hair

was done in a slightly different way. She had pinned her braids atop her head.

'Mrs Bradshaw,' the young man said, when she did not answer for herself.

'Well then you can take my photograph if it's all the same to you, Mr Felton.'

Mr Felton frowned, looking from Sykes to me. 'And yours too?'

'Perhaps but we want one of Jim, just on his own, to send to an elderly aunt.'

'Excellent.' Mr Felton drew back the curtain and ushered Sykes through to the studio.

I laid the *Bingley Bugle* on the counter, open at our announcement. 'Shall we go in the back, Mrs Bradshaw?'

She rose.

I followed her behind the counter. 'Who would have thought it,' I said loudly enough for Mr Felton to hear, 'I remember you from Scarborough, and we have a friend in common.'

She led me into a neat kitchen-cum-living room.

Had there been more time, I may have approached her in a more tactful, leisurely way, but Mr Felton may prove a quick snapper and have Sykes out of the studio faster than you could say, Watch the birdie.

She stood beside a well-polished round table and folded her arms. 'Now's not convenient.'

'The whole village will have seen this newspaper announcement by the end of today. You will need to think of something.'

'You'd no business advertising for us.'

I decided against telling her that there would have been no need to advertise had she told me the truth last week.

'All you need say is that a distant relation was sorry to have lost touch with you. Invent a legacy if that helps.'

'It's her isn't it, her ladyship.'

'Yes.'

'After all this time.'

'She won't bother you for long. She's dying and wants news of her child. Does Sophia know she is adopted?'

'No, and I'm not going to tell her.'

'It's up to you to tell her, before she finds out some other way.'

'Is that a threat?'

'No. I do know what I'm talking about. I'm adopted myself and I always knew it.'

'She's not ready to know.'

'At twenty-four? Then when will she be ready? I'm sorry to be so blunt, but knowing I was adopted made no difference at all to how I felt about the parents who brought me up. They are still my real parents.'

'It was supposed to be secret. How can I tell her, after all these years? It's as if I've lied to her.'

'It can still be secret, between you, Sophia and Lady Coulton. Don't you think Sophia deserves to know?'

I was not too sure of my own argument. The circumstances for Sophia and for me were so very different.

Mrs Bradshaw sat down heavily. 'What does Lady Coulton want?'

I took the chair opposite her. 'To know how you are, both of you. She was concerned when she lost touch. I've been searching for you for ten days. Everyone I met speaks highly of you and Sophia, including the staff at both schools. You've done a good job as a mother. No one can take that away.'

'She doesn't want her back?'

'No. But it may be she would like to see her once before she dies.'

'You've picked the right day to come. Bonfire Night, and you've put a firework under me, a rocket.' Mrs Bradshaw put her forearms on the table and interlocked her fingers. 'I wouldn't have had a child, if not for her.'

'Then tell Sophia, when she comes home from the library.'

'You've seen her?'

'Yes. She's a credit it to you.'

She nodded. 'Come back after tea. I'll tell her when she comes home.'

'Will Mr Felton be here?'

'No. I shut up shop at six. He goes home to his family. He'll be checking the bonfire with them, setting up the guy.'

'He seems a nice man.'

'Cedric Felton's my cousin's lad. He's been good to us.'

'I expect he's glad to have you here.' I stood up. 'Six o'clock then.'

'Make it half past.'

We took the few short steps from the living room back into the shop.

Felton and Sykes were emerging in jolly mood from the studio.

Mrs Bradshaw said, 'Would you credit it, Cedric, this lady bought fish from us when we had the shop in Scarborough.'

'Well,' said Cedric. 'It's a small world.'

Sykes paid for his photograph.

We walked back the way we had come. When we were a few yards along the road, Sykes asked, 'How did you get on?'

I told him, and that we had a few hours to pass in Bingley.

'Do you know what, this would be a good time for me to catch up with my old chum at the Ramshead Arms. Coming?'

'No. You go. It's a fine afternoon. I fancy a walk up to Cottingley. I'll see you back at the car at about quarter past six. Keep your fingers crossed that Sophia won't take the news too badly.'

I returned to the shop at twenty-five minutes past six. The sign on the door was turned to Closed. Not wishing to rush them, I once more looked at the photographs in the window.

It was Sophia who came to the door.

'You better come in, or we'll have the whole street gawping.' She held out her hand. 'I'm Sophia Wells, the person you've been looking for. I saw your piece in the paper today.'

'Kate Shackleton. How do you do, Sophia.'

'I don't know how I do. Come through. Mam's upset.'

'I'm sorry.'

'It's only natural I suppose.'

'But more of a shock to you?'

'Perhaps it will hit me later.'

'Sophia, I'm adopted, too. I didn't meet my birth mother until last year, though I knew about her.'

'Is that true? I thought you'd been spinning Mam a yarn.'

Mrs Wells was seated at the table, which was set with sandwiches, and cakes on a tiered stand.

Sophia pulled out a chair for me.

This was much more than I had hoped for.

Mrs Wells poured tea. 'Sophia wasn't as shocked as I thought she would be.'

Sophia shrugged. 'I've picked up hints that you didn't know you gave, and Dad too. He was worse at trying not to tell me why I didn't take after either of you. Of course a lot of girls imagine they must be from a different family, and that they don't fit.' Mrs Wells cringed, ever so slightly. 'Oh, I don't mean you, Mam. We're quite a good fit.' She turned to me. 'So who is this other mother? Mam hasn't given me any details.'

I looked at Mrs Bradshaw. She must have become so used to guarding her secret. Suddenly I felt a little fearful. This young woman was bright and too breezy for my liking. My task was to find Sophia for Lady Coulton, not to find Lady Coulton for Sophia. Had I overstepped the mark?

Mrs Bradshaw gave me a look that said, Go on then, you deal with it.

'She is a lady with a husband and sons.'

'Mam said my aunt Lily Tarpey was her nanny, so I can easily find out. If you work in a library that's the part you most enjoy, digging about for information. It would be no trouble to me.'

Mrs Bradshaw pushed dainty sandwiches towards me. The crusts had been cut off. At a different time of year, they would have been cucumber.

I took one.

'Take two, take three.'

They were small. I took two. It was pickled beetroot. 'Would you like to meet her?'

'Depends on who she is, and whether she wants to meet me. Oh and don't worry. I shan't spread it about to the world, not for her sake, but for Mam's.'

I took a deep breath, and polished off a sandwich. 'She is

340

Lady Coulton. She lives on Cavendish Square in the centre of London. Let us try and arrange a visit.'

'Good-oh. I'd like that. Will you come too, Mam?'

'No. I've never been to London and I won't start now. Take a slice of parkin, Mrs Shackleton.'

I took a slice of parkin.

'When will we go, Kate?'

'Call her Mrs Shackleton!'

'Kate will do.'

'And what about your job, Sophia?' Mrs Bradshaw asked. 'You can't just up and off to London like some flying duck. Who would take your place at the counter?'

Sophia suddenly drooped. 'I hadn't thought of that. I was thinking of fitting in a visit to the British Museum Reading Room. We can apply for a visitor's ticket through the library, you know, and I've never seen Buckingham Palace and . . . Oh I must go, now that you've said it.' Sophia fetched a calendar from a hook on the wall. 'I'll ask Mr Emerson tomorrow. He'll have seen your announcement in the paper. I'll tell him that a distant relative is on her death bed and very badly wants to see me because . . . ' She turned to her mother. 'What else might I say?'

'You are the niece of her much-loved nanny, and she has heard that you are a fatherless child.'

'That's perfect, Mam, like something out of a novel.'

I gave her my card. 'Let me know what Mr Emerson says, and we will try and arrange a date.'

Mrs Bradshaw walked me to the door and saw me into the street. 'She's fed up with her life at the library. She thinks this will change her world, but of course it won't. Nothing ever does. You take your world with you, wherever you go.

She's yet to learn that most of the time life is a slap in the chops with a wet kipper.'

Sophia bounded through from the house, a sudden excitement in her voice. 'Kate, did Lady Coulton tell you who my father was?'

I could truthfully tell her that she did not.

Mrs Bradshaw met my eye. Her look said, No good will come of this.

I wished them a cheerful goodbye, saying that I looked forward to hearing when Sophia would be able to arrange time off from the library for good behaviour.

Sykes was waiting in the motor. He stepped out so that I could shuffle into the passenger seat. 'You should have that wrist properly looked at.'

'The bandage needs tightening, that's all.'

'Inspector Wallis should charge Edwin Castle, Esquire with assault and battery as well as murder.'

'Perhaps I was one of the sprats the inspector used to catch his mackerel.'

As we drove back to Leeds, bonfires were being lit in back streets, in fields and on waste ground. We paused to look at a fire as Guy Fawkes was hoisted atop the pile of branches and rubbish. Children were outdoing each other with their fireworks: Catherine Wheels spinning their stars, Roman Candles shooting to heaven, and Jumping Jacks leaping where they pleased, sending screaming youngsters scurrying in every direction.

All the way home, the sky turned red, shot through with golden sparks.

Thirty-One

The train journey to London needed to be carefully coordinated since Sophia and I were setting out from different stations but could join forces in Wakefield. There was very little time for planning. She must have been formidably persuasive because on the day after my visit she telephoned to say that the librarian would allow her Saturday and Monday off. She seemed peeved that it was not longer. I thought it generous at such short notice, especially since he would let her leave early on Friday, in time to catch the 5.53 p.m. from Wakefield, arriving King's Cross 9.25 p.m. I flicked through my railway guide as we spoke. That train had a restaurant car. She would like the novelty of eating on the train, and it would be a good time to prepare her, warn her not to blow in on her mother like a storm.

Several times, I wrote and rewrote a telegram to Lady Coulton:

LADY POCKLINGTON'S NIECE MRS SHACKLETON IN TOWN TO PAY HER RESPECTS STOP *BRINGING NANNY TARPEY'S NIECE*

Try again:

MRS SHACKLETON IN TOWN AND WILL CALL STOP
NANNY TARPEY'S NIECE WISHES TO PAY RESPECTS

Finally, I picked up the telephone. Lady Coulton had said that her maid was old and deaf, so just the kind of person who might rush to answer. Fortunately, I spoke to the housekeeper.

'Hello, this is Mrs Shackleton, Lady Pocklington's niece. I shall be in London this weekend and hope to call and tell her ladyship about some progress on a matter that interests her, and to bring a young lady to meet her.'

There was a long pause. I guessed that the housekeeper was wondering how much I knew, what to divulge, and whether to put me off. In the end, she simply said that she would pass on the message.

What had begun to seem impossible was now almost accomplished. I was glad that we were to travel right away, before Sophia's feet turned cold. Of all the missing persons I had found, this case felt like both triumph and disaster. A triumph because there had been the race against time, and a disaster because mother and daughter would have no future, and because there would be no question now of my telling Lady Coulton that I had stumbled upon Sophia's unfortunate father.

On Saturday, just before noon, we sat in Lady Coulton's drawing room, waiting. Sophia, who had been the complete chatterbox on the train journey, was now silenced by the grandeur of her surroundings. She sat erect on a brocade-covered chair, her ankles touching, her eyes darting about the room to take in the rich furnishings, paintings and the ornate fireplace.

Her voice became almost a whisper. 'What a lot of room they have.'

'Yes. You wouldn't think it from the outside. All the houses round here are like this. Don't let it overwhelm you.'

'What must I call her?'

'Don't worry. Just say, how do you do, and see what she says. She will put you at your ease.'

'Is she coming down? You said she was ill. I thought we'd see her in her bed.'

'I saw her early last week. I now realise why she didn't come until afternoon, and what an effort it must have cost her.'

'Then should we not have come this afternoon?'

'No. Calls are made in the morning. If she did not want to see us, we would have been told she was not at home.'

'She'll be disappointed in me.'

'Why would she be? You've made your own way in the world, Sophia. Anyone with an ounce of sense will see that.'

We did not have much longer to wait.

The door opened. A maid stood sentry until Lady Coulton had stepped inside and then closed the door behind her.

Even in these last ten days, she had lost weight. Her face looked drawn, but she smiled a greeting.

We stood. Lady Coulton came to me first and took my hand. 'Thank you. I had not much hope, but you have fulfilled what I hardly dared dream of.' She hesitated. 'Sophia knows?'

'Yes. Mrs Wells, now Mrs Bradshaw, told her, just yesterday.'

Leaning on the arm of the sofa, she lowered herself gently into the seat. 'Sophia, come and sit by me.'

'I'll leave you alone. Excuse me.'

Lady Coulton looked up. 'The butler knows we are not to be disturbed.'

In the hall, the butler hovered. He gave the slightest of bows. 'Her ladyship informs me that you have a great interest in plants and would like to visit the garden room.'

'Yes. Thank you.'

As he led the way, I realised that this was the man who had followed Lady Coulton to and from the Cavendish Club last week, not to spy, but to help her if she stumbled.

The garden room was a space of utter tranquillity, the walls a pale green and the ceiling ornate and cream. Ferns and plants of every description filled the room. It led onto a garden with miniature fountains that even in November looked like spring, a fairytale place from a story book, creating the feeling that if I closed my eyes, it might disappear. I do not know whether ten minutes passed, or an hour. Time stood still.

The butler returned. 'Her ladyship has ordered tea, madam.'

I followed him back to the drawing room.

Lady Coulton stood as I came in. 'Give me your arm, Mrs Shackleton.'

I did so. She leaned on me rather heavily as we walked to the foot of the stairs. At the bottom of the stairs, she took hold of the banister. 'I can manage from here. Good days and bad, you see, and I have medicine that sees me through.' Suddenly she smiled. 'Sophia works in a library.'

'Yes.'

She whispered, 'She was conceived in a library. I almost divulged, but it is not the kind of thing the young need to know. Goodbye, Mrs Shackleton. Kate.'

'Goodbye, Lady Coulton.'

I watched as she climbed the stairs, realising that I was holding my breath, fearing she might fall as she took step by painful step. A nurse came onto the landing to meet her.

Slowly, I walked back to the drawing room.

There was tea and a plate of cakes on the low table.

I glanced at Sophia. 'I expect you should pour.'

'My hands will shake.'

'At least you have two good wrists. Go on. Try.'

She picked up the teapot and poured with the greatest of ease.

'To the manner born.'

She gave a wry smile. 'No such luck!'

We drank our tea slowly.

She took out a locket. 'My father gave her this.'

'It's pretty.'

'Yes. He was killed in the Great War. He was a student of philosophy.'

'Ah.' So that was what Lady Coulton had chosen to say. A wise move.

Sophia sighed. 'She asked me what we would do for the rest of the weekend. I told her I want to see the British Museum and . . . ' Her voice choked a little. 'I asked her my father's philosophy.'

Pretending not to see that she was close to tears, I spoke of where we would go next and where we would go after that and how it would be best to change our shoes before setting off.

It would not do to cry here and now. There would be plenty of time for weeping.

I was glad we appeared to be at ease when a few moments later the butler entered.

'Mrs Shackleton?'

'Yes?'

'I am instructed by her ladyship's man of business to hand you this envelope.'

'Thank you.'

When he had gone, Sophia said, 'What is it?'

'Not now.'

We returned to the Cavendish Club and put on comfortable shoes for our walking tour.

She came to my room and tapped on the door. 'I'm ready.'

I opened the envelope. It was a brief note of thanks and a cheque for two thousand guineas, one thousand guineas for Sophia, five hundred for Mrs Wells and five hundred for me. How gratifying that she trusted me so implicitly as to make the cheque out to me, and most generous of her. I wish my second thought had not been that now I would have to render tax on two thousand guineas.

It was a great pleasure to see the sights of London through the eyes of Sophia, who had never been farther than the distance between Scarborough and Bingley.

We had just finished breakfast on Monday morning, our bags packed and the taxi cab ordered, when a young lad brought a note from Lady Coulton's butler.

With deep regret, I must inform you that Lady Coulton passed peacefully in her sleep at 3 a.m. this morning.

Thirty-Two

The day for the funerals of Umberto Bruno and Dr Potter broke fine and clear, which was a great relief. I hate a funeral on a rainy day when dug earth turns wet and clay heavy. At Killingbeck Cemetery, I watched the coffin of Umberto Bruno lowered into his grave in the Italian section of the burial ground. Father Daley from St Patrick's read the prayers. PC Hodge and the ward sister, Miss O'Malley, were there, and a clutch of Italian women in their black dresses and shawls, holding rosaries. Two old men without overcoats came dangerously close to the edge of the grave.

Afterwards, the Italians stayed to talk to the priest. I slipped away with PC Hodge and Sister O'Malley, offering them a lift to town.

Dr Potter's funeral, that same afternoon, was an altogether grander affair, the university chapel being packed to capacity with his colleagues, students and former students. Mrs Carmichael and several library proprietors attended, including Miss Heaton who had taken a collection for a wreath.

Professor Merton gave a glowing oration, praising his colleague's intellect, his common touch and his popularity. The good Dr Potter would have proved a brilliant vice chancellor, Professor Merton said. He glanced with what might have been deep sorrow and a touch of malevolence towards the coffin of the man who had evaded the university's calling and left the mantle of unwanted promotion to grace his own morose shoulders.

In slow procession, the funeral cortege made the journey from the university to Lawnswood Cemetery.

Dignitaries, colleagues and students strode behind the hearse that was drawn by plumed black horses.

Close to the rear, I fell into step with Mr Morgan, too modest, self-effacing and cautious to claim his rightful place.

After the burial, we walked to the gates together. He had not been invited to the funeral tea. We spoke briefly. I asked him about his plans.

He rocked slightly on his heels. 'It is that I am staying on in the cottage and I am to take a post as university porter.'

'I am glad.'

'Yes. It will be better than the alternative of teaching the reluctant young on an hourly basis, and it will leave leisure time for working with Clever Archie on his numbers, to continue my master's work.'

This seemed a good moment to talk to him about Percy. 'You remember I told you about the Capuchin monkey Dr Potter was to have brought home, as a pupil.'

'Ah yes, the scheme of work concerning counting by digits, so neatly written. And how is the creature now?'

'He is well, and with me, but I don't want to keep him. Do you think he may be more at home in a zoo?'

A mad light filled Morgan's eyes. 'I will take him, if you

please. See you, another porter will move into the cottage, so we can manage the rent. Blenkinsop has a lady wife and a young orphaned grandson, so the monkey would not be left alone during the day. My fellow porter and his wife are animal lovers or I would not have agreed to them coming in the vicinity of Clever Archie, Dunce and Polynesia, crippling rent or no crippling rent. My master willed the animals to me, into my care, along with his Bible which you know about.'

We shook hands on the matter. I would bring Percy to meet Mr Morgan, and see whether they liked the look of each other.

'And please to give me news of the librarian's funeral. I should like to be there, to represent my late master and pay my respects to Mr Lennox.'

He was about to walk away when Professor Merton approached. 'Thank you for coming, Mrs Shackleton. It was a moving service.'

'It was indeed.' Morgan was about to slink away when I detained him. 'Professor, have you met Mr Morgan, Dr Potter's manservant? Mr Morgan this is Professor Merton.'

'How do you do, Mr Morgan.'

'How do you do, Professor.'

'Potter spoke highly of you.'

'Thank you for telling me. It is most gratifying that he ever mentioned me.'

'Well he did. Now you must come to the funeral tea.'

'I wouldn't dream . . . '

'Well I would dream. Come now, no arguments.'

Morgan smiled with pride as Professor Merton guided him away.

When I turned to go my own way, I almost bumped into Inspector Wallis.

'Mrs Shackleton.'

'Inspector.'

'A sad day.'

'Indeed.'

'Did you find the persons you were looking for, Mrs Bradshaw and Miss Wells?'

'Yes, I found them, thank you.'

'My driver is over there. May I give you a lift? We're going your way.'

I accepted his offer. We sat beside each other in silence on the journey back.

When we reached my gate, Wallis leapt from the car, came round to my side and opened the door. He picked up a brown paper parcel.

I smiled. 'Thank you, I can walk to the gate.'

'Am I allowed to see the monkey?'

'It hid the last time you came.'

'Clever monkey. By rights it should go to the Duchy of Lancaster. Its owner died intestate so it belongs to the Crown.'

We were on the doorstep. 'That is where you are wrong, Inspector. It was lawfully sold, remember? Dr Potter took delivery. His manservant inherits his animals.'

'I stand corrected.'

'Then come inside, and see whether Percy will say hello.'

His banter was hiding something, but what? I wondered about the brown paper parcel. Perhaps it contained spring bulbs. Wallis had appointed himself horticultural supplier to Catherine Shackleton.

We stepped into the hall. The inspector cleared his throat.

'If the monkey has found a new owner, the bag of sovereigns should go to the Duchy of Lancaster.'

'It is very noble of you, this desire to enrich the Crown. Do you really think the King needs fifty sovereigns from a poor Italian?'

'There were only forty-nine.'

'Oh dear. I let Percy play with them. He's probably tucked one away.'

'There would have to be a relative who could put in a claim for the sovereigns.'

'Then I'm sure one can be found. There is a priest at St Patrick's, Father Daley. He can be trusted to find the right way of channelling the money to some poor Italians.'

'It would have to be a relative with a claim.'

'I will pass that information to Father Daley.'

The drawing room door stood open. 'Percy's probably in here.' A slight rustle of the curtains told me that Percy was hiding behind the piano.

'Sit down, Inspector. He'll feel less threatened. Would you like a cup of tea?'

'No, I won't keep my driver waiting too long, I have a meeting.'

'Come on, Percy.'

Percy peered round the piano.

Inspector Wallis held out a brown paper parcel. 'Yours, I believe, Percy Bruno.'

Slowly, with his swaying knuckle-walk, Percy came closer.

The inspector put the parcel on the hearth rug.

Percy snatched it and took it back to the piano, keeping his distance.

'What have you brought him?'

Percy ripped the brown paper, tossing aside shreds until he sat in a den of litter. He held up his harness and lead for display.

'We found them in the basement. I'm assuming that Mr Bruno removed them, perhaps to give a demonstration of how Percy responded to commands without tugs in one direction or another.' He watched as Percy made a small mound of shredded brown paper. 'I believe Dr Potter was disturbed by Edwin Castle. The monkey got out. Either Castle did not see Bruno, or thought that he had also cleared off. I don't know yet.'

'Do you think the charges will stick?'

'I'll know more by this evening. We are still assessing evidence in relation to Dr Potter's murder. We can place Castle at the scene for the murder of Samuel Lennox. He may try to retract his confession on the historic charge of murdering his partner, but I doubt it. Mrs Carmichael will be able to arrange a proper burial for her father now that we have recovered his body.'

'Poor Mrs Carmichael. I dare say she'll never get over it, but at least she knows the truth.'

'Her mother always knew, and I think she did too.' His fingers played on the chair arm as if testing the material for flaws. 'I looked into several cases when I took up my post here, wondering what kind of place I had fetched up, including the case of embezzlement and the disappearance of Mr Nelson and the secretary. You see, Mrs Shackleton, I don't like people to disappear any more than you do. I went to see old Mrs Nelson. She was very hard up, having refused financial support from Edwin Castle, her husband's former partner. She never believed the story about her husband running off with a secretary. That same secretary came to see her two years after his disappearance and told her it wasn't true. The young woman was too afraid to go to the police. But Mrs Nelson went once a week for three years, and she wrote to the Chief Constable.'

'What happened?'

'Nothing.'

'Did you know that Pamela Carmichael was the Nelsons' daughter?'

'Yes, but I did not know that she had been watching and waiting all these years. Even she did not suspect that Castle was library president for a reason, the most foul of reasons. Why should she? He was everywhere, Chamber of Commerce, chapel, local council. I thought I would never be able to touch him, but he went too far, and he did not count on you . . . '

'And on the fact that Peter Donohue would never have been bent to his will in that way, and that Peter and Marian Montague were friends.'

Wallis smiled. 'An unlikely friendship. But such things happen.'

'Yes, across all sorts of barriers.'

'Even you and I might be friends, Mrs Shackleton.'

'Stranger things have happened.'

He stood. 'I had better be going.'

'Thank you for telling me about the background to the Castle case.'

I walked him to the door.

'You know, we had two women employed by Leeds City Police once. If we ever had the funds to employ a woman, I hope you might apply.'

I smiled. 'Never! I did a little of that in a volunteering way at the start of the war and it didn't suit me. But let me know if you need my help.'

'Likewise, I'm sure.'

I opened the door. He was about to say something else, but hesitated, pulled on his hat, smiled and turned up the path. At the gate, he waved.

Percy twitched the curtains, peering at the car and then at me in the doorway.

When I went back inside, Mrs Sugden opened the kitchen door.

'The kettle's on. Is it time for you to take a few hours off? Your mother was on the telephone.'

'I will speak to her later. Time for tea, I think and then I have one more job to do.'

'Oh aye?'

'Dr Potter's manservant wants to adopt Percy and teach him his numbers.'

'Thank God for that.'

'I think it will be good for Mr Morgan to have fresh company, and the sooner Percy goes, the sooner he will settle in.'

'Let's take him up there quick, before Mr Morgan changes his mind.'

I led Percy into the kitchen where Mrs Sugden gave him slices of carrot. I attached Percy's harness, and wrapped him up warm for the second car journey of his life. 'You're going to a new home, Percy, where you will be lavished with intelligent attention.'

'We must remember to tell Mr Morgan Percy's likes and dislikes.' Mrs Sugden poured cups of tea and a saucer of tea for Percy. He took it in his usual dainty manner.

Mrs Sugden said, 'We've hardly had time to share a word, what with everything that's been going on.' She cut a russet apple in quarters, one piece each for her and me and two pieces for Percy. 'Tell me, Mrs Shackleton, the young woman, Miss Wells, how did she get on with her mother, if that's not breaking a confidence?'

'I left them to talk together, but I believe they took to each other, I'm glad to say.'

'Well that's a blessing. Did she glean any information about her father?'

I felt a small stab of anxiety in case I had inadvertently given something away with regard to the unfortunate Samuel Lennox. But Mrs Sugden did not appear to notice my hesitation.

She handed Percy his second piece of apple. 'I expect Sophia must have been curious, in case her father was some bigwig who might want to acknowledge her one fine day. Might that happen?'

'No. Lady Coulton told Sophia that her father was a student of philosophy, and that he died in the war.'

'Did he, do you think, or was she just saying that?'

'If that is what she said, then who am I to question it?'

'A student of philosophy, eh? I wonder what he philosophised?'

Sophia had asked Lady Coulton that very question. On the train journey home, with tears in her eyes, she told me what Lady Coulton had answered. I thought there was no harm in passing on this philosophy to Mrs Sugden.

'His philosophy was that we must look forward, build a kinder world, and remember that we are put on earth a little while to learn to bear the beams of love.'

I could not quite read Mrs Sugden's expression, whether she was impressed, or sceptical. 'Is that philosophy? The last bit sounds like poetry to me.'

Percy crunched his apple with vigorous jaw movements, looking from me to Mrs Sugden, as if understanding every syllable, and believing not a word.

Author's note

The Leeds Library and the Cavendish Club are very special places. During the Great War there was nowhere in London for women of the Voluntary Aid Detachment to stay. At the end of the war, Lady Ampthill, Chairman of the Joint Women's VAD Department of the Order of St John and the British Red Cross Society, felt there should be '*A First Class Ladies' Club*' for all VAD women past and present, with charges that reflected the limited incomes of potential members. An appeal was launched, and shares issued. The Club's first home was Queen Anne House, 28 Cavendish Square. The Club's website quotes the *Spectator*: 'The work of decorating and fitting the club has been carried on extremely quickly, partly owing to the fact that many of the workmen engaged on it have during the war been in military and auxiliary hospitals where the VADs were serving. They therefore feel and express a real personal interest in the progress of the work and of the building being ready in time.' The Club opened on Friday, 14 June, 1920.

This summer, the New Cavendish Club, 44 Cumberland Place, W1, will close its doors for the last time. I am sad that

I won't be able to visit in future. Happily, Kate Shackleton will.

'In Leeds, where one would not expect it, there is a very good public library, where strangers are treated with great civility,' wrote James Boswell in 1779, revealing his prejudices eleven years after the opening of the Leeds Library, the country's oldest proprietary subscription library still in existence, housed in its present premises since 1808. I am indebted not only to present-day library staff but to those who have worked there over the years, written the history, served on committees and chronicled the mystery of the library ghost. The library welcomes new members.

Thank you to the usual suspects who have cheered me along during the writing process (you know who you are), and to agents Judith Murdoch and Rebecca Winfield for their encouragement, coffee and cakes.

Special thanks to Caroline Kirkpatrick and Grace Menary-Winefield for their superb editorial attention; to copy editor Robin Seavill; to the publicity and production staff at Piatkus; and to cover illustrator Helen Chapman for her evocative images of Kate Shackleton's world.

Frances Brody
Leeds, February 2014